Coast Walk

Frederick Regenold

Writers Club Press
New York Lincoln Shanghai

Coast Walk

Writers Club Press
an imprint of iUniverse, Inc.

For information address:
iUniverse, Inc.
2021 Pine Lake Road, Suite 100
Lincoln, NE 68512
www.iuniverse.com

ISBN: 0-595-25377-6

Printed in the United States of America

For Vivica,

Whose talent, personality, beauty and sexuality
inspired me to create the character,
Katherine Churchill, expressly
for her, and
nobody
else.

PROLOGUE

By midnight, a dense unseasonable Australian fog had completely enveloped the 45-foot Cabo Rico cruiser. Anchored off Bungaree Norah in the Tasman Sea, its isolated location in the dark foreboding ambience would have eroded the courage of a Navy SEAL.

Below deck on the cabin bed, the nude couple was evidently oblivious to the weather, the location, and the absence of light. The latter condition virtually prevented them from seeing each other as they vigorously copulated. Judging from her animalistic sounds, the female was seemingly the more enthusiastic, certainly the more orally demonstrative from a vocal standpoint. After several minutes, she actually expressed her innermost desire in words.

"Baby, please do it from the back...in my ass. I feel so good, but...I don't want to come right now. That way I can postpone it 'til later."

"My pleasure, dear. Hop up onto your knees," the male requested, with an unmistakable Aussie accent.

The darkness presented no problem for their change in physical positions. The switch was accomplished as if thoroughly rehearsed. Even in the pitch-black environment, the unruffled Aussie knew exactly where the condoms and Astroglide were...plus the relatively clean hand towel. As if sightless—and for all practical purposes he was at the moment—he dried the woman's natural vaginal secretions from his inflexible shaft with one agile stroke of the hand towel.

Then he dexterously rolled on a ribbed rubber before he gracefully smeared a glob of the lubricant over the sheathed length of his phallus. Within seconds, the man steadied her buttocks with his left hand on the small of her back, knowingly found her anus with the middle finger of his right hand and, with her manual assistance from between her widely-spread legs, guided his rigid penis to her anal entrance where he carefully and smoothly slid its complete length inside of her.

"Oh, Baby, that feels marvelous," she exclaimed in full voice, realizing no one could possibly hear her. "Take it easy at first. Let me adjust—then push it to me…deep. I promise not to come until you get on top of me."

He followed her instructions, skillfully varying the depth, angle, and velocity of his thrusts…but after 15 minutes, he paused. "It's a bit warm, Raquel. Let's go topside where I can give you more satisfaction in the fresh air. Don't turn any lights on however." Maintaining his physical position, he stayed inside of her and listened with amusement to her linguistically colorful reply.

She laughed bawdily. "Oh, shit, baby, that sounds like fun. We don't need any light. I prefer to do it in the dark. That turns *me* on. Promise me that tomorrow though, we can get the hell out of this place. Too fuckin' many sharks out there. Scares the hell out of me, even though I know we're safe on the boat. Let's sail back to Sydney. I need a week of civilization…and we're getting low on food too. Since the dinghy's in the water, let's go up on the foredeck," her voice suddenly registering delight, "where there's more room for me to perform." She giggled.

"That's a promise, dear…we'll sail to Sydney tomorrow." He smoothly withdrew his penis, wiping it with the same nearby hand towel and simultaneously removing the used condom. Then cheerfully, "Topside, for now. I hope you feel as good as I do."

"Oh, yeah, I feel great." She stood and began carefully feeling her way to the steps. "Should we bring an inflated pad or something cushy to screw on, especially if you're gonna pop it to me?" she asked in a matter-of-fact tone.

"Nah, there's no need for that. I've something else a great deal more pleasurable in mind…something I guarantee you'll remember the rest of your life."

"Hey, Brian, you devil…you're getting me excited and you know it. I'm gonna have an orgasm right here on the steps." She started up. "Let me go slowly," she requested. "I don't want to break my fuckin' ankle. I've been there, done that. That would take all the fun out of screwin' you…with a cast on." Another giggle.

"Of course. Take your time, dear," he cautioned.

Reaching the top, she arched her back, protruding her major-league breasts, and inhaled strongly. "Oooh, this fog is refreshing. I'm ready for you, Brian. I think I'm gonna eat you alive." She laughed loudly again, knowing the nearest human being was miles away.

Coming up the steps behind her, Brian slipped his hands under her arms and over her breasts, then gently fingered her aroused nipples. He whispered into her left ear, "Keep your voice down. You'll wake up the sharks." She could feel his phallus nudging the division between her buns.

"I'm so excited, Brian. I want you to make love to me for at least another hour." Staring straight ahead into the darkness, feeling his face over her left shoulder and touching hers, she told him sweetly, "I'm in heaven, baby. You're the greatest man I've ever met in my life…and the *first* Australian." She chuckled, wrapping the fingers of her left hand tightly around his hard cock. "You're also the sexiest man I've ever been in bed with. I'm so happy I found you. It all happened so quickly…I still can't believe it. It's like a fairy tale…or a dream…and I never want to wake up. My life was empty…until you came along."

He French kissed her ear, then, "I'm sure you know how much I love you, Raquel."

"Yes, baby, I do. I've never been so sure of anything in my life. You *are* my life, Brian. You know that, don't you?"

"Yes, dear, and I take a great deal of pride in that." Then changing his tone of voice, but keeping his dexterous fingers at work on her excited nipples, "What's that I see in the distance?"

Squint-eyed, she looked in vain. "Are you kidding? I can't see my fuckin' hand in front of my face."

Easing his fingertips away from her nipples, "I think there's a dim light, flickering," he suggested. Then snaking his right arm over her shoulder and under her chin. "Yes, I can see it now…off in the distance."

In a split-second, his arm tightened like a noose and he jerked it upward and sideways, breaking her neck instantly. She softly moaned, and her body twitched briefly…then silence and unending repose. Gingerly, he permitted his victim's naked lifeless corpse to slide down onto the deck, and immediately pulled a large diamond ring off the third finger of her right hand. He nimbly placed it inside his mouth. Then, swiftly, he lifted the limp body and heaved it overboard. At the sound of the splash, he spit the ring into his open palm and touched it momentarily with the fingers of his other hand before closing his fist on it.

Moments later, he looked into the fog where he'd thrown the woman's body, "Sorry, Raquel. I know you don't swim…but I'm quite sure the sharks will appreciate you far more than I did." For 30 seconds in the darkness, he listened to the frenzied commotion of the hungry sharks thrashing about in the water, then returned to the cabin.

CHAPTER 1

Frank Taylor had only been in La Jolla two months. The handful of people with whom he was acquainted knew very little about him, and that's the way he wanted it. There was certain background information he'd kept to himself. Wanting no distractions, he needed to focus completely on the important project that led his immediate agenda. Because of unexpected and uncontrollable happenings during recent years, it had been necessary to postpone this particular project until now and, being a newcomer to the area, he wanted no part of the usual informal inquisition customarily prompted by that status. Before coming here, he made an agreement with himself to keep the lowest possible profile. Of course, that's always easier said than done.

Sitting atop a bright yellow kayak, he faced the Caves, one of the natural attractions in La Jolla, California, a picturesque community in suburban San Diego, about 120 miles south of Los Angeles. Under him, the lucid ocean's temperature was in the high 60s, the air about 75°, with minimal wave movement. The black-and-silver Casio on his left wrist showed THU '02, 9–12, 9:32 a.m. It was sunny and cloudless, not a common occurrence at this hour along the shore. September, however, is considered by knowledgeable weather watchers to be the best month for beach visits. It was *mid*-September—more specifically a year and one day from that horrendous, world-changing day of terrorism that would never be forgotten—so the kids were back in school and most of the tourists had departed. The locals were fond of saying, "After Labor Day we get our town back."

Glancing down at his swim trunks, the only clothing he wore, he remembered childhood days in Memphis where he spent the summer weeks at Rainbow Lake public pool. During his 12th and 13th summers, he'd frequently report to the pool at 7 a.m., help clean it before the opening at 9 a.m., and avoid the 50-cent entrance fee. Then after five hours with his buddies—a short lunch break included—swimming, diving, hand-balancing, working out on the horizontal bar, and performing stunts from the swings, he'd leave promptly at 2 p.m. in order to throw his *Memphis Press-Scimitar* paper route. "Look at me now," he thought. "A senior citizen, kayaking in a place I'd never heard of, and didn't know how to pronounce correctly, when I was a kid".

Hundreds of birds—pelicans, cormorants, gulls, and sparrows—studied the man from their elevated perches along the cliff's face, approximately three to four stories high. The cormorants clearly predominated. According to what he'd read, there're seven caves in the side of the rock wall, most with names he couldn't recall. From his viewing angle about 50 yards out, he could see all seven openings. He'd intentionally picked this time of day because of prior research.

In a mental flashback he could picture his loyal friend, Jack McRae, telling him, "La Jolla's one the most scenic spots in the world, and the Caves area is my favorite." Jack had also told him, "Snorkeling there is fantastic, superior to Hanauma Bay in Hawaii, but most people, fortunately, are unaware of the La Jolla location."

Although he'd previously surveyed this area thoroughly on foot, today was his first time in the water. There's a designated spot down the slope from The Cave Store where he could've reached his present location by swimming, but he decided against it. Physically he was in fairly good shape, but in recent years his aquatic activities were close to nil. Also, peering down through the water, he remembered the movie, *Jaws*, and was content he'd rented the kayak. If he saw a fin approaching, however, he wasn't sure what he'd do…maybe ask a pelican for a ride.

The main reason for his visit to this specific location was to record a particular sequence of shots with his digital camera, but the fellow from whom he rented the kayak warned him about taking it with him, and he was right. After climbing onto the kayak at La Jolla Shores Beach and paddling two or three times, the first wave he encountered threw him off the kayak and into the ocean. That would've been the end of a rather expensive piece of photographic equipment. Fortunately, in the small pocket of his swimsuit, the only items he'd brought were his car key and a new laminated California driver's license, which he'd needed for identification at the kayak rental shop.

The lighting was perfect now, the sun beaming over his left shoulder, and there were no joggers or walkers on the path above. Around him, as far as he could see, there was no one else in the water. He glanced at his watch again. Then a female and a dog appeared directly over the cave nearest him, the last on the north side. It was a small terrier, black and white, and a woman with short dark hair and coffee-colored skin—maybe Mexican or African-American—wearing white shorts and an emerald bra. Her feminine physical attributes were easily visible. The dog wore a leash, the other end of it in the woman's right hand.

Apparently neither had anxiety concerning their closeness to the cliff's edge, as if they'd done it many times, when the pooch suddenly assumed his instinctual stance and answered nature's call. The man watched intently as she deftly flipped open, with her left hand, what looked like a plastic bag. She paused a few seconds, allowing the dog time to finish, then bent over to do her duty when a large aggressive pelican abruptly swooped near the canine pet as it actively pawed the ground with its rear legs. The terrier barked offensively, lunging in the pelican's direction at the edge of the cliff. The woman screamed, "Rocky!" spontaneously yanking on the leash and dropping the plastic bag. The dog safely flopped back on the turf, but when she'd jerked on the leash, the dog's weight caused the woman to lose her balance. After two quick, frantic steps on the very edge of the cliff, she dropped the red handle of the leash, put both arms out, as if teetering on a tightrope, made a hasty sign of the cross, and jumped feet first in what appeared to be a chosen but limited direction.

During her rapid descent to the ocean's surface, she crossed both forearms, holding them tightly over her bosom, and had brief eye contact with the man on the kayak before hitting the water in a nearly vertical position. The dog, evidently named Rocky, yelped ineffectually.

Momentarily hypnotized by the suspense, the man instinctively used the single kayak oar to point his craft toward the splash and, before she surfaced, stroked two or three times in her direction. When she emerged, gasping audibly, he and the kayak were only 10 yards away. Using the oar, he broke his forward movement, deftly rolled off the kayak, and breaststroked toward her. High above them, Rocky was throwing an anxiety fit.

The woman stretched her arms out toward the man, and he took both of her hands in his, treading water with his legs to stay afloat. "Gorgeous face," he thought, "around 35 years old, African-American," noticing the nipples of her naked breasts under the water's surface.

"Thank you," she said softly. Then actually startling him, she yelled, "Rocky. I'm all right." The terrier, apparently in disagreement, continued yelping, with a few groans thrown in for sympathy. The woman looked down briefly at her bare breasts and cried out, "Dammit, my bra came off." Then freeing her hands from his, she quickly covered her breasts and involuntarily submerged.

Alertly grabbing her hair, lifting her back to the surface, his face inches from hers, the man knew he'd never seen eyes so beautiful, so unusual, and so expressive. "Could be a lot worse," he grinned teasingly.

She forced a laugh, now keeping herself afloat. "You're funny."

"Are you okay?" he asked, attempting to distract her from the problem of her missing bra. "Looks like you know how to swim."

"Oh yeah, of course I know how to swim." She was looking directly into his eyes, thinking how warm and friendly they were, but mainly concerned about her exposed bosom. "*Think* I'm okay—maybe I've done something to my left ankle. Hurts when I kick. I'm mainly embarrassed. I'd like to kick myself in the butt."

Hoping her ass was as sexually attractive as her voluptuous breasts, he twisted around with his back facing her, and requested, "Hang on to my shoulders…and *don't* kick. I'll get us over to the kayak." It was only a few yards away.

Trying to keep her nipples from touching his back, she extended her arms and placed her hands at the base of his neck, instantly feeling its firmness. Unexpectedly, this suddenly awakened her libido. There'd been a lengthy gap in her sex life, to the extent that she'd forgotten the pleasant, fevered pelvic sensation that the nearness of a physically attractive man could generate. Her only recent association with that emotion had been accompanied by the use of her dildo, the use of which was giving her a minor guilt complex. But the dildo gave her pleasure, and she always slept better after it helped her have an orgasm. She quickly admitted to herself that being next to the real thing was far more exciting, at least to begin with, yet certainly riskier if it came down to the act of sexual intercourse.

Again, he used the breaststroke without his legs in order not to kick her. As he stroked, she noticed the prominence of his deltoids and triceps. Having been involved in high school sports, she automatically recognized those physical features. Gray hair came around from his temples, but it was mostly dark brown in the back and on top. She pegged him at approximately 55 years of age, perhaps 10 years younger than her father. "Must be a coach or an ex-athlete," she silently surmised, "considering his muscle tone."

Nearing the kayak, he grabbed the floating oar he'd left in the water, and placed it on top. He then pulled down a cloth strap near the rear section and, gazing into those divine eyes, said, "Okay, this is what I want you to do." Then, sliding a blue life preserver off into the water, "See if you can get this on—"

"No, come on, I don't need that thing. I'm an excellent swimmer. It's just that my ankle hurts."

"Thought it might help cover you—at least…the parts that need covering." Again, noticing her breasts were quite large and shapely, he was unable to conceal a slight smile.

"You're getting funnier by the minute." She wasn't smiling.

"Lady, I'm just trying to help." Politely making an effort not to look where he knew he shouldn't, he noticed a tattoo of a fox's head on the outside of her upper left arm, near the shoulder.

Fully accepting the noticeable spurt in her sexual desire, and relishing this stranger's proximity, she changed her tune, "I'm sorry. I know you are—it's a good idea. Let me have it, please." She reached out toward him with one arm, feebly shielding her breasts with the other, not really minding whether he saw them or not.

He pushed the preserver strap into her open palm, then twisted away to provide privacy. Noticing that, she mentally registered him in the "gentlemen's bracket." While she struggled getting her arms through the preserver openings, the man, stabilizing the kayak, scouted the shoreline for a place to take her. A small rocky beach not too far away looked like a good choice.

"Darn it, these plastic things on the front," she dramatically complained. "I can't snap them together. You're gonna have to help me—if you don't mind?"

Feigning embarrassment, he suggested, "Why don't you just put the vest on backwards? There's actually more material in the back and that'll give you better coverage."

Frustrated with the snaps, "Oh no, that means I'd have to take it off and put it back on again. Just do it for me, please—quickly, if you don't mind?" At this point, she didn't much care whether he saw her breasts again or not. "I'm sure it isn't the first time he's ever seen a woman's tits," she mentally deduced, "and, besides, it's sort of fun to watch his reaction. He looks embarrassed."

He wasn't sure why she tacked on the interrogatory clause. It was difficult to imagine any man declining her request. Now, with her left hand, she clasped the strap from the kayak and treaded water with her right arm, permitting him to work with the plastic snaps on the small cloth belts that would partially close the front opening of the life jacket. Presently, the front was completely open, clearly revealing her enticing bosom.

"Her nipples," the man reflected, "are like the eyes of a photographed person who'd been looking directly into the camera lens when the picture was taken." They stared at him unceasingly, challenging him not to look back.

Using his legs exclusively to keep afloat while his hands were occupied with the hitches wasn't easy. The plastic fasteners were the male and female types, the female having small releases on each side which could be squeezed to let the male enter, then released to lock it in place. It wasn't a question of the man's dexterity; his main concern was that his fingers were constantly brushing against her breasts and nipples, causing his cock to stiffen uncomfortably in the confined space of his swimsuit jock. The fact he was handling male and female coupling devices added a Freudian strain to his thinking process, which generated at slight tremble in his hands. In a way, he felt awkward, but on the other hand there was something pleasurable about the experience.

She watched his eyes as he worked. It was difficult to tell whether they were focused on the straps instead of her breasts, but she caught herself hoping the latter. Freud was at it again. Then she observed the muscularity of his arms and chest. "Here's an older guy who takes care of his body," she thought. "Wish my dad would do that. Look at those biceps. And the hair on his forearms…you could actually comb it. He's a sexy guy. I'll bet he's good in bed too."

The sight of her ample breasts prompted the man to remember why the inflatable variety of these jackets was called a Mae West, an entertainer from the past with whom the girl was probably not familiar. There were three sets of belts. After joining two, he was thankful that the lower half of his body was submerged because he felt a full erection. "Okay, that'll help," putting his right hand on the kayak.

"I think you're the one who's embarrassed." She suppressed a smile.

He was glad she thought that. It was the effect he wanted. "No, I'm just funny, remember?" He knew if she could see his erection that *she* would be embarrassed…but maybe not. Her smile exploded into a contagious laugh, and he caught it. "I *am* human, you know," he blurted out, hoping she was too. Quickly, both felt very comfortable in each other's presence. Putting the kayak strap back in her hand, he proposed, "Hold onto this with both hands. I'll push us over to that small beach."

"No, that's no good," she warned. "There's no way we can get up to my house from there. The wooden steps got washed out long ago. That dirt wall at the bottom is too high."

"Where's your house?" he asked, a little puzzled now.

"Above that cave…" she looked in that direction, "up there from where I fell. That's my backyard…or front, depending on how you look at it—except the path—that's public property. Are you new around here?"

"Yes."

"We have to get to the snork pad." She pointed south.

"The *what*?" His expression was comical.

"That's what I call it, the snork pad. Those rocks over there," pointing again in the same direction, "where you get in the water when you snorkel."

"All right. That's a pretty good haul. Be a lot easier if I could climb back on the kayak…but you think I'm funny now…if I tried that, I'd be hilarious." Remembering his erection, he chuckled. "I'll stay here in the water and push us over there. Hang onto that strap and *don't* kick with your sore ankle. Just let that leg relax."

As he shoved the front end of the kayak around in position to guide it toward their destination, she realized how difficult it would be to climb up onto the kayak from the water. Trying to minimize the drag she caused in their forward movement, she kicked with her able leg and, knowing he was doing all the work, remained silent.

Periodically he'd ask, "You okay?"

"I'm fine," she'd reply. After the second time he asked and got the same answer, they saw and heard Rocky racing to the snork pad, undoubtedly dragging his leash alongside. "He knows where we're going. He's brilliant." After he'd asked if she were okay the third time, and she'd replied with the same words, she added, "Take your time. Save your energy. The difficult part is after we get there."

He didn't know what that was all about and figured it best not to ask. Several thoughts popped into his mind during this watery trip: "Don't recall seeing a ring on her left hand…or right. She's probably injured worse than she thinks. After I get her ashore, I'll go to The Cave Store and call an ambulance. She's no doubt wondering who I am, what I'm doing out here alone on a kayak at 9:30 in the morning.

"So cute…really stunning. Very personable…easy to talk to. Couldn't help touching her breasts when I was fastening those straps. She asked me…to fix the straps, that is. Never seen a black woman so beautiful. Never seen *any* woman that beautiful. Her lips…never seen such sensuous lips…the kind actresses and pop singers pay thousands to have, surgically…such an expressive voice…perfect teeth. She seems so genuine…nothing phony about her. She's also the sexiest woman I've ever seen…and that's one helluva compliment, but she wouldn't have any way of appreciating it. Of course, I haven't seen the lower half. Definitely great tits though. I'd be delighted to kiss them.

"What are you doing, asshole?" he asked himself. "What are you thinking? What's happening to you? Forgetting who you are and your primary reason for being here? You'd better stop and think…carefully. Shut up and push…and kick. You've got a goddamned master plan, buddy, and you'd better stick to it."

While he was thinking, so was the young lady, kicking with her right leg only. "It costs about $25 to rent one of those kayaks, so he's not a street person, that's for sure. But what's he doing out here at 9:30 in the morning alone? Probably just a tourist…from Kansas…maybe Texas. Kind of rugged looking. Not a beach bum though…not tan enough for that. No wedding ring. Gay? No, don't think so…but maybe that's why his hands were shaking a little when he was hooking up those straps and his hands were brushing against my breasts. But, hell, I'd imagine any red-blooded man would be a bit nervous in the water next to a braless female stranger. Been fooled before, remember? You'd better. Not a handsome guy, that's for sure…but not really ugly. Shit, if I saw him at the Gulls Nest in a coat and tie, I probably wouldn't look at him twice. Nose is rather large…mouth is pretty small—practically lipless. Very sensitive face though. I like that. His eyes are what grab me…his fucking eyes, yeah. The irises are mostly green, I think, but next to the pupils there's some brown…different…never seen that before. When he looks at me—wow! And his voice…soft, low…not a loudmouth. Nice to listen to—the kind of voice you'd never get tired of.

"When he was close to me fixing the straps, his breath smelled so clean…no sign of halitosis or cigarettes. I like the way his hair's cut in the back...not zipped across high up on his neck. I don't like that. Good muscles—especially for a guy his age...any age. I've only seen the top third though...not even that, actually. Age-wise, could be my dad, except he's white. Wonder what he does for a living? Or did? Probably retired. No, he's not that old. Has to be something connected with athletics...not a banker or computer programmer...no way. Doesn't look pharmaceutical either...well, you never know. Maybe divorced...kind of has that 'been there, done that' look.

"Hands are pretty small, not much bigger than mine...not those big hams. When he was fixing my vest, I liked the way his fingers moved. I don't think he was trying to touch my nipples...but when he did, I have to admit I didn't mind. In fact, I liked it, damn it. Never in my life have I been attracted to a man this quickly...and he's white. Maybe it's in my genes. Remember mom...oh, shit. After what I've gone through, I better be careful. But it's almost as though I have no control...like I'm being drawn toward him...as if the reason I fell off the cliff was to meet him...like destiny. Wonder how tall he is? Bet he's over six feet. Hell, he better be. Wouldn't it be funny though, when we get out of the water, if he turns out to be 5' 4"...and I look *down* on the little asshole?" She laughed out loud.

"You okay?" he asked again.

"Yeah, just swallowed some water, I'm fine," she fibbed. "Oh, shit," she continued thinking. "It wouldn't be funny at all. I'd hate that. Gotta be careful. Don't even know this jackass. Might be a robber—or worse...goddamned sex fiend. They're all over the place. Don't know how he's gonna react when I ask him to help me up the hill to my house. What if he can't pick me up? Oh shit, wouldn't that be a laugh? Maybe I can walk. Maybe it's not as bad as it feels in the water...probably worse. And if he does pick me up, I hope Rocky doesn't bite him in the ass. Jeez, that's all I need. Hope I don't see anybody I know, with my boobs hanging out like this. And if we make it to the entrance, I can't just thank him, tell him goodbye, and walk in, locking the door in his face. I gotta take a chance on the guy.

That doesn't mean I have to invite him in for a quickie. Hell no. I can tell he's okay though, just by looking at him. My father would go into convulsions. This guy's nice though. I'm sure of it. I don't even know him...but I like him...very much...but I gotta see the rest of his bod. This talking head crap doesn't cut it. I gotta see the whoooole thing...including—yeah, you got it—that too."

There was a one-man welcoming committee at the snork pad: Rocky. No barking...only whining and running back and forth over the large boulders.

Not wanting to take a chance on damaging the kayak and having to pay for the damage, the man decided to purposely keep some distance between it and the rocks. Luckily, except for smooth swells, the ocean was quite placid, like a lake. He stopped the forward motion of the kayak at what he thought was a safe distance from the boulders, and swam around in front of the woman, between her and the snork pad. Rocky was very still now, in a kneeling position, whining loudly.

"Rocky, Baby," she used baby talk. "Your mama's okay."

"Hang onto my shoulders again and I'll get you over to the rocks. Don't put *any* weight on that ankle." She followed his instructions silently and willingly.

Unlike the shoreline of a sandy beach, there was a steep drop-off from the boulders into the ocean. Nearing the rocks, he turned his body toward hers, simultaneously forcing her hands off his shoulders. He then placed his hands under her armpits to pull her with him up onto the snork pad. A slight unanticipated surge lifted their bodies up onto the boulders, with the man under the woman, her partially exposed breasts close to his face. She watched his facial skin to see if it flushed. It didn't. Then Rocky, still whining, began licking her face, as well as his.

"I told you he's brilliant. He knows you helped me."

The man looked up uncomfortably from her breasts into those mesmerizing eyes. He was relieved that his erection had subsided. Otherwise, she would be physically aware of it at this instant. "Try to roll gently to your right so I can get out from under you...but careful with that ankle." Those lips again, inches away, caught his attention, and he knew if she didn't move pretty quickly his erection would return in full force.

Looking into his compelling eyes, she was reluctant to roll right or left—her present position was fine, as far as she was concerned. She'd never been on top of a sexy man in this position, and she was thoroughly enjoying it, especially with this particular man. That warm feeling she hadn't experienced in years was creeping into her pelvic area. She complied with his directions despite her impulse to ignore them and test his sexual arousal threshold, a suitable admission for next Saturday afternoon's confession at Mary, Star of the Sea. She hoped God and the priest would understand. Somehow, she knew God would, but she wouldn't bet on the priest. Well...that would depend on which priest listens to her confession. She'd learned that they too were human...some of them.

"Ouch". The pain was rather intense when her ankle rubbed against the boulder. Rocky squealed.

"Be careful," the man admonished. "Lift your bad ankle while I slide you farther up on this rock." He stood swiftly, again putting his hands under her armpits, this time from the back in order to drag her to a safer, more comfortable location just a few inches away. Again, he saw the fox head tattoo, as well as her breathtaking cleavage.

She was glad she'd shaved her armpits when taking a shower this morning. After moving her, he stood beside her. She tried to estimate his height, but decided it was too difficult from that angle. Nevertheless, she was sticking with "over six feet" at this point. No estimation was necessary concerning his derrière. "He's got a very attractive ass," she judged, "a physical attribute many white guys don't possess—and strong, well-proportioned legs...along with the absence of a pot gut. My interest is increasing by the minute. I'd forgotten what it was like to be turned on like this."

"What is Rocky?" the man asked, demonstrating his know-how with dogs by slowly moving the back of his right hand to Rocky's nose. The dog licked his hand appreciatively as the man briskly massaged the top of Rocky's head with his other hand.

"He's a Jack-rat…half Jack Russell and half rat terrier. Does everything but talk—actually does quite a bit of that. He's six and a half." Although mostly black and white, Rocky had gold blotches around his face, with two perfectly shaped oblong streaks above his eye sockets that resembled artistically placed brows.

"How'd he get the name Rocky?"

"Something about his face reminded me of Sylvester Stallone."

"Next time I see him I'll tell him."

"You kidding?"

"Of course. Just relax a minute while I pull the kayak out of the water." He eased himself back into the water.

Katherine sat with her right knee up and her left leg, the one with the injured ankle, stretched out. Rocky was in her arms, his favorite place in the entire world, licking fervently. She removed the leash collar from his neck, hoping he didn't get sick from lapping up the salt water on their skin. The kayak had drifted some 30 yards out. She watched her new acquaintance stroke toward it, this time using the crawl, very smoothly, as if he were a lifeguard or maybe had been. Shortly, returning with the craft, which was made of a lightweight plastic foam material, he managed to pull it up onto the rocks fairly easily, making sure the oar was still on top. She closely watched the entire procedure, happy for the opportunity to appraise his entire body. Her approval was reflected in a sensual smile, but the man wasn't looking.

Then she spoke. "It's kinda spooky. Maybe there's some kind of jinx on me." There was nothing humorous about the way she said it, looking at him solemnly.

"Come on, you don't believe in that stuff, do you?" He squatted near her left ankle, observing the slight discoloration and swelling, as well as the shapeliness of her long sexy legs. "What makes you say that?"

"I've had a couple of personal disasters living in that house."

"We all have personal disasters, regardless of where we live. If you've only had a couple...consider yourself lucky."

She was re-evaluating his personality. "Not very receptive," she thought, "and rather cold-blooded. But maybe he's had his share of disasters too." Then she informed him, "You can't see my house from here, but it's right over the farthest cave." A small pause to confirm she had his attention. "Do you know the name of that cave?"

"No..." He looked in that direction, then turned back. "I recall reading they have names. Sunny Jim, I think, is one. Don't remember the others."

"Sunny Jim's the closest, the one you can reach on a stairway inside The Cave Store—for a fee, of course. The one I live over," staring in its direction, gesticulating dramatically with her left arm, while keeping a grip on Rocky with her right, "is called..." pausing, looking squarely at the man for emphasis, "*White* Lady." She put a special inflection on the word, white, giving Frank several seconds to swallow what she'd said, then, "You know what I mean?"

"You must be from Haiti or Jamaica? Sounds like we're getting into voodoo."

Annoyed, "Noooo, I'm not from Jamaica or Haiti." Forgiving him, "Born and raised in good old Indianapolis."

"Your ankle doesn't look too bad," he volunteered, hopefully changing the subject. "What about the rest of you? Any pains internally?"

"Maybe this joker's a doctor," she reasoned. Instantly placing Rocky back on the boulder, "Don't move, Rocky," she began twisting her upper torso from left to right, right to left repeatedly, with her arms folded in ladylike fashion over her partially exposed breasts in order to give the impression she didn't want him to see them. "I feel sensational. Let me get an ice pack on this ankle for 20 minutes, once or twice, and I'll be fine. I have to go to work this afternoon—that's all there is to it."

He loved her spunk, but…"You realize you may have internal injuries that won't crop up for a few days? I want to run up to The Cave Store and call an ambulance. You should go to ER, get a physical. If you were my daughter, I'd insist on it."

"Now wait a minute, sir," a bit formal and somewhat irritated, "wait just a minute. First of all, there's not a way in the world I could be your daughter—"

"Oooh?" He jumped on that quickly.

Thrown off balance by his response, she tried to soften hers. "Well…perhaps…hypothetically—"

"That's precisely what I was thinking…hypothetically. What other way could there possibly be?" Now *his* face looked irritated, but actually he experienced delight in the confrontation. Rocky was still in the process of forming an opinion of this man, however, and the man, from his vantage point, was having great difficulty keeping his eyes trained on those of the woman, instead of her lovely breasts.

"Well, regardless of how you meant it," she said, "that's beside the point. Even if I *were* your daughter—"

"Oh, ho ho ho. Now you're telling me you *could* be my daughter?"

Both laughed. Rocky didn't know what to make of it.

"I told you, you're very funny," she observed. At this juncture she additionally considered him genial and had no fear whatsoever about taking him home, or rather permitting him to physically carry her home. She was now looking forward to it. "But you're distracting me from my main point, which I haven't got to…yet."

Instantaneously, the man became aware he'd never had this much fun with another human being in so short a time frame. His body and mind, by the second, were undergoing some strange alteration, being sucked into a magnetic medium from which he couldn't escape. It was like watching a movie and, all of a sudden, he was *in* the movie, having become an actor, sharing the scene with this gorgeous, sexually desirable creature before him, the leading lady. He was compelled to turn off the projector because he knew the entire scene was somehow a giant fabrication of his imagination, perhaps leading to another personal disaster for her—and certainly one for him. But how could he stop it? It was impossible. He was part of the scene, part of the fabrication, not outside of it. It was beyond his control. The only choice he had at this point was to play the part with what little talent he had, reciting his lines with as much conviction as he possessed, and to hope he'd remember his lines all through the final scene, trusting it wouldn't turn into a Greek tragedy, which he realized now was both in and out of his control. And if all went well during this artistic imaginative invention, surely there was some way he'd be able to get this sexy creature into bed so he could make love to her…or maybe she was the type who just wanted a good red-hot fucking. Either way, he'd be willing.

"Okay, let's have your main point," he invited. "You've got my undivided attention. I'm all ears." For the first time, he noticed the rest of her body. The white shorts were a sheer silk-like material and, because they were completely wet, accentuated her exceptional figure. One knee was up, but the other leg was fully visible, revealing a well-developed thigh and a ballerina calf, the kind he'd always admired in a woman.

"I was actually admiring your ears." She smiled sincerely. Then holding up her right hand, the left wrapped around Rocky, "Don't interrupt." With a cute smile, "Let me finish." Then a slight pause to collect and organize her thoughts. "I don't know where you're from—it's none of my business—but I don't think you know the economics associated with hospital care in this area. I saw a graphic example of it a couple of weeks ago. And by the way, I *have* health insurance—which isn't the main issue here. Anyway, one of the parking valets at the hotel where I work part-time was assaulted and robbed while retrieving a car. An ambulance took him to ER at the closest hospital where they treated him, scanned him, x-rayed him, medicated him, etc. He spent one night there, and was released to his parents *before* noon the next day. Take one guess what the bill was? And I'm talking about the hospital bill *only*—not the ambulance—that was another $600 plus. And not the bill from the attending physician who looked him over in his hospital room after he left ER—*that* was additional. And of course the hotel's insurance paid for all this because he was injured on the job. Again, that's not the point. Just tell me what you think the hospital bill was?"

"I don't know. I'd guess around $4,000." The man figured he was in the ballpark. Of one thing he was absolutely certain: He was listening to one of the brightest, most articulate young ladies he'd ever met—and certainly one of the most beautiful and physically enticing. He somehow felt the past slipping away from him, that his life was changing, never to be the same. He wasn't sure at this point if he really knew his exact identity…anymore. This had happened in the past, and invariably spelled trouble, but something about this was different…vastly different. The woman was unlike any he'd ever encountered.

"I keep telling you you're funny." She started to laugh, then stopped abruptly. "$21,000." She released Rocky, lifted both shoulders, showing her palms to the sky. "Had it been me, my insurance would've probably covered 80%. I'm not the world's best mathematician, but we're talking around $4,000-plus out of my pocket. And I'm not trying to compare his injuries with mine, by any means—he was beaten up *very* badly—lucky to survive. He looked terrible. It's just the idea of going to the hospital when I'm firmly convinced it isn't necessary—in my case, not the valet's. I'm old-fashioned. I'm certainly not poor, even by La Jolla standards. I live in a very nice home, and unlike most people nowadays, I take pride in my liquidity, instead of wallowing in debt…just don't like throwing money away. And I'm not stingy," smiling her punctuation, "just thrifty." She could tell he was devouring every word that came out of her mouth. "You're a complete stranger, and I understand if for some reason you don't want to get involved, but…I'd *really* appreciate it, Mr. Whatever-your-name-is…if you'd pick me up bodily and carry me home. If you won't, or you're not physically able…again, I'll try to understand…but there's no question in my mind about what *I'm* going to do…I'll crawl on my hands and knees up that hill, over the path, and into my house. I do *not* want an ambulance—I'll refuse it, if one comes—and I'm *not* going to the hospital."

The man stood there looking into her eyes. He remembered several people telling him that just before they thought death was imminent, their life reeled through their minds like a fast-forward video. He didn't see any video at this instant, but he sensed an intangible gnawing at his inner being, as if some omnipotent authority were stealing a part of him that he knew and had lived with all his life. Yet he also detected the pulsing, throbbing arrival of some fresh indescribable element that exhilarated him. There was guilt, as well as regret…even shame. But there was also joy, excitement, and a delicious anxiety. He was face to face with ambiguity and he unhesitatingly turned his back on it, almost defiantly, which for him was completely out of character…at least, *his* character.

From his standing position in front of the woman, his eyes never leaving hers, he slowly bent down, his face close to hers, "Put your arms around my neck." She did so immediately, purposely letting the side of her face touch his. He slid his right arm around her lower back and moved his left arm under her knees, lifting her sprightly. "You're not crawling anywhere. Not while I'm here."

Rocky's empty leash, one of those expandable types with retractable spring action in the oval handle, was in her right hand. "He'll follow us—or probably lead us," she indicated. Rocky was silent—and very happy, his small expressive face reflecting his best canine smile.

Tears welled up on the lower lids of the young woman's huge radiant eyes, seemingly contradicting her innermost feelings. The man knew the 250-yard trip, with her in his arms, up the slope and over the path, would be physically strenuous, but he knew the scenery—in his arms—would be the most spectacular he'd ever seen. Also, there was a self-confession that he somehow, during the last 20 or 30 minutes, through spirituality, or perhaps even sorcery, had been transformed into a different being. He wondered about the White Lady. He was also concerned about the possibility of a noticeable erection, which he'd have no way of hiding with this erotic gal in his arms.

CHAPTER 2

The scenery from the man's viewpoint, extraordinary but certainly not in the conventional way, was a close-up of the woman's exquisite facial features—and her inescapably alluring cleavage. Also, there was one minor distraction: He had to watch where he was stepping. He now understood what she'd meant about saving his energy for the hard part. A confirmation wasn't necessary, but he gauged her weight to be close to 125 lbs.—before he picked her up. Now he considered having underestimated by a few pounds…that, or the possibility his strength had diminished. She was a bit taller than he initially thought, and her beautiful legs, curled over his left arm, now seemed even longer than he'd suspected.

The first dozen or so yards were the most hazardous, with wet rocks and rough grooved sandstone. When they passed the rectangular observation platform on their left, three Asian men in dark business suits, cameras in their hands, gawked unashamedly. He was sure they weren't looking at him. Also, at that particular point, he became aware of her sweet-scented breath—no trace of cigarettes.

From the base of the wooden stairs, amid tall evergreens, they saw two joggers on the path above. During their ascent, he was unable to think of any woman who'd ever held him so affectionately—except his dear mother. At the top of the stairs, off to the left, their intended direction, two elderly ladies sat on a bench, eating something from a common plastic bag. In passing, the man's human bundle smiled at them, "Had a little accident, ladies—normally don't dress this way." Then looking back over her carrier's right shoulder and seeing their gaping faces, she quietly added, "Hope I don't see anybody I know."

Progress was good. Unaccustomed to being shoeless outdoors, the man's feet were taking a beating. Leading the way by several yards, knowingly preventing his master's carrier from tripping over him, the terrier strutted as if he were King Rocky.

"Look at that dog," he remarked.

"Actually he isn't a dog. He's a little person. My best friend, really…except my father, of course. But my father's a *big* person." Her beaming face was practically touching his. "There're three benches between here and my place…so please put me down on any of them if you get tired."

"I'll be fine, thanks." He made a mental note that her mother wasn't mentioned. "Just how big *is* your father, Goldilocks?" he jocularly inquired.

"Aw, he's not all that big—just in comparison to Rocky. Pretty big though. You called me *Goldilocks*?" She totally warped the pronunciation.

"Sorry, just a little regression to childhood. Besides," he remembered, "you haven't told me your name. Let's not pass your house."

"No, it's a bit farther. Katherine—with a *k*. However, only one person calls me that."

In a comic tone, he asked, "Shall I guess who that might be?"

"Go for it," she dared.

"Daddy." Close to baby talk.

Faking surprise, and with a little sarcasm, "How did you possibly arrive at that? By the way, I call him Dad."

"Not *quite* as dumb as I look."

"And you're probably a daddy. And you do *not* look dumb. On the contrary…"

"Oh oh, here it comes," he thought, sensing the first stage of his anticipated questioning, his face clearly mirroring it. "Now she wants to know if I'm married, how many kids I have, how many women I've screwed, and if I suffer from premature ejaculation or impotence?…my complete biography."

Reading it like neon, "Miss Nosy," she admitted. "I'm sorry."

"That's your nickname?"

"No, but let's just say that I'm naturally inquisitive. Can't help it."

"Just teasing," he assured her, glancing down at her tits. "Be as nosy, or inquisitive, as you want…" he couldn't believe he'd said that. "Up to a point."

"Whoa. The Mystery Man."

"From the cave of the White Lady," coating his words melodramatically.

Clinging to his neck with her left arm, and holding Rocky's leash with that hand, she feigned anger and popped him on the chest with her open right hand, thinking, "Wow. Nice pecs, too." Then wearing a big grin, she exclaimed, "This is it. Stop. Put me down on this bench and take a quick break. You'll have to climb those steps and go up through there," pointing with her right hand.

"No, if I do that I might not be able to pick you up again and, besides, I see a lot of ants on the bench…they'll make a meal out of you."

"God, you sound exactly like my father."

"Let's leave God out of it, please." He continued walking slowly toward the bottom step. "But it *is* funny—15 minutes ago you seemed reluctant to admit, *hypothetically*, I could be your father. Now…I sound exactly like him. Give me another 15 minutes," he again became melodramatic, "and I'll *become* your father."

"*Now* I know who you are."

"Who? Tell me. Sometimes I'm not quite sure who I am." He considered that a true statement.

"You're appearing at the Comedy Store. That's why you don't want to reveal your identity. You're a famous stand-up comic, and you're afraid I'm gonna ask for an autograph."

He shook his head. "No, you're way off. Comedy's not my thing. Up these steps?"

"Yes, please be careful—there isn't a lot of foot space—and I don't want you to fall. If you break a leg or get a hernia, you gonna sue me? That's probably the only way I'll ever see you again." Katherine shocked herself with the last sentence. She couldn't remember ever having been so forward with another man. In fact, she couldn't remember being forward with any man. It's always been the other way around, with men being the aggressors. She had never met anyone like this fellow though, whom she sincerely wanted to see again, and if she didn't verbalize it, how would he know? She hoped he wasn't shocked or offended.

"Careful," he thought. "See me again?" Then sardonically, he looked straight into her eyes and told her, "No question about it…I'll sue you for every penny you have," looking up at her impressive residence, "including this shack. I planned this whole caper—with the help of the White Lady—and, of course, my pet pelican. The only real concern was Rocky. My research indicated the possibility…he'd smell a rat."

The last line prompted Katherine to give him a phony laugh. "I take it all back. You must be a writer." She was admiring his thick, neat eyebrows, and noticing the lack of hair in his nostrils and ears. That pleased her.

Near the top step, plainly visible for any potential trespasser, there was a blue security sign, at the bottom of which read "ARMED PATROL."

"Is this when the Dobermans attack me—or will I get shot in the buttocks first?"

"Pit bulls," she emphasized. Then motioning with her right hand, "Around the right side, please, that's where the door is."

It was a large two-storied home of variegated brick. Inside, a couple of man-sized sculptures were luxuriating in the view through four huge, tinted picture windows across the front of the first floor. A spacious balcony with an ornamental wrought-iron parapet was above, and above that, a classic red tile roof.

Rocky, panting at the door, a side entrance, attempted to communicate that something out of the ordinary was necessary to open it.

"Has an electronic combo. See it on the right side?" She pointed toward it. "Just hold me there for a second while I push the buttons."

He positioned her. "I promise not to look."

"Oh, I do it so quickly it wouldn't make any difference..." She demonstrated, then pushed the green activator button, "in case you're the *Big Bad Wolf*." The door opened. Rocky dashed in.

"But I'm a fox," he quipped, recalling her tattoo. "I think extremely fast, and have a photographic memory."

"No, *I'm* the fox, buddy. Didn't you see my tattoo? I'll have you know I was a cheerleader for the Madison High Foxes—a good one too. Thanks for the warning anyway—as long as you're not a rat. The pit bulls, by the way, are inside—not out—" smirking, "and they'd love to attack a male fox. Don't just stand here, take me in, please." He did. She instantly dropped Rocky's leash on the floor. This is the part she was dreading somewhat, but she reminded herself about having to take a chance on him. He'd certainly done his good deed—and more. "This is fine, here in the kitchen. If you'll put me on that stool," again pointing, "it'd be great. Please shut the door we came in."

He nudged the door closed with his right foot, hearing the electronic device click, carried her to the stool with the red vinyl top, and cautiously lowered her onto it. Both were still rather wet, especially their shorts. Rocky however, had solved this problem with his canine version of the shimmy. The man stretched out both of his arms to expel the kinks, then arched his back.

"Any sign of a hernia?" She looked up from the kitchen stool, which was not low, and was now reassured he was over six feet in height. "I'm thinking about the lawsuit."

"Only a herniated disc."

"Oh, really? Well, everyone has those." Her good foot, the right one, was on the stool rung; the other, connected to the injured ankle, dangled in the air. Her left hand rested on the corresponding thigh, and her right elbow, atop the kitchen counter, supported her upper body weight. Rocky had curled up in his doggy bed 10 feet away, but missed nothing, with one eye open and one ear cocked.

Katherine stared deeply into her helper's green-brown eyes, thinking her last remark may have been overly flippant. Then in pseudo BBC, "Only jesting, my dear boy."

"What does everyone else call you?" The man moved another nearby stool under her left calf to elevate the injured ankle.

"Thank you," glad he'd changed the subject. "Kat—with a *k*. Meow." It was an excellent impression, and according to Rocky's sudden bark, an A+. "Last name is Churchill…no relation to Winston. And you are…?"

Although the man didn't blink or move, he paused for an eternity. Then with the straightest face imaginable and perfect enunciation, "Herbert Schmeelburger." Had he still been alive, Laurence Olivier could not have improved on it.

For Katherine, it seemed some invisible power had pushed the pause button. She sat motionless, intently watching his face for the slightest evidence of a ruse. There was none. Her lips parted slowly, as though her lower jawbone had increased in weight. Then suddenly, in a valiant effort to keep it all inside, she clamped her mouth shut, producing a sound not unlike that of a trumpeting elephant calf, accompanied by an outward burst of moist air. Had there been any mucous in Katherine's nasal cavity, the man would've regretted his fine performance. She began laughing uncontrollably while he stood there letting her get it out of her system. Rocky was up on all fours trying to evaluate the scene.

"Can I get some ice?" His expressionless face was the same.

"Now wait a minute, that's not your real name?" Her disbelief was obvious, but she was emotionally balancing, as she previously had physically on the edge of the cliff.

"Don't tell me," he challenged her, "you're one of those pusillanimous women who wouldn't be interested in a relationship with Herbert Schmeelburger?"

"Pusa—what?"

"Pusillanimous." Expressing total innocence, retaining his blank expression.

"What the devil is that? I'm a college graduate, but that's one I haven't heard."

"Now the devil's involved. Literally it means small-minded, but ordinarily it's used for lacking in courage."

"So henceforth, I should address you as Professor Schmeelburger? How about Herb or Herbie?" With the latter first names, she threw in a little New Jersey accent.

"No, you can call me Frank…only joking." Faint smile. "It's Frank Taylor. That's my real name."

Expansive smile, "Boy, am I relieved. Frank Taylor…beautiful name. Fairly common, you understand—but still beautiful. Something about Schmeelburger gives me the creepies. I almost believed you. But Frank Taylor…oh, man, you made my day."

"Clint Eastwood live around here? What about the ice? Don't wait too long."

"No, Pebble Beach, I think—Monterey area. Okay, first I have to get this wet stuff off. If you can help me into my bathroom, I can do the rest of it on one leg." Then in baby talk, "Give me your neck again."

Frank used the same arm placements as before. Kat moved her face even closer to his this time. She directed him.

"I'll sponge off real fast and put some clothes on—then comes the ice." Now in her bathroom, she pointed at the toilet. "I'll put the seat down and you can lower me onto it." She did her part.

He seated her. "Anything I can get for you before I leave?"

"Now wait a minute, you can't leave me," slightly freaked-out. "Everybody I know is at work right now."

"Well, I can't stay here in your bathroom with you." He smiled mysteriously, sensing another almost certain erection. "I'm not about to change your clothes."

"That certainly was *not* my intention, sir." The idea appealed to her though. Then, sugary, "Shut the door behind you and go down the hall to the right, second door on the left. That's where my dad stays. Another bathroom and a closet full of men's stuff are in there. There're polo shirts, cargo shorts, boxer shorts, undershirts, socks, and several belts—even some slip-on sandals. You name it—it's there. You and Dad are about the same size. His waist is considerably larger, but you can tighten the belt."

She snatched a pink terrycloth robe from a protruding bronze hook and skillfully tossed it over her shoulders, disregarding the sleeves. After rotating her torso a quarter turn to the left, she released the life jacket snaps with an ease that made Frank wonder curiously. Then sliding the soggy vest off her shoulders and arms, she tossed it in the corner on the tile floor and, as expertly as a quick-change artist, promptly stuffed her arms, one at a time, into the empty robe sleeves. As she turned back facing Frank, her hands were closing the lapels, then tying the sash in a neat bow. "That's better now. One of these days I'll snorkel down to the Cave of the White Lady and see if I can spot my bra. It was one of my favorites."

Frank stood at the bathroom door watching the mini-production, disappointed he saw nothing he shouldn't have seen, thinking she must have done some modeling in her past—or maybe present. "I think you've forgotten I have to return the kayak, the oar, and the vest you just removed so magically. My car's parked on a street next to the La Jolla Beach and Tennis Club. Can't your wonderful daddy help you?"

The standard routine of course, for security purposes, would be to acknowledge her father was asleep in the den upstairs, due to wake up any minute. "No, he's in Indianapolis and, I told you, I have to go to work this afternoon." With utmost empathy, *but*…"Frank, I know you must be a very busy man, even if you're here sightseeing—and I'm screwing up your day—but I'm depending on you. *Please* help me. I'll make it up to you somehow." She hoped he didn't get the wrong impression…that she was offering him sexual favors. She also realized her Freudian slip by using the verb *screwing*, and instantly thought, "Hell, it's too late now. Maybe it would be fun if he did get that impression. Let's see how he reacts. I'll play it by ear."

Frank was unable to take his eyes off hers, and he thought, "What the devil *is* going on here?" admitting to himself that perhaps the devil could be involved. He knew now that he was sexually attracted to her. "But this woman's anything but a devil," he decided. "She's angelic…possesses a face as aesthetic and celestial, or more so, as any I've seen in thousands of artists' representations." He openly submitted to and duplicated her compassion by asking her, "What do want me to do, Katherine? I'll help you."

So far, her hunches about Frank were correct. "You're a special guy, you know that? From the beginning I could see it." And she felt strongly that the end was nowhere in sight. "I'll phone the people at the kayak store and explain what happened. They'll have some kid take the stuff back and I'll cover the tip. Meanwhile, you can shower and dress in that bedroom—after you help me put on the ice pack. Last night I made a delicious tuna salad—my dad loves it—and we can have that for lunch. Then you can drive me to work—only a few blocks away—in *my* car, and I'll get a cab to take you back to *your* car in La Jolla Shores."

She covered it all, except for one item: "How can you possibly function at work on that ankle?" he asked sympathetically.

"No problem. I can sit during the class session...even prop my leg up on a chair. My students will love it."

"Your students?"

"I teach French, part-time—at Winthrop School—and I only have one class today. After class, somebody'll drive me home. When we finish lunch, I'll ice my ankle again and put a wrap on it. There's a cane in your closet. I can hobble around with that. It feels better already—I can tell—just don't want to put any pressure on it."

"My closet?" Frank thought, still standing at the bathroom entrance, "deeper and deeper." Then back to reality, he suggested, "If you don't mind, I'd like for you to call the kayak rental now. I was supposed to have it back in two hours."

"Great. Go back in the kitchen. Over next to the window, there's a cordless phone and, in the cabinet under it, there're phone books. One of them is small and blue—it's the *La Jolla Blue Book*—covers the La Jolla area only. Bring me the phone and the book, and I'll do it now." As he turned to leave, she told him, "Wait a sec." She jerked a bath towel off the rack nearest her and threw it underhanded to him. "Please wipe off your feet first, then throw it back to me so I can do the same."

After toweling off his feet one at a time while leaning against the doorframe, rather than throwing it, he walked the towel back to her, letting it slip from his hands onto her thighs.

"Katherine, listen to me." His voice now was more emphatic than at anytime since they'd met. The gravity of what he was about to say was amply reflected in his eyes. "We're total strangers. I know who *I* am." He quickly reminded himself, and expressed it to her, "At least, I think so—I'm beginning to wonder at this point...but I know practically nothing about *you*. Evidently you're fairly comfortable with that because you know who *you* are—and what you're all about, regardless of whether you're taking big chances with me. *I* know you're not taking big chances because I know who I am. But *you* don't—and that bothers me. It makes me uneasy.

"Put yourself into my shoes for a moment, Katherine," he continued. "You're not wearing a wedding ring, so that probably means no husband...but your boyfriend, 6' 9", 290 lbs., could stroll in any minute and I'd be in big trouble. And even if he's 5' 4" and weighs 130, I'd be terribly embarrassed. The only offsetting argument in my defense is I'm old enough to be your father...possibly your grandfather."

Katherine began to speak, but Frank quickly raised his right hand, tacitly discouraging her.

"The age difference...unless my imagination is running away with me and I'm participating in some sort of major self-delusion, seems unimportant to you. And *that* worries me even more." Brief pause. "I could go on for another 15 minutes, Katherine. What I'm trying to say is—and I don't recall ever having been at a loss for words—here I am, a perfect stranger in an elegant, magnificently situated La Jolla home, with the most...captivating creature I've ever seen...or heard of, or read about, in my entire life—someone who's presence...and nearness...is forcing me to frantically rethink my philosophical and spiritual principles.

"And you know what, Katherine? I can't do it while I'm looking at you...and talking to you. It's impossible. I've never been attracted to a woman like this. *Never.* You've caught me totally off-guard...not intentionally—it isn't your fault. I'm not trying to put the blame on you. But mentally and emotionally—and *spiritually*, more than anything—I need to catch my breath and do some very serious thinking. The truth is...and I'm accustomed to dealing only with the truth—as far as I'm concerned...I'm afraid...actually for the first time in my life. And I'm not afraid of you—that's not it at all. I'm afraid of myself...and what's happening to me. I'm also afraid of precipitating personal disaster number three for you...and that's the last thing in the world I want."

He gently took her right hand in both of his and continued, "The most intelligent action I can take at this moment—one that, years from now, you'll be happy I took...is to walk out of your house...and your life...and never come back." The look in her eyes told Frank that he'd hit the right notes.

Katherine fiercely held his wrists, looking through his eyes into his very soul. "No...No, please, Frank. Listen to me." Then quietly, she began sobbing. Rocky, as if by magic, appeared next to them...not barking, only observing with canine empathy.

Frank knelt on one knee, using the towel that had fallen from her thighs as a cushion. Rocky licked his leg affectionately. Frank never thought he'd kneel before a woman while she sat on a toilet, and have a dog tongue his leg.

Between sobs she tried to communicate. "I'm not married." One sentence at a time, "I don't have any boy friends." With labored breaths. "I'm not romantically involved with, or even interested in, *any* man. Please listen to me, Frank. You can't just walk out. Everything you said about your feelings for me is exactly how I feel about you. Never, *never* have I met anyone like you, and I've never felt this way about any man."

She was merely crying now, enormous tears flowing over her high cheekbones. For the very first time, Frank saw a woman who, although in the act of crying, remained beautiful. He begged her to stop, but she continued.

"I don't care how old you are," she proclaimed. "What's that got to do with it? It's what's inside that counts. It's what kind of person you are that's important. And you're a very special person. I know that. Otherwise I wouldn't be sitting here talking to you like this."

He interrupted. "But that's the point, Katherine. You *don't* know that." He spoke calmly, attempting to halt her unstable exhibition by throwing the truth in her face. "You *think* you know it, like a hundred thousand other people thought they knew it—*before* the divorce proceedings. Sure, it's too late then. They wished they had known each other a little better, wished they had talked about a few more things in greater detail. But they didn't. Infatuation is what they call it. There's passion—no question about it—but it's irrational and has absolutely no foundation...except physical attraction...and physical attraction is important. I'd be the first to admit it." And based on what Frank had seen during the last hour or so, the physical attraction that this woman had for him was incomparable. "But the end result can be disastrous, perhaps like your two previous experiences you haven't discussed."

Her composure was returning, and she turned on her persuasiveness. "Frank, you can be too rational, too analytical. You're older than I, and no doubt have many more acquaintances. I wonder how many couples you've known appear to be genuinely in love. And I wonder how many of the ones who appear to be genuinely in love, actually are. Based on my own somewhat limited exposure, I cannot come up with one single couple—not one—and that includes my mother and father."

She had already released his wrists, tenderly holding his hands in hers. "Regardless of the age difference, the cultural and sociological differences, regardless of the racial difference—whatever...in this life, if you meet one person for whom you feel *love*—in the true meaning—and that person feels the same way about you...and you're lucky enough to spend one year with that person—even one month...even one day, Frank—like today...you're one of the most fortunate..." She resumed weeping, "human beings...or *creatures*," she referred to what he'd called her, "who's ever lived on the face of this earth."

Frank had to control his own emotions. It was a new experience for him. Her emotional and verbal reactions were beyond his expectations. Rocky tilted his head and whined twice.

Katherine, almost whispering now. "That's how I feel about you, Frank. I know it sounds crazy. And you must think I'm a crazy creature." Prelude to a smile. "But I'm not proposing marriage to you. You know that." Stunning smile, especially in contrast to what he'd seen during the past moments, "I'm only asking you to let me get better acquainted with you—and give yourself a chance to know more about me."

Frank didn't know what to say. Confusion, happiness, and apprehension were all creeping up on him. This was superior to any script he could've written. In fact it reminded him of his friend, Jack McRae, and what Jack had told him about his girlfriend, Ann Rockford, when they were students at Duke University. After knowing Jack for only a few days, Ann invited him to her dormitory on the East Campus. There was a special alcove in a downstairs waiting room where a female student/resident was allowed to talk in semi-privacy with a male friend for a limited time period. Ann actually got down on her knees in front of Jack, with tears streaming down her face and, aware that Jack couldn't possibly be in love with her in so short a time span, beseeched him to let her love him because she was hopelessly smitten.

Frank knew that mentally, and in writing, he would later deal with this scene in an altogether different fashion, but he was now unable to ignore the similarity with his current predicament. This brief memory affected the expression on his face.

"Frank, are you still with me?" she asked, waving her hand in his face.

"I'm sorry, Katherine…In God's eyes, we're all creatures…and as I told you, I guess…I'm afraid. It would be impossible—and I underline the word *impossible*—for you to know or comprehend the turmoil that's going on inside of me."

She loved the way he brought God into it, and sincerely hoped he was a Christian. Her intuition told her yes. "Frank, you never have to be afraid with me. There's no way I'd ever do anything to hurt you."

"Sure," Frank thought, "not intentionally." He was familiar with those words…and the scenario that customarily followed them weeks, or even months, later. From a kneeling position in front of her, he got up. Ashamed of what he'd just thought, admitting the guilt wouldn't be hers but his, and convinced she was an honorable young lady, he smiled at Katherine. "I know that," he said quietly.

"Let's postpone the phone call," she suggested, "until after we clean up, if you don't mind. They'll pro-rate the kayak rental charge, and I'll take care of it…no problem. After all this talk…which I'm very pleased took place, I'd prefer to clean up first and then apply the ice. Is that all right with you?"

"It's fine."

"Please shut the door as you go out. Rocky'll stay here with me. Take your time. I know I'll finish before you, but knock before you come in," followed by an unnatural smile used only as a punctuation mark. "The cane I referred to is in the extreme left corner of the closet, leaning against the wall. If you can find it bring it. I'll be sitting here," she chuckled, "on the toilet waiting for you."

Both grinned.

CHAPTER 3

When Frank knocked on Katherine's bathroom door, although carrying a cane, he felt like a teenager approaching his first date. The proverbial lump was very much in his throat. There was another lump, caused by his partial erection on the right side of the oversized cargo shorts he wore, but fortunately the fabric bulge due to the fit differential sufficiently concealed it.

At the sound of Katherine's melodious voice when she responded, "I'm ready," accompanied by Rocky's eerie moans, Frank knew he was about to take his "first giant step" onto a different, completely unknown planet. It was a cosmic journey from which he'd never return…surely not in the emotional and intellectual capacity of the man he'd lived with for many years.

Turning the knob, he pushed open the door. Before him, standing on one leg, her right index finger touching the vanity for balance, was the most striking female he'd ever encountered. By simply combing her pixie cut and expertly glossing her sensuous lips, Katherine accomplished something Frank would've thought impossible: She elevated the beauty of her extraordinary face. Of course her multicolored, florally designed skirt, black sleeveless blouse, and simple turquoise necklace contributed nothing negative, but Frank had ended his appraisal with her visage and the incomparable smile it wore.

"You'll *never* see me sitting on a toilet again. That's a promise." The smile was now restrained, but those heavenly eyes reflected the swirling fervor set free inside her.

Katherine, in turn, was impressed by Frank's new look, especially in her father's clothes, included in her assessment...except the shorts were too big. Mainly, she liked the way he combed his hair, parted on the left, with the areas above his ears apparently trained to lie horizontally; and secondly, she appreciated the fact that he had a good crop of it...at what she estimated was his age. The khaki cargo shorts were noticeably bunched around the waistline where her father's belt had forced a substantial size reduction. Her dad's dark green polo shirt looked fine. On his feet, Frank wore between-the-toes type sandals.

"That's a promise I wouldn't necessarily make you keep," Frank said, his face clearly imaging his pleasure. Then he thought, "I like this planet...might stay." And slightly paralyzed by the nonfiction persona before him, his personal thoughts continued, "I wish she were the only inhabitant...and I didn't have to deal with all the other jackasses." Then looking down at the sensitive face and talkative eyes of Rocky, no doubt recording every word, perhaps every thought, he added, "Except for Rocky...he can stay."

"I wiped off the cane with my towel," Frank said. "Was a little dusty," holding it out, crook first, toward her. "Used your dad's comb—I put it back, after cleaning it."

"That's fine," smiling. "He'll never know." With her left hand she seized the crook, let the cane swing downward, and swiftly hobbled from the bathroom, favoring her left leg. "Follow me. Rocky, you go take a nap." She led Frank back into the kitchen, where she returned to the red-topped stool. Rocky returned to his doggy bed. Motioning to the refrigerator with her right hand, "If you'll open the freezer section below, look in the back on the right side, you'll see a couple of packs with synthetic ice and Velcro straps."

They had light blue plastic covers and Frank spotted them easily.

"Follow me again," as she started out, grabbing a kitchen towel from the sink area. The terrier watched, not budging. Going down the hall in a different direction, they went through a large oval doorway into a spacious, luxuriously furnished living room.

The life-sized sculptured figures, one resembling a conquistador, the other a Grecian maiden, were still searching the horizon. Many other art objects had been tastefully placed on the various wooden or marble, intricately designed tables of mixed sizes and shapes, reflecting exquisite workmanship. A vast carpet-to-ceiling, built-in bookcase monopolized the far wall. In it, the spaces devoid of books were few, each occupied by objets d'art. On the wall nearest the doorway from which Katherine and Frank entered were several large impressionist paintings, two of which Frank thought could be Renoirs—or maybe Monets.

In an area away from the windows, beyond the bookcase, there was a built-in, professional looking stereo unit. Between the bookcase and the stereo unit, against the wall, there was a sumptuous sofa flanked by two rectangular, mahogany lamp tables: one with a cabinet, the other with three drawers. The tables were graced with impressive matching lamps and marble compotes containing artificial fruit. Atop the table with three drawers was a telephone.

Three commodious, modern designed chairs in beige fabric that matched the sofa, one with an ottoman, were thoughtfully arranged on a thick lime-colored carpet, which completely covered the entire living room floor. Unquestionably, the center of attention was the grand piano, situated in front of the paintings.

Still barefoot, Katherine limped directly toward the end of the sofa by the phone and seated herself, leaning the cane next to the cushion. "Oh, this feels good. Frank, please slide the ottoman over here—it's lighter than I. Let me hold the ice packs while you do it."

"Sure." Giving them to her, he gently picked up the ottoman, put it in front of her, and quickly retrieved the blue packs.

"Thanks." She opened the middle drawer of the end table, pulling out what looked to be a plastic dust cover, maybe for a computer keyboard. Spreading it on top of the ottoman, she then neatly folded the kitchen towel and carefully positioned it over the dust cover. After closing the middle drawer and opening the top one, she removed what, according to her previous description, appeared to be an additional *La Jolla Blue Book*, and put it in her lap. "Now we're making progress." Stretching out her left leg, holding her injured ankle over the kitchen towel, she then reached for the cordless phone with her right hand. "Dr. Taylor, see if you can fasten the ice packs—it's gotta be easier than the life jacket—and I'll look up the number and call about the kayak."

Frank smiled sheepishly, a bit of redness invading his face, "Won't be as much fun though."

Big laugh from Kat, "There you go. You're admitting it—you were having fun. I kinda thought you were. I was watching your eyes in the water. Baaad boy."

He started on her ankle as she began flipping through the yellow pages. Stopping on a particular page, Kat perused ads under the kayak heading. "Is it the Kayak Company?"

"That's it," finishing with the Velcro straps. "How's it feel? Not too tight?"

"Perfect," from New Jersey, letting her ankle sink into the kitchen towel. "Take a break, leave this up to me. Please remind me when 20 minutes are up." Having memorized the phone number, she tossed the Blue Book back into the drawer, closed it, picked up the cordless phone, the type with the Caller I.D. window above the numbered buttons, and began tapping certain digits.

Unless Katherine needed specific information, Frank figured it best to stay out of it. Setting the timer on his watch for 19 minutes, he walked toward the big tinted windows and sucked in the rather unique aura. Although periodically hearing Kat use his name two or three times, Frank was mainly concerned about whether his head was screwed on properly. Glancing at the Steinway, he recalled when Katherine mentioned the multitude of couples who are apparently in love, but in reality are not, she expressly included her parents. That carried an insidious dark significance for Frank.

Standing next to the conquistador, Frank was overwhelmed by the breathtaking scene: the still cloudless sky with Del Mar, Solana Beach, and perhaps even Oceanside near the horizon. Several walkers and joggers moved along the path. He could see the spot from which he thought Katherine fell. "If I lived here, with this view," Frank reasoned silently, "my concentration would be limited to fucking Katherine at least once a day. On the other hand, if my fate were to turn into stone and become a statue…not a bad location." From a nearby table, Frank picked up a framed 8"x10" of what was undoubtedly Katherine, as a teenager, and her parents. A mystical look invaded his unblinking eyes.

"It's all set, Frank. No problem," Kat announced.

Frank knew there wouldn't be. Katherine's personality exuded confidence. If the woman said she'd do something, you could bet on it. Wearing a controlled smile, he turned, "I didn't expect any," and ambled in Kat's direction. Pausing briefly before the bookcase, he noticed several Thomas Hardy novels in a row. One of them, *Far From the Madding Crowd,* was slightly awry. As he repositioned it, "After some serious consideration, I've decided if one must have a personal disaster, this is an ideal place to experience it."

She burst into laughter, then suddenly stopped when she evoked the particular disasters in her own life.

"You could open it to the public, charge an exorbitant fee, and guarantee a disaster," he added, "and become even richer."

"Frank, you're making fun of me. I'm as rich as I care to be." Simulating a hurt expression, but also genuinely feeling it, "Maybe when you hear my *whole* story, I'll get some sympathy."

He sat next to her on the sofa and carefully adjusted the cane's position, making sure the weight change caused by his body didn't disrupt the ice treatment. Her left leg with the injured ankle was between them. It was the first time they'd sat together.

Softly begging her pardon, as he indulged himself in marveling at her bewitching eyes, "Forgive me, Katherine, I…I've never joked with anyone like this, since maybe high school. I don't know how to explain it. I feel so comfortable with you, like I've…known you for many years." Frank heard himself saying the words, but had difficulty admitting it was he who spoke, as though his hearing was related to a separate entity than his speaking…as though his old self, floating away in some mystical nebula, listened bemusedly to this new and different person he could feel himself becoming.

"That's exactly how I feel, Frank. It's wonderful. I swear I've never felt this way about anybody."

"Don't swear…please." He looked at his watch. "You're into the last 10 minutes. You're pretty good at this," looking at the ice packs. "Most people start squirming after two minutes."

"I've done it a few times."

"You look like you've been active in sports."

"Oh yeah, most of my life."

"For example?"

"I did a lot of different things. Pretty good at springboard diving—one and three meters…never went off the platform, however…until this morning," she chuckled.

"That explains how you hit the water so well today."

"I suppose so. Soon as my legs entered the water, I knew I had to quickly pike my body to decrease the depth of my plunge, otherwise I *would* be in the hospital. Plus I've snorkeled there hundreds of times and had a pretty good idea of how deep the water was. Luckily, it was close to high tide, and I knew it before I fell. I was mainly trying to push myself out beyond a clump of rocks on the bottom. I could actually see those rocks when I was on the edge, trying to regain my balance. When I knew I'd lost it…that I was going to fall, I just tried to jump beyond that clump. Fortunately, I made it."

When Katherine spoke more than one sentence, Frank found himself mesmerized just looking into her eyes. He'd snap himself out of it, nevertheless, wishing he could sit there and listen to her forever.

"So diving and what else?" Not big on small talk, he was sincerely interested.

"Some gymnastics. Wasn't on the team, but I used to practice with them. My girlfriend was—this was all in high school. In floor exercise, I wasn't bad—I was above average on the uneven parallel bars, but otherwise, forget it. Took too much dedication. I was doing too many other things—a cheerleader during football and basketball seasons." Then pointing to the fox tattoo on her left arm, "Here's the fox I was talking about. All the cheerleaders had one. My tennis game's not bad—even now. And aside from sports, most important of all is the piano."

Nodding at the piano, "I was wondering if you played." Frank extended his arm and took her left hand in his. "Great hands…beautiful fingers for the piano."

Squeezing his hand, smiling, "My teacher used to tell me that too. You play?"

"No, no—radio, that's about it. Joking around with you…that was thoughtless of me to bring up your personal disasters. That's absolutely none of my business. I'm very sorry." Actually he was curious to know what they were.

Irritated a bit, "What do you mean, none of your business?" Facing him head on, "I want you to know everything about me, Frank, and I intend to tell you everything. Or maybe you're trying to tell me you're not really…that interested."

Searching for something in her eyes, but unable to find it, thinking, "Sure, and you want to know everything about me too, right?" Then back to Kat, softly, "I didn't say that, Katherine—or think it." Once again he was dealing only with his conception of the truth, and the truth was that he wanted to know all about her. Yet she had a perfect right to know all about him, but he had no intentions of sharing that information. "What happens with the kayak?"

"He knows precisely when to change the subject," she thought. Then aloud, "Some kid who works for him'll be at the front door within an hour. I'll give him the vest and the money…he'll walk down the slope, hop on the kayak, and be back at the shop in less than 30 minutes. Then everybody'll be happy—Oh, I forgot. Please go back to my bathroom and pick up the wet vest. I don't want you to take it through the house, dripping, when the guy rings the bell. Go out the side door where we came in. Don't close it behind you though…you'll be locked out. Haul the vest around to the front porch steps so it'll be there when he comes to the door—"

"Wait a minute," Frank interrupted. "What happens when your neighbor spots me escaping through the side door with an unidentified object…and phones the police?"

"Frank, you're too much. You obviously have a criminal mind." Smiling, "Where do you come up with all that stuff?"

"I read the paper, watch the TV news, and I'm an accomplished cat burglar—with a C. What else do you want to know?"

"A lot. Remember, I'm nosy by nature," smiling more broadly, but catching herself in time. "Okay, how's this…go back to the kitchen, look in the cabinet under the sink. There's a box of plastic bags. Grab one. Take it to my bathroom and throw the wet vest into it. Bring it back out here. Go up those steps," she pointed to the only area in sight where Frank hadn't been. There were three steps up into what evidently was a dining room section. "That doorway on the left leads to the front door. You can drop the vest on the steps just outside the front door. How's that for organization? Oops, one other thing. What I'm wearing, I had in the bathroom closet, but my purse and sandals are in my bedroom. It's the one diagonally across from my dad's. Remember? Can you get them for me? The purse is black suede, on the dresser. The sandals are tan leather, and should be peeking out from under the dresser."

Frank started in that direction. "Be right back."

Kat closely observed Frank's walk, his erect posture, and the manner in which he moved his arms. In the baggy shorts, she was unable to see his attractive butt. The swimsuit was more revealing. She silently gave her full approval. "Maybe he's only 50 or 51," she silently conjectured. "That would only be about 15 years difference...not bad. Now it's only a matter of giving the money to Frank, so he can in turn give it to the kid at the front door, then removing the ice pack, and going into the kitchen and preparing lunch. And during lunch, possibly ask some harmless questions in order to find out a little more about this interesting, physically exciting man who's unlike any other I've met. Not only that, he has so many of the qualities I've always looked for in men, but seldom found. And I'm still betting he's great in bed too."

"This it?" Frank held the bag in one hand and the sandals in the other at shoulder height.

"Right on, sweetie. Let me get the money so you can give it to him." The term of endearment created a smile on Frank's face as he approached her. "What're you smiling about?" She knew exactly, and she knew if he could read her mind, his smile would be gigantic.

"Nothing," his smile widened. "Just in a good mood." Those eyes of hers had him again.

"You're a *very* sweet man...and I'll bet you're always in a good mood. I can't imagine you being angry. How much time left?" Proving she could also change the subject swiftly.

Checking his Casio, "Four and a half minutes."

She'd taken two bills out of her purse, a $20 and $5, and closed it. "Here, put this in your pocket so you'll have it when the bell rings."

Frank was folding the bills when Rocky streaked from the hallway door as if chasing a rat, barking at the top of his lungs. His destination appeared to be the front door.

To Frank, "That's our man." To Rocky, "It's okay, Rock, we know who it is. Calm down." To Frank, "Just open the door enough to give him the money, otherwise, Rocky'll chew him up in little pieces. Only kidding. It's best not to let him get out though—he's kinda aggressive, in an affectionate way. Sorta like me."

Frank started toward the kitchen. "First, I have to get the plastic bag and put the wet vest in it."

"Oh yeah, I forgot," she smiled, watching him disappear, and then sprang to a standing position, snatched the cane with her left hand, and rapidly made her way to the bookcase, curious as to what book he'd touched. Because all the Hardy books were bound in bronze leather, she knew it had been one of them, but she didn't know which. Frank reappeared from the hallway door, carrying the bagged preserver, and went in the direction of the front entrance. Kat returned to the sofa and waited there until Frank came back. When he did, she asked, "Any problems?"

"Not a bit. Said he'd take care of everything. Rocky got a little frisky, but it worked out okay. Thanks, Katherine."

"Hey, I appreciate your help very much. Let's eat something. I'm fine now. I'll take off the ice packs in the kitchen and put them back in the freezer. Are you hungry? I am. Didn't have much breakfast."

Katherine, leaving her sandals and purse, and still barefoot, walked more normally now. Rocky accompanied her.

Frank watched her cautiously. "As usual, I had a good breakfast, but the swimming worked up my appetite."

"So you like breakfast, huh?"

"My favorite meal. Grew up in a breakfast-eating family."

"That's one reason you're so healthy looking."

Back in the kitchen, Kat stood the cane up in the corner between the counter and the wall, sat on the red-topped stool, propped her left leg up on the nearby stool, and began removing the ice packs. Frank held them while they both eyeballed the injured ankle. He also scrutinized every other visible part of her body. He noticed how perfect her skin was. Rocky went back to his bed.

She gently squeezed the hurt area. "See, it's fine now. I told you," slowly rotating her foot to prove it.

"Yeah, it looks a lot better, but take it easy. What can I do to help?"

"That's a deal," touching his hairy forearm tenderly. She'd wanted to do it. "You could sell that hair to some baldheaded guy."

"Never thought of that. If I ever get financially strapped, might try it." He replaced the ice packs in the freezer, went to the sink, and started washing his hands.

"Guy's hygienic too," Kat mentally noted. "So far, batting a thousand. Lying next to him in bed, he's probably one of those guys who have a natural fragrance. Bet even his cock tastes good. Damn, he's sexy." Then to Frank, "Look on the second shelf, under the milk and juice, and you'll see a white bowl covered with plastic. That's the tuna. Next to it, in that covered blue dish, there're some stuffed eggs. In that slide-out drawer below, wrapped in plastic, there's red leaf lettuce that I thoroughly washed last night. And up above, there's milk, orange juice, or that pitcher of tea…whichever you want. I'll have the orange juice. If you want tea, look on the fridge door, you'll see a plastic baggie with a lemon already washed and quartered."

As Kat spurted the directions, Frank smoothly followed them, only seconds behind.

After sliding open a plastic cabinet door above her head, Katherine reached in, pulled out a box of Ritz Crackers. "Is it okay if we eat here at the counter? I can keep my leg elevated. It feels fine now."

"Absolutely." Placing the bagged lemon on the counter and pointing, Frank asked, "Are the plates over there?"

"Right. There're utensils in the drawer below—and the paper napkins are there. Please bring them." Kat, equally conscious of sanitation, moved gingerly without the cane to the sink and began washing her hands.

Frank watched closely, admiring the elegance of her hands and the dexterous manner in which she squished the liquid soap between and around her graceful fingers. He was unable to recall ever having seen a woman wash her hands so artistically...and sensually. He was on the verge of an erection, just watching her. With a paper towel, she dried them very well.

From the corner of her eye, she'd caught Frank in the act of observing her. She grinned magnificently, revealing those perfect teeth. "I kinda like being a captivating creature." Both laughed. "Let's eat," she proposed. Returning to the red-topped stool, hardly limping, she reached above once more, removing two large glasses that she placed on the counter.

Frank seated himself on another stool, on the opposite side of the counter, directly facing Kat, who adroitly uncovered the food, placed open leaves of lettuce on both dishes, and served a helping of tuna salad and a stuffed egg, first to Frank, then to herself. She pushed the salt shaker and pepper grinder toward him as she re-elevated her leg.

"That's sea salt, by the way. Hope you like my salad. I'm sort of a health nut. I use white albacore, celery, egg, and a soy-based mayonnaise, which I also used for the stuffed eggs." She noticed Frank put the pitcher of tea on the counter. "Don't you want some ice for your tea?" She broke open the plastic bag containing the cut lemon and slid the sugar bowl over to him.

"No thanks, it's cold enough. I *am* sort of a lemon freak though," squeezing lemon into his tea, "but I'll pass on the sugar. Don't use the stuff."

"Same here."

"Saw the soy milk in the fridge. That's what I use. We must be on the same wavelength." Frank didn't give Katherine a chance to respond. "Tell me about the piano. What kind of music do you play?" As he looked across the counter at this absolutely stunning female, he could feel himself becoming sexually aroused. Her mere presence did that to him. She was fully dressed, but he could mentally see her in the nude, with her luscious breasts, tiny waist, and seductive ass. Frank was hungry for food, but he was also hungry for Kat.

She was a bit hesitant with her answer…and disappointed, because she'd planned to talk first about an entirely different subject. Both had put small amounts of tuna salad on crackers, slowly eating and looking into each other's eyes.

"The piano's certainly a major part of my life, Frank. It would be impossible for me…to think of life without the piano. But trying to do what you asked me to do—put myself in your shoes—I think there's something else, from your standpoint, that's more important for me to tell you before I tell you anything else. I'll make it as brief as I can, and excuse me for talking and eating at the same time, but I really want you to know about this from the beginning."

"Beginning of what?" Frank thought. "Here I am on this strange planet with this captivating creature I physically desire, and the surprises are starting to unfold. The suspense may be too much for me."

Katherine interpreted Frank's silence as an approval to continue. "I'm 36 years old. In my entire life, I've had romantic relationships with two men. The first one lasted about six months. I was a senior in high school—'Miss Everything'…captain of the cheerleaders, beauty queen, and all the rest of that nonsense. He was quarterback and captain of the football team…guaranteed a scholarship to a top-level college—also very handsome and, I believed at that time, extremely nice. To make it short, on several occasions he tried to come on to me, and I made it quite clear that I had no interest in a sexual relationship. He told me that was the only real interest he had in me, that he could have sex with any girl he wanted, and that his primary interest was football—take it or leave it. That was the end of *that* relationship, which never went beyond a kiss. My decision required less than one second. The last I heard, he's already been married and divorced twice. Before that, he flunked out of college. Don't know the details. Don't really care.

"That had a poisoning effect on my feelings about men for a long time. Shouldn't have, but it did. My father, who's my hero—he's the greatest guy I know—in every respect—helped me climb out of the gloom. If I'd had any sense, just looking at my father, I should've known that somewhere there had to be at least one other guy out there like him.

"A little over six years ago I thought I'd met that guy. I was modeling in Paris. Met him through one of the designers. That should've told me something, but I wasn't paying attention. He was charming, intelligent—into biotech stuff, doing heavy research. Had the necessary sophisticated French accent...not movie star handsome, but good-looking in a very Gallic way. Not extremely masculine though...I realized that even then.

"How does the expression go? 'He swept me off my feet.' Wined me, dined me, danced me. Showed me off to all his intellectual, scientific friends—and of course his family—never once making a sexual advance of any kind—a perfect gentleman. I was beginning to convince myself there was no such thing. And guess what? He and an American friend were coming to La Jolla—I'd never been here, but had heard nothing but great things about it—to patent and start producing, from a newly formed corporation—*their* corporation—they were the owners—this top-secret product 'that would overwhelm the pharmaceutical industry,' he told me.

"He proposed marriage. You gotta realize I was on the edge of 30. And even though he wasn't the Prince Charming I'd expected to hook up with someday, he *was* charming...and a gentleman. I figured I'd probably never meet that real prince, and if I were ever interested in making the big blind jump into matrimony, this was the guy I'd more than likely be *reasonably* happy with. And it sounded like a kind of adventurous future...living in a great place like La Jolla, with occasional trips to France. So, like millions of other fools, I did it."

Katherine managed to eat between sentences, periodically sipping her orange juice, practically never taking her almost unblinking eyes off Frank, who was hopelessly under her spell.

"My mother," Kat continued, "went ballistic. Antoine—that's his name—Antoine Gabin—everybody calls him Andy—is white, and she didn't want any part of it. That didn't bother me a heck of a lot because my mother and I were never the very best of buddies, but I felt bad about my dad, who was extremely understanding, getting caught in the middle. Because of the friction—and a few other things—we decided it was best to get married in Paris, at a small Catholic Church near his parents' home. Surprisingly, both my parents flew over. I knew my dad would, but would've bet big money my mom wouldn't. She had more fun than she thought. Got a little drunk on the champagne, but…" Katherine shrugged her shoulders and grinned.

"Was a beautiful wedding, mostly his crowd. Some of the people I knew from modeling were there. Then two or three weeks later, we were off to La Jolla—I hope you're not getting bored—the important part is coming up."

"Not at all." Frank tried to smile sincerely, but it was noticeably weak.

"Are you sure?"

The feebleness of his smile was due not to his lack of interest in what she was saying, but to his mixed and confused feelings about her having been married in the Catholic Church. "If she were Catholic," he pondered, remembering her making the sign of the cross just before coming off the cliff, "fine, but…" Then he brought himself back to reality. "Absolutely," he said firmly to her, strengthening his smile.

"For me it was love at first sight…as far as *La Jolla* was concerned. I was crazy about the place from the very beginning—and still am. With Andy, it's a different story. I had this strange feeling from the start that something was missing, but couldn't put my finger on it.

"Looking back of course, the signs were all there. I simply didn't know how to interpret them. He was wrapped up in his research and I fully accepted that—expected it—but there was no way I could've guessed how many long hours he'd spend on that project. He'd be gone for two and three nights in a row without phoning me. His explanation was always about some unexpected business meeting in San Francisco or Dallas, or a research phase of the project that couldn't be interrupted 'for any reason,' he said—even if one of his parents died. When I'd quiz him about why he couldn't make a one-minute phone call to let me know what was going on, he'd shrug it off with, 'Darling, you have no conception of the potential numbers involved here.' By numbers he meant dollars, money. That's the driving force behind Andy…money, and one other thing that I'm getting to."

Frank saw that Rocky was as engrossed as he by Kat's story. He wondered if Rocky had previously heard this same monologue.

"Romantically, I was an infant…guess I still am. Sure, I had dates with different men, heard all the lines you can think of trying to get me into bed, but basically I had meals, saw movies, went dancing, and that sort of thing—and that's it—nothing more. I was never sexually promiscuous. I was a virgin until I met Andy." Katherine knew that she'd derived sexual pleasure from her dependable dildo on numerous occasions, but that was a personal matter. "He's the only one I've had any…" Her steady gaze had a spellbinding effect on Frank. "sexual experience with. I'd read books on it, but I had no real exposure to it—only with him. And with him, it certainly was *not* the wonderful emotional high I expected and read about."

Frank interpreted that to mean she had never been sexually satisfied and, from the look in her expressive eyes, he was perhaps being considered as a desirable candidate. He liked the idea. At the moment, there was nothing he would've liked more than to have sex with her.

"With Andy, it was as if he were playing a video game. He was completely detached. Instead of expressing his love for me physically, he was deriving pleasure from using my body, like he had put his money into the machine and wanted to see how close he could get to the highest score. I never felt that any personal gratification on my part was under consideration at all. I just happened to have been there, and was the one he was doing it with. The surprising part is, that several married women I know have told me they've experienced the same feelings with their husbands...but they're still married. Can you believe that?

"Again in retrospect, I know how stupid I was. He got his U.S. citizenship because of his marriage to me. That's probably all he wanted from me, tell you the truth. I let this go on, believe it or not, for three and a half years. I'm talking too much. I'll get to the meat."

Rocky sprang to all fours, his eyes frozen on Kat's.

"No, not that kind of meat, Rocky. Go back to bed." He did. "I started asking questions for which Andy had no intelligent answers. And many of his answers were completely inconsistent with the truth. I did some checking around, confronted him with the information. He admitted he had a vasectomy only weeks before we married. Then a couple of days later, I found out through a reliable source that Andy and his American business associate, companion, lover—whatever you want to call him—were having an affair—and had been, even before he met me. The first thing I did was go to the doctor and get checked for HIV. Fortunately, I was okay."

Katherine broke down. Rocky didn't move, only moaned two or three times.

"Katherine, you're making yourself sick. I don't want you to do that. Please," Frank urged her. "You can tell me all this stuff some other time."

"No, that's basically it. I wanted you to know now—not later." Under control now, "I can't begin to tell you how that affected me. I thought that was the end of me. It was the end of my world. Dad came to my rescue, thank God.

"The divorce was a *very* distasteful experience. Financially, I came out fine, but emotionally...devastated. All the legal proceedings took nearly a year. Luckily for me, at the very beginning, Andy and Chuck—that's his buddy's name—sold the corporation to some British conglomerate for $112 million. I got this house, the one in front of it, a sizeable cash settlement, and a comfortable monthly income from a trust fund for the rest of my life." Katherine considered it unwise at this point to reveal she was actually a multimillionaire.

"But if I could push a button," she went on, "go back to pre-Antoine, I'd do it in a heartbeat. Also, I got my maiden name back and, because of the circumstances involved, had no problems—just a lot of paperwork going through the San Diego Catholic Diocese—having my marriage annulled, as far as the church is concerned. If I could push another button and make the nightmares go away, that would be nice too." She reached across the counter and ran her fingers over his.

"I don't think our nightmares go away, Katherine." Frank expressed the words with a steady voice. "They're something we have to learn to deal with...and live with. We all have them. Believe me, I have my share...maybe more. But when you're putting your make-up on, Katherine...brushing your teeth, combing your hair...just stop and look at yourself for a second in the mirror. You'll see this gorgeous young lady who has it all...I mean everything. I...I don't know how to say it to you. You...are...a dream girl, in every respect. You should thank God from the bottom of your heart."

"I do, Frank. I really do."

With his right hand, the one she'd been fingering, Frank fondled the little finger of her left hand. Since she hadn't mentioned her mother with reference to the divorce, and he didn't want to appear inattentive or uncaring, he inquired, "Did your mom die?"

She gave him one of those puzzling smiles. "I believe you've been paying attention, Professor Schmeelburger." She laughed.

"You don't get to be a professor daydreaming. Besides, I want to pass the final exam."

She squeezed his hand lovingly. "This is one of the most enjoyable days of my life. If it gets any better, I don't think I can stand it."

Frank grinned, and had a very clear conception of how it could get even better…getting her spectacular ass into bed, but he decided to contain himself. "You're really putting the pressure on me." He smeared more tuna salad on another Ritz Cracker and continued eating.

"About two and a half years before the divorce, my mother walked out on my father. She didn't walk, she ran off with a man who evidently had some connection with her job in marketing. No one really knows the details on that. He appeared on the scene from out of nowhere. A white guy, wouldn't you know it? I have to admit that I derived some sort of secret, twisted satisfaction out of that. She was almost 50 at the time, but *easily* looked 39 or 40…and I mean a *very* sexy lady. She had all the right stuff in the right places. Much better looking than I. My dad, who's a pediatrician—I didn't tell you that—was totally surprised—no warning whatsoever…absolutely blind-sided.

"He didn't know the man. In fact, none of the people my mom worked with knew him. The guy was in some kind of international trade—import/export stuff. Evidently, she dated him outside of her work. Listen to this…my mom left Dad a note, basically saying she was bored, felt like she wanted to do something a little more exciting with the rest of her life. She didn't even leave me a note—*nothing*! She was probably ashamed because my father soon discovered she'd taken $82,000 out of *their* savings account. That was nearly five years ago. We've never heard from her—no letters or phone calls. At first, Dad wanted to find them and prosecute, figuring the guy was behind it all. Then his professional partners, the doctors with whom he has a very successful medical practice, convinced him her notoriety all over the news media would have an adverse effect on their business...that actually finding out what kind of woman she was might have been worth the money he lost. Of course, part of that money was hers anyway. He bought that, but he still wanted to hire a private eye, trace her, just in case she'd possibly been murdered. I begged him to forget it. 'She did what she wanted to do,' I told him. 'Leave her alone, and if she's been murdered, there's nothing you can do about it now.' The note he received from her was clearly in her handwriting. The signature on the withdrawal slip was definitely hers, and the bank branch manager, who was brought into the scene when she got the money—because of the large amount—clearly recalled that she was in a very happy mood, and entirely alone when she did it. If there had been any invisible coercion by the stranger she'd met, the bank manager told my father, she could have informed him very easily. Dad asked the bank manager to forget about the whole thing. He did. 'If you meet some nice lady and want to get married, that can all be worked out legally,' I told Dad. 'In the meantime, let's chalk her off.'" A set of tears made its way slowly down Katherine's face. "Dad's still dealing with the legal issues, but according to certain information that hasn't been proven, my mother and that man both died in the World Trade Center last year. But that's based primarily on a letter that was generated from a word processor, which only has my mother's initials on it. The insurance people will probably pay off my dad *after* he's dead." The flow of tears increased. "It's kinda hard to chalk off your mother."

Frank's pause was long. "It's even harder not to judge her. That's God's domain." His face reflected perfect composure as he spoke the words. "Her eternal destiny is in His hands now."

For what was only 10 seconds, but seemed a full minute, Katherine sat quite still, peering at Frank through her teary eyes. "I think I'm the one who's dreaming...but this isn't a nightmare. It's the most beautiful dream I've ever had. And you're the most thoughtful person I've ever met." She was becoming more and more aware of Frank's refreshing wisdom, something to which she was unaccustomed in her everyday life.

"How's the ankle feel?" he asked.

"He's a master at this change of subject business," she silently decided. Raising her ankle slightly from the stool top, gradually moving it, "Much better. I could probably do without the cane, but I'll still use it." She stood, while using the counter as support, and tried to walk…and did, without the cane. "You see, what'd I tell you? That's the end of the ice. It makes it too numb and I really don't need it any more. Did you have enough to eat?"

"Plenty…very tasty."

Reaching for her cane, "We finished the tuna and the eggs. If you'll just put the tea and the orange juice back in the fridge, we'll leave the rest of this stuff here—I'll get it later—and we can go back to the living room for a little while before I go to work. Okay?"

Having already replaced the juice and tea, "That's fine." As they walked through the hallway again, Frank was happy to see the assured manner in which she carried herself, particularly the seductive manner in which she moved her hips as she walked. He wanted to ask her to play something on the piano, but hesitated due to her injured ankle. He loved the piano, but wasn't that knowledgeable concerning the foot pedals and thought they could present a problem for her. Rocky followed in silence.

Once in the living room, she went straight for the piano bench, placing her cane on the floor between the bench and the wall paintings. Rocky sat next to the wall. Kat then motioned for Frank to sit in the large chair that faced the piano. When he'd asked earlier about the piano and if she played, Kat regretted cutting him off and switching to topics she felt compelled to cover, but now that she'd done so and had seen his interested response, Katherine knew this part of the program would be much more enjoyable.

"Infatuation, love at first sight, absurdity, maybe asininity—whatever you want to call it," she thought. "Maybe just raw carnal desire. All I know is, this is a very special day in my life and, regardless of what happens, I'm gonna express exactly what's on my mind, and let this wonderful man know how I feel about him. Naturally, I'm not gonna tell him how much I want to go to bed with him and make passionate love. That *would* be asking for trouble. But I've never felt this chemistry before with any man, and there will be no regrets on my part that I didn't verbalize what's in my heart, even though that's being heavily influenced by what's going on in my pelvic region. The truth is the truth, and I have to accept it."

All the joy inside Katherine radiated from the irrepressible smile on her face as she sat there silently admiring Frank Taylor. She knew nothing about the man, past or present, only what she saw and the sound of his voice. And his voice hadn't revealed one bit of information about his identity, what he did, where he was from, or his plans for the future.

Having been coached by her father as far back as she could remember to always use common sense, she carefully considered that Frank could be a criminal, that he could rape her, murder her at this moment, and the only witness would be Rocky—if he weren't also killed. The seconds zipped by and she was running out of time. She decided if she were that mistaken about this man, for whom she felt this uncontrollable physical attraction, she'd deal with those eventualities as they unfolded. Her affirmative conviction was not going to be changed at this point.

Smiling at Frank, Kat informed him, "I'm sure you'll be delighted to know I've decided not to give you…a final exam." They both laughed. "*However*, at a later date, I'm requesting a term paper."

Frank gesticulated with his right hand. "I figured there'd be a catch." Then in his secret thoughts, "But as long as I get to fuck you, it'll be worth it."

"Without the piano," she explained to Frank, "I don't believe I could've made it through that dark period in my life. The piano, Rocky, and of course my relationship with God are the things that saved me. My father, naturally, but he wasn't here most of the time. The piano is my means of expression. I don't compose music, but I like to play around with arrangements. What kind of music do you like?"

Pausing to answer her unexpected question as accurately as possible, "Some classical—depends…some jazz. You have to realize I grew up in a different era. I really don't care much for what I hear on the radio. When I was a kid, the big bands were popular: Dorsey, Goodman, Basie, Ellington—and vocalists like Sinatra, Bing Crosby, Ella Fitzgerald, Doris Day…and there were the Broadway musicals—Rodgers and Hammerstein were my favorites. Even a non-musical person like me could remember their tunes and lyrics."

Katherine was delighted that Frank had an appreciation for music. Evidently his tastes were not all that broad, definitely with reference to contemporary music, but he knew what he liked and could name the artists.

"Let me play something…especially for you."

She began with a rather sophisticated introduction to what Frank correctly guessed was 'Some Enchanted Evening' from Rodgers and Hammerstein's *South Pacific*. During the initial 30 seconds, her keyboard mastery was audible and visible. Her injured ankle presented no problem. Frank leaned back in the comfortable chair expecting to hear the remainder of a melodious instrumental. He was mistaken. From the moment Katherine first seated herself on the piano bench, she hadn't removed her eyes from Frank's. As she began to sing, her face took on a magical quality and, if she blinked, Frank missed it. Her interpretation was strongly jazz oriented, and may not have pleased either Rodgers or Hammerstein, but Frank was completely taken in. The creative knack she displayed in breaking up the lyrics with her commanding contralto, elongating certain words, pausing unexpectedly, and filling the verbal gaps with short virtuosic displays of piano technique, brought to Frank's mind one of his favorite performers. And her probable unconscious ability to not blink made him think of Ross Perot during his early 90's presidential campaign.

Occasionally, as she replaced certain key words in the lyrics with specific ones that applied to their meeting, Kat grinned deliciously, knowing unequivocally at this point there was a special bond between Frank and her.

It was a very impressive performance both vocally and instrumentally, and Frank applauded in his characteristically unobtrusive, polite manner. His face, however, said everything Katherine hoped for. He was speechless. Sitting there in a supernatural lull, he soaked up every nuance of the real-life painting before him. With a certainty that was questionable as well as intoxicating, the realization came to him he would never voluntarily leave this new planet. Severing communications with earth now was not an option, but a desirable necessity. Tears collected in his eyes. His master plan was up in the air now…totally.

Katherine rose from the piano bench, walked slowly without the cane to Frank, and sat on the arm of his chair. Seemingly embarrassed by a substitute replacement, Rocky cantered over to investigate. "Rocky, go back where you were," Kat warned. He did, hastily but reluctantly. She then placed her right hand behind Frank's neck, caressing the soft hairs with her fingers, looking directly into his face. "You have tears in your eyes."

Without speaking, he took her left hand in his and then, "You're incredible Katherine." Softly, quietly, selecting his words with great care, a personal characteristic she admired, "I just…had no idea how talented you are. I'm not surprised…no way. Again, you simply caught me off guard. I'm wondering, how many more surprises will there be? It's amazing how you sat there…and off the top of your head rewrote some of the lyrics. You're terrific. And your style…reminds me of one of my favorites."

"Who?" With startled interest.

Just for fun he almost said Ross Perot, but thought she might not grasp the humor. "Nina Simone," somewhat apprehensive he may have named an artist she didn't like, but knowing it was too late now.

"Oh Frank, you made my day—again. She's my idol—along with Herbie Hancock—another Herbie," she chuckled. "I have all Nina Simone's recordings. And you know her music—I can't believe this. That surprises me very much. You're full of surprises too."

"Why?" He was holding her left hand in both of his hands now. "You do this professionally?"

"Not really. On Friday and Saturday nights, I play the keyboard at a lounge up the street, but it's just part-time, kind of a fun thing for me. Gives me a couple of good practice sessions every week. Most of the clientele is middle-aged and older, so they request a lot of songs you probably like—and me too. For most of the stuff I do there I don't use this style…I play and sing conventionally, otherwise they may not invite me back. But occasionally I ask them if they'd like to hear *my* version, and they seem to appreciate it."

Before destroying radio contact with earth so to speak, Frank felt he should make one last attempt to bring Katherine—and himself—back to reality…but she interrupted his thoughts.

"You know what I've decided?" Not waiting for an answer, she continued, "My ankle's fine now. I'll take the cane just for psychological support, but let me drive you to your car, then I can drive to work from there. But…" she reinforced her right-hand grip on the back of his neck, noticing again how firm it was, and clenched his left hand tightly with hers, "look at me, Frank." He already was. "You're not going to pull a disappearing act on me, are you? Obviously, you've got many other things to do. If you can't see me tonight, tomorrow I have an early staff meeting at school and, following that, one morning class. Then after 11a.m., I'm free for the rest of the day. Tomorrow's Friday, so I do have to be at the lounge by eight o'clock.

Please see me tomorrow. Maybe you can come by the lounge, visit me for a little while just to see what I do. I'd love that."

There was a slight hesitation on Frank's part. He was thinking of his personal puzzle, and how he could fit all the pieces together. "That works out fine," he agreed. "Tonight I really should spend some time on my project, which I'll explain to you later. I can come by around noon. My place is pretty sloppy right now. I'd be embarrassed if you saw it. It's a tiny garage apartment in an alley here in the village."

"There're no alleys in La Jolla, Frank. You'd better get that straight right now, or you'll be in deep—you know what—with the locals. There's Bishops Lane and Drury Lane and several other lanes, but *no alleys*…in La Jolla." Standing in front of him now, she tried out her ankle.

"My place is on Bishops Lane near the Empress Hotel."

"Yeah, I know the area well. Get my hair done at Nadya's in an arcade near there. Since you know how to get here, I'll go to your place some other time. I'll show you how to get in here off Prospect. There's a house between this one and the street. It's a little tricky, if you haven't been here before. The taxi drivers get it all screwed up. That's why I always use Jewel Transit. They're the best." She caught herself using the word, screw, again.

Frank remembered aloud, "I have to get my swim trunks out of the bathroom."

"Why don't you grab another plastic bag and put 'em in that?"

Frank was off to the kitchen. "That's great."

When Frank left, Rocky came over to Katherine as she was picking up the cane near the piano. She sat on the bench and rubbed his head. "Mamma has to go to work. You be a good boy now and take care of everything, okay? And listen to me…don't be jealous. You're my best buddy. You know that." She smiled and whispered to Rocky. "But this guy really turns me on." Then back to her normal voice, "There's plenty of food and water for you. If you have to pee pee, you know what to do." From the way Rocky looked at Katherine, it was easy to see that she was his sun, moon, and god, but *he* hadn't quite made up his mind about Frank being on Katherine's planet. Perhaps Rocky could see something in Frank's eyes that Katherine couldn't.

Taking her cane and purse, she slid her feet into the sandals and accompanied Frank to the driveway area, where they got into Katherine's red late-model Prelude. She showed Frank how to enter the driveway to her place off Prospect.

Driving her car presented no problem; she didn't use her left foot. On the way to Frank's car, which was in La Jolla Shores, they exchanged phone numbers in case of an emergency, Frank scribbling the numbers down on a pad from the glove compartment. He left his number on the top sheet of the pad. Then, after folding it neatly, he put the sheet on which he'd written her number in the pocket of the shorts that were too big, along with his new California driver's license and car key.

As Frank had mentioned, his car was on a street that bordered the La Jolla Beach and Tennis Club, a private, rather exclusive resort facility with red tile roofs, well-kept tennis courts, an expansive beach, and a pitch-and-putt golf course on meticulously gardened entrance grounds.

After Frank agreed he'd be at her place around noon the next day, he smoothly eased out of her vehicle and shut the passenger door very gently. Not at all surprised, she had expected him to do it exactly that way. Door slammers were one of her pet peeves, especially if it were *her* car door they were slamming. Intuitively she knew Frank didn't fit into that category, and he proved it. He was smooth, gentle, and very attentive. She knew he would be that way in bed too. The fact that he didn't give her an affectionate kiss, at least on the cheek, did disappoint Kat somewhat.

CHAPTER 4

Katherine experienced noticeable difficulty while attempting to concentrate during the initial phase of her afternoon class. Her new acquaintance had put her in heat. Her libido was in high gear, and it was a fresh experience, certainly taking into consideration that it was brought about by the possibility of feeling a live penis inside of her, instead of the usual dildo. But once into the swing of her classroom routine and the specific lesson, she was able to push Frank's image into the back of her mind. Her ankle was much better. Maybe she'd exaggerated the pain in order to enlist his help. She smiled inwardly at the thought. She smiled again when she pictured herself in bed with Frank, fornicating delightfully.

On the way home she stopped at El Pescador on Pearl Street for a salmon sandwich on sourdough and salad to go. She'd have it later that night. Upon entering her home, after putting the food in the fridge, her first priority was Rocky. It was a behavioral pattern to which the little guy was addicted...an almost mandatory drill. He would pounce on his doggy bed, twirl over on his back with all fours extended upward, and wait for Kat to give him a vigorous rubdown with both hands. Hearing the funny noises she made while doing it enhanced his enjoyment. Next on her agenda, was the matter of going with a plastic bag to the spot from which she had earlier fallen, so she could gather Rocky's droppings and properly dispose of them.

That required about 10 minutes, including a couple of minutes of her gazing down at the area of the ocean surface where she'd hit the water.

Then, after washing her hands just as thoroughly as when Frank had watched, she rinsed the dirty dishes with hot water and a scrub brush, and placed them in the dishwasher until there were enough to constitute a sufficient load. Choosing the comfort of her living room, she checked the Caller ID record for in-coming calls. There was one call only, from Winthrop School pertaining to a task she'd already performed. She almost pushed the memory button for her father, but following a pause of at least 30 seconds, decided against it. Her impulse was to share her happiness with him, however, she knew very well he'd have many questions for which she had absolutely no acceptable answers.

Replacing the phone, she walked to the windows and again viewed the spot from which she'd fallen. That started the entire mental video of what had happened that morning. She reviewed it all, remembering the dialogue, the feelings, and Frank's face, regretting an unseen videographer hadn't captured every instant on tape so she could watch it over and over…at age 80.

Katherine asked God to help her, to guide her so she could make intelligent decisions. Attempting to distract herself to pass the time, she turned on the TV news. That didn't work. She had no interest in the happenings of the world or San Diego. Wherever she looked, she only saw two images: Frank's sensitive face or his sexy body.

She reminded herself of who she was: a college graduate, a pianist/singer, a French instructor, a 36-year-old divorcée with considerable financial and physical assets, including a hefty assured monthly income for the rest of her life, a beautiful home in one of the most desirable spots on earth, an incomparable father, and Rocky, the greatest dog alive.

After her divorce two years ago, she thought it best to go the rest of the way single. "Why get married again?" she questioned herself.

"Why go into another potentially unhappy legal relationship with a partner whose antecedents are questionable?"

Most of the guys her age seemed shallow and materialistic, mainly interested in money and a good quick fuck, and the various items they could buy with the former. And she had no interest in being the latter, particularly since, in her judgment, the *quick* obviously took priority over the *good*. She wanted no part of the one-night stands. She'd dated a few men in that category who'd approached her with that apparent objective in mind, and had been terribly disappointed, not by their performance in bed because she never went that far, but by their attitudes in general. Yet, none of them had lighted her fire the way Frank had. If so, taking stock of her current bodily sensations, she may have tumbled into bed with at least one of them.

The middle-aged ones, who apparently had the money *and* the toys, gave her the impression any money or toys they shared with her was conditional, namely sexual favors, and she wanted no part of that. But there again, none of them had been in the same quality category as Frank. Her fire had not been lit. She'd concluded that life was less hectic and simpler with Rocky, that there was no such animal as Prince Charming, who only existed in fairy tales, romance novels, and the imagination of naïve young ladies. Urbane women like her knew better…until now.

Now there's Frank Taylor, most definitely at this point an unknown entity. His background has to be 180 degrees different from hers, a totally dissimilar human being, unlike any she'd been around. She tried to attribute it exclusively to the age disparity, but horse sense clearly validated that, among his contemporaries, Frank Taylor would doubtless be regarded as an oddity or, more accurately, a standout. He didn't fit the mold. Frank Taylor was an individual in the purest sense. He'd never go along with the crowd if it meant doing something against his principles, and Katherine, at least in her own eyes, had very high ethical standards…bending them somewhat with reference to getting into bed with Frank.

This is the kind of man she'd always searched for and not found. He was the type of man she'd always wanted to look up to. Since her teenage years, when Katherine had thought of marriage and raising a family, Frank fit exactly the image of the man she had in mind. He wasn't African-American, but Katherine had always considered herself racially colorblind. She could easily picture herself sitting next to him in church. She freely admitted to herself that Frank sexually aroused her, that as his wife she would take great pleasure in expressing her love for him sexually. The truth was, and she openly accepted it, wife or not, she would love to fuck him...and that's what she planned to do.

Katherine did a great deal of thinking in the early evening that Thursday. After eating her salmon sandwich and salad, she and Rocky went for a short walk. Then she took a shower and decided to go to bed earlier than usual. On Friday she wanted her mental faculties to be razor-sharp. With Frank, it was paramount that her questions and responses be accurate and explicit, without deception, without equivocation.

Sitting on the side of her bed, she asked herself in all honesty, "Is it really possible that I could be falling in love with a person I've known for only a few hours? Or is it purely carnal desire?" Katherine stared at the carpet for 60 seconds without answering, then went down on her knees before a crucifix on the wall, as she did each night, and began to pray.

With one eye and both ears, Rocky watched and listened from his additional doggy bed, situated in the far corner of Katherine's bedroom.

"Dear Heavenly Father, thank you for the many blessings you've given me throughout my life. Thank you for my life itself—I take nothing for granted—and thank you for my health. Thank you for my loving family. Bless my wonderful father—and my mother, wherever she is, and my Uncle Gordon, who is always very close to you. And thank you for Rocky, my best friend. I couldn't do without him.

"Thank you, Dear God, for letting me survive the fall this morning without a serious injury. My ankle is fine now, but I'm fully aware I could be in a hospital or dead. I appreciate you letting me be here in my room in this comfortable home. And thank you so much, Dear God, for letting Frank Taylor be there when I needed him, like an angel. Thank you for bringing him into my life. I place myself in your hands, Dear Father. Please guide me and help me know what to do. Since I was a little girl, I've prayed that you would help me find the right man to love and to make happy, a man who will love me as much as I love him. I've been mistaken twice. I sincerely think Frank is the one, but I need your guidance. Please tell me, Dear God. Please show me in some way that Frank is the right man for me. Above all, please help me to be a better person, a true Christian in your eyes. Amen."

Katherine slid into bed and tried for the next 15 minutes to fall asleep, but her hyped-up libido wouldn't release Frank from her mind. She wanted him to stay, if not physically, imaginatively. Pulling up her mini-nightie with one hand, she removed the dildo from her night table with the other, and visualizing Frank's nude image for the next 20 minutes, gave herself an orgasmic treat. She then quickly fell asleep, with the dildo comfortably in her favorite spot…and Rocky closed his other eye.

CHAPTER 5

Friday morning's weather was a carbon copy of yesterday, perhaps even clearer. It was 7:28 a.m. and Katherine had already eaten breakfast, glanced over the newspaper, and dressed. Grateful to God that her ankle was in good shape, she was ready to leave for the staff meeting, except for Rocky's constitutional, which this morning would have to be somewhat shorter because Kat was a little behind schedule.

For now, she decided to stay off the subsidiary path from which she fell. Rocky desired to revisit it, hoping he could attack the same pelican that caused all the trouble on Thursday, but Kat restricted him to the main path. Momentarily caught in reverie, observing the rhythmic groundswells, she reassured herself yesterday's drama wasn't a fantasy. After Rocky answered nature's call, she locked him in the house and was off to Winthrop School.

Nothing eventful occurred at the staff meeting. It was primarily a semi-monthly coffee break during which the administrative personnel called upon the instructors to inform them of any problems, present or foreseeable. Since the school year had just begun, there wasn't much ground to cover.

Her French class was as smooth as always. The students adored Katherine. It was almost like she was one of them, although she stood for no nonsense. Despite being a disciplinarian, her sense of humor was in the realm of their experience. Also, it didn't hurt that she was the best looking and cutest teacher at the school. She was also the sexiest. She kept the male students fully aroused. Some of them signed up for her French class just so they could admire her bod during class and engage in vivid sexual fantasies with her—all of this while she lectured. Those particular male students usually paid the price at test time.

At the 11 a.m. bell, Kat left promptly, got into her car, and drove the six or seven short blocks to her home. Quickly, she sprayed and cleaned the windows of her car, then entered the house for Rocky's rubdown. Next, a shower, teeth brushing, hair combing, make-up, and into a different casual outfit: stretch jeans and a deep red polo top. She wished for more time to re-polish her nails, but it was too late.

While she was putting dog food and water in Rocky's kitchen bowls, he sprinted without barking toward the front door area. Kat knew it was Frank. The doorbell rang. Her watch indicated 11:59 a.m. He was still batting a thousand. She didn't bother to tell Rocky who it was. He knew. Entering the dining room from a door at the other end of the kitchen, Kat briefly smiled, twisted, turned, and took three or four broad dance steps before a ceiling-to-wall mirror that made the space look even larger. She was checking her entrance appearance, although it was Frank's entrance, especially the snug fit of the stretch jeans and the profile of her derrière prior to presenting herself to Frank. She took a deep breath to see if her breasts looked prominent enough. They did, and she smiled in approval.

As she reached for the front door knob, "God, please don't let him see my goose bumps." Rocky, waiting patiently at the entrance, had a puzzled look in his eyes.

She swung open the door and grinned directly into the eyes of…her father. And behind him, stood Frank.

"Hi, Baby. Surprise." Her father hugged her intensely, kissing her on the cheek.

Reciprocating, "Wow, this *is* a surprise," she gasped. "I was expecting Frank. So was Rocky." The taxi that brought her father drove away.

"Frank and I've already introduced ourselves," said her father. "I figured for sure he was a real estate agent." Looking at Frank, "They all want to sell this property, so they can get the commission. Can't blame them…they could live off that for a couple of years." He bent down, energetically massaging Rocky's head and neck. "Rocky, Baby, you little rascal, I missed you. You been a good boy?" Rocky responded, whining and licking.

Frank stood by looking agreeable and knowing that family matters took precedence. He was well aware that Dr. Churchill's visit wasn't scheduled, and that Katherine was embarrassed under the circumstances. His only option was to play it by ear.

"Where's your car, Frank?" Kat inquired.

"I walked over. Do we need it?"

"Not at all. Just wanted to make sure you didn't get a parking ticket if you're on Prospect." Then to her father, "Why didn't you phone me from the airport, Dad? I would've come after you."

"I did, but I got the answering machine, and I'm glad. I don't like for you to do that."

"Oh, my gosh." She was ashamed. "I'm sorry, Dad. I was on such a tight schedule after I got off today—I forgot to check it."

"No problem, Baby."

"Let's go inside," Katherine requested, preparing to pick up her dad's suitcase.

"No, I'll get that, Katherine." Lifting it, "Here we go." Her father led the way through the door.

"Come on, Frank." Kat motioned for Frank to follow and, as he passed, she whispered in his ear, "Don't mention my fall."

Frank nodded in agreement, giving her a plastic bag. She was certain it contained her father's clothes Frank had worn yesterday. Fortunately, the bag was opaque. They went into the living room where

Katherine's father put down his suitcase and addressed them. "Listen, you two evidently had something planned and I don't want to intrude."

"I invited Frank to lunch—not here. We were going out, and we'd like for you to come, Dad."

"No, Baby, I'm bushed. The convention in LA got boring, so I decided to leave...swing by here before taking the 'red eye' home. As you know, I don't make a habit of barging in on you like this. It's Friday, so I guess you're gonna work tonight, aren't you?"

"Yes, Dad."

"You'll be coming back here before that, won't you?"

"Sure, I have to shower and change clothes."

"Then why don't we do this? You two go on and do your thing. I've got a couple of kids I'm concerned about, so I'll make some phone calls and touch base with my staff. Then I'll clean up, maybe take a short nap. I can't sleep on those planes. And we can be together and talk for awhile before you go to work. But I want to make one thing very clear...you're not taking me to the airport. I'll take a cab. Is that agreed? Otherwise," chuckling, "I'll sneak off before you return."

"Okay, Dad, if you're sure that's what you want to do?"

"Oh yeah, I've already had two airports today, and that's two too many. I can spend 10 hours with sick screaming kids, but 30 minutes in an airport and I'm a basket case. All I need is to unwind for awhile."

"Frank and I'll go on then." She thought it best to keep the plastic bag, hoping her dad didn't later look for the dark green polo shirt or his sandals. "Your room's all set. There're fresh towels in the bathroom. I'll be back by six, maybe sooner, okay? If I'd known you were coming, I would've made some tuna salad for you," smiling at Frank. "Are you hungry?"

"No, I'm stuffed, Baby. Don't need to eat for a week. You and Frank have a nice afternoon."

"Happy to meet you, Dr. Churchill." Frank extended his right hand. "Sorry I didn't have a chance to chat with you."

"Same here, Frank, and please call me Sam." They shook hands. "Maybe some other time."

"That would be my pleasure."

Listening to every word, Rocky was down on all fours near the wall. With her hand on her father's left shoulder, Katherine kissed him on the cheek. "See you in a little while," looking at him affectionately. "Rocky, take good care of Dad. Let's go out the side door, Frank. We'll leave the car and use our legs, if that's okay with you?"

"I prefer that," Frank said, following Kat toward the kitchen.

"Dad, if you need my car for anything, you know where the extra keys are."

"No, Baby, I won't be using it. Thanks anyway."

Katherine swiftly placed the plastic bag in a top kitchen cabinet, winking at Frank.

After they exited the side door and Kat confirmed it was locked, Frank looked directly at her and spoke, "Katherine, we can do this anytime. I think you should be with your father. I know you don't get to see him that much."

"That's exactly what my dad would've said. Maybe you *could* be my father, after all." She raised her eyebrows, giving him the most captivating smile she could generate. "I want to be with *you*—and *nobody* else. Besides, you heard what he said."

At the bottom of her steps, and before they started south toward downtown La Jolla, Katherine turned north on the dirt path and guided Frank by his arm. "Before we start to the village, let me show you the spot where I lost my balance."

"I saw it from your window yesterday," he replied, "when you were phoning the kayak place."

"But I want to show you my favorite bench too…Rocky's and mine." She momentarily nestled her head against his shoulder, as they approached it, not far away. Like the others Frank had seen yesterday, it was securely attached to a slab of concrete. Its two side supports were also of concrete, but the sitting area was made up of four wooden planks. The backrest consisted of three planks. "Rocky and I call this 'our bench.'"

Frank looked down at it. "Is it your bench? Did you have it put here?"

"No, no." She chuckled. "I'm only joking. But we've spent hundreds of hours here together. He loves it, and so do I."

Frank looked out over the ocean. "It's a beautiful spot. I can see how anyone would love to sit here and take in this scene. You can see all of La Jolla Shores. Look at those homes along the cliffs over there." Scripps Pier and beyond, all the way to Oceanside, could be seen.

"It's a commemorative bench. Someone put in here in memory of a loved one. Here, let me show you." Katherine walked to the south end of the bench and bent over, indicating, "There's a metal plaque here, see?"

Frank bent over also and looked.

Kat read it aloud, "It says,

'LOVE AND TIME ARE DEATHLESS
DOLORES M. HARBER
11/12/24–8/24/01'

"She made it to 76—almost 77," Frank observed. "Not bad. Hope she had a happy life. What's this over here?" He pointed to some letters that had been carved into the wooden seat of the bench.

"Oh, that was done shortly after the bench was put here, which was about a week before 9/11..." she read it,

"TABBY—Y—FEDERICO"

"What's that all about?" Frank wanted to know. He fingered the letters.

"Must be Mexicans," she answered. "Tabby is probably a nickname, like my Kat. Federico is a man's name, and *y*, in Spanish," she pronounced it like an E, in English, "means *and*. I guess it's the equivalent of Tabby loves Federico." She turned and pointed dramatically at the spot from which she'd fallen yesterday, "And that's a location I'll never forget for the rest of my life." Kat embraced Frank. "I'm so glad you were there. Okay, let's go back the other way."

They began retracing their course toward the snork pad on the main path leading to The Cave Store.

"This was more fun when you were carrying me. You spoiled me," Kat teased.

"What about the lawsuit?"

"Aw, forget it then. I don't want any part of that. I'll walk." She squeezed his arm.

For the most part, the path was wide enough to walk side by side, but occasionally a jogger or someone coming from the opposite direction would appear, and they'd have to walk single file. For nearly 100 yards, they walked in silence. Katherine could see that Frank was admiring the scenery, and she let him.

At a specific point on the path where it was clearly in view, Kat pointed out, "There's the snork pad down there. One day we have to go snorkeling."

"That would be great. Don't forget to wear a bra though."

Kat laughed. "I knew you'd say that."

"Oh, I'm just kidding." He looked at her seductively. "You don't have to wear it."

She popped him on the arm, and got slightly aroused sexually by his last remark. "You're baaaad, boy. I'd better wear it. I don't want to get arrested."

Quickly noticing the impression of her breasts through the red polo top, and sensing the start of an erection, Frank chose to change the subject. "So this is public right of way?"

"Yes, it is. They call it Coast Walk. Most of the tourists don't know about it. They assume it's private property in the backyards of these homes built along the cliff. No matter how many times I walk on this path," she looked out over the ocean, "it's just an awesome scene. It's like being in another world. Growing up, I never saw anything like this."

Frank understood the feeling. He'd had that sensation for the last 24 hours. As they approached the empty bench where the two observant elderly ladies sat yesterday, Kat suddenly took hold of Frank's left arm, pulling him down toward the bench.

"Let's stop for a minute. Remember who was sitting here yesterday?" She tested him.

"Sure. Three Asian guys." He tested her.

Slapping him on the shoulder, "You're getting funnier every day. The Asian men were down there on the platform, silly, and you know it."

"Yeah, and I think they were sneaking some snapshots of your cleavage."

"Cleavage? You mean my naked tits. How about you, Professor Schmeelburger? Even *without* a camera," laughing and knowing she'd caught him.

"Hey, I told you I'm human."

"Well, I'm so glad to know that. The way you suddenly appeared in my life from out of nowhere, I wondered if you were an alien from another planet." She looked through the tall evergreen trees that separated them from the rocks and ocean below.

"It's strange that you say that," declared Frank, "because I have this weird feeling…that I'm on another planet."

Katherine cuddled up very close to Frank, pointing her face directly at his, her eyes devouring his, "I've walked here many times, Frank, and it's always breathtaking…but I've never had this feeling before. I've had some rather extraordinary moments in my life…in music, sports, modeling…but at this very moment—*right now*…this is the biggest thrill of my life…just sitting here on this bench…with you." She gently placed her head on his shoulder.

Frank could feel the warmth from her forehead on his cheek. He could smell her natural fragrance. Two joggers went by, but Katherine and Frank were oblivious to them.

"That's a pretty heavenly assessment, Katherine." Frank said the words quite slowly, pausing between each one. "I think you'd better come back down to earth. Look at me." In very gradual movements, Katherine turned her face toward Frank's, revealing her magnetic but watery eyes. "You don't even know me, Katherine." He spoke with exaggerated deliberation. "You don't know where I'm from, why I'm here in La Jolla, what I do, what my future plans are. You know absolutely nothing about me."

As if waking from a coma, she put her hand on his shoulder, focused her eyes, now rather piercing, on his, "Frank, I know everything I need to know about you. All the things you just mentioned—what's that got to do with who you really are? Where you're from? Why you're here? Et cetera. Nothing. I see the man you are—in front of me. I hear the sound of your voice. I've heard the responses you've made to my remarks. I've heard your opinions on several subjects. I've felt your arms around me. I've smelled your breath. And I've looked deeply into your eyes, as I'm doing now—and I see this man…I'm in love with." She sat up more erectly. "I think I understand, Frank." Her voice took on a different tone. "And I have to accept it," not really wanting to verbalize the next sentence. "I have a feeling you're not *really interested*." She underlined the last two words with those huge eyes.

Now Frank did a Ross Perot imitation—no blinking. "If I agreed with that, Katherine," A middle-aged couple strolled by. Frank lowered his voice. "I'd be the biggest liar in the world." When they were out of earshot, "The truth is…I'm crazy about you." Katherine's face started brightening. "I went back to my place yesterday, planning to do some work. I couldn't do anything. All I could think about was you. I hardly slept last night. I feel like I've aged about five years—and I'm already too old for you. I thought about what a nut I am to entertain the idea…someone as beautiful and talented as you could possibly be in love with *me*? I keep wondering if I'm not the subject of a prank. Maybe you're suddenly going to come up to me and tell me you'd made a bet with someone that you could make me think you're in love with me, and now that you've won the bet and collected your winnings—goodbye Frank. I'm completely out of my element, Katherine. I'm not really sure what to do about it."

Putting his hand in hers, "Please don't think like that. It's terrible. Don't do anything, sweetie. Just be Frank Taylor and let me love you."

"Oh my God," he thought, "this is a replay of a scene at Duke University." Then Dr. Churchill's image interrupted his plea, and Frank inquired, "When you go home later, what's your dad going to say?"

Standing immediately and looking at two nearby gulls, "He'll go into convulsions." The gulls, frightened, flew away.

"No kidding?" Frank was serious.

"Well, not exactly…but he'll have 150 questions and I won't be able to answer any of them. He's trying to protect me. I know that. He's a wonderful father, and he's concerned about his only little girl. And, as you know from what I told you about my mother's disappearance, there's more to it than that."

"What're you gonna tell him?"

"I don't know," pulling him to a standing position. "Let's go eat. I'm hungry. Maybe I'll get an inspiration on a full stomach."

Again, they embraced. Frank kissed her on the cheek, realizing at this point, when he felt the pressure of her braless nipples against his chest, he should permanently break off radio contact with his former world. As Katherine turned to resume their walk, and Frank saw the tight fit of her perfect ass in the stretch jeans she wore, there was no question in his mind.

Just prior to reaching The Cave Store, Katherine brought to Frank's attention a sign attached to a wooden fence adjacent to the store, which read: "Historical Landmark No. 288, The City of San Diego, 1860, Coast Walk Trail."

While Frank was reading the sign, Katherine admired his casual outfit: khaki trousers, short sleeved blue denim shirt, dark blue belt, and white-and-blue running shoes.

They started out of the small parking area in front of The Cave Store. "1860," said Frank. "Wow, that was just before the Civil War."

"Path has been around for a long time." Curious about a little black case on his belt, she asked, "Is that a pager on your belt?"

"No, no, it's a camera. I wanted to take some shots of you, but not now—you've been crying."

"Am I ugly when I cry?"

"Matter of fact," Frank was quite serious, "you're the only woman I've ever seen who is still gorgeous when she's crying."

A cute roguish look invaded her face. Then imitating W.C. Fields, "Sounds like you've seen a lot of crying women, Kiddo. Want to explain that?" Back in character, "I'm just joking." Hitting him on the arm, "After lunch, when I'm feeling better, if you promise to let me take some of you. Pretty small though…sure you can actually take a picture with that thing. What is it, one of those throw-away types?"

"No, that's why I didn't take it on the kayak yesterday. It's rather expensive, and it would've been completely submerged in the ocean. Fortunately, the guy warned me. I wouldn't have thought you knew who W.C. Fields was."

"Oh sure. Seen him in old movies on TV."

"Then you're probably familiar with Mae West."

"Of course." Imitating her, "Why don't you come up and see me sometime, Baby?"

Frank laughed. "You keep surprising me."

Katherine and Frank were on the sidewalk now passing Goldfish Point, walking toward the Cove and Scripps Park. The Point is a bare sandstone peninsula approximately 300 feet in length and, at the highest spot, around 50 feet above the sea. Near the middle, a huge section of its underbelly has been eaten away by erosion, and it's possible to see through from one side to the other. Posted signs warn people to stay away from the sheer unstable cliffs, that a collapse in the overlying ground surface is imminent due to the ongoing erosion.

Frank continued, "That's pretty spectacular. Does it have a name?"

"Goldfish Point."

"You can see all the way through down there."

"Don't ever swim down there. It could cave in anytime."

"No, you won't catch me down there."

"I'm sorry to take you back where you came from, Frank. I'd planned to drive us over to Coronado and do something special, but my father's surprise visit prompted a last minute change."

"We'll do anything you want to do."

"There's a restaurant in Hotel Milano—Robilio's. Have you eaten there?"

"No, that's fine. I presume they have fish."

"Yeah, the filet of sole's yummy. You're a fish eater, huh?"

"I love fish. Eat that and poultry, and of course fruit and vegetables. Haven't had beef or pork in several years."

"That's incredible."

"What is?"

"In the last two years that's been my menu."

Giving her a sly glance, "You gave up meat with your divorce?"

"Aw, come on, Frank, that was coincidental. I suppose it was about at that same time that I started eating healthily and trying to take better care of myself."

"Good for you."

"We could go to The Yorka, but we'd get interrupted every two minutes. That's where I work on Friday and Saturday nights."

"The Yorka?"

"I'm sorry, Hotel Mallorca. The locals call it The Yorka. You know where it is, don't you?"

Pointing up the hill to their left, "Up above, on the next street—Prospect?"

"Uh-huh. I'm at the Gulls Nest. It's a nice lounge, very pleasant atmosphere, casual. Please come see me tonight. If you can't do it tonight, maybe tomorrow night?"

Frank stopped abruptly and faced Kat. Then he imitated W.C. Fields. "I'm coming tonight, my little chickadee. Wouldn't miss it for anything in the world."

"All right! Not quite as good as mine, but not bad."

"You know what a chickadee is?"

"Oh, here comes my lesson for the day. A little chicken, I guess."

"No, my dear. It's a titmouse."

Her laugh was more like a spontaneous uproar. It got the attention of several people. Hardly able to talk, she forced out the words, "This has gotta be a joke. I'm supposed to ask you what a titmouse is now, and you're gonna tell me it's a mouse that sucks tits, right?" Then, after reprising her contagious laugh and noticing the attention she was getting, she covered her mouth and whispered, "If you're trying to sexually arouse me, I got news for you." Nodding her head dramatically and stifling another one of those laughs, "You're succeeding."

Frank laughed then. "You're absolutely nuts. You know that, don't you? How could you think I'd do such a thing?"

She kissed him on the cheek, purposely rubbing her right breast firmly against his arm.

He physically pulled back sharply. "Hey, careful now, that works both ways." Then he stood there for a second with a mischievous smile on his face. "Okay, I'll visit the Gulls Nest tonight, but just for awhile though," he added. "I'm not one of those guys who hangs out in bars." They continued walking and Frank, using his right hand, gestured toward the La Jolla Cove and Scripps Park. "This is the type of place I prefer to hang out."

"If I could play the keyboard and sing here instead of the Gulls Nest, you know I'd pick here. I'm not a singing B-girl, if that's what you're thinking. It's not my style."

"Just kidding. I understand. This," referring with his eyes to the multitude of gulls, all facing the sun, "is the *real* gulls nest."

Scripps Park is at the end of Girard Avenue, one of the principal roads in the village, where it meets Coast Boulevard after coming down the hill from Prospect Street, another main drag. The park is a well-kept oblong plot of greenery, approximately a fifth of a mile in circumference, sprinkled with tall palms and unusually shaped Torrey pines, a coniferous type of pine tree native to the San Diego area. In the section near the Cove, there're public restrooms and, adjacent to that, facing Boomer Beach, which is a favorite spot for seasoned bodysurfers, there's a white structure, The La Jolla Cove Bridge Club. As Katherine and Frank strolled, the park was situated between them and the ocean.

"Since you're into healthy eating," Frank had already told the woman he was crazy about her, and would now explore the territory of personal habits, which could possibly change his mind, "I'd be surprised if you drink alcoholic beverages."

Kat knew exactly what he was doing—and loved it. "I'm not a drinker. Every once in awhile with a meal, especially if it's Italian or Mexican cuisine, I might have a glass of wine or beer."

"Aw, even I do that." Frank smiled.

"And when you do, Professor Schmeelburger, what kind of wine do you prefer?" Returning the smile.

"Merlot."

"Excellent selection."

"What about those small white paper tubes that people," pursing his lips, he inhaled quickly through his mouth, "suck on?"

"I despise those. They're called cigarettes—unless you're referring to joints," giving him a grotesquely synthetic grin. "I just *love* those." She stopped, looking in both directions to make sure no passers-by were approaching, grabbed one of his arms, made her eyes bigger. "I'm really into smack, Baby." Then repeating, but not in any way matching, her laugh suppression and elephant trumpet when Frank first told her his name was Herbert Schmeelburger, she took both of his hands in hers, "Look at me, Frank. I'm just a plain simple Catholic girl who tries every day to lead a Christian life. I don't use any drugs of any kind, but I appreciate your asking. I really do. I told you I want you to know everything about me, and that's why it's great we can get together like this and talk. I think it's wonderful. You ask me all the questions you can think of."

She turned, holding his arm, tacitly urging him to continue walking up the hill to Prospect Street.

Frank raised his face, pretending to address an imaginary judge, speaking to him with a pronounced Southern accent, "Your Honor, I rest my case for this..." he looked directly at her lovely breasts, then tilted his head at an exaggerated angle so he could obviously admire the curvature of her tight fitting butt, "plain simple Catholic girl. The prosecutor has the floor."

Kat quickly choked down another laugh and mentally snapped herself to attention, realizing she somehow hadn't included law as a possible occupation for Frank. "Maybe that's what he is, an attorney," she silently reasoned. "It fits him perfectly."

"Your Honor," she looked at the same make-believe judge, "since there're no other witnesses present, I'm forced to put the defense on the stand."

Frank reacted instantly. "Objection, Your Honor. I only witnessed the fall off the cliff and...uh...two other..." He was now looking at her tits, "uh...relevant items."

She slapped Frank on the shoulder, laughing, "Whoa. You're a *very* baaaad boy."

"The prosecution," Frank continued, "has completely misconstrued my response, Your Honor. My reference was to the life preserver and the kayak."

"Uh-oh, that makes me a baaaad girl." She faked crying, dropping her head sadly.

They had a small audience in the box seats, a restaurant balcony where luncheon guests were enjoying their meal…until the distraction. Kat and Frank were so engrossed in their mock court scene they were unaware of the onlookers.

Frank lifted her chin with his index finger, patting her leniently on the shoulder. "Nobody's perfect, honeychild."

She remained in character, blubbering audibly. "But I thought *I* was."

At La Terrazza, an Italian restaurant on the Girard Avenue gradient, four luncheon customers at an outdoor table, two men and two young women, applauded loudly. Probably in town for Sunday's preseason Charger game, sufficiently inebriated, they cheered, "Bravo. Bravo."

Katherine blushed as she and Frank sped up the hill to Prospect, crossing it and continuing on Girard.

"We're silly, aren't we?" She admitted, embarrassed that Frank would think her childish.

"I thought it was kinda fun actually. It's something entirely new for me." Deciding to razz her, "You probably do it everyday."

"Oh yeah, sure. *Never*! These have been the most unique two days of my life." Both were still walking rather fast, but not so fast as to prevent her from beaming fondly at Frank, "And I'm loving every second of it." She had no difficulty countervailing his long strides with her shorter yet brisker pace and Frank, exceedingly grateful and rather amazed Katherine wasn't wearing a caste on her left leg, wittingly put her to the test.

"How long have you been in town?" Kat recalled during the fantasized courtroom drama that Frank had rested his case, given her the floor.

"Two months."

"Like it here?"

"Better everyday," glancing at her sexy ass. He tried not to laugh out loud, but didn't quite succeed.

Knowing exactly where he'd looked, and loving it, "You rascal, you're in another good mood, aren't you?"

"You mean it shows?" He laughed again, thinking of his past erections.

"Like a lit-up theater marquee. Your face radiates when you're happy. And you're not really a smiley type of guy, are you?"

"That's true. Coworkers have come up to me and asked very seriously, 'Are you okay, Frank? Is something wrong?' And of course nothing's wrong, it's just the way I normally look. I explain to them I don't go around with a smile on my face all the time—" Still moving at a rapid clip, periodically dodging oncoming pedestrians, Frank, nevertheless, looked away from the route so he could focus on Kat's face—and periodically her tits, "—until I met Katherine Churchill."

"To hear you say that really makes me happy."

"And it makes me happy to know that. You deserve it." And there was something else she deserved too. Frank would have to figure out how and where to give it to her. "My only problem is trying to determine why *I* deserve it. Or even if I don't deserve it, why am I having this marvelous dream?"

"This ain't no dream, Herbie." Shaking his arm forcefully, "I'm for real. You want me to bite you to prove it?" She blatantly displayed her impressive and beautiful set of teeth.

"When you mentioned the *White* Lady, the vampire possibility tickled my brain."

She played the part. "It's dark in Robilio's. I'm gonna getcha in there."

Thoroughly enjoying Frank's sense of humor, Kat decided to save her next line of questioning for the more secluded surroundings of Robilio's, which aside from superb food and attentive service is why she chose it.

"I guess you know your way around La Jolla very well by now?" Thinking that question shouldn't cause any problems, "or maybe you've been here before?" That one might.

"No, this is my first time in La Jolla...or San Diego. A friend of mine told me wonderful things about it."

Kat thought, "Well, at least he has a friend. That's encouraging—unless it's like the one Andy has. But maybe it's a female friend. I'd better shut up on that subject." Resuming a blander avenue, "We have the best weather there is. People come here from all over the world—affluent people who could live anyplace they desire—and they pick La Jolla. Don't tell anybody though...it's getting kinda crowded."

"I promise. The lack of humidity is what got my attention. I didn't know there was such a place."

"All right," she thought, "enough of the weather." Again deviating conversationally, "Up ahead in the next block, on the left, is where I go to church...Mary, Star of the Sea." She hoped that wouldn't upset him.

Solemnly, he asked, "Are we praying the rosary before lunch?"

Kat stopped in her tracks, holding Frank by one arm, looking at him seriously. "You're not an atheist, are you?"

Frank wanted badly to attempt another Laurence Olivier performance, but, unable to contain himself, he broke into a gigantic grin, even laughed a bit. Passers-by took notice, but Kat and Frank ignored them. Taking both of her hands in his, lifting them to his chest, he looked deeply into her eyes, "Katherine, I'm a Catholic. I worship in that same church. I'd planned to tell you at lunch, but I suppose now is as good a time as any." Frank again looked up at the imaginary judge and talked Southern. "Sorry, Your Honor, I had no intention of withholding circumstantial evidence."

Kat's mouth ajar, her brain painstakingly replicating the words from Frank's lips, she studied his entire facial configuration as if seeing him for the first time. The skin imperfection near the tip of his nose, the clearly visible surface vein under his right eye, his noticeably narrower left nasal passage, and what appeared to be a mole showing through the hair around his left temple, were all unconditionally accepted by her. Evolving into a reflected mixture of serenity, gratitude, and willingness, her troubled features improved dramatically.

"There's no way I can express how...much pleasure...and relief...that gives me." Kat could feel the pulsation of Frank's heart with her right hand, which he clutched on his chest. Then, distantly, "The Catholic Church is going through a crisis now."

"It'll survive...always has. I guess I cheated though. Please forgive me."

That remark about cheating emotionally jolted Kat. "What do mean?" She swiftly retracted her right hand, the one next to his heart.

"Yesterday morning when you went off the cliff, I saw you make the sign of the cross. I knew then you were Catholic."

She pulled his hand close to her face, partially blocking her mouth, slightly muffling her words. "My gosh, Frank, you're gonna give me a heart attack."

At that instant a patrol car from the San Diego Police Department skidded to a stop near the curb. A handsome olive-complexioned officer with black hair sprang from the driver's seat and spoke loudly over the top of the car. He was alone. Katherine and Frank could look through the car windows and clearly see his hand on the grip of his holstered pistol.

"Kat, you okay?"

Katherine felt Frank's grasp tighten on her arm. "Hi, Burt, you startled me. Something happen?"

"An RP called in a couple of minutes ago, said you were back there—" he pointed in the direction from which they'd come, "—below Prospect crying on the sidewalk."

She smiled at Frank and felt his firm hold on her arm relax. Then, to the police officer, "Oh Burt, I'm so embarrassed. Frank and I were goofing around, just having fun—I was acting like I was crying. This is Frank by the way. Frank, this is Burt."

"Nice meeting you," said Burt.

"Same here. Sorry about wasting your time. We didn't know anybody was watching." Frank shook his head.

"Hey, that's all right. Somebody thought you were in trouble. They were concerned about you." Burt tried to make the best out of it. Displaying a great smile, easily qualifying as a leading man in the movies, "Wish I had someone to watch over me like that." Laughing, "Okay, you folks have fun."

"Thanks, Burt. Please relay my apologies to the dispatcher, especially if it's Mary. I know her."

Burt was back inside the car and gone in a jiffy.

"I'm gonna be teased about this. I wonder who the heck called in. Should've been obvious we were joking around. Those people applauding...they knew we were playing."

"Burt got the message. He understood," Frank explained.

"He's terrific. Been around here for years. He knows the scene well." She guided Frank across Silverado, turning right on the sidewalk, down the left side of the street. "Let me stop for a 'sec' and see if Paul has something I need." Opening the door at Jewel Shoe Repair, she ushered Frank inside.

A short stocky middle-aged man, perhaps 50-or-so years old, with balding blond hair and a photogenic smile, was behind the counter. "Kat, how are you?"

"Hi, Paul. I'm fine. This is Frank."

Frank quickly extended his right hand and shook Paul's. "Hello, Paul. Very nice to meet you."

Paul returned the welcome. "Likewise, Frank."

"I need a new shine sponge. You got any?"

"Yeah, sure," reaching under the counter, Paul pulled out a small rectangular box. "Gonna be at the Nest tonight? My girlfriend and I might drop by."

"Oh, sure. Come on by—I'll sing a special song for you…something *very* romantic." She chuckled, holding the box up. "I love these. We're gonna have lunch at Robilio's. How much is this?"

"That sounds good. Best cannelloni west of the Mississippi." Referring to the box of shine sponges, "They're three bucks, plus tax."

Kat placed four ones in Paul's left hand. Frank glanced over some of the shelved merchandise, as Paul rang up the sale and gave Kat her change.

"Thanks, Kat. You and Frank have a great meal."

Frank held the door open for Kat.

"I'm sure we will. See you next time." She exited and Frank followed. Continuing on Silverado toward Fay Avenue, the next street, "They do good work."

Turning left at Fay and staying on that side of the street, they walked a half block to Hotel Milano's entrance, where Kat pointed out a display window with menus, photos, and reviews concerning Robilio's. About to enter the lobby, "Let's go next door for a minute," Kat tossed in an afterthought. "I have to change an appointment with Nadya, my stylist."

Just beyond Hotel Milano, they turned left at a walkway leading through an arcade with shops and offices on both sides. Nadya's door was open. She was combing one client's hair and another was sitting along the wall with her head in a dryer. All three looked up as Kat went in. Frank stalled at the entrance.

Tall, svelte, and with lustrous black hair, Nadya, maybe 27, gushed with sex appeal and smiled brightly. "Kat, what are you doing?" She had an exuberant way of speaking.

"Hello, Nadya." Kat unconsciously matched her stylist's effervescence. Then to the customers, "Sorry, ladies, only a quick interruption. Come in, Frank. I want to introduce you to my buddy, Nadya."

Frank made three steps into the shop, simultaneously greeting all those present.

Ratcheting her vitality up a couple of notches, widening her smile, Nadya gave Frank a speedy once-over. "Hi, Frank, where're you from?"

Without the slightest hesitation, Frank responded, "Finland." The lady under the dryer tilted her head to get a better look at Frank.

Kat gulped furtively, realizing that within 15 seconds Nadya had learned more about Frank than she had in over 24 hours.

"Finland, wow." An expert on small talk, Nadya didn't miss a stroke combing the woman's hair. "What you doing out here?" Her Russian accent was quite noticeable, as were her tits.

Frank, having already spotted the latter before he heard the former, grinned, "Corporate planning."

"Nadya, they added another class to my schedule—" Fearing Frank's reaction, Kat decided to barge in, "—and, wouldn't you know it, it's exactly when my appointment with you is next week."

"No problem, Lovey." She caught Frank's eye, "I have many talents," then looked back at Kat, "and rearranging schedules is one of them, but…not as much fun as some of the others." After winking at Kat, Nadya revolved a 180 degrees, placed the comb on the counter at the base of the mirrored wall behind her, and picked up a spiral notebook and pen. "Tell me when you'd like to come."

"Would be great if I could come an hour earlier than planned—if you don't have anything then."

Nadya licked one of her fingers seductively as she glanced at Frank, turned a couple of pages, browsing their contents, "That's Tuesday, right?"

"Yes. Was at two—I'd love to come at one."

"Gotcha." After scribbling in the notebook, she put it back. "We're all set." Picking up the comb again, "I'll see you then."

"Thanks, Nadya. Frank and I'll run along."

"Okay. Let me know when you need a haircut, Frank. I do men." Nadya flashed her knockout smile.

There was no question in Frank's mind about Nadya *doing* men, and Frank would love to be one of them. He instantly decided that the next time he needed a haircut, Nadya would do him, and he would love to *do* her. He smiled at her and waved good-bye. "See you around, Nadya. Nice to have met you."

They headed back to the hotel entrance. Kat grabbed Frank's arm rather tightly. "The way Nadya looked at you, I'm not sure I want her to cut your hair." She beamed playfully at him. "I'm jealous already."

"I kinda like that." He returned the smile.

"Me being jealous, or the way Nadya looked at you?"

Removing her hand from his arm and taking it into his, "There's only one answer to that question…silence…meaning neither."

At the hotel entrance, a personable valet greeted them, "Hi, Kat. Good afternoon, sir," and opened the heavy glass door.

Kat, with a smile, "Thanks, Ted." Frank nodded at the valet. Inside the marble-floored elegant lobby, two desk clerks, a male and a female, waved at Kat.

One step inside Robilio's entryway, adjoining the hotel lobby, a plump diminutive brunette smiled from behind a large wooden hostess lectern. "Kat, where've you been, honey? So glad to see you." She danced out quickly, giving Kat an affectionate hug.

"Hi, Felicia," hugging her tightly. "Been a busy girl. I should've called for reservations…looks packed," and it was. "Can you squeeze us in?"

"You got lucky. Must be living right. There's a booth in the back." Felicia, scooping up two menus, "Right this way."

Kat and Frank followed her into an adjacent room. Each table and booth was occupied, but the last booth, all the way back, was empty. That's where Felicia took them. Kat, delighted, knew they couldn't have chosen a better spot.

Felicia placed the menus on the table and turned around. "How's this, honey?"

"Perfect. Thank you so much." Kat, putting her hand on Frank's arm, "Felicia, I want you to meet my friend, Frank—and Frank, obviously this is Felicia."

Having the savoir-faire not to shake hands with guests before their meal, Felicia smiled and quasi curtsied. "Nice to meet you, Frank. You two have a wonderful meal. I'll send Enrique over." Kat and Frank sat down. "If there's anything I can get, let me know. Thanks for coming in, Kat." She walked away.

"You know everyone's first name. I like the informality of not using last names." Unfolding his napkin, Frank placed it in his lap. "Is that typical of La Jolla?"

"You know—" Kat retraced the last three or four faces they'd encountered, "—the fact is, I don't know their last names. Well, Felicia's is Robilio. She's the owner's wife. But the others…they don't know mine either, so no big deal." Putting her napkin in place, Kat opened her menu. "Just want to clarify—you're my guest—I invited you. That understood?"

"That's fine, provided you order for me. How's that?"

"*Très bien, Monsieur.*" Perusing the menu, "Ouch. I don't see the filet of sole I recommended."

Also looking over the menu, Frank put her at ease, "They have halibut. I'll have that, broiled."

"Kat, so happy to see you. Good afternoon, sir." It was the waiter, Enrique. Scandinavian in appearance with the baritone voice of a six o'clock news commentator, he had a heavy Spanish accent. "Would you like to start with something to drink?"

"Hi, Enrique. This is Frank." Kat smiled politely.

"Hello, Enrique. I'll have ice tea with my meal. We'd like to order now."

"What would you like, sir?"

Kat spoke up. "Frank's having the halibut, broiled."

"Do you want pasta or vegetables with that, sir?"

"Vegetables, please," Frank replied.

Enrique, looking at Kat, "And what can I get for you?"

"I'll have the chicken Marsala, also with 'veggies,'" responded Kat, who then looked at Frank. "Would you want to split a Caesar salad with me, Frank?"

"Sounds good."

"I'll have ice tea also, Enrique."

Enrique, jotting it all down on his pad, "I'll bring your salad and tea in a few moments." He backed away from their booth.

Kat informed him, "We're going to wash our hands."

"Very well," answered Enrique, moving quickly toward the kitchen area.

Kat escorted Frank from the restaurant to the restrooms, which were down the hallway past the hotel manager's office, around the corner to the right, adjacent to the elevators. Kat told Frank Hotel Milano was a small European-style hotel with about 100 rooms and, reportedly, the accommodations were quite comfortable and spacious. After washing his hands, Frank waited 30 seconds by the elevators for Kat and they returned to their booth.

It was difficult for Kat to wait until they got back to the booth before asking, but she did, "So it's my understanding you're not a native-born American, you're from Finland?" She'd clasped her hands together, eagerly listening for his answer.

"Here we are, folks." With their salad and tea, it was Enrique, neatly putting everything in its place. "I've already divided the salad for you. Would you care for water?"

"No, this is fine, Enrique," answered Kat. "Thank you." Once again, he disappeared rapidly.

Kat peered obliquely at Frank. He was simply enjoying her beauty as his lips created a miniature pithy smile.

"I'm not from Finland." Looking directly into Kat's eyes, he still had trouble thinking straight. "Just a stock answer I provide to strangers."

Now he'd really piqued Kat's interest. "You mean yesterday morning after you'd lifted my head out of the water and told me it could've been worse, if I'd asked you where you're from, you would've told me Finland?"

Frank hastily reflected and chuckled, in particular about the sight of her naked tits under the water, "I suppose so—it's sort of a trained response...like Pavlov's dog." Squeezing lemon into his tea and having a little fun now, but not sure if Kat shared in or appreciated his humor, he then started on his salad.

"But why Finland? Your ancestors from there?" She also began eating, but had no intention of dropping the subject.

"No, that has nothing to do with it. I'm primarily Dutch and English, with a little French and American Indian thrown in. Regarding the Finland thing, guess you could say I'm a very private person. When people I don't know ask me where I'm from, I feel it's none of their business. I tell them Finland because there're only about six million people who speak that language. The odds against having someone speak back to me in Finnish are rather slim. Whereas if I told them Ecuador or Argentina, there's a fairly good possibility they might start blabbering in Spanish to me...and I don't know Spanish—only a few words. In fact, I don't know any foreign languages—certainly not Finnish." He chuckled again.

"Well, hopefully, I'm no longer a stranger. Do I get to know where you're from, Professor Schmeelburger, or is that some deep dark secret known only to you...and your pet pelican?" Now Kat was having fun. They both laughed.

As he lifted his glass of tea for a sip, "Chicago—*touché*. The salad's excellent."

"Oh, Chicago. Everything's excellent here. It's an outstanding restaurant, and I'm having my own little private ball, sitting here with you. I'm glad you like it. What about the...corporate—what did you call it—planning? Is that another Pavlovian salivation?"

Frank was impressed by the manner in which she asked the questions. "Precisely. Except the odds are reversed. Everybody's in corporate planning—or financial planning or financial consulting. Of course...here in La Jolla, everyone seems to be in real estate. No, I'm not in corporate planning, not by a long shot." He knew what Kat wanted to know, and he was going to tell her...according to his master plan. "A friend of mine...has been in prison for many years."

The expression on Kat's face visibly changed.

"I'm *not* an ex-con," Frank interjected, stressing the negative adverb, "so relax. We were kids together in school—not really friends, but played sports on the same team." He took a deep breath. "It's a lengthy...complicated story—"

"Frank, you don't have to tell me all that now—"

"I want to, Katherine. It's important to me for you to at least know the outline of what it's all about—just as you wanted to tell me about Andy and your mom. It's the primary reason I'm in La Jolla. You should know—I want you to. I feel bad that I've waited this long." Frank drank some tea. "Every time he's up for parole the committee shoots him down. To a large degree that's because of the warden...more correctly ex-warden, who's since retired, but still exerts a lot of influence on the parole board.

"The first day Jack—that's his name, Jack McRae—was in prison, he was physically bullied by a correctional officer who didn't like the way Jack was looking at him. Jack was in handcuffs, and the officer backhanded him across the face, and told Jack not to look at him that way again. They were alone at the time. Well, Jack has a temper—didn't take his eyes off the guy. The officer outweighed Jack by at least 50 pounds. When the guy put both hands up and lunged at Jack, as if he were going for his head, even though Jack was handcuffed, he instinctively used a judo move he'd learned in the navy. Grabbing the correctional officer's hands, curling up and rolling backwards on the floor in front of the man, utilizing the man's forward motion defensively as he placed both feet near the officer's stomach area, Jack catapulted his assailant's body up and over, against a wall behind them. The man's heavy body, which was upside down when it hit the wall with a great deal of force, slid to the floor…breaking his neck instantly. The guy lived…but as a quadriplegic. He died a few years ago. It's a sad story. Coincidentally, the guard was the warden's best friend and fishing buddy. The warden solemnly promised Jack—privately of course—he'd keep him in prison for the rest of his life, a promise he's managed to keep.

"Personally I think Jack's paid his dues and deserves to spend the few remaining years of his life in freedom. He made a terrible mistake, but he's atoned for it. Forgiveness, however, isn't part of some people's make-up…and here we have the added element of revenge."

"How do you plan to help Jack?" asked Kat.

"I want to do a biographical paper on Jack—not for publication as a book, but expressly for the parole board…and more importantly, the media. If the media buys into it, I feel confident about getting him out of there."

"Where is he?"

"Northern Illinois."

Enrique, beaming enthusiastically, arrived with their chicken and halibut. "All right, folks, here we are. Hope you're hungry." Placing it on the table, "The rolls are nice and hot. And here's your butter.

Looks like you're still working on your salads—I'll leave them. Are you okay with the tea?"

Kat and Frank responded, "Yes, fine."

"Wave if you need me." He was gone again.

"Looks great." Frank inhaled through his nose, "And smells wonderful. Hope my story didn't destroy your appetite."

"No," with a slight smile, "I'm a realist. That was then…this is now. I know you'll love the food. Never been disappointed here." She held up her fork with a small piece of chicken on it. "You gotta have a nibble of this before you taste the fish." She moved it close to his lips. He opened his mouth, not looking at the chicken, but into those remarkably expressive eyes. She placed it inside his mouth. It was one of those precious moments that draw two hearts closer together, and they both recognized it. At this point, however, Frank didn't know how strongly Katherine was sexually attracted to him. Glancing down at the two clearly visible impressions of her nipples pressed against her deep red polo top, he decidedly became aware of his own sensual arousal in the form of an erection. Frank shifted the piece of chicken with his tongue, savoring its distinctive taste, then bit into it.

"What do you think?" Kat asked.

"Using your word…yummy." He wasn't thinking about the chicken though.

And neither was she. "The sauce has Marsala wine. I love it." She started eating.

"The halibut looks great too." He broke open a roll.

"So, you're doing some kind of research here in La Jolla?" she inquired, not really wanting to return to that subject, but aware the opportunity was here and that she should take advantage of it.

Trying without success to ignore her nipples, "Jack spent time here in the navy—in 'Boot Camp' at the Naval Training Center in San Diego, which no longer exists, and about 13 months at North Island—the Fleet Air Photo Lab. He was a photographer. That was his job in the navy. He's the one who got me interested in photography." He pictured Katherine in the nude, and wondered what it would be like to photograph her...and better yet, what it would be like to fuck her. After a slight pause, "My research here in San Diego shouldn't take much longer."

"And what other locations are involved?"

"He spent two years at Ford Island in Honolulu. That's in Pearl Harbor. The photo lab where he worked there was about a 150 yards from where the U.S.S. Arizona monument is now. And after the navy, he spent two and a half years at Duke University in Durham, North Carolina."

Kat stopped eating, placing her fork on the plate. Then she reached over and slowly moved her hand across Frank's hairy forearm. Sadly, she asked, "You have to leave here and do research at those places?"

"That was my plan, Katherine," partially covering her hand with his, and quickly sneaking another look at her nipples before he focused on her eyes again, "Until I met you."

Their eyes were now locked. Frank knew all the escape hatches were sealed. He didn't care. Whatever happened would have to happen. He would deal with the consequences as best he could. More and more, everyday he was realizing how human he was, that he simply wasn't cut out for sainthood, not that he ever truly thought he was. But he did have a plan, and it was up to him to make it work. He'd learned from past experience that dreams only materialize through dedication and diligence. Just having the dream wasn't enough. But his sexual desire for Katherine kept getting in the way. He weighed the possibility of adjusting his plan.

She slid across the seat closer to him, putting her right arm behind his neck, then very discreetly and sweetly kissed him directly and sensually on his lips. "I love you, Frank." She nudged him gently with that same arm. "Look at me," as if he weren't. "Do you know that? I love you. I know now that I've never been in love before, but I'm very much in love with you. I'm so very happy." Afraid she was attracting attention that may embarrass Frank, not her, she removed her arm from behind his neck. "I'll do everything I can to help you with your project. Maybe I can arrange my schedule so we can go to Hawaii and North Carolina together."

She hadn't given him time to slip his tongue into her mouth during the kiss. He was disappointed. "That would be nice...but I think I can get most of the information I need on Hawaii and Duke University from the computers at either the public library or UCSD."

As if from a magician's hat, Enrique appeared. "Is everything all right? Can I get anything for you?"

Kat told him, "Delicious as always, Enrique. Thank you." He left.

They sat in silence for a few minutes, simply enjoying the meal and looking affectionately into each other's eyes, completely comfortable with the absence of audible conversation, as if their feelings for each other could easily be communicated telepathically. Neither had previously experienced this shared phenomenon, and both relished it, recognizing its significance. The intensity of Frank's erection was increasing.

"Last night, not able to sleep, I lay there thinking." Frank's verbal delivery was more passionate now. "When I was in high school—and I know this couldn't possibly happen chronologically...perhaps hypothetically," he grinned. "If someone had asked me to list all the attributes I would want the girl of my dreams to possess..." looking into her eyes as he had never looked into any other woman's eyes, "the personification of all those things...would be you. If I had known you in high school, my life would've been entirely different." Only Frank could possibly know the full significance of that statement. And, in his mind, it was absolutely true. "I think I would've kidnapped you, or tried to persuade you to run away with me. So I'd probably be the one in prison now, not Jack.

"You play the piano, sing, speak French, you're athletic—even into gymnastics—you're angelic, you're gorgeous, and the way you talk and walk...I don't know what I would've done. Of course, you were so popular at that time in your life you probably wouldn't have known I was alive, or even looked at me. So I suppose it's better this way," he laughed softly. "Except I'm running out of time. I wish I could program the whole thing all over again so we'd know each other in high school, and I could live through that period of my life again…with you."

Kat was completely under his spell. If privacy and a bed had been immediately available, she would have been in the bed with her clothes off, and ready for Frank to screw her. But she wondered, "Where'd you go to high school?"

"Memphis Tech."

That instantly brought her back to reality. Her response came slowly, with a tinge of disbelief. "Memphis, Tennessee?"

"Yes."

"Frank, I know you're older than I…as I told you, I don't care…but Memphis, Tennessee? When you were a kid, we're talking separate water fountains, separate restaurants, back of the bus…and separate *schools*. We couldn't have gone to the same school…and if we had dated, I'd hate to think of what would have happened to us…especially *me*."

"I was thinking of that last night, and how stupid it was. I knew it was stupid then. At five or six years old I knew it was ridiculous. I wasn't brought up that way, Katherine, thank God. Fortunately, I was able to see through it, although I'm a product of that environment. If I had been of your race as a kid, I would never have made it to my 20th birthday."

Kat fingered the hairs on Frank's left forearm. "Your telling me this comes as no surprise whatsoever. The instant I saw you in the water yesterday, I knew that about you—everything you just said. I could read it in your beautiful eyes. You were led to that spot yesterday, Frank. You were supposed to be there when I fell from the cliff. There's no question in my mind—God meant for us to meet and be together. We're soul mates. The timing is just *too* perfect to be a coincidence. God wants us together."

The last sentence reverberated in Frank's mind. His erection disappeared. It was difficult for him to finish the food in his plate, but he did, not wanting Katherine to think he didn't like it. She also finished, waved for Enrique, and paid with her credit card. After letting Felicia know how much they enjoyed the meal, they left the hotel and started back toward Scripps Park where the plan was to take some photos.

At the corner of Silverado and Fay, Kat asked Frank about his apartment, whether she'd be privileged to visit it. He wanted in the worst way to take her there and have sex, feeling certain that she'd gladly comply, but his better judgment screamed at him to wait, to be patient. One hasty, selfish move at this point would easily destroy his entire plan, and he knew it. He begged off, explaining the current state of sloppiness in his apartment would cause him a great deal of embarrassment, but promised to invite her at a later date. She understood.

Taking a different course, they continued on Fay to Prospect, rounding the corner past the Hard Rock Café, then down Jenner to Coast Boulevard, where they crossed to the ocean side and spent time watching the seals rubberneck the tourists...and them. Strolling along Coast Boulevard in a northerly direction, they entered Scripps Park again, this time on the sidewalk near the sea.

For an hour and a half they took pictures of each other with Frank's digital camera: on the rocks, on the bench, next to a tree, with the ocean in the background, etc. Kat had never used a digital type camera and, as she had indicated earlier, this particular one was quite small. Like most people, she was fascinated that immediately after snapping the photo, you could see the results on the view screen, then keep the image or erase it.

Kat's modeling experience was evident: the way she posed, either smiling or, in vogue during the past several years, glowering—and like Ross Perot, never blinking. Frank had a photographic feast. From whichever angle he shot Kat, her image was repeatedly delicious. A delight for close-ups, her skin was flawless and, now having seen her posing in stretch jeans, Frank was convinced she had the most beautiful ass in the world. He looked forward to seeing it naked…and up close.

Kat, on the other hand, was once again surprised at Frank's photographic technique. She'd worked with at least 30 different professional photographers in her modeling experience, and Frank was right up there with the best when it came to directorial ability. He had an obvious knack for using the right words to get her to pose a certain way and, at the same time, making her feel perfectly at ease. And he did it seemingly with no effort. If his finished photos were in the same league as his directive talent, then maybe photography was his real occupation.

Finally, after taking a full-length shot of Kat with La Jolla Cove in the background, Frank moved the camera away from his face and suggested, "You know, I think you should go home and be with your dad for awhile."

"Okay, sweetie, you're right."

"I'll walk you up to The Cave Store, then I can go up those steps to Prospect and back to my apartment."

They did that. Frank was reluctant to pinpoint the time at which he'd make an appearance at the Gulls Nest, somewhere in the vicinity of 9 p.m., and not for too long. He simply felt out of place in cocktail lounges. She understood. He wondered if a blazer and tie would be all right. She approved. Their *au revoir* consisted of a subtle but affectionate kiss on the lips. Frank stood there watching her stride up Coast Walk, past the bench on which they had sat hours ago. At the point where the path curves right and Kat knew she would disappear from Frank's view, she turned around, absolutely certain he would be there, and threw him a kiss. He returned it, thinking, "I like the image, but the kiss in Robilio's was better. I know she's gonna be fantastic in bed."

CHAPTER 6

The possibility that her father had taken a nap prompted Kat to use the front entrance rather than the side, which had the audible electronic locking device. As she inserted her key, there was Rocky's unmistakable whine. She opened the door, entered, and eased it shut behind her while whispering to Rocky, "You all right? You've been a good boy? Try to be quiet because Dad's asleep. We don't want to wake him up, okay?"

Anticipating a vigorous rubdown, Rocky rolled over on his back, all four paws extended upward. Kat went to work on him. First, she zestfully tickled the inside of his front legs near his chest; then she energetically rubbed the sides of his body from his shoulders down past his ribcage to his hips; and finally, she tickled the inside of his back legs, not too far from his private parts. Not having been neutered, Rocky preferred the last phase. The expression on his face didn't change, but Kat could read it in his eyes.

"That you, Baby?" The voice of Katherine's father came from the living room.

"Hi, Dad. Thought you'd be taking a nap." Kat stood up, walked quickly over to her father, who was sitting in one of the big chairs, his legs stretched out to reach the ottoman.

"Had to change my plans. They found an acceptable organ donor for one of the kids, so I have to get back a little quicker. Was able to do it through Memphis and arrive almost two hours sooner." He was fully dressed, his suitcase on the carpet next to him.

Kat's heart stopped when she heard Memphis. Already nervous about confronting her father, the sound of that city's name hastened her need to use the bathroom. "Dad, let me go wash my hands. I've been playing with Rocky."

"Sure. There's a taxi on the way."

Kat and Rocky went through the door to the hall en route to Kat's bedroom. Four or five minutes later they reappeared and Kat, still visibly uneasy, was hoping the cab would arrive sooner rather than later.

"I'm sorry about the cab, Dad. I don't like for you to have to do that. I hope you called Jewel Transport. They're the only ones who can find this place."

"I did. Talked to Rhonda." Suddenly he got up. "That's all I'm gonna to do is sit—I'd better stand for awhile. Come on over and sit in this chair, please. I want to talk to you for a minute."

Something in his tone of voice amplified Kat's anxiety. By instinct, she was aware of her father's probable supposition, yet unable to fathom how he could possibly arrive at it so quickly. Kat learned at a very early age that playing dumb to her father was not an intelligent decision, but at this instant she was trying desperately to buy time.

Without using the ottoman, Kat sat erectly where her father had been. Rocky was at her feet. Dr. Churchill stood with the large windows behind him and, because there was still plenty of daylight coming in through those windows, it was hard for Kat to clearly see his eyes. Conversely, her eyes were perfectly illuminated as if Frank, with his digital camera, had positioned her there for a photographic portrait.

Dr. Churchill, a large stoutly built man with impressive features, resembled a professional football coach more than the stereotypical pediatrician. His voice and manner of speaking, however, were very much stereotypically what one would expect from an African-American stage actor of the highest echelon. With very little imagination, one could easily envisage Dr. Churchill portraying Othello and, even in a spacious theater, hearing his every word…from the last row. Only his gray hair and eyeglasses would preclude him from being perfectly cast.

Looking directly at her ample breasts and clearly seeing the rather large nipple impressions on the surface of her red polo top, her father asked sternly, "Are you wearing a brassiere?"

It was the last question out of a possible 100 that Katherine expected her father to ask. Plainly shamefaced, and unable to focus on his eyes, she avoided his face, peeking down at the subject of his query.

"Katherine, please look at me when we converse."

Now looking where she knew his eyes were supposed to be, "No, sir, I'm not wearing a bra."

Vocally reaching for his lowest range, "Don't you think that's…asking for trouble?"

"Oh, come on, Dad, there're certain private decisions a woman of my age should be able to make. Going braless isn't considered vulgar in this day and age. For heaven's sake, some girls would give anything to have tits like mine—and they do it—they pay for it, and they get breast enhancements. I happen to have the real things, and I'm rather proud of them."

"Okay, let's drop that topic. If you want to show your tits, go for it. Who's Frank Taylor?" Knowing there wasn't much time, her father chose not to waste it.

The way he said it, the fact that he remembered Frank's name told Kat everything. "I'm in love with him." Rather than answer her father's question, she decided to challenge him by getting to the heart of the matter quickly. This was a new experience for both.

"I could tell that from the way you looked at him."

Surprised by his response, Kat decided to throw back a question, "Could you tell anything from the way he looked at *me*?

"I didn't look at *him* that much. I was watching you. But I'm quite sure he noticed your tits, even if he's severely myopic. Never seen you behave that way around any other man."

"Dad, I've never felt this way about any other man." She realized her father was carefully studying her well-lit face, searching for any trace of weakness in her conviction. "I know you're concerned about me…because you love me, and I appreciate that more than I can possibly express to you. You're the greatest father in the world, and I love you with all my heart…so please have confidence in me, Dad. My eyes are wide open."

Sam Churchill, very still, with both hands in the pockets of his trousers, watched the expression on the face of his only child. "What about your brain, Katherine, is it wide open?" Her father had an incredible vocal range, and during the remainder of this conversation he utilized it to the fullest. "What does Frank Taylor do for a living? What's his occupation…or perhaps he's a professional?"

"He's working on a biography." She knew her father wasn't into literary stuff, and maybe that would get him off her back.

"Ooooh, I see, he's an author. Biography of whom?"

"It's about a friend who's in prison." Kat knew that would draw flak. "Frank thinks it may help him get out."

Without any response to the prison reference, "Did he grow up around here?"

So far, her dad was asking questions for which she could provide harmless answers, and she was surprised he skipped over the prison thing, but her response to this one, she was certain, would generate a pointed reply. "No. Memphis, Tennessee."

Tilting his head forward for emphasis, "Memphis?" The harmonious manner in which he pronounced the city's name was aurally fascinating, bringing to mind it's original Egyptian namesake.

Notwithstanding her father's profusely backlit position, she was able to see his large eyes widening. Attempting to defuse the bomb, "Yes, but he's actually been living in Chicago for several years."

"How long have you known him?"

Kat would have preferred that the bomb exploded, but it was too late now. "Oh Dad, I haven't known him very long, but, believe me, he's a *very* special man."

Both hands came out of his pockets dramatically—like Othello. "Believe you?" The level of his voice increased. "Very special man?" He was clearly agitated, as if his wide receiver had dropped a game-winning pass in the end zone. "Yeah, Andy was a *very* special man too. Turns out he wasn't even a goddamned man—not in my book."

"Don't be unreasonable, Dad. That was an entirely different situation." Rocky sat next to Kat's chair, not moving a muscle and quiet as a mouse, but permitting nothing to escape him.

"Unreasonable?" Five decibels up, "For God's sake, Katherine, come to your senses." Taking short steps in different directions, obviously quite disturbed, then abruptly stopping in front of her, "Look at me, woman…you're *not* a girl anymore. You're a woman—a 36-year-old woman." Kat hadn't seen her father come unglued like this since her mother left him, "And you're my daughter—you're all I have—and here you are messing around—showing your tits off—to some stranger who looks old enough to be your father."

"You don't even know the man, Dad." Now Kat was getting upset.

"*I* don't know the man? Baby, *you're* the one who doesn't know the man. Come on tell me, do you know him? I want to hear it from your lips. Do you *really* know him? Listen…you can live with somebody 30 years and not know them…at all. Ask me about it. I'm the expert on that. The only way I think you get to know someone is by working with them—eight hours a day—under all kinds of stress conditions. Then you get to see how they respond emotionally…how they perform under adverse conditions. Then you get to know who they are…what they're made of…what kind of character they have. Just everyday life with a person—no matter how close—even making love to them periodically…doesn't cut it."

Though dressed comfortably in a light gray polo shirt and dark blue cotton slacks, beads of perspiration had collected on Dr. Churchill's forehead and cheeks. Continuing, his demeanor was evangelical, "There was an article in the paper recently where a guy was arrested—now listen to this, you'll get a kick out of it—at his own wedding rehearsal. He was wearing a Super Bowl ring...that he never earned, was getting married...with a fake name. They had a long list of warrants on him. In one place he told them he was a Navy SEAL, another place a professional skier, someplace else a professor of psychology, in another city he told them he'd played for the Dallas Cowboys—" a short laugh, "—that wasn't in Dallas I guarantee you—and on and on. This guy's a complete fraud...and this poor dumb broad—maybe a very nice young lady with a first-class education—another of the thousands of educated idiots—that's what I call them—was going to *marry* him, entrusting him with her future—her life—for God's sake. What happened to her common sense? Somewhere along the way she evidently closed her eyes...and turned off her brain...her *educated* brain.

"Now that's the kind of guys who're running around out there...all over the place—like the bastard your mother got hooked up with. They go from state to state—even country to country, throughout the world—making acquaintances with women who have financial assets—and you fit right into that category, Katherine. They attract these women, entice them to fall in love with them, then they get married and then...in some cases, the women mysteriously disappear—like your mother—or die from a freak accident...and guess who gets all the assets—the money?" Rubbing his fingers against the thumb of his right hand, "The lying, cheating bastard gets it...that's who. The son of bitch who took you mother away from me could very well still be out there—very much alive—and using what's left of that $82,000, which probably isn't a hell of lot. In fact, I'm sure that's long gone. He's probably already latched on to some other decent gullible woman who's looking for excitement...like you. I'll remind you, just in case you've forgotten...you're a multimillionaire...and I have absolutely no idea why you continue working...it's beyond me."

There was a tinge of disrespect in Kat's voice and look when she said, "Thanks, Dad...for scaring the hell out of me. What I do—and I've tried to explain this to you before—isn't work...it's fun. I actually enjoy it, believe it or not. I guess that's hard for you to understand. It makes me feel good. And I can tell you there's nothing particularly exciting about Frank Taylor. He's just a wonderful man, a good solid citizen...basically a simple guy. And there's no question in my mind...he'll make a *great* husband."

"I'm trying to wake you up, Katherine. When I leave in a few minutes—I know you have to be at work at eight—but just take 15 minutes. Don't turn on the radio or the TV, don't play the piano, don't even pray—just sit there in the chair—don't let Rocky distract you—just sit there and," with his right index finger he fiercely prodded his temple, "*think*. Use the brain God has given you. He can't do it all. He can't use your brain *for* you. You have to *think* for yourself."

There were no tears from Katherine, but her face was alarmingly sober. "One of the books you gave me...when I was a teenager—it's on the shelf over there somewhere...I can't recall the author. The story is something about a cockroach and a cat—archy and mehitabel—I remember the characters' names, I guess, because mehitabel was a cat, and I'm Kat. The cockroach supposedly wrote it, but because he didn't have the strength to press down on the typewriter's shift key there were no capital letters. He wouldn't have that trouble today, using a computer keyboard. Anyway, there's a line or a quote that's one of my favorites: 'If you make people think they're thinking, they'll love you; but if you *really* make them think, they'll hate you.'" Leaning forward in the chair, her elbows on the armrests and her hands tightly fingered together in front of her, "You're *really* making me think, Dad." A tear rolled down the right side of her face between the nose and cheekbone, and her lip trembled. "But there's no way in the world I could ever hate you. You're a *great* father."

Sam Churchill immediately went to his daughter, kneeling beside her on one knee, getting as close as possible, putting his arms around her, and crying like a 10-year-old whose dog had just been run over. "Baby, I'm sorry. Please forgive me." At this moment there was no resemblance to Othello. "You know how much I love you. I'm just trying to help you."

Patting him tenderly, "I understand. Please don't cry. I love you too. You have a long—"

Rocky barked noisily and chased an imaginary rat toward the front entrance. The doorbell sounded.

"Perfect timing," exclaimed Kat. "Are you all set?"

"Got everything right here," springing to his feet, he jerked a pastel blue hanky from his back trouser pocket and wiped the tears from his face.

Kat grabbed the same hanky away from her father, using it on her face. He picked up his suitcase, took back his handkerchief, and stuffed it in his pocket with his free hand. Rocky was near the doorway, no doubt wondering why the delay. Kat checked through the peephole. She opened the door.

"Hi, Dan, how are you...how's the family?" After she and her father went through the door, Kat released the night latch on the inside knob to prevent locking herself out, made sure Rocky stayed indoors, and closed it.

"Everyone's fine, Kat. Thank you." A tall, thin, nice looking man in his 50's with well-groomed, pepper-and-salt hair, Dan shook hands with Dr. Churchill. "I believe you're Kat's father."

"Sam Churchill, yes. Nice seeing you again, Dan."

Lifting the suitcase, Dan gently placed it in the open trunk of the late model, white Lincoln Town Car, not an unusual sight in La Jolla. Father and daughter embraced and kissed; the former climbed into the back seat.

Before closing the rear door, looking up at his daughter, "Might come back pretty soon. That okay?" he asked politely.

Her hand on the edge of the opened car door, Kat leaned over to see her father's eyes, and softened her voice, "Dad, you're welcome here anytime. Consider this your home." Then giving him that unique Katsmile he'd been waiting for, "Please don't worry. I don't know about my brain being wide open, but my head *is* screwed on." Both laughed.

"I wanted to wear my green polo shirt, but I couldn't find it." Her dad appeared genuinely disappointed.

"Got to be in there somewhere." She knew exactly where. "I'll have it for you next time. I promise."

"Goodbye, Kat," Dan smiled. "Thank you." From the other side of the car, he gave her a high-five, as if her hand were next to his.

"Thanks, Dan. Give my love to Rhonda and the girls." Kat shut the door and waved to her dad through the tinted glass as Dan drove away.

Back inside, Rocky expected a rubdown but didn't get it. Kat usually took a shower, but didn't. She decided on a bubble bath. After confirming the answering machine was on, she headed for her bathroom. She stood naked in front of the full-length mirror, visually scanning her firm, perfectly shaped body, especially noticing her well-formed breasts and dark protruding nipples. She regretted that after her bubble bath she wouldn't be able to give herself sexually to Frank, before going to the Gulls Nest…and after she returned. She needed him…badly. A dildo had definite limitations.

CHAPTER 7

One would expect to find Hotel Mallorca in Spain or on that Mediterranean island, but quite possibly would not. One would certainly *not* expect to find it, of all places, in Southern California. But there it is, on the edge of a picturesque slope overlooking the Pacific Ocean and La Jolla Bay.

The same, of course, might be said of La Jolla itself. Thousands of tourists and business visitors have frequented Southern California, including the city of San Diego, but somehow have failed to see this veritable gem. The residents are continuously grateful for that because, having seen La Jolla once, a visitor will assuredly return many times with friends or relatives—and their cars.

The availability of both living and parking space in this lovely community is at a premium. Parking one's car can become a dreadful exercise in frustration. Fortunately, for the past several years there's been a height limitation of 30 feet in the building code. Otherwise, the parking situation could become more unbearable than it is.

The climate and scenery are the primary attractions. People whose occupations involve global travel, with an opportunity to visit many different spots in the world, for example: intercontinental airline pilots or international businesspeople, who also amass sufficient funds on which to comfortably retire, do so in La Jolla. Having been practically everywhere, they're able to compare La Jolla's low humidity, abundance of sunshine, cool summer nights, and moderate winter weather with all the overrated, sweaty tourist traps promoted in the travel and senior citizens magazines. Admittedly, it's expensive, but you do get your money's worth...*if* you can afford it.

Hotel Mallorca is *THE* hotel in La Jolla. It's intrinsic to La Jolla. Without Hotel Mallorca, La Jolla would not be La Jolla. It's as simple as that. Established in the 1920s, in its infancy it was highly regarded by many of Hollywood's top stars as an ideal hideaway for trysting. Current visitors find its elegant Old World ambiance, laced with cozy seclusion, rather intoxicating. From the moment pedestrians turn off the sidewalk into its entranceway, walk through the gardens and enter the lobby, they immediately sense a tangible escape from the mundane. A diminutive elevator, enclosed only with decorative ironwork and still requiring an operator, is a significant and popular vestige.

At 7:45 p.m., the parking valets at Hotel Mallorca anticipated the arrival of Kat in her red Prelude, as they did every Friday and Saturday at this time. Each prayed they wouldn't be absent—parking or retrieving a car—when the physical embodiment of their wildest, most lecherous dream drove up. They were never disappointed. Agreeing even if she wore Levi's, a sweatshirt, and an old full-length raincoat, they wouldn't be disappointed...well, maybe a tad. But invariably she came in the sleekest, "chicest," sexiest—but always tasteful, never vulgar—most ravishing dresses they'd laid eyes on. And all the rest: high heel shoes, necklace, bracelet, ring, earrings, fingernails, toenails, coiffure, and make-up—nothing but superlatives—plus the one ingredient without which all the others would add up to little more than a fashionably attired Olive Oyl: natural beauty in its very highest form.

Tonight was certainly no exception. When Kat rolled up to the entrance, the attention of all five valets was riveted on her alone. The lucky valet who opened her car door was privileged to glance surreptitiously at those long sexy, remarkably alluring legs he would gladly give his left testicle to have wrapped around his nude waist...especially tonight, when she wore a knee-length dress, the hem of which as she exited, crept well into her upper thigh area. Admittedly, it required split-second visual quickness however because, realizing her exposure, Kat sprang tactically from the car without hesitation.

"Good evening, Kat." In a uniform consisting of a green polo shirt and khaki shorts, he was a young clean-cut chap with red hair whose optical range was inescapable, evidenced by the ape-like grin he flashed back at his coworkers.

"Hi, Mick. Thanks," Kat answered, noticing the excitement in his face, and vowing next time to shift both legs at the same time, thus minimizing his viewable intake of her thonged vulva. Enthusiastic applause from the remaining valets was the usual routine at her arrival. At one point in the past, she asked them to refrain because of the minor embarrassment, however, when they continued, apparently not in defiance but rather in a display of affection and admiration, she let them. After all, it gave her psychological propulsion into the evening's next stage. Also, she knew they looked forward to it and deserved some fun. Who was she to throw a damper on their sexual fantasizing? They weren't literally screwing her in public; they were simply admiring her in an imaginative, prurient manner. Besides, they parked her car in a special secluded spot and babied the hell out of it. There's no way you could buy that kind of attentiveness, even with a handsome tip. What the hell, maybe she'd continue to let her thonged vulva be glimpsed in the future. And why not? Since her early modeling days, she'd taken great pains in completely shaving her pubic area, eliminating any possibility of a single hair showing along the edges of her thong.

Over the top of her car, she beamed that photographer's dream-of-a-smile and waved, "Hi, guys. What's happening?"

All gave different answers as she walked, swinging her butt seductively, around the back of her car. As a group, the valets had unanimously given her the title: "The Best Ass in La Jolla." She now had the absolute attention of every pedestrian and car occupant within 50 yards. Twice in the past, rear-enders resulted from the out-of-control gaping.

She wore a fuchsia, cotton chenille dress with shoulder straps displaying a low-cut, but discreet, neckline. The absence of a necklace eliminated any distraction from the natural grace and voluptuousness of her exquisite cleavage. At the waist, accentuating its small size, was a multicolored sequined band. Her high-heeled shoes matched the dress's color, along with the tiny leather purse she carried in her left hand.

Equal regard followed her through the crowded lobby, onto the elevator, and into the Gulls Nest. As usual, on Friday and Saturday nights there was a good crowd in the lounge. A stately room with ornate chandeliers and an extra thick carpet, it contained 25 tables, each with four chairs, and a bar counter with 17 stools. A high-technology keyboard, with all the switches and controls to provide sophisticated accompaniment, was situated near the wall farthest from the hallway entrance. Soft lighting provided a relaxed atmosphere, and the noise level was surprisingly low, attesting to excellent acoustics. Throughout the Gulls Nest, literally hundreds of visual reminders corroborated beyond any doubt the customers' location: ash trays, paintings, wall paper, taxidermy, photographs, statuettes, tablecloths, napkins, china, centerpieces, and glassware. There was no escape from the ubiquitous seagull.

Most of those present, having seen Kat perform, applauded enthusiastically when she appeared. En route to the keyboard, she smiled, waved, and stopped momentarily to greet acquaintances. Some were regulars who came on Friday or Saturday nights, customarily sitting at the same tables, automatically reserved for them by either of two veteran Hispanic-American waiters and the host.

After briefly acknowledging four or five familiar faces, Kat paused for several seconds to embrace Horace Bagwell, standing at his table with two attractive lady friends beside him. A handsome well-dressed man with striking silvery hair and a majestic mustache of the same color, Mr. Bagwell looked to be in his early 70s. He owned a great deal of La Jolla property, predominantly commercial from which he derived reputedly astronomical monthly lease income. A well-fixed Friday evening fixture, he had in the past periodically entertained the thought of asking Kat out for a sumptuous evening, but wisely decided hearing the word "no" from her lips would be more than he could suffer. Although batting a thousand financially, he'd struck out romantically on several occasions during his adventurous life, and the thought of hearing the "umpire" bellow "Outta here!" with reference to Kat would be intolerable. Because of her incredible beauty and sexual magnetism, he'd even considered making an extremely lucrative proposition for her to spend the night with him, but wisely reasoned, if her response were negative, he'd henceforth be regarded as persona non grata at the Gulls Nest.

Kat stopped next at the table nearest the keyboard, affectionately hugging and kissing the cheek of its sole occupant, also a loyal Friday-nighter. Kat joked with the hotel staff that an earthquake wouldn't keep Paulina Fontanals away. An ageless teenager at heart, with the vivacity of a 19-year-old, Señora Fontanals would put anyone chronologically near her to shame. A proud native of Barcelona, Spain, her inner beauty was reflected by a dazzling smile not even Kat could exceed. Invariably dressed to perfection, preferring Carolina Herrera, Armani, or de la Renta, she came this evening in a leather two-piece gold ensemble with eye-catching accessories—her trademark—and impressively coifed, auburn tinted hair, a stylist's pièce de résistance by Nadya. Characteristically, she displayed the poise and demeanor of a queen.

Normally accompanied by friends or relatives, following dinner in either the Café Cielo or Spanish Room, tonight Paulina, the name she insisted Kat use, was alone. After embracing Kat, she stood there admiring the younger woman's youth and pulchritude. Kat, who considered Paulina the epitome of class, remembered a glorious painting of her as a lovely young lady in Spain and hoped, when the years had passed, that Father Time would be as generous to her as he had to Paulina.

"You look absolutely gorgeous tonight, Paulina."

"Only tonight?" pretending sadness and demonstrating her cerebral alacrity.

"*Siempre.* I love the leather." Kat slid the chair back so Paulina could sit. "Just relax and tell me what song you'd like to hear."

Although fluent in French, Kat's knowledge of Spanish was limited. Nevertheless, due to her fondness for the incomparable Catalonian, coupled with Paulina's undeniable devotion and lavish gratuities, Kat zealously memorized lyrics to certain selected songs in Spanish.

"How about '*Besame Mucho*?'"

"*Muy bien*, señora. I think I have that one down pat, but if I forget the lyrics I'll just fake it with Spanish jive-talk. Okay?"

"Of course, dear," having no idea what Katherine was talking about. "Anything you do is fine."

Placing her purse inside the keyboard bench, Kat seated herself. A staff member flipped on a semi-spot to softly illuminate her. Tapping the microphone once to verify its connection, she adjusted it to the proper height and began playing the introductory notes for "*Besame Mucho*."

Enraptured throughout the number, Paulina's vivid eyes never left Kat's image, especially during the vocal passages as Kat clearly revealed her virtual mastery of Spanish pronunciation. Hands clasped together near her face, Señora Fontanals appeared not to breathe.

To avoid isolating the rest of her audience while performing this special number for Paulina, Katherine carefully, but briefly, established eye contact with all, including sporadic surveillance of the bar section from which Frank agreed to observe her.

Making her promise not to highlight his presence, namely dedicating a song to him, Frank had emphasized, "Just let me be a fly on the wall. I'll watch three or four numbers, then disappear. I'm very shy." Accepting the last sentence as true would be impossible for Kat, but she thought it best to honor his wishes.

At the end of "*Besame Mucho*" there was warm applause. Horace Bagwell rose to his feet, projecting a passionate smile. Kat wisely knew not to settle her eyes on his more than an instant. Many times in the past, she'd read their message and preferred not to enlist the "umpire." Paulina threw a kiss to Kat.

A silver request/tip bowl was on a small marble-topped table, easily within Katherine's reach. On every table and at the bar, a supply of sky-blue miniature envelopes with the Gulls Nest logo was available. The practice was to put some folding money inside the envelope, write the name of a song on the outside, along with that of the requester if they wanted it announced, and then place the envelope in the silver bowl.

Two customers were now involved in that activity. Preferring a more direct and personal arrangement, Paulina Fontanals, prior to her departure, would inconspicuously slip Kat a crisp $100 bill.

"Hi, everyone. My name's Kat. Meow." Laughter "Welcome to the Gulls Nest." Looking at the ceiling, then smiling at her audience, "If one flies over your head, be veeery careful." More laughter. Relaxed as if in her living room, Kat exuded a remarkable array of qualities any performer dreamed of. She made everyone present, including waiters and bartenders, feel she was talking and singing only to them. "If you have a special request, don't be bashful, use the little envelope. If you can't think of anything, just leave it up to me. I'll improvise." Gigantic smile. Applause. "This is one of my favorites…a Gershwin composition. I'll give you *my* version. Buckle up, and get ready for the curves." She did *her* rendition of "Embraceable You," meaning the jazzed-up version. They loved it.

Seemingly four hours later—in reality only one—she looked up near the final notes of "Love Me Or Leave Me," glimpsed Frank's face at the entrance and, although the last song was from the repertoire of Nina Simone, one of Frank's favorites, was exceedingly happy he hadn't heard it. She loved the song, yet Kat wouldn't have chosen it at this particular time in her relationship with Frank. It had been requested anonymously.

Frank had no way to foresee the scene before him. Having pictured in his mind a much smaller room, not nearly as elegant, he was completely overwhelmed. During the interim before coming, he'd reviewed on his desktop computer the digital photos he'd taken of Kat that afternoon, his practiced eye repeatedly proclaiming the validity of her beauty, but was totally unprepared for what he saw tonight. The bartender finally prodded Frank's shoulder with his finger to get his attention.

"I'm sorry," Frank offered an apology. "I'll have bottled water and a squeeze of lemon."

"In a glass, sir?"

"Yes, please," easing up on the barstool.

Katherine's impulse was to go to Frank and embrace him, but a promise was a promise. Her scheduled break was at 10 p.m., which meant Frank would be gone. Although she had the freedom to do as she pleased, some of her regulars, Paulina Fontanals for instance, left at the end of her first session and Katherine would never consider disappointing them by taking her break earlier.

The next two pieces, "Killing Me Softly with His Song" and "Forever in Blue Jeans," were requests. Because Frank hadn't seen her in this setting, Kat naturally felt the pressure of wanting to excel. She handled it like a pro—no butterflies. Then she decided to break her promise...and keep it at the same time.

Moving her lips close to the microphone, giving Frank a sweet little smile, she softly spoke, "I never break a promise." Not quite. She then began the introduction to a song made famous by Doris Day: "Again."

When Kat started with the lyrics, looking directly at him, Frank got instantaneous goose pimples. As a senior at Memphis Tech, dating a cute blonde named Shirley, "Again" was *their* song. "How strange fate is," Frank thought. "All those years ago, there I was double-dating, necking in the back seat of my buddy's car with Shirley, and listening to Doris Day sing 'Again.' Now, here I am in a place I'd never heard of then, watching a gorgeous African-American woman—a woman I could not have gone to the same school with then—with whom I'm now undeniably in love, sing the same song *to me* in the presence of 100 people." With each tick of a second, as he watched and listened to Katherine, Frank felt stranger and stranger.

There was nothing jazzed up about Kat's version, an unhurried melodious love-song technique—pure female crooner style, perhaps even Doris Day would've acclaimed. The accompaniment sounds produced by the electronic keyboard components created an instrumental backup comparable to any talented combo. Eye contact between Kat and Frank was laser-like.

During the number and immediately after Kat finished, an indescribable invisible energy permeated the Gulls Nest. No one escaped it. The regulars, especially Paulina Fontanals, were aware they'd never seen and heard Kat perform with such emotional impact. Because of the lighting and the number of customers, Frank wasn't singled out by anyone, although Kat had obviously been looking toward the bar.

Frank was a basket case, utterly incapacitated over what he'd just witnessed. Quite certain he'd be unable to handle the untouched drink, although is was only water, he somehow, despite teary eyes and a trembling right hand, managed to pull a $10 bill from his wallet and place it in the bartender's opened palm.

"I'll get your change, sir."

"That's all right. Thank you. Goodnight."

Physically, Frank navigated his body along the hallway, down the stairwell, through the lobby, and out onto the street, but mentally he was wavering. The fresh salt air was a relief. Rather than crossing to the other side and heading for his apartment, he followed the descent of Prospect to lower Girard, then to Scripps Park and the Cove.

Others had a similar idea. The weather begged for an evening stroll. Floodlights around the Cove area lit up the beach and breakers, revealing a handful of swimmers. Still dazed, Frank leaned against the rail and looked seaward.

Understanding why he'd reacted so strongly to Kat's singing—that was uppermost in his mind. Based on years of occupational experience, accustomed to analyzing problematic situations in order to arrive at solutions, or to at least open avenues in that direction, Frank replayed the "Again" scenario in his thoughts, this time attempting to break down his feelings, rather than concentrating on Kat's mentally reprised performance.

The heart of the problem, according to his interpretation, was that two separate and distinct periods in his personal life had been immediately and dramatically drawn together by the music and lyrics of one song. He was revisited by the notion of his present day self and a totally dissimilar self from yesteryear encountering one another, the latter now representing a personality he would prefer to revive, perhaps even become, because of his relationship with Katherine. Unlike reincarnation, which reportedly involves two or more separate lifetimes for the same soul, this would imply two different beings occupying the same body during its lifetime, but within divided time boundaries...not simultaneously however, as in a multiple personality disorder.

Swiftly, Frank trashed the thought. It was inconsistent with his basic philosophy and horse sense. After a 30-minute inner monologue of self-reproach and self-examination, he wanted to dismiss the matter as an example of retro-audio stimuli eliciting extreme nostalgia, à la Pavlov's dog. In Frank's mind, the only thing *that* elicited was B.S.—having nothing to do with Bachelor of Science.

Never a conscious practitioner of self-delusion, Frank remembered his pal, Cicero, from 2,000 years ago and what he said: "If the truth were self-evident, eloquence would be unnecessary." It took Frank awhile to get there, but the truth was patently self-evident and there was no necessity for eloquence...only clear thinking.

Staring out into the darkness over the ocean, beyond the lights, and listening to the surf, Frank admitted, "For the first time in my life, I'm in love. It's that simple. I've never known love. Thought I did...but I didn't. I've talked to a lot of people about love, but I didn't know what I was talking about. I've known hatred and the results of that. I know all about duplicity...and betrayal. I'm an expert on those subjects. I'm well versed in the myriad chambers of darkness that constitute the inner workings of many human minds. There's a huge segment of my past from which I'd like to escape...never to return, however...

"When I see Katherine...she's so refreshing...so unique. When she looks at me...when I touch her...I never dreamed I'd experience this much happiness. If I had...things would be different. My life would have been different. And at my age...falling in love at my age must be like jumping from a plane, thinking you have on a parachute, realizing three seconds into your free-fall you don't. There's no ripcord, no chute, nothing. I'll just have to 'wing it' on the way down. Whatever happens, happens. And on the way down, I'll know it's never happened before...and when I reach the bottom...I'll know it will never happen again, that's for sure." Frank walked back to his garage apartment, mentally and emotionally disturbed by the twisted road that brought him to this major intersection in his life. The memories of the one relationship responsible for his meeting Katherine were choking his conscience. He wasn't sure he could survive with that memory...and with Katherine. He felt that was a challenge he would not be able to overcome. Much of his life had been a training ground for dealing with evil, and that had never presented a problem. Confrontations with evil, or the devil himself, were matters in which he'd excelled. That was his element, his comfort zone. But now, he was face to face with decency and goodness. Adjustments would have to be made...huge adjustments...a complete reversal in his method of thinking and acting...*if* he were to survive...*if* he were to exist as his different self...*if* his master plan was going to work. "And maybe," he thought, "maybe...my master plan should be shit-canned! Maybe Katherine is far more important than any master plan."

After the applause died for "Again", Kat was unable to spot Frank's face near the bar. She panicked, thinking it was her mistake to sing so directly to him. And yet she was so certain of his love for her, the little voice within convinced her to calm down, that a rational explanation would be forthcoming.

"Kat." It was Paulina, standing close, plaintive, her left hand on Katherine's right shoulder as she looked down into Katherine's eyes. "What is wrong, dear?" The lilting manner in which she spoke unmistakably validated her geographic origin. "Something happened. I can tell. Are you okay?"

Speechless, with tear-brimmed eyes, Kat, strangely feeling for the first time the emotional pain associated with the departure of her mother, looked up at Paulina, who was a marvelous surrogate, benevolent and infinitely more understanding, possibly because she had no daughters. Paulina's magnificent face radiated her compassion for Kat.

Her voice breaking noticeably, Kat answered softly, "I'm...in love."

In a split-second Hyde-to-Jekyll transition, Paulina's countenance registered unbelievable joy. Bending closer to Kat, moving her face directly in front of Kat's, with those enormous Spanish eyes figuratively devouring her, "That's wonderful. Who is he? Have I met him?"

Instantly feeling 100% better, "No, but you will. I promise." Kat patted Paulina's hand. "Let me sing a song—especially for you."

Paulina, raising both arms triumphantly, backed away from the keyboard and returned to her seat. Katherine went into a vibrant rendition of "Spanish Eyes" that thrilled Paulina and everyone else.

Kat's first session ended four songs later. She and Paulina hugged, the latter, secretively transferring a gratuity from her hand to Kat's, departed as usual, on this occasion happier than she could recall. It was 10:01 p.m., time for a 15-minute break. After pulling her purse from the keyboard bench, Kat, about to deposit the tip she'd received from Paulina, realized there were two $100 bills instead of one. "She's the kindest, most generous person I've ever known," Kat thought, promising herself to politely scold Paulina the next time she saw her for being overly rewarding. On second thought, the possibility of hurting Paulina's feelings dissuaded her. She quickly gathered the tip money, which she'd already separated from the envelopes, pushed it into her almost empty purse, and made her way to the payphones in the hallway outside the lounge entrance.

When Frank's phone had rung for the 15th time, Kat got the message—after she hung up: silence. And silence, of course, meant there was no message. "He has no answering machine—or it was turned off," she thought. "He probably wasn't there...probably." The little voice once again reminded her to take it easy. She went to the restroom.

Something was missing in Kat's final session and she knew what it was, or rather who he was. This was a new experience for her. The relationship in high school and the one with Antoine were bland in comparison. She wanted to spring from the keyboard bench and run to Frank. But where was he?

So she played...and sang. Glancing at the request slips, Kat turned herself on cruise control for the remainder of the evening, not once referring to sheet music. Although having religiously learned to read and to use it in piano classes, most definitely for the classics, Kat daily expressed her gratitude to God for his gift: the ability to play by ear—an innate ability that's essential for a lounge keyboardist or pianist.

Between numbers, there were the unavoidable but brief conversations with regulars—or with two or three newcomers who wanted to compliment her. Occasionally some unknowing admirer would try to buy her a drink, but Katherine had trained the waiters to courteously inform them she was a teetotaler.

Finally it was midnight. After collecting the rest of the gratuities, saying goodnight to five or six people, she was tempted to use the payphone again, but nixed that idea. She calculated mentally that getting her car, driving the four blocks home, giving Rocky his rubdown, letting him pee near the side door, washing her hands, and checking the answering machine would take her to 12:45 a.m. minimum. Maybe this one time she'd skip washing her hands.

Hardly recalling her trip through the lobby, she found herself out front surrounded by waiting guests from the hotel and its popular restaurants. Willie, one of the valets, had already taken her parking stub and would return momentarily with her car. Reviewing the faces, Kat knew all eyes were on her. She accepted it willingly and returned their smiles, realizing she was indeed an attraction. "No reason to be uncomfortable about that," she'd reminded herself frequently. "I'm a very lucky girl—always have been. And now I have Frank."

She gave Willie a five, watched his eyes watching her legs, and got into her Prelude. Not too much traffic. With the necessity to encircle an adjacent block in order to head in the direction of her home, the four-block drive became seven. U-turns were prohibited. Into the driveway, past the front house on Prospect, she then quietly glided to stop near her front door. Rocky's whining began.

His rubdown was considerably shorter and he noticed it, looking up at Kat with disappointment in his eyes. Kat knew better than neglect nature's call to Rocky. She'd pay for it in the middle of the night or when she got up to eat breakfast. Afterward, ignoring the golden rule of sanitation, Kat went directly to the answering machine. One call. Push play. First, the robot voice: "You have one new call. Friday, 10:07 p.m." Then, "Hi, Baby," it was her dad. "I'm between planes in Memphis. Knew you'd be at work, but just wanted to tell you I love you and ask you to forgive me for upsetting you this afternoon. Hopefully, everything will work out. If you say Frank is a great guy, he must be a great guy. I look forward to…spending some time with him…and of course you. I'll be calling. Love you. Click."

Kat, smiling at the machine, "I love you too, Dad." There were no more calls. She grew tense. Having stored Frank's number in the phone, she pushed *talk*, *mem*, and *2*.

On the first ring, "Hi, Katherine."

"You have caller ID?" She was surprised.

"No, I knew it was you," His calm voice was so warm and so direct, as if his lips were next to Kat's ear.

Trying to emulate him. "Hi, sweetie. I'm sorry to call so late."

"You kidding? I've been waiting. If you hadn't called by one, I would've called you."

Emotionally, Kat zoomed from the bottom to the top in four seconds flat.

"And if I'd called you," he continued, "and you hadn't been there, I would've had a nervous breakdown."

Both laughed and Kat, despite Frank's denial of musical talent, was becoming aware, moment by moment, of his skill in playing the full range of her emotional keyboard.

"And if that happened," still on the subject, threateningly, "you know what it would mean?"

"No, tell me," joining the game.

"I'd have to sue you." More laughter.

"You're crazy. You know that?

"About you, yes."

"You disappeared on me tonight. What happened?"

Short pause. "You know, Katherine, you...uh," remembering his reaction at the lounge, Frank choked up a bit. "Let me say this first. There's no way I could've been prepared to see you at the lounge. When I walked in there...oh my...it's...hard for you to understand—I know. I'd seen you in shorts and jeans...but when I looked over at the piano—or I guess they call it a keyboard—and saw you in that...stunning dress, with the lights and the keyboard that sounded like a topflight combo...your voice over the speakers, the way you sang, your virtuosity playing the keyboard...I was overwhelmed Katherine. You're a *very* talented young lady." He said the words slowly, pausing between each one. "What's gonna happen, Katherine—it's right out of a movie...one night a producer or director from Hollywood will go in for a drink...and see you—hear you...and you'll be gone—right out of my life. I'll never see you again."

"Wait a minute, Frank. Listen to me, will you? I've had those offers—several of them—from Hollywood to New York—even Paris and—funny but true—Tokyo. Baby, I don't care about any of those offers. I'm not interested in that stuff—none of it. The only thing I'm interested in is *you*. Don't you understand that? I'm in love with you, Frank. I want to spend the rest of my life with you."

Frank was silent, not sure what to say. He liked everything he heard, but his mind was whirling. "The correct way you should say that is, *you* want to be with *me* the rest of *my* life."

"Be quiet, please. Don't talk that way, Baby." Kat wasn't ready to stop. "Frank, if we're gonna to know each other—and you're the one who brings this up, not me—we're gonna have to pull out all the stops. We're gonna have to talk about every single thing on our minds. Oh, Frank...I love you so much, I want to crawl inside of you, be part of you. I *am* part of you. I know that." Pause. "Are you still there?"

"Of course, I'm here," he replied calmly. "Please understand...those are my feelings too." Frank wondered if she was in her nightgown or naked. He wished he could see her.

"Then please—I don't know if you're in your pajamas or whatever—but slip on something and come over here."

Frank gulped and thought, "That's what I get for wishing for those things." Then to Katherine, "To your house?"

"Yes, of course, that's where I am." Surprised that he asked. "Spend the night with me, Baby. I want to be with you. We can be together...and make love."

Long pause. "Oh, Katherine...let's...you see..." Another long pause.

"Oh, this is a perfect example of some kind of weird, supreme retribution." She belted out the words as if singing an up-tempo number.

"I don't follow you. Are we back to the White Lady?" Frank usually picked up on things swiftly, but not in this case.

"Yeah, maybe that's it—the White Lady. No, silly. Remember my first boy friend—the king of football?"

"Oh, yeah."

"He could've had any girl in that school...but he wanted me—and I declined—I gave him a big fat no."

Frank remained silent.

"Here we are," she was emphatic, "almost two decades later...and you know who you remind me of?"

"You?"

"Right on."

"Told you, I'm not as dumb as I look."

"Don't give me that stuff, please. And you know who *I* remind me of?"

"Him."

"Exactly. And it hurts...badly. I never really knew how he felt. I wasn't interested enough to even think about how he felt. I didn't give a...darn. I was disgusted with him. Now I know. Perhaps—"

"Do you feel sorry for him?"

"Frankly, Frank," she laughed. "That's kind of cute—I like that. But I'll revise it. Truthfully, Frank, I don't feel sorry for him. More correctly, I didn't feel sorry for him—at the time of the incident...maybe a little now. But mainly I feel sorry for *ME*—because I don't think you have any idea of how much I love you."

"Now, slow down, Katherine. You're getting ahead of yourself."

She could hear some excitement in his intonation, which made her feel better.

"Don't think for one minute," he challenged, "that I wouldn't love to come over there, jump in bed with you, and make love to you. I'm crazy about you. I told you that. You don't think I fantasize about that stuff? You're constantly on my mind—"

"Now, you're talking my language." She was ecstatic.

"By the way, you look great in the photos I took—"

"What?" Amazed. "Frank, you're changing the subject again. You always do that. You just told me you want to make love to me, and I'm inviting you to come over here and do it. What's wrong with that? We're in love. Everybody else does it. I want to do it, Baby. I want to express my love for you physically. You know the history of my sex life. It would be different if I was promiscuous, but I'm not. I want to go to bed with you, Baby, because I love you and I want to give myself to you."

"Katherine...we're not everybody else. We're a special couple. You're a very special woman...and I want to keep it that way. I don't want to do anything that would cast a negative spell on our relationship. A few times during my life I've failed, but I could always honestly tell myself that I'd tried for excellence. For us...I want sublimity."

"Wow. You make me feel like an angel, Frank—"

"You are an angel. You're also beautiful—inside and out...and wonderfully gifted in so many ways. You're everything I ever dreamed of—and one day I'll explain that in greater detail. I'm much older than you. It's my responsibility to act properly, to do the right thing. If I don't, I'll never forgive myself. I can't forget Jack, Katherine. He's been in prison all these years. I'm sure he's wondering what I'm doing. I can't turn my back on him now. He's the reason I'm here in La Jolla. If it weren't for Jack, I wouldn't have met you. You have to help me concentrate on my project. I have to do my best...to get his freedom."

Tears flowed from Kat's eyes. Rocky was concerned. After seeing her tears, he gently placed his head on top of her right foot and moaned. "Okay, Baby." Rocky looked up, thinking she was talking to him. She wasn't. "You're right...of course. What do you want me to do?"

"You said something about a class you teach at the 'Rec' Center tomorrow morning."

"Yeah, it's...exercise and tumbling for middle school girls."

"At what time?'

"From 10 a.m. to 11."

"Unless you have something else on your agenda, I could come by during your class and see you in action. Then we could do something in the afternoon."

Obviously pleased, "That's wonderful. I'll bring a top and some jeans so I can change at your place, okay?"

"Katherine, my place is a wreck. You don't want to see it...and I don't want you to see it. I have a little pride."

"Come on, I'm just gonna sponge off real quick. I promise not to bring the white gloves."

"White gloves? Listen, I'm gonna blindfold you before you come in this dump."

"Heeeey." Then seductively, "Let's do it. Sounds like a lot of fun."

"Cut it out, will you. I have to sleep tonight."

"Well, then you better not come over here, Buddy. You won't get any sleep with me around. If fact, you'd get the workout of your life."

"Shame on you, you plain simple Catholic girl."

"Angels are no fun."

"You're the only one I've ever met personally, and you disprove that statement. You can present your verbal treatise on that subject tomorrow. It's way past my bedtime. I'm usually in the sack by 10."

Kat, full of mischief, "Well, we're gonna see about changing that habit real soon."

"You are really bad, young lady...but you're so cute, I guess I'll forgive you."

"You say the nicest things, Professor Schmeelburger."

Frank chuckled. "I'll never escape from that, will I?"

"Never." Conceding defeat, realizing his wall was impenetrable. "Okay, sweetie, you have a good night's sleep, but dream about me, will you? Dream that I'm making passionate love to you. Is that a deal?"

"It is. See you in a few hours." Without any prompting, Frank told her, "I love you."

Slightly overwhelmed and extremely happy, "I love you, Frank. Goodnight."

After she put the phone down, Rocky and Kat traded looks. Kat spoke first...and last: "I tried, Rocky. I'm captivating, but...not a very good seductress."

CHAPTER 8

The "Rec Center" is short for La Jolla Recreation Center, located a block and a half from Frank's excuse for an apartment on Bishops Lane, a paved strip of asphalt, fit for vehicular travel, between the rearmost properties on the two nearest parallel avenues, Fay and Eads. In other communities this lane would be called an alley, but this was La Jolla.

Fairly typical, the "Rec Center" stands out somewhat due to the excellent condition of the six tennis courts. The green surfaces and the white marker lines appear to have been painted within the last year, and all the nets are in good condition. The two outdoor basketball courts actually have decent nylon on all four rims. In most public parks, that's unheard of; the rims are either net-less or have metal nets. Two separate kiddie sections include comprehensive mixtures of above average swinging, hanging, and climbing equipment, either in plastic or with requisite rubberized coatings, one area with a sand surface, the other with all-weather safety mats.

At the edge of the "Rec Center," fronting Prospect, is a buff stucco building with arched windows where Kat's class had begun 30 minutes earlier. In the same structure, there are staff offices, restrooms, and a weight room for "iron-pumpers."

Kat was on stage demonstrating an exercise for the buttocks and hamstring muscles when Frank entered. On her hands and knees, she was alternately curling one leg at a time, up and over her gorgeous ass and the small of her back. Ranging in age from 12 through 14, 23 girls in almost identical positions on floor mats were intently watching Kat, and trying their little hearts out to duplicate her phenomenal movements. Most wore appropriate attractive outfits. Kat, in blue-and-white Nikes, white skintight bottom, and a cutoff, navy blue-and-white, horizontally striped tank top, resembled a supermodel from a glitzy workout video.

Frank, infinitely more at home than last night at the Gulls Nest, leaned against the wall like some of the parents, and watched Katherine do her stuff. Acknowledging his presence, she grinned happily. Continually jumping off the stage to personally instruct a participant, then back on again, her ankle apparently presenting no problem, she went from one routine to another, showing no sign of fatigue. Next, there were high kicks, then a twisting motion for trimming the tummy and hips, followed by jumping jacks, and so on. Once again, Frank privately crowned her derrière "The Most Beautiful Ass in the World," as he felt his penis stiffening.

During the last five minutes, she emphasized the importance of drinking water, eating properly—especially a good breakfast—and getting enough sleep. She closed by explaining how consistency was the key element—encouraging them to do some form of exercise each day in their den or bedroom, that it wasn't necessary to go to a fancy fitness spa. The kids and their parents applauded as she made her final leap off the stage. Quickly walking to the nearest corner and grabbing a dark green backpack, she started in Frank's direction.

The "laser-link" connection resumed instantly as she strode the length of the room. Watching her approach, Frank had to convince himself it was real, that this captivating creature, this girl of his dreams, this plain simple Catholic girl was in love with *him*, not the guy standing behind him. Of course, there was no guy standing behind him—only the wall.

Realizing it would embarrass him, she didn't kiss him, but she wanted to…badly. Frank could see it in her eyes, and he wanted her to, so he kissed her—on the cheek.

"That was a pleasant surprise," her face very close to his so no one could hear.

"I'm full of surprises," he admitted. "Mostly pleasant." Giving her a foxy smile, "You look so cute. Got a fantastic figure," purposely letting her see him ogle her buttocks. "I'm glad I got a chance to see you here." Giving her a white plastic bag, "Thought you could use this."

She looked inside the bag, removing its contents, "Oh, Baby, you sure are full of surprises." It was the emerald bra she'd lost falling off the cliff. "When did you get it?"

"This morning. I swam out from the snork pad, figuring you or Rocky would probably see me during your walk…and *knowing* for sure that Jaws was gonna swallow me whole. Already had my obituary composed."

"Oh, give it to me quick. That's the only way I'm gonna find out anything about you."

"Just mentally," pointing to his brain. "It's up here."

"Shucks, you got me all excited. Well, anyway you deserve another kiss." She kissed him quickly on the lips. "Sorry, I'm all sweaty, but I just couldn't resist," flashing her inimitable smile and laser-look. "That's so nice of you to do that," holding up the bra. "The snap in the back broke—I can fix it…no problem. You could've been hurt. Did you have trouble finding it?"

"No, I have a face mask—saw it on the first dive. Came up, got some air, went back down and got it. Right in front of the White Lady. Kinda creepy down there alone. I thought I saw her stick her head out of the cave, but I just gave her the finger."

"Please shut up." Giving him a mischievously reprimanding expression, "I won't be able to sleep tonight." Then smiling seductively, "Unless you're in bed next to me." Not wanting to press her luck, she put the bra in her backpack, "You're my hero. As for

Rocky's walk, I'm not going near the edge anymore…learned my lesson. He was trying to pull me over there this morning. Uh-uh. He can do his business on the main path—that's it."

"I'm glad to hear that."

"Thank you again. That was *very* thoughtful…and daring." Changing her tone of voice and smiling cutely, "Although I'm one of those rare people who doesn't have body odor, I'd like to sponge off."

"Off to my penthouse then." They started out.

"Did you drive?" she asked.

"No, my place is a short distance down the street. Have an all-night spot, so I just left it there. Parking's tough, as you know. Where'd you park?"

"Draper…front of the church. Better change it though. I don't want to get a ticket, so let's take my car. If I can't find a place quickly, I'll drop you at your place, go park, then come back."

"I'm not letting you out of my sight, young lady," he said very deliberately, checking out her tits.

Happy, "Hey, I love this conversation. What's gotten into you? This is the Frank Taylor I've been searching for. Where was *this* Frank Taylor around midnight, when I needed him?" Unhappily, "You disappointed me on the phone though. You know that, don't you?"

They skirted the basketball court, moving along a walkway through the children's play area toward the Presbyterian Church across Draper Street.

"After I told you goodnight, I had a long talk with myself." He sounded serious. He knew he had to in order to convince himself.

"To use your expression, I wish I could've been a fly on the wall. Bet that would've been fun?" jabbing his arm.

"Probably been a very bored fly."

"Well, I brought the blindfold, so I guarantee that *you* won't be bored," sneaking a look at him. "And I know I won't."

"You're really something, young lady."

"I'm *huuuman*, Frank," elongating and exaggerating the pronunciation of human. "I'm not an angel. Oooh, just kidding...I really am an angel. Go on...change the subject. I know you will." Laughing, she unlocked her car and they got in.

Frank admired her legs, and thought he should ask, "How'd it go with your dad?"

"Well..." She turned on the ignition, carefully backed out of the diagonal space, taking advantage of a long pause and drove south on Draper. "Please direct me."

"Turn left here at Kline," he responded.

"Aside from..." turning left at Kline, "trying to convince me you're a serial killer, everything's super." Thinking it humorous, she chuckled.

Eerily straight-faced and looking ahead, "I'd turn left here at Eads, just to check the availability of unlimited spots. My place is at the other end of the block. If we can't find something along here, maybe on Silverado—we're not staying long."

Thinking about changing his mind, depending on the condition of his apartment, "Think I see an empty one way down there."

"That's a loading zone in front those condos."

"Right here then. Perfect." Looking ahead, she almost went past it. Another diagonal space, she easily turned into it. "You sure there's no time limit?"

"Hey, this is my territory...trust me. We'll only be here about 30 minutes. Lock it up though...according to the 'crime watch' in the newspaper, there's a lot of car theft around here, and they love Hondas."

It was mid-block. Snatching her backpack from behind her seat, Kat made sure the car doors were shut and activated the alarm. Walking toward Silverado, she waited for his reaction to the "serial killer" remark.

Frank figured she was waiting, so he picked up on the subject. "Your father's right, Katherine."

Without missing a beat or changing her pace, "You mean you *are* a serial killer?"

With a touch of sarcasm, "Right on...I didn't think it would take you this long to come to that conclusion."

Grabbing his arm dotingly, with her best redneck impression, "Ya shore don't look like one t' me, Bubba."

Again, without changing his expression, "Theodore Bundy didn't look like one, sound like one, or act like one, but, to the tune of about 30 women, he *was* one. He was also a former law student...and a rather sophisticated and charming fellow. He completely fooled a lot of women. What you see, is not always what you get."

Continuing the impersonation, "You're scarin' the hell outta me, boy."

"I'm not trying to scare you—that's not the idea...far from it. Your father has a good point though. He's a very intelligent man."

Rounding the corner from Eads onto Silverado, she stopped him abruptly, switching to a TV quiz show delivery, "That was the correct answer, sir. You have just won..." She adjusted the backpack strap, the only one she was using, over her left shoulder. Then arching her back, nearly throwing her right hip out of joint to emphasize certain physical endowments, namely her large breasts, Kat looked at him lasciviously and spoke the same way, imitating Mae West again, "I'll show you when we get inside, Baby. I got a little game I want to play with you."

After a muted chuckle, shaking his head, "You're the one who belongs at the Comedy Store." Walking again.

"Just trying to lighten things up. My dad, bless his heart, takes life too seriously. And I believe we're supposed to have a little fun as we make our way through this kinda crazy adventure." Approaching Bishops Lane, Kat leaned over, cupping her hand in simulated secrecy, and whispered, "Don't tell anybody I told you now—you gotta promise me—but this is actually an alley—not a lane."

Now, he played her game. "Ooh, that's a definite no-no—means automatic and instantaneous exile from La Jolla. I'll pretend I didn't hear you."

"They can exile me, Baby…as long as you come along with me, and do every single thing I tell you to do…including what you're thinking about. Hah, hah. Gotcha on that one."

"But I like it here in La Jolla." Then referring to his apartment in front of them, "But *you* may not like it *here* in my apartment…and prefer exile."

"Just try me, sweetie. That's all I ask," she teased. "You'll never regret it."

Frank chuckled again, and tried to politely dodge her invitation.

Not really a garage, but a two-car carport with an outside stairway to a door one flight up, this was Frank's residence. One of the cars belonged to Frank; Kat presumed the other was the landlord's. Surveying the surroundings, Kat spotted the back of the Empress Hotel.

"Come on, I'll lead the way," said Frank. It was a wooden structure, painted white, and the stairway's width could only accommodate one person. Frank unlocked and opened the door, standing inside as Kat entered. Considerably neater than she foresaw, it was however a great deal smaller than she imagined. Kat was all eyes.

"Okay, put the microscope away. I'm not a professional housekeeper." Frank shut the door.

"Not bad. Nicer than you described. A little claustrophobic, but what the heck. I'm sure it's just fine for your needs. And it's definitely big enough for my needs." She gave him a queen-sized wink.

"Careful now. Remember, you're a plain simple Catholic girl."

"Well…I'm just giving you the facts."

Sidestepping the innuendo, "You're right. It's all I need. Here, let me show you." Frank motioned for her to follow. He led her to the tiny bathroom. "There're clean towels, a face cloth, and fresh soap. Please take a shower, Katherine. It only takes five minutes longer, and you'll feel better. Okay?"

"Sounds great," she grinned with exaggeration. "Right out of the movie, *Psycho*," giving him a spooky ghost-like laugh and wiggling her eyebrows.

Fifteen minutes later, Kat emerged ready for the cameras. Having already seen her in four different ensembles, Frank was prepared for anything. Like the parking valets, he was curious to see what she'd come up with, especially considering what she'd brought had been folded or rolled up in her backpack. In dark green stretch jeans that once again accentuated her voluptuous butt, with tan leather sandals, Kat wore a smashing, deep gold halter-top, displaying the balanced proportions of her arms, shoulders, and back—plus her flawless complexion—and, once again, thanks to her father's absence, no bra, which meant...clearly visible nipples.

Frank stood when she came in from the bathroom carrying her backpack, which she placed on the floor in the corner. For some unknown reason she had not yet applied her glossy lipstick. The mystery associated with that reason was swiftly disclosed when Katherine came close to Frank, putting both arms around his neck, and French kissed him in her most seductive mode. He responded like any healthy red-blooded man, but Frank, not only healthy and red-blooded, was older, wiser, and apparently more appreciative. Consequently, his response greatly exceeded her expectations...and she enjoyed it immensely, delighted she had miscalculated. It wasn't their first kiss, but it was the first one in complete privacy. And privacy, judging from the activity of her tongue, did make a difference. As if, without any warning or notice, discovering an original exotic delicacy, Frank and Katherine were unable to resist savoring the next one...and the next one...and the one after that.

Gently releasing the pressure of her lips on his, looking into his greenish brown eyes, Kat spoke softly, "Oh, Frank, I'm not very patient. Please forgive me. I'm so in love with you. I want you so much. Don't you want to take my clothes off, Baby," with a subtle smile, "and throw me on your bed?"

Frank was human too, and his desire was just as real as hers, but he had a master plan to which he had re-pledged his dedication, and experience had taught him that plans had to be followed if objectives were to be attained. "It works both ways, Katherine. I told you I'm crazy about you. It's just that...I want...everything as it should be. You're so very special...you deserve the best. That's what I meant when I said your father's right. Based on what you know about me at this point, you have absolutely no business being in love with me."

Kat started to speak, but Frank put his finger over her lips.

"No, listen to me. I'm only suggesting that we know each other better. You've told me so much about yourself, but you know practically nothing about me. Let's go some place—we have all afternoon—some place where we can talk with a little privacy," chuckling. "Not this much privacy," smiling, looking into her eyes. "If we stay here, we both know what's gonna happen—and it's not that I don't want it to happen." Glancing down at her scantily covered nipples, he could feel an erection starting, and knew if they didn't leave soon, he'd be screwing her in his bed within 15 minutes...or less.

Katherine was combing through the hairs on his forearms with the tips of her fingers. That didn't help matters.

Frank continued, "I want to make love to you—you know that—but that's not the right way. I don't want either of us to have any regrets." He touched the side of her face with his fingers. He wanted to caress her marvelous breasts, but knew better. "I want our relationship to be endless. Am I asking too much?"

Without hesitating one instant, "Of course not, how can I do anything but love you more for feeling that way—and actually having the self-discipline to do it? That's one of the reasons I love you so much...I respect you." For an instant, Katherine lost her own self-respect. She knew that she truly wanted to make love to him now, at this moment, but didn't have the guts to press on with it. There was the possibility of offending him, and losing him forever. She didn't want to take that chance. "Why don't we do this? See if it sounds okay. We'll go to the Marine Room for lunch, then walk along La Jolla Shores, find a nice private place where we can sit next to the sea wall...and we can talk our brains out. Or *you* can talk *your* brains out...I'll just listen." She laughed.

"That's great," Frank concurred. "I'm all for it. Let's go."

Now trying to conceal her disappointment in not taking him to bed, "Let me say this before we go. It's difficult for me...maybe I'll say it the wrong way and upset you...which I don't want—but I have to say it."

"What's that?" He was curious now, and admitted to himself that, if she repeated her invitation to go to bed, he doubted his ability to decline again.

Her concern showed. "Yesterday I told you about the generous monthly income I have. Later I'll tell you the details. What's important now is, I want to pay for our expenses. I do *not* want you paying for anything. I've got it, I want to use it, *but*...please don't feel uncomfortable. Will you promise me that?"

"I'd planned to talk about that today, among other things. It's important, and you have a right to know it. I receive a few dividends from investments I've made over the years—also a monthly social security check. My retirement income is minimal. The fact is, financially, I'm not very well off, Katherine. *However*, if you were penniless, it would have no bearing on my feelings for you, my love for you. Money's never been foremost in my thinking. That's one reason I don't have much." Frank wasn't ready to tell her the other reason, at this point.

"There's no problem then," kissing his nose. "And there never will be."

"That you have it and want to use it, is wonderful. I'm sure you know if the situation were reversed, I'd feel the same as you." He raised her hand to his face, "You're gonna laugh when I change the subject. I wanted to show you the photos we took yesterday—on my computer—but if we get involved in that now it's very time consuming. Let's do it some other time, okay?"

"Sure, you can bring them to my place."

"You have a computer?" He hadn't spotted it.

"Yeah, upstairs in the den. You haven't been up there. You're welcome to use it anytime you wish," kissing the end of his nose again.

"Fine. Let's go then. Don't forget your backpack."

"Just a sec." She moved quickly into the bathroom, pulling lipstick out of her front right pants pocket, and applied it, the glossy type, to her sensuous lips. Then replacing it in her pocket, she lifted her backpack. "Okay, I'm ready."

Picking up a khaki narrow-brimmed hat as they left, "I'll take this along for the beach," Frank indicated.

"Good idea. Mine's in the car."

The Marine Room is next door to the La Jolla Beach and Tennis Club, south of it. Katherine parallel parked on the street just two or three spaces south of the restaurant rather than in the Marine Room's outside parking lot because, "There's no time limit, and we can leave it here after we eat and walk along the beach," Kat explained. Frank left his hat on the front passenger seat.

Being a Saturday, the restaurant surprisingly wasn't as crowded as Katherine expected. Apparently she was acquainted with the hostess and, after a short wait, they were seated at a table by the tinted windows, which were all that separated the guests from the beach. The sand was only about five feet lower than where they sat, and a continuous parade of people, all sizes and shapes in various swimwear, plus the ocean and sky, composed an impressive scene.

Despite the attractive scenery and delicious meal, Frank and Kat would've rated their privacy near the bottom of the scale. At a table nearby, an elderly couple sat speechless, as if adjusting their invisible antennae for improved audio reception. Immediately catching on, Kat and Frank decided to postpone their planned subject matter, simply relax, and enjoy the food and scenery. After a few minutes however, Kat, deciding to mischievously stir up the interest of the eavesdroppers, was eager to see if Frank would pick up on it.

"You seriously think Herbert's going back to Finland...or stay here?" She kept a remarkably straight face, slightly raising the volume of her voice to make sure the couple heard her.

Frank's penetrating look and convincing response confirmed his signal reception. "He told me approximately a week ago he planned to spend the rest of his life here...even intends to be buried here." When he saw Kat's eyes light up and the left side of her top lip quiver, he quickly added, "He said if Penelope doesn't like it, she's welcome go back to Venezuela and live with Alfredo and his pet pelican."

Once again, Frank exceeded her expectations. Aware of his mental sharpness, Kat was in no way surprised he caught on, but the ingenious and comical manner in which he did so, caused her to lose control. Jerking the large cloth napkin from her lap, she covered her face, faking a sneeze, but in reality suppressed an ungovernable laugh.

Frank, realizing what had actually happened, went along with the cover up. "Jemima, you're catching cold. It's because of that top. Your back and shoulders are completely *naked*," stressing the last word without changing his facial expression.

This added to the discomfort of Kat's attempted containment. She was on the verge of bursting at the seams—into laughter. The elderly couple, spellbound, hadn't uttered a single word, but evidently the imitation sneeze generated sufficient fear to force a speedy decision.

The woman's speech pattern smacked of panic, "Are you ready, Charles?"

Her husband's eyes were clearly focused on Katherine's nipples. His answer came slowly and reluctantly. "Yes." He stood with a great deal of effort and deliberation and, after extricating his wife from her chair and taking one final peek back at Kat's nipples, he escorted his wife toward the exit, but not quickly enough to satisfy Katherine.

Under the table, Kat playfully kicked Frank. "You rascal, I almost had a cardiac arrest…and I'm not joking. Jemima! That almost killed me on the spot."

"Who started it?" Frank asked provocatively.

"Never again," she waggishly promised. "I learned my lesson." Then sotto voce, "Maybe you really are a serial killer. You are *very* cold-blooded. I honestly thought I was going to die." She was serious, and was still trying to resume breathing normally.

"You can't say I didn't warn you," smiling devilishly and almost convincing her. Then changing character and subject, "The meal was first-class. The star ingredient of course…was you. And this is quite a scene, but…agoraphobia is setting in. Shall we leave?"

Still a bit uncomfortable from suffocating her laughter, "Okay, prof…educate me." Without much enthusiasm, "What does that mean?"

"The opposite of claustrophobia, like my apartment, remember?" Aware of her discomfort, "I'm only kidding though. I love it here. But we do need to talk. Hey, I'm sorry, Katherine. I hope I didn't make you sick. I was just having fun, playing along with the game that you started."

"Yeah, but my gosh, how can you come up with that stuff off the top of your head and keep a straight face—as if it's real? You should've been an actor. You would've been terrific. I'm serious."

His response to that puzzled Kat. Frank simply shrugged his shoulders without changing expression. "Let's get some fresh air, shall we?"

"All right, sweetie." She needed it too.

Kat took care of the tab, leaving a tip. They made a short visit to the restrooms. Out front, she requested they stop briefly at her car, where she opened the trunk, removed two colorful beach towels and her straw hat. Frank got his hat from the front. She then asked him to remove his Nikes and socks, which along with her sandals, she put in the trunk space. Giving one towel to Frank, she then took some folding money from her purse, put it into her pocket, hid her purse under what looked like a blanket, and stuck a plastic tube of suntan lotion in her other pocket before closing the trunk and activating the car alarm.

They walked attentively in their bare feet down a narrow passageway between the Marine Room and the property to the south. The concrete surface ended with several steps down onto the sandy beach where, to their left, were the cliffs and the seven caves of Thursday and, to the right, was the wide, mile-plus La Jolla Shores Beach. It extended to the pier at Scripps Institute of Oceanography…and beyond that, depending on the tide.

Katherine and Frank went to the right, or north, which would take them past the La Jolla Beach and Tennis Club, the Sea Lodge, Kellogg Park, and the remaining half-mile or so to the pier. Inland, east of the beach, there were prominent hills filled with deluxe residences.

After rolling up their pants a couple of notches, they walked hand in hand, beach towels over their shoulders, on the wet sand near the tidemarks where the footing was firmer.

Kat wondered, "Have you been to this beach?"

"Only when I rented the kayak…and got thrown off of it by a wave."

"That's right," she grinned. "I'd forgotten."

"Quite a setting," admiring it as he spoke.

"Perfect for walking and jogging. Down and back, it's pretty close to three miles. I try to do it once or twice a week." She twisted his hand and pulled it close to her body. "Maybe we could do it together once in awhile."

"Yeah, I'd like that." Studying her carefully as they walked, Frank still had difficulty accepting all this, his mental and emotional reactions in particular. "So what else did your father have to say? It must've been embarrassing for you, knowing so little about me."

"I don't know if embarrassment is the right word…just very uncomfortable. He's never been upset like that before—at least I've never seen him that way—even when my mother left him."

"Did you actually tell him you're in love with me?" The words in that order, with *me* on the tail end, were totally unfamiliar to Frank, as if he were talking about someone else. Perhaps, subconsciously, he was.

"Sure, right up front." They were walking at a slow pace, so people were passing them, not only from the opposite direction, but also from behind. Flags identified specific areas of demarcation for surfing or swimming. Periodically a lifeguard could be heard with his bullhorn, warning a violator. Swimmers, surfers, and boogie-boarders moved in and out of the water perpendicularly to the path of Kat and Frank.

She continued, "Please understand Frank, my father does *not* run my life. He's my dad, and he has been, and is, the greatest. I'll never know exactly what happened between him and my mother—and it's really none of my business—but there're two sides to every story—you know all about that—and that's his problem. My life is my problem, and I intend to live it according to my personal design." Kat was walking in a relaxed fashion and could easily have been talking about any number of insipid subjects, but she was on a roll, the words flowed without obstruction as she endeavored to make her point, so much so that she stopped, directly facing Frank. "What I'm saying is, my father is not going to screw up my life—or my relationship with you—even though I love him and I know he loves me. If anybody's gonna screw up my life it'll be me, and I'll take that responsibility…and suffer the consequences."

After throwing the beach towel she was carrying over her left shoulder, she put both of her hands on his upper arms, her face only inches away from Frank's. "Do you really have any idea how much I love you?"

Instantly, "Yes, I know very well, Katherine," flipping his beach towel over his left shoulder and drilling his gaze into her dark pupils, "because I feel exactly the same way." Placing his hands on her waist, pulling her close, Frank kissed her fervently, disregarding the minor problem presented by their hat brims. Now in front of the La Jolla Beach and Tennis Club, they turned and resumed walking northward.

"When we pass the Sea Lodge and the park, there're less people—also a long seawall where we can find a good spot to sit and talk."

"I'm concerned about your back and shoulders getting sunburned." With the fingertips of his right hand, he skimmed over the surface of her back, from the halter knot behind her neck to the small of her back.

"Careful, I'm huuuman," she giggled. "I'll cover up." She threw the beach towel over her shoulders so it would cover the intended area.

Tacitly they agreed to save the serious talk for the sea wall. Holding hands as they walked, expressing their love for each other through fitful eye contact, Frank and Katherine sporadically embraced and kissed, oblivious to those around them, as they basked in a real-life fairy tale. Scenery and weather fully cooperated, a milieu any postcard photographer would have found enticing.

Passing the north end of Kellogg Park, Kat pointed out the sea wall, the initial part of which was gray and depressing. Not too much farther, in the direction of the pier, there was a section of white sea wall that was considerably more inviting. They looked for a relatively clean area and found it. Double folding the beach towels and placing them next to the wall, the idea was to sit facing the ocean, using the wall as a backrest. The water's edge was some 50 yards away and, although hundreds of people were in view, the distance between any one of them and the two lovers was so great it realistically qualified their location as private, for all practical purposes.

Kat helped Frank get situated, then surprised him by quickly kneeling, face to face with him, and straddling his thighs with her sexually enticing legs and ass. "Can I ask you anything I want?" Her smile was completely disarming, resembling that of a 15-year-old who had just fallen in love for the first time.

"On one condition." Noting her physical posture in relation to his, the obvious zipped through his active imagination.

"You rascal, you always come up with something that complicates things."

"It's called covering one's...position—"

"You mean ass."

"Shh, hush, hush—no profanity, please. You know I disapprove of verbal inelegance."

She removed her hat and his, rubbing her nose against his. "All right, Mr. Smarty Pants, what's the condition?"

"When you state your request, I'll reveal my condition."

"Oh, that's absolutely unfair and you know it, Professor."

"'All's fair in love and war.' I'm sure you've heard that before."

"Seems to me I have...and you probably know who said it."

"Of course. General Nathan Bedford Forrest."

Shaking her head in disbelief, "You must really be a professor." Their faces were only two inches apart.

"My real name—" kissing her lightly on the lips, "is one of the topics I plan to cover today."

"Oh, for heaven's sake, don't tell me it's really Herbert Schmeelburger?" She had fun with her pronunciation of the last name. "Or maybe worse?"

"Meaning if it is, our relationship has ended, right?"

Kat looked back and forth, first at his left eye, then at his right, for some hint of a joke. "No, it just means I have to learn how to call you Herbie." She used her phony New Jersey accent.

Frank chuckled. "Now *you* gave the correct answer, and *you* win..." kissing her nose, "a kiss on the nose. Call me Frank Taylor. That's my real name. Also...you may ask me anything you want."

"What's the condition?"

Pausing, looking at her, and thinking, "Um...that I can eat your left ear," feigning a giant imaginary bite into the air with his mouth and head.

She instantly pulled back from his fake bite. "You're not one of those Hannibal guys, are you?"

With a phony laugh, "If I were, your tuna salad would still be in the fridge—unless daddy ate it—but *you*," pointing his finger directly at her, "would be here," pointing the same finger at his stomach.

"In that case, I accept your condition. Do you want to go first?" The devilish look again. "I'm looking forward to it."

"No, the question first. That determines if I swallow your ear."

She returned the fake laugh. "All right." Then dead seriously, "How many times have you been married?"

"Oooh." Holding his throat, pretending a look of horror, "You go for the jugular, don't you?" Then leaning back against the sea wall, "Well, let's see, now..." With the fingers on his right hand, he started pulling to one side, one at a time, the fingers on his left hand. "Patricia, Diane, Margarita—"

"Oh, my gosh, is this one of your unfunny jokes?"

Frank detected a little weakness in her vocal delivery, but carried on with his idea of fun. He couldn't remember having this much fun, one-on-one, in his entire life, definitely not with a woman he wanted to screw as much as he did Katherine. "And if it isn't...it's all over?"

There was obvious uncertainty in her face. "That depends."

"On whether I've been married nine or ten times instead of three, right?"

Throughout this charade, as Frank listened and answered, his mind raced over the parallel with a scene from the past. The similarity was scary, and Frank recalled having utilized the two-person drama in other instances. According to his intellectual reconstruction of the scenario, Jack had told him, while visiting Ann's home during that fateful holiday season, sitting with her in a car, she had point blank asked how many girls he'd made love to. After carefully evaluating each past relationship in order to give an honest answer, Jack told her, "Seven." Ann began crying, then asked him how many of the seven had he truly loved. Again, Jack thought back with great care and reiterated, "Seven." Unable to rationalize such behavior, Ann challenged him on the validity of his response. Jack explained quite rationally that it would be impossible for him to make love to any girl without being genuinely in love with her. To do so, in his mind, constituted empty sex or, what in contemporary terms is referred to as, recreational sex, and Jack wanted no part of that. For him, that would've been totally out of character.

Ann was devastated, figuratively coming apart at the seams and, for all practical purposes, that was the end of their relationship. Had Jack lied and said he hadn't really been in love with any of them, which in conscientious analysis is closer to the truth, possibly assuaging Ann, he wouldn't be in prison today. But who can honestly and accurately say that life with Ann would have been preferable to life in prison…or even death. Only her present husband, whoever that may be, could answer that question…if he dared to.

A more carefully thought out retrospect would have confirmed that Jack *thought* he had been in love with each of the seven girls. If he had indeed been truly in love with them, he conceivably would have married any one of the seven. But the truth was, he had not been in love with any of them…except one.

Given the opportunity in a less stressful, less emotionally charged confrontation with Ann, Jack no doubt would have offered that interpretation, but Ann slammed the steel door in Jack's face…forever.

On Kat's face, Frank could easily see the proliferation of puzzlement, so he chose humor: "You know, I really need a calculator to do this...accurately." No ophthalmologist had studied Kat's eyes so meticulously. With the last remark, he could see the beginning of a smile creeping in from the left. He couldn't wait. "You know I'm playing with you, Katherine. Come on...the answer is *never.* I've never been married to *anybody*...and that includes my pet pelican. There's nothing conjugal between us—I assure you—she's just a pet. I think she's a she."

"Let's leave your pelican out of this." Now it was Kat, painstakingly doing a refresher course on Frank's face. "That is *very* difficult to accept, Frank Taylor. I'm not calling you a liar and, hopefully, you understand what I'm trying to say."

"Well, I'm not a liar, and I'm certainly not about to start with you. Remember, dear, it takes two to tango and, as I've told you, my dream girl has never appeared...until now...and I'm looking at her."

That merited an amorous kiss, and he got it. Then, "How many women have you made love to?"

There was no escape from the Jack-and-Ann dialogue. Or maybe it was the White Lady after all. The coincidence of having just mentally reviewed that scenario, only seconds ago, brought an understandably strange look to Frank's face.

Katherine's perceptivity gauge was highly accurate. She chose disengagement: "Don't answer that, Frank. I'm sorry I asked that question." Giving him an affectionate kiss on the mouth, "Whatever the answer would be, it would have absolutely no effect on my love for you. I'm not in love with your past. I'm in love with the Frank Taylor I'm looking at right this minute. To some extent, we're all products of our past, but that particular item is none of my business."

She was still sitting on his thighs, presently more on his upper thighs, having slid forward slightly, toward his torso. Anyone looking from 50 yards away could be wondering about...hanky-panky.

Learning from Jack's incident, Frank figured his best option was silence, but finding her last statements so eminently noble, he was unable to resist a compliment: "Wow. You impress me so much, Katherine…in so many ways."

Wearing the demeanor of an acutely preoccupied district attorney, "I didn't say it to impress you, Frank. I said it because I want the question stricken from the record."

Expressing humility, he decided to comfort her. "Hey, it's no big deal."

Closing in on him with a menacing tone, "In that case, Baby, how many women have you screwed?"

Their combined laugh explosion attracted attention 100 yards away. Kat, hysterical, rolled off Frank onto the sand. Frank completely cracked up.

She stood quickly, grinning down at him, pulling the tube of suntan lotion from her pocket. "I can play that game too, but that's all I'm doing, playing. That's the end of that subject. Here," dropping the lotion container in his lap and repositioning herself in front of Frank, straddling his thighs again but with her back to his face, "make yourself useful and smear some of this gunk on my back and shoulders. I don't want to look like a lobster at the Gulls Nest tonight."

Frank was tremendously relieved, but tried not to flaunt it. Luckily, she faced the other direction, revealing the most ravishing expanse of African-American skin Frank had ever seen, thanks to the halter-top designer. Having not so secretly glimpsed the opposite side in the ocean on Thursday, he could now leisurely experience, visually and tactually, this natural work of art. Placing an ample amount of the squeezed lotion on the fingertips of his right hand, Frank repeatedly applied it with the artistry of a finger-painter, the dexterity of an accomplished masseur, leaving no open areas untouched.

"Baby, you're hired. The only catch is, we have to stay here. You have to continue this *forever*."

With disappointment, "Oh, that's not long enough."

Manifesting drowsiness, "It's so relaxing, I may have trouble performing tonight."

Momentarily forgetting, "Performing what?"

Jumping at the opportunity, "Ooh, I know what I'd like to perform."

"Please, we're having a polite conversation."

"Oh, I can perform *very* politely," twisting her neck and sneaking in a sly grin. "I'm sure you'll be delighted."

"Naughty girl. Shame on you," vigorously kneading her deltoids.

"You know, Frank...?" For a change, she was going to switch subjects. "You should write a screenplay about our relationship. I love the beginning, with me falling off the cliff. I can just see it in a movie," spreading her arms and hands dramatically in front of her, "on the big screen."

"Just leave Jack sitting there in his cell?"

A little hurt that Frank would even consider her that indifferent. "No, of course not. I didn't mean that. I meant after your project."

"I don't know anything about screenwriting." But playing the game, "Besides, who would play your part, you?"

"No way. I don't know anything about acting, but a few people have told me I look a little like Vivica Fox. She'd be great for my part. You know who she is?"

"I don't think so. Maybe I'd recognize her face if I saw it. She'd probably be okay, but I've got news for you. Don't let it go to your head though."

Kat, interested, twisted around to see his face, "Tell me."

Looking at her profile reinforced his conviction. "You're much more beautiful than any Vivica Fox could possibly be."

Pleasantly shocked, "Are you kidding? She's a knockout."

"Then you're a double knockout—and definitely...sexier."

"Ooh, Baby, you're saying all the right things. Gimme a kiss," resuming her original position. "That's enough lotion," proceeding to devour him. After finishing, "That's not really fair to Vivica though. If you ever saw her in a movie, like *Two Can Play That Game*, I know you'd change your mind. And besides, you haven't seen her up close and personal—like this." She planted another big one on him.

"No, and I'm sure I never will. I'd much prefer the real thing—you."

Continuing the game, Kat wanted to know, "Who's gonna play the infamous Frank Taylor?"

Chuckling sarcastically, "Oh, those imaginative people in Hollywood'll get some handsome dude/star like Sean Connery or Clint Eastwood—which is a radical departure from reality. But I guess that's what movies are all about."

Somewhat baffled, "How do you mean?"

"Well, just take a good look at me. I'm an average Joe Blow…with less than average looks…not even remotely in the leading man category."

"Listen, you…I think you're extremely attractive, and *very* sexy—and nobody could play Frank Taylor better than you. You proved that in the Marine Room. Your performance almost killed me. And besides, you *are* Frank Taylor—the real thing."

"But you're slightly opinionated. The international movie audience would not be so biased in my favor. Of course, that's the premise, which makes or breaks the theme of our story. And if Vivica Fox did play the part, successfully convincing the audience she'd truly fallen in love with a guy who actually looks like *me*," chuckling, "she'd go down in cinematic history as the greatest actor of all time…supplanting Meryl Streep."

"Meryl Streep—she's the greatest—and Oscar winner Halle Berry's my favorite—but the guys you mentioned…Connery and Eastwood, are too old to play your part."

Genuinely taken aback. "What do mean too old? All three of us are the same age."

Jumping to her feet, "What!?"

"Born in the same year. They may be a few *months* older than I. How old do you think I am?"

"Not over 55. Well…maybe 56." Trying to revive by wetting her lips with her tongue, "Right? Probably younger, huh?"

"Sit down, I don't want you to fall on your face."

She squatted beside him. "Okay, tell me. I'm ready."

"No, you're not. In that position, you're gonna fall on your back. Put one knee down for balance."

Following Frank's instructions, "Let's have it."

"I'm not responsible for a cardiac arrest. You understand that? No lawsuits, okay?"

"If you don't hurry up and tell me, I'm gonna have one…and I *will* sue you, even after I'm dead. And I'll come back and haunt you."

"That's an easy way out for you…just die on me. What about poor old me?"

"Hah." Fake grin. "You'll have the pleasure of dealing with my father. Won't that be *fun*?"

"Preferring death, I shall pull a Romeo stunt. I'll mix the suntan lotion with a few seagull droppings. That should do the trick. Horrible flavor though."

Kat chuckled. "Are you going to tell me or not?"

"Well, it's been such a wonderful relationship. Can't you see I'm trying to postpone the ending?"

Sweetly, with anticipatory sympathy, "Trust me."

"All right. I've given you sufficient warning." Long pause, then pronouncing the number very distinctly, "71."

Frozen for five seconds, then with a bizarre quasi-smile, minutely eyeballing every square inch of Frank's face, touching the surface vein under his right eye, touching the bump on the end of his nose, putting her hands above Frank's ears and moving his scalp back and forth, up and down, to possibly expose a hairpiece. Then, jabbing and confirming the muscularity of his pectorals, briskly seizing his right biceps, then his deltoid, and then his forearm to validate their size, and, with the fingertips of both hands, certifying the firmness of his neck, Kat finally trained her eyes directly on Frank's and slowly repeated the age he had just given her…"71?"

"Fifth of November—only a few weeks away—72," Frank inserted.

Now emphatically, "You are *not* 71 years old, Frank Taylor. This is another one of your silly jokes. If you're 71, I'm Donald Duck." Kat stood.

Putting his right hand on top of her nearby left foot, "Such a lovely foot. Sorry to see it change into that strange webbed variety." Then, turning sideways in order to take a wallet from his left back trouser pocket, he flipped it open, displaying his new California driver's license, and gave it to her.

After 20 seconds of silence, she repositioned her feet, one on each side of his thighs, and lowered her body, facing him in her initial straddling position, placing her extraordinary ass on his thighs. Folding the wallet, she placed it between their crotches. Then delicately, she placed her hands on his shoulders. Looking at him understandingly, she spoke the words he'd anticipated: "Quack, quack, quack, quack." By forcing air into the cheek area between the teeth and jaw hinge on the left side of her mouth, Katherine sounded almost as good as Donald himself.

Frank looked at Kat with amusement, putting his hands around her waist. "Does that mean I have to start talking like that? Or were you telling me goodbye?"

Nodding, then shaking her head. "Quack, quack."

Inviting her compliance, which she provided silently, he pulled her close, caressing her lips with his. By nature a somewhat unrestrained individual, Kat's desire dictated an even more demonstrative and pleasurable approach, which she expressed with a soul kiss. Frank was very receptive.

Her face touching his, her words yielding and velvety, "Baby, I don't care if you're 100. I'm in love with *you*—not your chronological age." She pulled away from him in order to get a fuller picture. "And look at you. There is no way you look 71 years old, or anywhere near that. My father's 65. You look 10 years younger. Are you taking some kind of youth pill? Tell me what it is so I can get started immediately. I want to look as good when I'm almost 72."

Squeezing his arm muscles with her hand, Kat continued, "You don't get muscle tone like that watching TV, man. Come on, you're holding out on me. Instead of sleeping, you must be going to the gym at night, correct?"

"Staying with the Disney theme, I have a little Mickey Mouse workout I do every day."

"Tell me," Kat was interested. "What you do?"

"I try to do 50 pushups...usually make it to 46 or 47. I don't want to kill myself making it to 50. Then I simulate 120 chin-ups, using an imaginary horizontal bar."

"Why 120, instead of just 100?" she queried.

"It's the last 20 that make the 100 worthwhile. You know about that. I do 30 or 40 sit-ups. Then I do 200 toe presses—that's what I call them—where you go up and down on the balls of your feet. Basically, that's it. Takes about 20 minutes, with a little in-place running thrown in between."

"Why don't you do 220 toe presses?" she grinned.

"Next time you're exercising do 200, and that'll answer your question."

Katherine laughed. "Yeah, I bet at 200 your calves are about to catch on fire."

"You guessed it. With exercise, the important thing—what you told the kids this morning—is to be consistent. As you know, most people aren't. *But* you also have to consider, when I was 12 and 13 years old I was walking on my hands and performing on the horizontal bar—something I continued all through high school—so a lot of what you see are leftovers."

This all made sense to Kat. It explained her first impression of Frank when he got out of the water at the snork pad. It was one of the reasons she was physically attracted to him.

"A lotta guys would like to have those leftovers, Baby. And you eat properly," she added. "That's great, Frank." Kat was closely inspecting his facial skin. "You don't have any deep wrinkles, practically none on your forehead and cheeks. Some crow's feet from smiling—I have those. What's this little vein?" Her fingertip was under his right eye.

"I picked that up pretty early, I think from all the hand-balancing. After we threw our paper routes—the *Memphis Press-Scimitar*, an afternoon route—three or four of us used to have a contest to see who could walk the farthest on our hands. I usually came in second—nobody could beat Konrad Dieterich—but I think I created this surface vein trying."

"And this small blemish on the end of your nose?" she asked.

"That's from squeezing a pimple when I was about 14. Should've known better."

Kat kissed it affectionately. Looking above his face, "What about your hair? Most guys your age who're lucky enough to have hair…it's completely gray. You've still got a lot of brown in there. Do you use something on it? Come on, tell me the truth."

"No, I don't care what color my hair is. It is nice to have some though. I guess it's just heredity. You don't have any control over that. Not yet, anyway," Frank grinned. "Maybe in another 20 years, you'll see all these 90-year-old people with black hair that's for real."

"You're funny. I told you that right after I met you. When I lost my bra, you said it could've been worse, meaning I could've lost my shorts too." Kat chuckled. "I'm getting to know all about you, and I love it. November 5th. You're a full-blooded Scorpio. I'm a Leo. I love every square inch of you, Frank." Her huge brown eyes were hypnotic. "Did you ever dream a woman would say that to you?"

"No." Frank could feel his emotions getting the best of him, a sensation to which he was totally unaccustomed until he met Katherine. He could also detect an erection and, considering her position, wondered if she could detect it too. "I don't...know...there's no way...I can express to you...how I feel about you."

Kat curled her fingers on both hands around Frank's head, grabbing his hair in the back, pulling him to her, and soul kissed him. He relinquished all controls to her. It was a breathtaking trip. His erection was increasing.

Frank, coming up for air, "I can't believe this is happening, Katherine. I'm having trouble thinking straight."

The look on Kat's face spelled passion. She was well aware that her normally smooth-running control system was presently malfunctioning, and that sexual desire had taken over the pilot's seat. Never having been in this situation, she struggled to distinguish between desire and love. Intellectually, she would always choose love. This was not a matter of choice however, but recognition, and sexual desire was a skillful impersonator. Her new exposure to sexual desire over the last 24 hours, though quite limited, was fascinating and physically exhilarating, whereas her past experience with what she erroneously identified as love was infinitely disappointing. Her reasoning at this point, admittedly suspect, suggested an enhanced familiarity with sexual desire would increase her qualifications to make a wise decision. With Frank representing her safety net, she decided to move in that direction. A dangerous road, but Frank would be her guide. In view of his last statement, however, Frank's condition was dubious at best. Her primary objective, nevertheless, at this point, was to fuck him, regardless of the consequences. And once Katherine Churchill sets her mind on something, she usually does it.

"We'll just love each other forever—that's all." She slowly rubbed her lips over his. "I don't want you out of my sight. I think I'll go crazy without you." She held his head between her opened hands, looking desperately into his eyes. "Please, Baby, listen to me. Please come live with me. There's a large bedroom upstairs, and you'll have the den and the computer. I promise you I'll behave myself. I won't do anything you don't want me to do." That was a lie and she knew it. She hoped God would forgive her, but as she had admitted to God many times, she was human…she was a sinner. That's why she went to confession some Saturdays. "I promise. Please say yes."

In Frank's mind, it would be impossible to reconcile such an arrangement with his personal philosophy…and his master plan, which at the moment was the more important of the two. Nevertheless, curiosity compelled him to seek certain information. Thinking his search would cause Katherine to believe he'd entertain the request, he hesitated momentarily, but feeling her moist lips against his and the movement of her braless breasts against his chest, he decided in favor of verbal exploration.

"What happens when your father unexpectedly pops in?" He rubbed noses with her, Eskimo style.

"Don't worry, I'll take care of that," she assured him, running her tongue over the outside surface of his lips.

Pulling his face away slightly to avoid her tongue as he spoke, "I'd be in the middle—and very uncomfortable. He's your father. He gave you life. You owe him respect."

Moving her face closer, sliding her tongue around the inside of his lips, then, "I love my father, I respect him. I do not owe him my life. My life is mine. I want to give it to you." Another soul kiss. "That's my desire. I want you to have my life." And she also desired to screw him as soon as possible. She was bored with her dildo. She wanted no more of that. There was nothing like the real thing. That was her educated supposition at any rate, but based on her past experience, she certainly couldn't argue the point.

Frank, thinking of a distraction, "I'm concerned about your getting sunburned."

Instantly, without moving her arms from around his neck or reducing the one-inch distance between their lips, "The other beach towel is on the sand beside you. Throw it over my shoulders." An Eskimo kiss.

Using his right hand, without looking, Frank found the other beach towel. He jerked it partially open, flipped it up and over her back and shoulders, then, adding his left hand, unraveled it completely, neatly covering her naked shoulders and back. As if it had been rehearsed, Kat swiftly withdrew her arms from Frank's neck, located the edge of the huge towel with her fingers, pulling it up from the back of her neck over both of their heads, then tucking it against the sea wall behind Frank's back. From under this towel-covered, two-body clump against the sea wall, an on-looker would only see Frank's protruding outstretched calves, ankles, and feet. Kat immediately replaced her arms around Frank's neck and French kissed him.

In the shade created by the towel, Kat eased her face away from Frank's, her eyes cemented to his, "I've got you all to myself now. Let's stay here forever. As far as I'm concerned, you're just a kid, but when you do get to be an old man, I'll put you in a wheelchair and push you to my house."

Their laughter generated the interest of several beach-walkers, naturally wondering what was going on under the towel.

"You're actually getting nuttier by the minute," Frank proclaimed. "You know that, don't you?"

Defiantly, "Who cares? I'm having fun. I'm not hurting anyone." Remembering her physical position, "Maybe you're getting tired of me sitting on you?"

"No, I'm comfortable." He was except that his rigid penis was cramped.

"Aren't you having just a teensy-weensy bit of fun?"

Kissing her lips and wishing a private bed were available, "What do you think?"

With an elfish smile, "I think so." Reverting to her proposition, "Please stay with me, Baby." Putting her finger over his lips to prevent him from talking, "My dad's really not a grouch. I can handle him. When I tell him all about you—"

"You don't know all about me, Katherine. Basically, my age is the only thing you know about me now that you didn't know a few hours ago."

"I know you've never been married," she reminded him.

"Well, that. I'd forgotten."

"Okay, let's see..." Thinking of other questions, "Where did you go to college?"

"Undergraduate, Loyola."

"A good Catholic school. You also went to graduate school, huh?"

"Yes, Fordham."

"Hey, another good Catholic school. Any pedophilic priests running around?"

Frank smiled. "Not to my knowledge, but you never know...unless you're a kid."

"Denzel Washington, the Oscar man, went there, didn't he?"

"Yes, Alan Alda too."

"Oh yeah, the 'Mash' guy. What was your major?"

Frank realized, sooner or later, this would come up. It came sooner than he expected and, although he would cover this topic thoroughly at some point in the future, he felt this was not the proper time to do so. That would definitely have an adverse effect of his master plan.

Attempting to pick an esoteric subject with less finite boundaries, and therefore one hopefully Katherine would shy away from conversationally, "Philosophy," Frank answered.

"No wonder you're such an *in-depth* guy." A soul kiss, "I like that."

"Careful with the double entendres, you might—"

"Maybe that's what I want to do," she was quick on the trigger, followed by an Eskimo kiss.

"Thought you were a 'plain simple Catholic girl,'" quoting her.

"Just having a little fun. At those Catholic schools you attended, maybe they taught you it's bad to have fun?"

"That's a debatable inference. Where did you go to college?"

"Started at Marian College, also a Catholic school, but got involved in modeling. One thing led to another, and I dropped out. My parents were very upset. Later, with the money I made modeling, I got a degree in French from City College, New York. You don't wear glasses?"

"Had the laser job two years ago."

"Really? How is it?"

"Great. Wore glasses more than 40 years. They told me I should, but I don't even like to wear sunglasses...it feels so good without them. Got the 'mono'—left eye for reading, right for distance."

"No kidding? Work out okay?"

"Fine for me. Some people have trouble adjusting. I'm pretty adaptable."

"I can see that. You're very youthful, Frank. Are your feet sticking out beyond the towel?"

"Yes."

"Pull 'em under the towel, Baby. Otherwise they're gonna get cooked."

He did...and kissed her. "Thanks." Now the towel-covered, two-body clump had no legs.

She wanted to go back to her proposition, which was her secondary objective, but he was encouraging her to ask more questions, so..."What have you been doing over the years?" She tried to sound harmless, "Anything exciting?"

This was the other side of the coin he preferred not to deal with at this time. Her question was not very specific or clearly defined, so Frank chose to answer it in general terms.

"Unexciting...and insignificant. Corporate beehive stuff," watching her eyes for a reaction. "Nothing to be proud of...on the other hand, nothing to be ashamed of. One day you're looking in the mirror shaving and you realize most of your life has zipped by, and you haven't lived up to your own expectations. That's why the project about Jack is so important. In my lifetime, I'd like to do something constructive to help, at least, one other person."

Giving him a light kiss on his lips, "I know another person you can help." And she knew precisely how he could help her. And she knew he would enjoy it...maybe as much as she.

"That person doesn't need my help," retaining the third-person form that Katherine started. "She wants my love...and she has all of it."

"What about my ear? You haven't eaten it yet. I'm disappointed."

Smiling, Frank imitated the sound of a lion, then French kissed her left ear.

"Ooh, I love it. When you finish, eat the right one."

The lion again—then the right ear.

In view of their relative, towel-covered privacy, Katherine seriously considered raising her halter-top so Frank could kiss her naked breasts—just the thought of it strongly aroused her—but suddenly a natural urge changed her mind. "Guess what, Baby?" She raised her eyebrows.

Removing his mouth from her right ear, "What?"

With exaggerated animation and distorted enunciation: "I have to pee pee."

Frank chuckled, "Me too."

"Here, take your wallet," removing the towel, handing his wallet to him and standing. "Let's take the towels, or they won't be here when we get back. It's not far. We can come right back. You like it here?" She extended her arms toward him, offering to help him rise.

He grabbed her hands, and she pulled him to a standing position. "I love it." Then he glanced down to make sure his partial erection wasn't noticeable. It was, but he quickly hid it with one of the beach towels he picked up.

After putting their hats on, they walked to the water's edge and south, to the restrooms.

CHAPTER 9

When they returned to the sea wall, Katherine and Frank sat with their backs to the wall as they'd originally planned. Because of the sun's more acute angle, their hats were now tilted to shadow their eyes. One towel protected their ankles and feet from the rays of the sun; the other was draped over Kat's shoulders and back to cushion her skin from the sea wall and to provide some protection from the sun.

"Maybe you told me, but I've forgotten…exactly what did Jack do to wind up in prison?" Kat thought it was an appropriate time to learn more about the mysterious friend.

"He killed a guy…in a one-punch fight…that Jack claims he didn't start."

"Ugh. That's pretty serious."

"You're right, it is. No one has a right to take another's life." Frank paused for an eternity. A faraway look invaded his face. "But Jack's not a cold-blooded murderer…that's my point. What he did was completely unpremeditated, impulsive, more importantly, accidental—and even more importantly, self-defensive…when you consider that he was outnumbered and knew he had to make a strong physical statement. Those guys would've taken him apart. Basically, it was a case of a very fine young man in the wrong place at the wrong time. My objective is not to prove his innocence—he was guilty…but I want to show that, considering his true character—and he had more character as a teenager than anyone I knew—and value as a human being...I want to show that the punishment was far too severe."

"You think pretty highly of this guy." Kat's curiosity had been aroused. "What's that based on?"

"I met Jack when we were 10th-graders at Memphis Tech on the basketball team, which was a pre-season pick to win the city championship. Jack never had a basketball in his hands until the ninth grade at Bellevue Junior High School. Said his family and all his buddies used to laugh at basketball as a sissy sport, with guys running around in shorts bouncing a ball. Well...he fell in love with the game, practiced all summer, alone in a 100° temperature gym at the Oak Park YMCA, developing his skills in order to make the team his first year at Tech.

"We both made the team. I was on the 'B' team, but Jack was the number three guard on the 'A' team, a heck of an accomplishment when the 'A' team was picked to be champions."

"Sure was," Kat agreed. She was interested. Had Frank read the phone book aloud, backwards, she'd have probably been interested.

"Just before Christmas vacation in a practice game," Frank continued, "a pre-season game that had no bearing whatsoever on the league standings, our coach used a couple of transfer students from a rival school as substitutes. The coach of the rival school, which was very much in contention for the championship, learned of this...also that it was against the rules. He reported it, and we were kicked out of the league for the *entire* season—meaning no basketball for Tech High...not even practice.

"I vividly remember the team meeting at which our coach revealed this to us. Some of the senior players actually broke down and cried. Three of them had served in the military, and had come back to school for their senior year just so they could play sports. There were a couple of senior players who would definitely have been All-Memphis, and probably would've won college scholarships. Jack sat across from me. I can see his face now—I'll never forget it. He didn't cry, but you could figuratively see the wheels turning in his brain, remembering all those hours, dripping with sweat, preparing for tryouts. Then to actually make the team, be a second stringer on a team that's picked to win it all, and to have it thrown out the window because of a minor rule infraction—not by a player, but by the coach—well…"

"That was totally unfair," said Kat in disgust.

"Some of the guys just couldn't understand why the players were being punished for something the coach did. It was all written up in the sports section of the newspapers. There was no TV then. And, of course, the only explanation from the coach was…'A rule is a rule.' He apologized, said he wasn't aware of that rule. At any rate, that was on a Friday, a couple of days after Christmas. We'd been having practice games, and practice sessions, during the holidays. The following Monday, Jack, who learned that the Memphis Board of Education administrative offices were not closed for all the school holidays, only for Christmas Day and New Years Day, paid a visit to the office of the Superintendent of Public Schools—the top dog. Jack went directly into his office, jumped up on top of his desk—the superintendent stood—and Jack urinated directly in his face."

Kat applauded and cheered, again attracting attention along the beach. "Oh Baby, I'd love to have seen that."

"You weren't even born."

"What happened then?" she was hyped up.

"They took him to jail—not Juvenile Hall—regardless of his age. Naturally, it was all over the papers and the radio, not only citywide, but nationally. The good citizens of Memphis got up in arms. There were meetings, hearings, and everything else. Jack told the authorities—he was quoted in the papers and on radio, 'They might as well execute me—basketball's my life and nothing else really matters. I don't want to live, if I can't play basketball.' The Tech High Yellow

Jackets were reinstated. We won the city championship—and get this—the Tennessee State Championship."

Tears were in Katherine's eyes, her upper lip quivered. She was close to crying. "None of that would have happened if it hadn't been for Jack. That's quite a story, Frank. They should let him out of prison for that alone."

"He was the school hero, but you know what? It had no adverse effect on his personality. To him it was like nothing happened. That tells you a lot about the guy."

"Is there more? This guy's interesting. I can see why you want to help him."

"Not too long after graduation—approximately a year—the Korean War started. Being in college, I got a deferment, but Jack, who had dropped out of Memphis State after only one quarter, joined the navy. In 'Boot Camp' here in San Diego, because he was issued marching boots a size-and-a-half too small, Jack developed infected blisters on both feet. He reluctantly complained to his company commander when it got to the point where he could hardly walk. He was a chief boatswain's mate who was a 16-year veteran of mine sweepers…an 'old salt' as they were called. The 'old salt' told him to just stick it out, that everything would clear up, he just had to march it off like a man. The 'old salt' was also from Memphis, and he knew the other company recruits knew that, and he didn't want to be criticized for showing Jack any favoritism.

"Jack ended up in 'sick bay'—the hospital. They told Jack and the 'old salt' if another day had passed, gangrene would have set in and Jack would have lost both feet…maybe legs. The 'old salt' came very close to being court-martialed. Jack, after three days in 'sick bay,' receiving a shot of penicillin in his buttocks every four hours, was sent back to his company, number 50–172—"

Kat, amazed, "Good lord, you know all that stuff."

"Normally, I'd say let's leave the Lord out of it, but in this case, I think the Lord had a great deal to do with Jack McRae's evolvement.

And remembering all that stuff is easy when it's been part of your life for several years."

"Sorry I interrupted. Please go on."

"Well, when they sent Jack back to his company after being away three days, the 'old salt' refused to accept him. He felt that Jack's missing three days would have a negative effect on his performance, and that would in turn affect the company's performance, thereby greatly reducing its chances of finishing high in competition and winning honors. The 'old salt's' superiors told him Jack's absence was due to his bad judgment, that he was stuck with him whether he liked it or not.

"Jack said the 'old salt' looked very much like Spencer Tracy, that his uniforms were all imported gabardine from Hong Kong with three perfect pleats down the back of his shirt, making the other company commanders appear second-class.

"After marching the company around with their rifles for an hour and a half on Jack's first day back, the 'old salt' had them march to an area in front of a wooden stage. Climbing the three or four steps, he walked out onto stage, looking at them threateningly, and reminded them they'd been told a week ago to study the semaphore and be prepared to perform it that day.

"Referring to a notebook that contained all the recruits' names, he called one out. That recruit then mounted the platform and faced the company members. He was instructed by the 'old salt' to lead the company in the semaphore, shouting the letters out as he demonstrated them with his arms, using imaginary flags. Recruit number one regretfully admitted he was not prepared and was sent back, with a heated remark from the 'old salt,' to his spot in the company marching formation. Recruit number two repeated that performance. Number three, likewise. When recruit number four heard his name bellowed, trying to minimize his embarrassment and save a futile trip, he declined on the spot. Not wanting to disappoint him, the 'old salt' hotly requested his presence on the stage, chewed him out in the language for which the U. S. Navy is famous, and literally screamed him off the stage.

"Following three more 'copy-cat' acts, the 'old salt' turned to pepper—red, not black. He walked to the center of the stage and…" Frank grabbed his own throat with his right hand, causing his facial color to redden and, while actually keeping his voice down, simulated shouting through facial expressions, and imitated the 'old salt,' "Does anybody in this company know the semaphore?"

Watching Frank, Kat cracked up. His acting ability didn't surprise her. He'd already demonstrated that. But this was more of a comical, character acting performance. He saw her reaction from the corner of his eye.

Frank then posed the obvious question, "Guess whose hand went up?"

Kat, grinning, "Jack's?"

"The *only* hand that went up. Still raging at the top of his voice, the 'old salt' asked him," Frank continued his impression, "'How can you know the semaphore? You've been in "sick bay" for three days. Get up here.'

"Jack marched onto the stage, making all the turns in military fashion, coming to a halt at center stage, then did a crisp left face to front the company. Still at attention, he began shouting the letters, starting with *A*, simultaneously snapping his arms in position to semaphorically convey that corresponding letter. It was a flawless demonstration. Between butt shots of penicillin in 'sick bay,' Jack had the Bluejacket's Manual propped up on his lap, studying the semaphore. That's where and how he learned it. The company commander complimented him in glowing terms in front of the entire company.

"Near the end of the three-month training period, the approximately 80 recruits were asked to choose the outstanding man in their company as 'Honorman.' The guys in 50–172 picked—you know who—Jack McRae."

"What a guy. Hey, give me a kiss."

He did. "I was wondering how long I'd have to wait."

"Well, it's kinda tricky when you're motor-mouthing, especially as the 'old salt.'"

Chuckling, "All right, I'll have designated pauses for a kiss. Just one small footnote...several months later, the 'old salt' was killed in a freak car accident here in San Diego. The funeral was in Memphis. Jack's mom went to the funeral home after reading the obituary in the local paper and realizing who he was from letters Jack had sent her during 'Boot Camp.' 'Old salt's' brother was there and actually showed Jack's mom the notebook in which his brother had kept thumbnail profiles of the recruits. There were several gold stars by Jack's name, and he'd written, 'Jack McRae, an outstanding recruit, will make a fine naval officer.' Isn't that something?"

"Sure is. I see what you mean about this guy. So where did he go next in the navy."

"He qualified for what they called Airmen School, a two-month exposure to the 13 different jobs for enlisted men in the aviation branch of the navy. Coincidentally, it was in Memphis at the Naval Air Station at Millington. Jack was going home every weekend to see his mom, grandparents and friends, so his grades weren't very impressive. In fact, they were bad. Of the 13 jobs, the most appealing to Jack, and practically everybody in his class, was photography.

"Jack told me he'd never taken a picture, that his uncle—also named Jack—always took the family photos, and he, Jack McRae, knew absolutely nothing about photography. What they showed him in Airmen School about this particular job assignment attracted his attention. That was his first choice. In an interview with counselors, however, he was told that because of his poor grades in Airmen School there was no way he could possibly go to the Naval School of Photography in Pensacola, Florida, that he should seriously consider other job possibilities. Apologetically, Jack explained why his grades were low, in contrast to the high grades and 'Honorman' award in

'Boot Camp.' He also told them he understood how they felt, but that if he changed his choice on the 'dream sheet,'—as they called it—he would never forgive himself, because that's what he wanted to be as a career navy man…a photographer. That was his dream."

Kat shook her head. "Mr. Determination, huh?"

"You'd better believe it. He was one of three who went to Photo School, which was very tough for him because of his lack of knowledge on the subject. In that three-month school, which was five days a week and involved lots of homework, they got into photographic chemistry and everything else you can think of regarding photography. How about a kiss?" He got it. "I'm trying to bring you up to that fatal day of the accidental killing. Tell me if you're bored."

Kat put her thumb and index finger on his chin, turning his face toward hers. "Baby, I am not bored. I could sit here with you forever. Just love to be with you. I don't have to be doing anything. Matter of fact, this is quite interesting. I just hope, if for some reason your efforts don't work out, regarding Jack's freedom, you won't be terribly disappointed."

"No, naturally I'd be disappointed, but it's sort of like Jack wanting to go to Photo School. I want to be able to say to myself that I tried. It's also important that you know the story. I wrote Jack about you."

With much enthusiasm, "Really? What'd you tell him?"

"That I'm nuts about you."

"Oh, Baby, I'm sorry to interrupt, but please be with me tonight. Don't worry about my dad. I'm nuts about you too."

"First, let me get through this."

"Okay, after Photo School, what happened?"

"By the way, talk about fate. While he was in Photo School he was offered an opportunity to try for Naval Air Cadet Training School, also at the Pensacola base. He had one quarter of college credits from Memphis State before he dropped out, and was told he was recommended very highly and could possibly qualify, if he was willing to take a few more college courses. The next day, by sheer coincidence, Jack saw a Memphis Tech kid, Billy Mac Quinlan, who graduated a year ahead of him, walking by the officers' dorm for air cadets.

"They got together that night and Billy told Jack he wasn't happy with the situation, that after finishing basic training in Pensacola, he'd be sent to Corpus Christi for advanced training, and then directly to Korea for combat against the North Koreans who were flying superior planes. Reports from overseas were grim. Two or three days later, Jack declined the air cadet offer. About a year later, he learned Billy was missing in action. They never found him."

"That's horrible," Kat said. "If Jack hadn't seen Billy, he might've gone the same route. It's all timing. If I'd fallen off the cliff 15 minutes sooner or 15 minutes later, I probably would never have known you." She hugged him ferociously. "Oh Frank," looking at him intensely, "I'm so glad I fell off that cliff. I love you so much."

"After Photo School, Jack spent the summer of '51 off the coast of Korea on the battleship New Jersey, having a chance to go ashore occasionally in places like Yokosuka and Sasebo, Japan.

"The New Jersey was hit in Wonsan Harbor, a direct hit on the number one turret—that's the huge metal casing that has three of those gigantic 16-inch guns sticking out." Using his hands and curving his fingers to illustrate, "They're 16 inches in diameter. There're three of those turrets on the ship, with three guns in each. The number one turret is the one closest to the front of the ship. One guy was killed, about 20 injured.

"After breakfast every morning, Jack and his buddy, Reese Harley, stood outside the hatch—the doorway—to the photo lab for a few minutes and talked. Jack, knowing Wonsan Harbor was enemy territory, had planned to get a Speed Graphic camera and cover the deck area for possible action photos. A first-class petty officer named Shea told them to come in and develop some film, something Shea had never done before. They were quite upset about his timing—there's your word—because they didn't want to miss any of the action. Jack wanted to photograph it—that was his job.

"While they were 'souping' the film, as they call it, the number one turret was hit and several other shells exploded around the ship. When Jack and Reese looked outside the Photo Lab afterward, they saw that the metal mesh racks, which held rope and cork flotsam in case the ship went down, had been blown apart. Had they been there, talking—and that's exactly where they would've been—death would've been sure and swift."

Cuddling close to Frank, "More fate, huh? More timing. That's creepy."

"Not too long after that, Jack and I learned our Tech classmate, Charlie Norman, who was in the marines, got killed. That was a blow—to us and to anybody who knew Charlie. He was just a great kid. If you had a son, you'd want him to be like Charlie Norman. Charlie and I had a tandem routine on the horizontal bar. We used to draw applause at the public pool."

"You were at Loyola when you heard about Charlie?"

"No, that was during the summer. I was in Memphis. So from the New Jersey, Jack came back to San Diego, where he was stationed at North Island at the Fleet Air Photo Lab—a 13-month period. This is when he was selected to specialize in color photography. There wasn't a lot of it then, only one color specialist at that particular lab, a guy named Richard Silverman, a reservist who was being discharged. The officer in charge of the lab asked Silverman to carefully pick someone meticulous enough to learn and fulfill assignments in color photography. I'm sure I don't have to tell you his choice.

"Something else happened at North Island that changed Jack's life—for the better. He told me that during the first two years in the navy he had no real goals, no long-range objectives, most of his free time was spent drinking beer, having fun, and all the other things sailors do on liberty. One day at the Fleet Air Photo Lab, an older fellow who was being discharged, another reservist called in when the

Korean conflict began—a guy by the name of Henry Foxworth—gave Jack a book, and said he might get a kick out of it. Jack told me he never read anything except some of the sports section in the newspaper and a few comic books, and went all the way through high school without reading any books.

"This book was entitled, *Thirty Days to a More Powerful Vocabulary* by Wilfred Funk and Norman Lewis—"

Kat gesticulated with both hands, "My gosh, Frank, I can't believe you remember all those names off the top of your head. I mean—*Henry Foxworth, Wilfred Funk*—for heaven's sake."

"Henry Foxworth is an extremely important guy in Jack McRae's life. And the sad part is, every time Jack talks or thinks about Henry Foxworth, he gets tears in his eyes. That's what Jack wrote me. He said Henry was like one of those angels you read about in stories. He gave this paperback book to Jack, the book dramatically improved his life, and he never saw Henry again, never had a chance to thank him, to tell him how much that book helped him, without Henry even knowing it.

"The book started Jack on a reading journey, an unquenchable reading journey that never ended. He began reading the classics. He read literary magazines such as *Saturday Review of Literature* and *Harper's*. He read two or three daily newspapers. He started night classes at San Diego City College—used to walk from what they called the 'nickel snatcher' pier, a couple of hundred yards south of the Broadway pier, to the college campus near 11th or 12th and Broadway—roundtrip. A week or so later, Jack was transferred to Ford Island in Pearl Harbor. At first he was furious—didn't want to leave San Diego—but after he got settled in Hawaii, couldn't have been happier."

Kat, completely hooked, "I can understand that. It screwed up his night school after he'd gone to the trouble of registering and paying for the class."

"Classes," he corrected her. "French and psychology."

"French. Good man. I like this guy." Putting her arm around Frank's neck, "You see, he liked Hawaii. One of these days I want to take you. Okay?"

"We'll see."

"We'll see? You're so noncommittal. Don't you ever just come out with a big fat *yes*?"

"I have to be careful saying yes to you."

"Yeah, I know what it is. You think I'm gonna rape you, don't you—"

"Katherine, please..." Looking upset, but not really being, however trying to appear that way, "I thought we had an understanding not to talk like that." There was nothing that would've pleased Frank more than Katherine raping him, but it was out of the question for the time being.

Staring him down, "Baby, you told me you fantasize about that stuff, didn't you?"

Looking for an escape hatch, but not finding it, "Yep."

Gleefully, "I bet you've fantasized that I raped you, right?"

"Nope."

Kat, disappointed but determined, "Then I'm sure you've imagined us making love, haven't you? Tell me the truth now. Don't try to smart talk your way out of it."

Suppressing a chuckle, "Yep."

Triumphantly, "Then, *Baby*, if you can think about it, why can't you talk about it? What's the big deal?"

"Someone said—I can't recall a name." Frank put his hand behind Katherine's neck, drawing her close, "Give me a kiss first." A very passionate one, perhaps to compensate for the hiatus. Then, "Are you listening?"

"All ears." Kat grinned goofily.

"That reminds me," touching her left ear with his index finger. "I have some unfinished business," licking his chops. "Where was I?" Remembering, "Oh, yes, 'Be careful,'" speaking melodramatically, "'of what you think. What you think becomes what you say or write. Be careful of what you say or write because that becomes what you do. And be careful of what you do. What you do becomes a habit. Be *very* careful of your habits, because your habits become…your destiny.'"

Kat, awestruck, "Magnificent. You may eat my ears whenever you wish…one at a time."

Frank, smiling, then didactically, "I have a strange feeling the gist of that thought-provoking quotation completely escaped you."

"Baby," back to earth, "this is us. Thinking, talking—talking, thinking…We're not two people anymore, don't you know that? We're one. We're Frank slash Kat…or Kat slash Frank." She rapidly twisted her body toward him, ending up in a kneeling position, fiercely seizing his right forearm. "You think this is *your* arm? Uh-uh, Baby, this is *our* arm."

Frank was transfixed.

"And this hand," holding out her hand, the one with which she'd just held his arm. "This isn't *my* hand, it's *our* hand." Searching Frank's face to confirm his comprehension, then very slowly, "I still don't think you get it—"

"Please don't say that, Katherine. You really…you hurt me when you say that, and I don't think you want to hurt me."

Kat propelled herself into Frank's arms, "I'd never hurt you, Frank. You're my life."

"Then you have to understand…that my objective—my obligation to Jack—was in existence for quite a few years before I met you."

"How long has this guy been in prison?

"It happened on Christmas Eve, 1956—10 years, almost to the day, from his meeting with the Superintendent of Memphis Schools. This is September of 2002. That's…46 years."

"Terrible. I'm sorry. I can see how important Jack's predicament is now. That's so sad. Did he stay long in Hawaii—in the navy?"

"Two years. He took night courses at the University of Hawaii…finished his freshman English there. Wrote a term paper on Thomas Hardy's agnosticism. I noticed you have several of Hardy's books in your living room."

"I think they're all there. I didn't know he was agnostic."

"According to Jack he was, and Jack received an *A*+on the paper. His instructor told him he should think about being a writer. She was very impressed with his work. His girlfriend in Hawaii was Nisei, meaning both of her parents were from Japan. Her name was Jean Nakamura. She spoke Japanese fluently…English too. Evidently she was a very bright girl—a little older than Jack—and quite intellectual. He said they used to go to the beach, discuss Dostoyevsky or Balzac. She was really the love of his life, and the biggest regret of his life is not marrying her."

Kat cuddled closer. "You're not gonna pull a Jack on me, are you?"

He embraced Kat amorously, kissing her and keeping her face directly in front of his. "You are so funny. I'm not gonna pull a Jack on you. I'm pulling a Frank on you—"

"Uh-oh, I'm afraid to ask what that's all about."

"Means I'm gonna jump into a wheelchair and leave the driving up to you."

"Oh yeah? Well, if you can jump *into* a wheelchair, Buster, you can jump right *out*." Both laughed.

"You're kinda mean…and cold-blooded too. Back to the islands—otherwise I'll never finish—while Jack was stationed in Hawaii—by the way, that was his last duty station. He was discharged after leaving Hawaii. While he was there, stationed at Ford Island, he received a Letter of Commendation from the Chief of Naval Operations, the highest ranked officer in the U.S. Navy, for his photographic work. That was Admiral Arthur Radford."

"That's incredible."

"Especially when you consider he never had a camera in his hands before the navy. I doubt even one percent of navy photographers have one of those letters in their personnel records...probably not even a half percent. Don't forget this is the same guy who never touched a basketball 'til the ninth grade. And I forgot to mention...after the 10th grade when we won the championship, he was a starting guard the next year. Then as a senior—poor guy—because he was a little over six feet tall, one of the tallest players on the team—heights have elevated since then—and ambidextrous, coach made him play center. He hated it, but he did it. Would've been a cinch for All-Memphis at guard. That's the only time I can remember being happy I wasn't ambidextrous. Otherwise it could've been me because I'm six, one and a half. I was a forward. Jack had to play against two guys who were six, ten and a half...those guys were physical oddities then."

Frank twisted his head toward Kat's left shoulder and kissed the fox tattoo. "Never thought I'd kiss a fox right in the face."

"Life is full of surprises," she ran her fingers across his face.

Rubbing his lips over hers, "All through high school, my nickname was Phoxy."

Instantly pulling back from him, "What? You gotta be kidding?"

"I'm not kidding at all. You could ask people from my graduating class, people I didn't know very well—it was a large class, a big school. You could ask them if they knew Frank Taylor, and they'd probably say, 'No, I don't remember any Frank Taylor.' But if you ask them about Phoxy," he smiled, "they'd look at you and say, 'Yeah, I remember Phoxy.'"

With contagious ebullience, "That's absolutely incredible. How'd you get the name?"

"I was pretty tricky with a basketball—no-look passes...and occasionally behind the back, even though Coach didn't approve. As long as the pass was good, he didn't care. Oh, and I spelled it with a PH instead of an F."

"What do you mean?" She'd lost him.

"Phoxy. I spelled it PHOXY instead of FOXY."

"That's weird. Why? I've never heard that."

"I don't even remember...that's probably why I did it...guess I just wanted to be different. Now that I think about though, a friend of mine, Freddie Thompson, started it all. He was very artistic. He checked with me first, then he printed my name, Phoxy, with PH, all over the place, mostly in very inaccessible locations—like ceilings and the tops of high walls. It was his idea to use the PH. He thought it would be unique, and I sort of liked it too. He was a good gymnast—a small fellow, but extremely strong.

"One student would stand on another student's shoulders, in one of the boy's restrooms for example, and Freddie would climb up and stand on the shoulders of the highest student, then neatly and artistically print PHOXY, in big block letters on the ceiling. I got called to the office a couple of times by the Assistant Principal, Miss Effie, and of course I denied any knowledge of it."

Katherine shook her head and smiled. "Miss Effie? Was that her real name?"

"Oh, yes. That's what we all called her...*reverently*, believe me. Her nonsense toleration was a flat zero. Wish I had a picture of her to show you. You'd get the message, kiddo. She could lay a belt on your butt with a force you wouldn't forget very quickly."

"Back in the good old days, huh?"

"Yeah, they actually were. I had a lot of fun."

Chuckling, with her face directly in front of Frank's, "I can't believe this. Phoxy. That proves it, Baby," gesticulating with both hands. "We're suppose to be together. God wants us together—two foxes." Both arms around him now, "I love you so much, Phoxy." Tears collecting in her eyes, "You're my big fox. And I'm your little fox. I'm so glad you told me that. It's beautiful."

"You're my little Kat. What's beautiful is you. You're the most beautiful woman I've ever seen in my life." Frank kissed Kat with a refreshed passion.

They sat silently looking at each other and touching each other for at least a full minute, then, "What happened to Jean?" Kat asked. "Did Jack just ditch her in Hawaii?"

Shaking his head, "No, the last few months before he was discharged from the navy, Frank made a decision concerning college. His dream at the time was to become 'The Great American Defense Attorney.' I'm skimming over the surface, so I can get you to December, '56. Almost went to Columbia University, but realized, even with the GI Bill, living in the Big Apple would necessitate having a part-time job. He was actually accepted by Columbia, but after some thorough research and an interview with the legal officer at Ford Island in Hawaii, he chose Duke University."

"Great school." Kat popped Frank on the knee with her open hand. "Coach 'K' wasn't there yet. I'll bet at Tech High, there's no way you could've imagined Jack would go to Duke University."

"Impossible's the only word I can think of. He had no interest whatsoever in academics. I told you—sports section and comic books. I would've bet my life savings he wouldn't, and couldn't, go to Duke. Funny you mention it, because he told me when he got back to Memphis, after the navy, and one of his uncles found out he was planning to go to Duke, the uncle looked him straight in the face and said, 'You can't go to Duke University. Don't you know that?' Jack said he looked at his uncle, for whom he had tremendous respect, and said, 'Watch me.'"

With anxiety on her face, "I'm worried about Jean. What happened?"

"Well, Jean gave up a good job in Honolulu and went to the University of Missouri to study journalism. Jack got out of the navy at the end of April, '54—"

"Still don't understand how you can remember all this stuff…not only names, but dates."

"This has been the major subject in my life for at least a decade."

Sadly, "What about poor little me?"

"That's different. I'm not in love with 'this stuff,' as you call it. But I feel strongly obligated to complete what I started. You...I'm crazy about you. And I'm asking you to help me concentrate on it. That's the only way...I'll ever finish it."

Caressing his hand, rubbing it against her face and kissing it, "You are the *greatest.* Jack is wonderful, but you're more than wonderful—"

"No, no, I'm not in the same class with Jack McRae. He could've been anything he wanted to be—done anything he wanted to do...and he's spent 46 years of his life in prison. Rips my heart out, just to think about it."

Katherine noticed a strange distant look on Frank's face as he spoke that last paragraph. Massaging his right hand in both of hers, "Come on, take it easy. You're doing your best. So Jack got out of the navy...?"

"And classes at Duke didn't start until September, so Jean was a house guest at the McRae's place in Memphis that summer. Jack said they were inseparable. He used the same expression you used about us...soul mates." Pause. "Let's move on to the interesting part."

Turning toward him, "Don't tell me it gets better."

"No, as a matter of fact it gets worse, but more interesting. Just listen. When Jack arrived at Duke, the only thing on his agenda was the entrance exam, which was a requirement. By the way, he scored second highest in the vocabulary phase, thanks to Henry Foxworth. He learned that later from a dean, when he tried successfully to switch from a political science class to psychology.

"The only other matter on Jack's mind was going out for football. At Ford Island in Hawaii, Jack was a star on the basketball team. There's a lot I've skipped over because it's too time-consuming. What I'm saying is, Jack was in good physical condition. He worked out daily, and at this time he weighed 190 lbs. Also, he was a heck of a football player, outstanding receiver and excellent passer.

"He knew football practice had already started when he arrived on campus, but was planning to check it out the next day. There was nothing to do that night, however. He didn't know a soul on campus. Walking past Page Auditorium—"

"I thought you hadn't been to the campus yet?"

"I haven't."

"But you know all these names."

"I told you, lots of correspondence with Jack and many notes."

"Okay, he's walking by Page Auditorium—"

"And he heard these rather loud voices, as though in conversation. They were having tryouts for a play, a William Saroyan play entitled, *The Time of Your Life.* A great play—takes place in a bar. You'd be right at home."

"Shut up, you," teasing.

"He walks down front, where other students are watching the ones on stage read for parts. It's a large auditorium—1500 seats. He sits and watches for awhile. Then it hits him. Now here's a guy who's never seen a play. At Tech High? No way. He'd seen hundreds of movies. By the way, I did...avoid the truth on one count, regarding my love life."

Sitting very erect now, twisting toward him, huge eyes on his, "I'm listening."

"I told you I'd never been in love." Pause. "Right?"

The district attorney, cross-questioning, "Right. That's exactly what you said. And what are you saying now? You changing your tune?"

Slowly, "The truth is...I was madly in love...with Greer Garson."

Slow smile of relief, "You rascal. You almost got me on that one."

"You know who she is?" Surprised if she did.

"Yeah, I've seen her in old movies on TV. Nice looking woman...English."

A little irritated, "Nice looking? She was gorgeous...had class."

Faking extreme gravity, "Now let's not overdo this, Buster."

Frank, in a dream, "She was the epitome of feminine pulchritude, with the poise of a queen...and incredible charm. And her voice...oh my gosh. *Random Harvest* with Ronald Coleman—saw it three times, just to watch Greer Garson...and listen to her."

Kat, back to reality, "How old were you?"

"Around 12."

Laughing and hitting him on the leg, "You had a crush on that lady."

"My buddies thought I was nuts. They were all after Lana Turner."

Closing in on him and talking softly, "I'm sorry I'm not Greer Garson, but don't forget, they tell me I look like Vivica Fox." Suddenly it dawned on her, "Hey, another fox. Funny, I never thought of that. Isn't that something?"

Enclosing her with his arms, Frank whispered, "Come here, Vivica, you little fox, you. Phoxy wants to show you something." They kissed passionately.

"Oooh, Phoxy, I like that." She gave him an Eskimo kiss. "Did Jack try out for that barroom play?"

"He got the part of Tom. Wasn't the starring role—that's Joe. But it was a principal part. He was all through the play. Frank's French professor—"

"He got back to his French—that's great. This guy's all right."

"Yeah, Dr. Graham...hypercritical with a biting wit, came up to Jack the morning after opening night, before his French class started, told him quite seriously he'd seen hundreds of plays, including *La Comédie Française*—in France, during summer vacation—and many others on Broadway. He told Jack he should seriously think about acting as a career, that his performance was excellent. Jack was flabbergasted.

"Let me throw in a small side dish before I go on. Every male freshman was required to take a physical fitness test at the beginning of the school year. It consisted of a consecutive series of individual physical tests with time limits, for example: pushups, sit-ups—no crunches in those days—chin-ups, sprints, etc. This was required of every freshman, including—get this—all scholarship athletes in all sports. We're talking about some guys in pretty good condition. The second highest score of all these students was Jack's. The football coach actually approached Jack a day or two later, personally inviting him to come out for the team. This is when Duke had a good football team. One of Jack's classmates was Sonny Jurgensen, an NFL star quarterback later. Well, Jack was already rehearsing *The Time of Your Life*, so that was the end of that.

"He went back to Memphis during the summer months, but not for vacation. Deciding to accelerate his academic schedule and finish in three years instead of four, he enrolled at what then was called Southwestern at Memphis, taking an intermediate French course. There's your French again. Jean joined him in Memphis that summer. The class instructor was dying of leukemia, something never mentioned by the students or the teacher. One of their projects was to read André Gide's *La Symphonie Pastorale*, naturally in French, and to then write an epilogue of their own compositional theme in French. Jack made an A+, and the teacher, the one who was dying of leukemia, told him he should pursue writing as a career."

Smiling mysteriously, Kat asked, "This is the same guy who peed in the superintendent's face?"

Nodding and grinning, "You remember that."

"Don't think I'll be forgetting it. That's what I call serious drama. That's heavier than *Hamlet*. I wouldn't want to play the superintendent's part in the movie. They might go overboard for realism in the scene. Did Jean go back to Missouri?"

"At the end of the summer, Jack returned to Duke, but Jean…went to live with a friend in LA. That was the last time they saw each other. Jack said it was an *awful* experience, putting Jean on the train, relatively sure he'd never see her again. He has frequent nightmares about it. He's wished many times he could go back in his life to that point—he'd never let her go again. Said he would've taken her back to the Duke campus with him, where he knows—with her background as a secretary—she could've easily found a job. He knows now, sitting there in his cell, that Jean was the love of his life. He would give anything in the world to have her back."

"Very sad story," Kat remarked. "Hard to understand how a guy that smart could do something like that. That was kinda dumb on his part. She was probably too good to him. He took her for granted. What do you think?"

"Could be. But according to Jack, before he left Honolulu Jean had an operation—an ovary removed—and the doctor explained she probably would never have kids. Jack said that was in the back of his mind. He'd always wanted to have children, and it was that negative aspect that caused him to let her slip away. He knows now he made a big mistake. And of course he has no children…never will.

"Back at Duke for his second year, Jack met Ann Rockford. At first, they used to flirt with each other on the shuttle bus between campuses. Did you know Duke has two campuses?"

"No."

"Well, you know about Coach 'K' so I thought you might. They're approximately a mile and a quarter apart…maybe with all the added construction during the past 45 years or so, even closer now. The West Campus, the men's campus, has Gothic architecture, and the women's East Campus has Georgian. It's a very impressive place, based on the photographs I've seen. There was—maybe still is—a shuttle bus that hauled the students back and forth from one campus to the other. Some of the male students, who lived in dormitories on the West Campus, had classes on the East Campus, and vice versa. On the bus, Jack noticed this girl with dark hair and gigantic attractive eyes, like yours, and…" Frank looked directly down at Katherine's breasts, noticing her prominent nipples again, "also…"

Katherine knew what he was looking at. "Gigantic sexy boobs like mine." She started laughing.

"Hey, wait a minute," Frank interrupted. "I was gonna use different words."

"Okay," she insisted, "overgrown sensual mammary glands." Holding her laugh back, she playfully watched his eyes.

He smiled bashfully and remained silent, but focused now on her magnetic eyes. "Anyway," Frank attempted to resume, "he had difficulty avoiding her eyes, like me—" and glanced at her breasts again.

"And her tits, like you." Katherine was unable to contain her laugh.

"Come on, Katherine, I'm never gonna finish this story if you keep that up." Frank tried his best to look serious, but in actuality he was thoroughly enjoying the fun.

She took his hand in hers and brushed it against one of her nipples. "Baby, why don't we go back to my place and go to bed? You can kiss my breasts and make love to me. That's what I really want to do. You can finish the story after we make love. Okay? I want you, Baby."

Frank was stumped for an acceptable and credible answer. He wanted to make love to her, but he could see his plan starting to unravel. Experience had taught him how important it was to be patient, especially when the leverage was in his favor, as it appeared to be at this moment.

"I'm right at the end, Katherine. Just a few minutes longer, then we can go."

With a monstrous grin, "To bed?"

"Katherine, you're embarrassing me. You've got a one-track mind."

"You're right. I admit it…sorry to embarrass you though. All right, Baby, forgive me. They got attracted to each other on the bus. They couldn't take their eyes off each other…and I can probably tell you what happened? But you're gonna tell me that in those days they didn't do things like that."

"No, no, you're on the wrong track now. One thing led to another; they had coffee together, talked, and had a few dates. Early on, Ann, tears streaming down her face, told Jack she was deeply in love with him, but understood it would be impossible for him to love her in such a brief period. Nevertheless, she implored him to allow her to love him, hoping she could win his love.

"It was a very awkward, though somewhat pleasant situation for Jack, having recently permitted the love of his life, Jean, to board a train and ride away. Jean gave up a secure job, and without doubt risked her life's savings on the possibility that Jack would take her as his wife…and lost. She lost Jack, that is, and probably most of her savings. Hopefully, in LA she gained something, or someone, of equal or superior value. Ann, on the other hand, was much younger, probably 19 years old, from a well-to-do family, her father an executive with an internationally known company, and, by toying with Jack, had absolutely nothing to lose, save a speck of pride.

"Virtually broke, without a car, and living from one monthly GI Bill check to the next, Jack warned Ann it would be a test in asceticism for her, accustomed to having more or less anything she wanted. Once in awhile, Ann, unable to own a car until her senior year, according to regulations, borrowed one from a sorority sister, and she and Jack would park somewhere in the vast acreage of the surrounding Duke Forest for a necking and petting session."

Kat perked up on that note. "Shame on them." Pretending surprise, "I didn't know they did stuff like that back in those days."

Frank, defensively, "Jack said they did, but I don't remember anything like that."

Hitting his left biceps with her fist, "Now you're gonna tell me you never kissed anybody."

With zeal, Frank pulled her close and kissed her. Then, "I must admit…I have."

Kat, looking at Frank through half-closed eyes, "You know what I mean, Herbie—before me."

Raising his *left* hand for an oath, "On my word of honor," one word at a time, "I…have…never…kissed…" then, quickly, "a man."

Laughing out loudly, "That beats the hell out of my first husband's record."

"Please, we don't need the profanity. And speaking of records, you said *first* husband." Suspiciously, "What's the implication here?"

"That's easy." Positioning herself for what she hoped was coming, "I want one more…you."

"Lady, you won the jackpot." An extremely passionate embrace and a soul kiss, after which they sat with their shoulders together, holding hands and looking out toward the horizon.

Kat, wondering if Frank had already forgotten her proposition, but not wanting to appear overly aggressive, spoke first. "This is the most divine day of my life."

Frank was looking at her left hand, the fingers of which were entwined in his right. He squeezed it gently to make sure it was there, that he wasn't dreaming. "That's a very strong, very significant word…divine."

"Yes, Godlike. And when I'm with you I feel very close to God."

Those words precipitated a brainstorm for Frank. They brought him back to reality and reminded him of his urgent need for contemplation. He'd promised himself that tonight, before going to sleep, he would resolve this complex issue, which was eating away at his conscience, in order to be at peace with himself during the coming weeks. In telling Katherine more of Jack's story, it reinforced the priority of his master plan…the true reason for his coming to La Jolla. It was also a refresher course in human frailty.

Kat continued, "You sound like my uncle."

"How's that?" Frank queried.

"My uncle used to tell me the word, divine, is very special, that it's so closely connected with God, it should only be used in a religious way, or in some reference to God. I don't think he'd be upset with me for using it the way I did, because I was simply saying that my closeness to you makes me feel close to God…and to me, that's divine."

Frank appeared a bit stunned. He wondered if he'd ever get accustomed to the manner in which Katherine could shake his emotions to the foundation.

Frank also wondered aloud, "Is he your dad's brother?"

"Yeah, he's 62. He's my uncle, but I call him father."

Chuckling, Frank commented, "That's kinda weird, isn't it? You call your father, dad, and your uncle, father. What's that all about?"

Gleefully, "Because he's a priest…and definitely *not* a pedophile—no way!"

Apparently Frank was caught off guard. "Your uncle's a Catholic priest?"

"Yes, and a wonderful uncle."

"Well…you hadn't mentioned that."

"It didn't come up in conversation."

"Yeah, well…that's true. Thought when I told you on Girard I was a Catholic, you might have mentioned it."

"Didn't occur to me then."

Interested, Frank asked, "What type of…is he a…parish priest or—"

"He teaches…theology at Georgetown. He's a Jesuit. Been there many years." Giving Frank a big kiss on the nose, "So when Jack and Ann were doing all that hot necking in that huge forest, did anything," lifting her eyebrows, "exciting happen?"

Looking at Kat in complete astonishment, "You are a very funny lady. There couldn't be a dull moment living around you."

"Oh, I don't know. I can be pretty boring. You just haven't seen the complete me. Ask Rocky. He'll give you the lowdown. But with Jack and Ann, I thought maybe we were getting to the good part…the sexy part…the only part of a novel that holds my interest." She giggled.

"Now I'm meeting the real Katherine Churchill, and guess what?"

Still wearing a goofy smile, "As usual, I'm afraid to."

"Don't be." He licked her ear. "I like her. Don't ever change. Anyway, by now Jack had switched from a pre-law political science major to economics, planning with his fourth year of the GI Bill to attend the Pasadena Playhouse College of Theater Arts in California and study acting.

"During his second year at Duke, he played Bert Jefferson in *The Man Who Came to Dinner*—was also stage manager—and played Ponza in *Right You Are If You Think So*, a Pirandello play which was performed on an arena stage. He received excellent reviews in both productions. In the last semester of his second year at Duke, he was asked to be president of the Duke Players during his senior or third year. A bit apprehensive about accepting the responsibility, since the two previous presidents reportedly had suffered nervous breakdowns, he agreed only after persuading two of his classmates, John Hewlett and Bill Sharpton, close friends who previously had no interest or experience in play production, to join the group and work as stage managers.

"In order to graduate in three years, he had to take some courses during the summer between his second and third years at Duke. First, he took a full year of accounting in six weeks at Duke summer school. He said that was an absolute nightmare—the worst academic experience he'd ever had. It was six days a week in a class that took up most of the day, then staying up until 2 or 3 a.m. many nights doing homework. After that, he went back to Memphis State for a history course during the last half of that summer.

"The first and only Duke Players production during his cut-short senior year—this was before the fateful Christmas holidays—was a comedy entitled, *Reclining Figure.* He had the romantic lead, a character named Sam Ellis, who was played on Broadway in the original by Mike Wallace of '*60* Minutes' fame. Few people are aware of Wallace's acting stint and, who knows, he looks and sounds so great at his age, he may have exceeded Christopher Plummer's terrific performance in the movie, *The Insider*, if he'd played himself. Wallace is one of my favorites. I admire his professionalism and drive…and smarts. And '60 Minutes' is my favorite TV show.

"Jack received fine reviews for his performance, and was told by a Duke Players faculty advisor from the Speech Department he was the best president they'd ever had.

"As Christmas vacation approached, Ann asked Jack to come home with her as a house guest through the holidays. Jack fully realized the main reason was so her parents could scrutinize him, and Ann, without academic distractions, could analytically compare him with her hometown boyfriend, John Sawyer. Not really pleased with Ann's smoking habit or the fact she was an overindulged teenage girl he'd never be able to financially satisfy or psychologically cope with, Jack was very much physically attracted to her and, with the absence of Jean in his life, enjoyed her feminine companionship. Attempting to conceal his restrained enthusiasm from Ann, Jack accepted her invitation, hoping he could pull off an acting performance at her home in Lake Forest, Illinois comparable to those he'd given in Page Auditorium on the Duke campus.

"Okay, they flew to Chicago, where Ann's parents met them. The father, of course, paid all of Jack's expenses. They drove the 30 or so miles to Lake Forest. Now there're many details about his stay at Ann's house, but I'm just giving you the information on two basic incidents.

"The party was on Christmas Eve at Ann's home with about 50 invited guests. On the night before, Ann and Jack were parked in one of the Rockford family cars along Lake Michigan, discussing their relationship in depth, when Ann turned to Jack and asked him how many girls he'd made love to—"

Kat with verve, "Wow, talk about déjà vu. That's pretty scary."

"Well, you saw the look on my face when you asked *me*."

Shrewdly, "Yes, I certainly did see that look on your face, young man. I know how *you* wiggled out of it. Jack, of course, was much younger—"

"I didn't do any wiggling. You dropped the subject. Ann didn't let Jack off the hook so easily though." He gambled with that answer, hoping Kat wouldn't pounce on it. "So, in his mind, Jack ran through the various faces—"

"Faces?" Kat laughed, "Yeah, I love your choice of words."

"Naughty girl. You know what I mean. He reviewed the *images* in his mind. Came up with the number, seven. Ann broke down, starting crying uncontrollably. When she partially regained her composure, she wanted to know how many of the seven he actually loved. Again, Jack..." Frank tried to think of a better way to say it, "reviewed the *relationships* mentally and told her, 'all of them.' She began sobbing again, and asked to be taken home. That was the end of *their* relationship.

"Jack had no way of knowing what Ann told her parents and friends but, along with the climate outside, it got pretty chilly inside. Jack, looking back, knows he should've grabbed his personal belongings and left. He didn't. The party was a fiasco, with all of her friends ostracizing him. Two of John Sawyer's friends impolitely told Jack to get out. Then John walked between them and shoved Jack against the wall, telling him to get his...redneck tail—he used another word—back to Memphis. Jack, from the 'Make-the-first-blow-count' School, faked a left uppercut, then launched a two-by-four right jab aimed at John's nose, but John had quickly moved his head sideways to avoid the fake uppercut, and the jab caught him at the temple. He fell to the floor...dead.

"The trial was one-sided. Jack's only support was his court-appointed attorney, who wasn't very competent. His mom, who made the trip from Memphis, was the only family representative. Her husband, Jack's step-dad, much older than she, was physically in no condition to travel. Jack has no brothers or sisters. Every witness was biased against Jack, who told me about several incriminatory lies he had no way of contesting. It was their word against his, and his amounted to zilch. So there he sits, with the extra time thrown in for permanently crippling, in self-defense, a prison guard who happened to have been the warden's best friend."

Kat, looking somber, interlocked her left arm with Frank's right, "46 years down the drain—what a waste. The guy probably would be a well-known actor or writer."

"Hasn't really been a complete waste." Frank looked meditatively toward the Pacific Ocean. "For the last 25 years or so, Jack's been teaching English grammar and composition, plus a course in appreciation of photography—no cameras, of course—to some of his fellow inmates. A couple of his so-called graduates have done rather well. Rick Parrish is a best-selling novelist and Andrew Brandon, a photographer, is known internationally. And I'm sure Jack has changed the lives—for the best—of many guys who've been around him. It's possible that he's done more good in prison than he would've done on the outside. I doubt that. Only God knows." Then looking over at Katherine, "John Sawyer's parents have lived with a terrible memory too."

"At least Jack's done something constructive with his life," Kat pointed out. "It's still a shame. I think he would've been very prominent in society, very successful. Being such a talented writer, it's surprising and unfortunate that Jack hasn't produced some sort of written material in his own defense."

"He tried several times," Frank clarified, "and the pages somehow disappeared very mysteriously. Obviously, all of his activities are closely watched. He's given up now, and looks to me as his only chance. It's probably hard for you to accept that a prison warden would do something like that, but, going back to my favorite TV show, '60 Minutes,' they had a segment last summer in which an innocent man spent 30 years in prison. There are reportedly FBI memos clearly indicating that J. Edgar Hoover was aware of his innocence. Unfortunately, that type of behavior goes on at the very highest level. They mentioned something about legislation being filed to remove Hoover's name from the building at FBI headquarters."

"They should. That's horrible. Baby, I'll do everything I can to help you," kissing him lightly. "Thanks for telling me the story. I have a much better understanding now of your motivation." She glanced at her watch.

"It's three," Frank confirmed. "You have to work tonight, so I think we should wrap it up and get you home," Frank suggested. "I'm glad I don't have to do what you're doing tonight."

"Well," she explained, "once I get into the swing of it, everything's fine...like an exercise routine...the first minute is the hardest. After that, you start feeling like a million dollars."

"True. Nice to hear you say that."

"Please do this for me. Since we have to go right by my place on the way to yours, let's stop just for a moment so I can show you the upstairs." Seeing he was about to interrupt, she put her index finger against his lips. "I promise I'm not going to trap you or trick you, just want you to see it. Please."

"No problem. I'd like to see it, but just for a minute."

"Agreed. Love you." French kiss, quickie style. "I had a wonderful afternoon. I want to have about...100,000 more."

"Me too. You're a doll...a foxy doll."

They stood, shook the sand from the towels, and checked to see if they'd forgotten anything, then started back toward her car. Throughout their return walk, Katherine had one primary objective on her mind: getting Frank into bed and fucking him. During the next 20 minutes, she had to figure out how to do it.

CHAPTER 10

Although it was mid-September and the tourist season was over, the weather resembled August—83°F. Hundreds of people from inland areas like La Mesa, El Cajon, and Escondido had flocked to La Jolla to enjoy the seacoast climate—at least 10 degrees cooler than their neighborhoods. Consequently, Torrey Pines, Prospect, and most of the other main streets in the village were congested. Kat's home, fortunately, was only six or seven blocks away from their parking spot near the Marine Room.

As she pulled into her driveway, passing the frontage property on Prospect, a secretly motivated smile crept over her radiant face. Katherine felt confident that she had the solution to successfully seducing Frank. In the next 30 minutes, she'd find out if it worked.

Frank, noticing her enigmatic smile, "What's that all about? You got something up your sleeve?"

"No, I promised, remember? Just occurred to me that this should be the end of the line. We should both be living here…together."

"Don't tempt me. Remember, I'm human too."

She turned into a parking area near her front door, and they got out of her car, Kat snatching her backpack off the rear seat. After activating her car alarm, she and Frank approached the door. Rocky was squealing dramatically.

Five feet from the door, Kat stopped Frank's forward motion by pulling his arm. "Rocky sounds like he's trying to tell me something."

"Meaning there could be an intruder?"

"His voice is higher pitched than usual. The only other person who has a key is my father."

Frank, in a negative tone, "Something tells me I should head for my place."

Kat, considering aloud, "How could it be him? He said there was some kind of transplant emergency at the clinic. And if it isn't him, you're not gonna leave me alone, are you?"

"No way."

"And if it is him, he's probably looking through the peephole, so you can't just walk away." Dropping her backpack, putting her arms around Frank's neck, and in a low voice, "Let's give the peeping Tom something worth looking at."

"What about the neighbors gazing through the windows?" Frank smiled, playing the game.

"My neighbors don't gaze, they *spy* on me. They might as well get used to it. They're gonna see a lot of this." Kat kissed him very passionately, and he didn't resist. "I'm sure it's nothing. Rocky smells you, that's all."

Frank, feeling suspect, "Are you trying to tell me something?"

Picking up her backpack with a grin, "Only that everything's fine. Let's go in," removing a set of keys from her pocket, she prepared to unlock the door.

The front door quickly swung open. It was Dr. Churchill, and of course Rocky. "Katherine, I thought it was you." Her father wore a forced smile, and Rocky raced back and forth between Kat and Frank.

"Dad, what a surprise. If you'd looked through the peephole, you'd have seen us." Although Kat was pleased to see her father, she was, at the same time, genuinely ticked off at his timing. Figuratively, at least in her vivid imagination, she already had Frank in bed with his clothes off.

Dr. Churchill fibbed, "I always forget about that peephole."

Rocky knew better, looking at Dr. Churchill accusingly while Frank stroked him.

"What about the transplant?" asked Kat.

"I'm just the coordinating physician. It's all set up for Tuesday. I'll be there." He gave Katherine a fatherly kiss on the cheek, extended his right hand to Frank. "How are you? Frank, I believe, is that correct?"

They shook hands. "Yes, Frank Taylor. I'm fine, thank you."

Kat, after placing her backpack on the ground, gave Rocky his anticipated rubdown on the doormat, while Dr. Churchill kept Frank under his microscope.

Feeling stress from the magnification, Frank decided, "Katherine, I've got a lot of work to do. I think I'll run on—"

"No, please, Frank," Dr. Churchill interrupted. "I have something rather important I'd like to discuss, and since it involves you, I hope you can stay for a few minutes. It won't take long."

Katherine, her face tense, immediately straightened up from her Rocky massage. Disappointed, his legs pointed skyward, Rocky continued to lie there on his back. Kat's voice, reflecting anxiety, "Dad, what are you doing?" She wasn't sure what he was about to do, but not wanting to take any chances on her wonderful relationship with Frank, she suggested, "Frank, you don't have to stay if you don't want to—"

"Katherine." Othello was back.

She'd never heard her father say her name in that tone of voice. It made her cringe.

Dr. Churchill continued, and his words and delivery could not have been more emphatic, "I'm asking Mr. Taylor to stay. I wish to speak to him. Please come inside."

Again, Kat picked up her backpack. They entered, and she closed the door, "I know Rocky wants to pee, but he'll have to wait—"

"No, he doesn't," replied her father, instantly. "I took him five minutes ago. Let's go in the living room."

Once in the living room, Kat decided to skip washing her hands. She didn't want to leave Frank alone with her father. Looking worriedly at Dr. Churchill, she distinctly declared, "You've never done anything like this, Dad. I'm really embarrassed. I hope you know that."

"You've never put me in this position before—"

"Put you in this position?" Kat was openly agitated, roughly tossing her backpack near an end table. Rocky sat next to it. "I didn't put you in this position. You put yourself in it. You're the one who got on the plane and flew back out here. I've always appreciated your help, Dad, but this time I certainly didn't ask for it."

Raising his voice to the next level, Dr. Churchill responded, "No, but you sure as hell need it. If I'd been in Paris when you were dating *Antoine*," giving the French pronunciation of Katherine's ex-husband's name a rather curious twist, "I could've saved you a lot of suffering. I knew what that guy was all about the split-second I met him, but I didn't have enough guts to tell you. I didn't want to break your heart."

"That was an entirely different situation, Dad."

"It was different all right, and maybe this situation is different from that one—I certainly hope so—but this is *another* situation, and I'm not about to sit back and watch it happen without doing anything. I'd never forgive myself."

This was obviously between Katherine and her father. Frank, not really upset with the scene because he sensed it was coming, sat in one of the large chairs trying to keep a low profile. Once again, he would have preferred to be a fly on the wall.

Kat put an end to that notion right away, pointing in Frank's direction, "And do you know what this guy's all about?"

Her father, looking at Frank, "No, I don't. And that's what scares the hell out of me after seeing some of the Westerfield trial on TV this summer." Katherine had never heard these particular forceful and implicative speech patterns used by her father.

"Well, Frank and I just spent four hours together at the beach, talking, and Frank did most of the talking, so I know what he's all about."

Quickly picking up on the last phrase, her father responded, "You've already told me what he's all about—trying to help a friend get out of prison—I know that. What I'm interested in is," talking to Katherine, "who is *Frank Taylor*? I'm not that interested in his friend." Then turning to Frank, "That's what I want to know. Who are *you*? And what have *you* been doing for the last..." opening his palms in front of himself, "30 years of your life?"

Frank was about to speak, but Katherine beat him to it. "Dad, for heaven's sake, will you just take a breath and think about what you're doing—"

"I've had several hours to think about what I'm doing, going and coming round-trip on the plane. You're the one who needs to think about what you're doing. I know what I'm doing, and I know what I intend to do." Dr. Churchill was almost frothing at the mouth. Looking back at Frank, "You give me some intelligent answers, Mr. Taylor—and I mean right this minute—or you can get your butt out of my daughter's home."

Kat, screaming, "Stop it, Dad! That's enough." Rocky, was all eyes—on all fours.

The doctor to Frank, relentlessly, starting quietly and building to a crescendo, "Just a little warning to you, Mr. Taylor...you look maybe 10 years younger than I, but I grew up in the toughest part of Indianapolis. I did my share of street fighting as a teenager, and I can whip your ass in five seconds flat."

Not screaming, but still quite loudly, Kat answered, "He's not younger than you, Dad. He's 71 years old."

Othello, the ex-street fighter, looked as though he'd just taken a punch in his stomach. Mouth open, eyes glazed, and not a clue of what his next words would be, he attempted to focus on Frank, then back to Katherine, then back to Frank. "Sev…" not able to get it out, he tried again, "71 years old? Good lord, man…you could be my daughter's grandfather."

Only the hint of a smile on Frank's face, but a very noticeable twinkle in his eye as he said, "Hypothetically."

Katherine, despite, and possibly because of, the previous stressful exchange, broke into laughter and rushed to kneel beside Frank. Putting his left hand in both of hers, "You are the greatest. I'm crazy about you—"

"Crazy is the right word." Her father jumped on it, "This is worse than the woman with the big boobs who married the old guy from Texas, the one who died and left her all that money that his son is contesting. *You're* the one with the money. I'll bet *he*," pointing accusingly at Frank, "doesn't have a damned cent."

Frank smiled at the doctor. "Social Security, that's it."

"Oh, my god." The doctor couldn't believe it. "Aren't you ashamed of what you're doing? Okay, you're 71. What've you been doing the last…*50* years? I want some answers or you're outta here."

Standing to confront her father, "He's not out of here! He's *my* guest. This is *my* house. This is *my* life. And I love him with all my heart. I don't give a damn if he's 100 years old. There's a 35-year age gap between Clint Eastwood and his wife, Dina…and they're *very* happy."

Her father wasn't going to give up. "Maybe according to last week's *People Magazine*, but next week you may read where she beat him up with a baseball bat. Don't you realize he'll probably be dead within five years?"

"Clint Eastwood or Frank?" Kat questioned.

"Both!"

"You know what, Dad? It'll be the happiest five years of my life. I know many women who haven't had one year, or even one week, of true love in their entire life. If I can have five years, I'll take them. And you know something else? The girl with the big boobs—maybe she actually loved that old guy. Maybe he was the only man she ever dated who didn't try to fondle her boobs. Maybe he treated her like a lady, and she loved him for it. People can't accept that, and you know why?" Not waiting for an answer, "Because most people have never *really* been in love. They wouldn't know what love was if it bit 'em in the ass. They don't have any conception of what true love is—selfless love, love that doesn't require any rewards in return...divine love. The same kind of love God gives us. The kind we should give him...and each other."

The father suddenly realized what a remarkable daughter he had. For Frank, there was no big surprise. He knew Katherine well, though briefly, and was very proud of her. He also knew that inevitable point in time had arrived, and there was no choice for him but to face it. It was the vital hinge for his master plan. Without it, there was no way for his master plan to work. Frank recognized it instantly because he had anticipated it from the outset. The only question had been *when*? And the answer was *NOW*.

Frank stood and walked to Dr. Churchill, putting his right hand out for a handshake, "I'm sorry Dr. Churchill. I owe you an apology." The doctor shook hands, not knowing why. "You've been very patient," acknowledged Frank, then smiling, "I'm sure you could whip my tail in about *two* seconds flat." He then turned to Katherine, who seriously doubted Frank's last remark. "I suppose your only excuse, Katherine, is you were blinded by love. But that *is* a legitimate excuse...for anyone," looking back at her father, "who believes in love. Being neither patient nor blind, I don't have an excuse. I'm the guilty party here. I'm the...real villain in this scenario...and I fully accept all the blame."

Frank's eyes now fixed on Kat's, he continued, "I'd planned to tell you everything not later than next week, Katherine, preferably sooner. I wanted to pick that ideal moment, but of course…there's no such thing. If you think about it for a minute, you'll realize I haven't had much time to myself since we met." Looking back at her father, but still primarily addressing Katherine, "In front of your father is not exactly what I had in mind…but here we are, and I'm aware that you can't wait any longer—you shouldn't wait any longer."

Now directly to her father, "Yes, I am ashamed, Dr. Churchill…more than you'll ever understand." Taking a deep breath and expelling it, "I'm also…very much in love with your daughter, and I doubt you'll ever understand that either—"

"Frank, you don't have to be ashamed of anything. We love each other and that's all that matters. What is it you're driving at? Is it something of a personal nature you haven't shared with me?"

"Yes," he replied.

It was such a simple word, but in this case Katherine felt her life depended on it. Glancing at her father, she thought her heart would stop. She tried to keep her upper lip from quivering. Finally, preparing for the worst, almost whispering, she asked Frank, "What?"

Loud enough for the doctor to hear, because it was he who asked the question, but looking at Katherine, Frank answered, "For *almost* 50 years…I've been involved…in the same profession…as your uncle."

Kat and her father, in unison, as if rehearsed, "You're a Catholic priest?"

"Yes, a Catholic priest…and I am not now, and never have been, a pedophile."

As if not only a rug or carpet had been pulled out from under her, but the whole house had disappeared, Katherine felt suspended in air, looking at the bump on the end of Frank's nose, the surface vein under his right eye. She remembered him disliking both profanity and the use of God's name in a non-religious way. All these seemingly insignificant details now made sense. Somehow, suspended there, managing to move her body close to his, taking his hands in hers, and not really caring if her father heard, she asked, "Why, Frank...why didn't you tell me?" The answer was plainly written on his face and, as usual, she covered his lips with her index finger, noticing the tears welling up on his eyelids. She whispered the question, "You were afraid of losing me, weren't you?"

Emotionally unable to speak, Frank nodded in agreement. Then seeing Dr. Churchill disappear into the hallway, he said, "I've never been in love, Katherine. It was like...having one of those...beautiful dreams, in which you know you're actually dreaming...but you want the dream to continue because it's so enjoyable...you're afraid to do anything or say anything that might end the dream. The thought of being in love hasn't entered my mind since becoming a priest. I solemnly vowed...never...to have a romantic relationship."

Katherine was sure she'd heard her father leave. She turned to confirm his absence, then led Frank to the sofa where they sat together. "Frank, you've given what most men would consider the best years of their life, in your case virtually most of your life, to God. You know better than I—you're an expert on the subject—that He's a God of love. He's not going to punish you for breaking your vows. There's no way I can believe that. If we're together, I may be taking you away from the priesthood, but I'm not taking you away from God, Frank. I'm joining you and we'll worship Him together as man and wife. As I told you, we're one, we're not separate. I want the coming years of your life to be the best, and I want to be part of those years, part of your life...and I want you to be part of my life. I sincerely believe God wants it that way."

Sensing relief from his disclosure, yet experiencing a bizarre sense of guilt from his words and actions, he brushed his fingers through her hair, "It's impossible, Katherine, for you to understand how serious this is."

"I suppose I'd have to be a priest in order to fully understand it. But I do understand how much I love you. I know that. And I know how much you love me. Remember Frank, God brought us together. My falling off the cliff at that precise moment was no freak accident. It was an act of God. I'm convinced of that. He wanted it that way. He wants you to experience the happiness of a family life with a loving wife and children. We'll have beautiful babies. Don't you want that?" Her smile was luminous.

Frank noticed Rocky, waiting for his response. "A man would have to be absolutely insane to say no to you." He attempted to match her smile...impossible. His felt insincere, and he was certain that it looked the same way. "I need some time. I have to think. Why don't you go talk with your dad, and phone me tomorrow?"

"It's funny, on that first day, I was afraid *you* were the big bad wolf. Turns out, it's my father—"

"Don't say that. He's trying to protect you. He loves you very much. That's obvious."

Kat, smiling again, "That was so cute when you said, 'hypothetically.' That cracked me up."

"Just don't call me Gramps."

She chuckled. "You want to leave?" Kat was concerned about Frank pulling a Jack on her, but didn't want to bring it up. "Tomorrow? That's an eternity."

"I'm sorry. I need the time—alone."

She didn't like the look on his face...or the inflection in his voice. "Well, are you going to call me...or am I going to call you?"

"Whatever."

"Oh, Frank, I'm not a 'whatever' person. When you walk out the front door my heart's gonna stop. I have an answering machine, so why don't you call me as soon as possible. You know I want to see you or talk to you as soon as I can, so please call me at any time. I don't know how I'm gonna get through tonight."

They started toward the front door, Rocky leading the way.

"I'll walk home. You don't need to take me." Frank had the same look and the same tone of voice.

"You sure? I'll be glad to take you."

"No, that's the idea. I need some space."

Rocky watched them closely at the front door as they embraced and kissed. Kat noticed the kiss was affectionate, but not very passionate.

After saying their good-byes, Frank walked through the door and down the walkway. Eight paces away, Kat called him, "Frank."

He turned around, wearing that same look.

Grinning, she reminded him, "I love you," trying to connect with his soul, but somehow feeling she'd failed. "My answering machine will be waiting, and it's not very patient."

He smiled, a little better this time, and waved.

CHAPTER 11

The door to the bedroom Dr. Churchill customarily used was open. Kat went in, followed by Rocky. Her father was sitting in the Lazy Boy. Their eyes met instantly. She didn't like the look on his face. Walking to the side of the bed next to him, she sat on it, facing him. Rocky relaxed in the corner.

"You okay?" she asked her father.

"Not really," sounding more like Othello again.

"What's wrong now?" Kat figured he'd be happy to know Frank wasn't a serial killer.

"You mean what's right now? I don't see that anything has changed for the better, Katherine. As a matter of fact, it's worse. He's supposed to be wearing a ring like Gordon…like any Catholic priest. I didn't see any ring. Where is it…if he's a priest?"

"Dad, you're so negative. He doesn't want anyone here to know his background, certainly not any of the priests at Mary, Star of the Sea. They'd immediately have him involved in church work, and he's trying his best to concentrate on finishing his biographical project. Now you know he's 71, and you know he's a Catholic priest—and not a serial killer. Doesn't that give you some relief?"

"A Catholic priest would *never* remove his ring…certainly not for that reason. Maybe Frank Taylor isn't a serial killer or a pedophile, as he seemed to unnecessarily emphasize, but it should occur to you that he could possibly be a priest who's been defrocked because, in his past, he impregnated some innocent young girl who fell for his charm…like you! And I suppose you're still in love with him?"

Kat, defensively, "His emphasis on not being a pedophile was a humorous reference to our conversation at the beach. It was primarily for me—kind of a private joke—not for you. The same goes for when he said 'hypothetically' in response to your observation that he was old enough to be my grandfather. He and I had discussed that before. And yes, at least some of the puzzle pieces have fallen into place. That's for sure. I knew he was a wonderful man, contrary to what you thought, and his being a priest confirms that. Yes, I'm still in love with him—even more so. And concerning your premise that he may have been defrocked for knocking up some lustful teenage girl, that's preposterous and you know it. But hey, Dad, I didn't know you were that imaginative."

"My god, girl. You're up there floating around in the clouds somewhere. You'd better get your tail back down here on earth. You'd better wake up, young lady. You have absolutely no idea of the seriousness of this."

"That's what he said."

Chuckling, "He's not a complete idiot, after all."

"Please, Dad, this has been a very disturbing afternoon. He's an extremely intelligent man."

"I agree with the first part, but I don't know about the last. I'll tell you one thing, if he *is* extremely intelligent, you can kiss him goodbye. You know that, don't you?"

Straightening her posture, hands on her kneecaps with both arms stiff, she inquired aggressively, "What are you talking about?"

Jiggling her memory, "Don't you remember the episode between your Uncle Gordon and Rebecca?"

"Yeah…I'd forgotten her name, but as soon as Frank said he was a priest, I thought of her."

"That's a perfect example. Rebecca would've given her left eye if Gordon had run away with her. She was *crazy* about him—to use your word."

"And Uncle Gordon was actually in love with her, wasn't he?"

Reluctantly, "I guess you could say that." Then quickly, "But that's the point," shifting the Lazy Boy from a reclining position to a more erect one. "He's a Catholic priest, and he's taken a solemn vow to *never*," barking the last word, "have a romantic relationship with another human being. And *never* means *never*," still barking.

"So my uncle just walked away from the…friendship?"

Her father scratched his nose and rubbed the top of his mouth with his index finger. "After searching his conscience for a couple of years, he had to make a decision."

Kat, with a drop of sarcasm, "You mean after searching *for* his conscience. That was a rather long search if it took two years. I have a strange feeling that while the search was going on, Uncle Gordon was having a little fun on the side."

"Well, he *is* a man."

"However, at the end of two years he turned back into a priest." The playful gleam in Kat's eyes was quite visible. She continued, "Reminds me of something an Italian told me about everybody addressing a priest as father, unless they happen to be his kid. Then they have to call him uncle."

"Your uncle wouldn't find that very amusing."

"I think he would. Uncle Gordon has a great sense of humor. Wouldn't surprise me if he were the author of that joke. I don't know about his guts though."

Dr. Churchill, evidently taking exception, "Katherine, my brother is a fine man."

"I know he's a fine man, Dad. I'm not contesting that, and I love him very much, but if he had truly loved Rebecca—and I think he did—he should have had the guts to marry her and leave the priesthood."

Her father was now exasperated. "It's not a matter of guts, Katherine, we're talking about breaking a solemn religious promise to God."

"If we're talking about the same God of love whom I've worshipped all my life, I simply don't comprehend the problem. Maybe you're telling me that every priest who's ever fallen in love, left the priesthood, and married—and I know there've been more than a few—will surely be sent to hell by God? I cannot accept that. And, if I did, I'd go right up to Frank Taylor this very minute and spit in his face, kick him in the ass, and call him an SOB." Tears ran down both of her cheeks. "I'd do anything necessary to make him hate me and leave me—so he wouldn't go to hell. I wouldn't want to be responsible for sending anyone to hell—certainly not someone I love. And I *love* Frank Taylor." She began to sob. Rocky stood. "I love every single thing about him. I love his fingernails. You just don't understand." Uncontrollably now, and louder, "I even love his *toenails*."

Her father tried desperately to grab Katherine before she and Rocky rushed from the bedroom, but unsuccessfully.

CHAPTER 12

With a box of Kleenex on the passenger seat, Kat drove along Prospect, wiping the tears from one eye at a time, watching the street, and looking on both sides of it for Frank with the other. She knew her father meant well, but her heart was burning from the confrontation with him. Throughout her life, their daughter-father relationship had been exemplary. Acknowledging he no doubt was under a great deal of mental and emotional strain from his work, now compounded by his overblown and misunderstood interpretation of the romantic bond between Frank and her, Katherine, nevertheless, was miffed by the tactics he'd employed.

First of all, his behavior was totally unlike any she'd ever witnessed, making him resemble a stranger instead of her beloved father. Next, his unfounded presumptions concerning Frank seemed to give her no credit whatsoever for character evaluation, a particular attribute in which she'd always taken a lot of personal pride. Of course, she'd forgive him. He's her father. An apology from him would be nice though.

Thinking she saw Frank near the entrance of Hotel Mallorca, she slowed for an instant. No, it wasn't him. The valets yelled and waved at her. She waved back.

Approaching the intersection of Prospect and lower Girard, she had to make a decision. "Could he have gone to Scripps Park or the

Cove?" If so, she'd have to turn right. "Or did he go home, so he could be alone and think?" In that case, she'd bear straight and proceed back to upper Prospect, near the entrance to the Colonial Inn. She decided on the latter, turned left onto Fay at the Hard Rock Café. After turning right on Silverado at the Empress Hotel, then left at Bishops Lane, she quickly saw his car in its designated spot. She reminded herself that meant nothing because Frank mostly walked around the village.

Just this once ignoring the rules, she whipped into a reserved parking space, bounded from her car, not bothering to activate the alarm, and raced up the flight of steps to Frank's entrance door. After knocking rather loudly, she noticed a doorbell button and used it. Nothing. Again, the bell. Again, nothing. She returned, disappointed, to her car.

Sitting there momentarily in a trance, she noticed the car clock. It showed 3:59 p.m. Her mind sped to arrive at some possible location at which Frank could be found. There would be a Mass at Mary, Star of the Sea at 5 p.m., followed at 6:30 by another in Spanish. Presently, the only activity would be in the confessional stalls near the church entrance. It would be a perfect time for Frank to pray and think in relative seclusion.

Revving the engine slightly, she backed out and zipped onto Silverado. Crossing Fay, she proceeded to Girard where she turned right toward the church, a block away. There were no empty parking spots on Girard. In front of the church, she turned left onto Kline, quickly seeing a diagonal space on the left beside the church, and made another hard left into it. Activating the alarm, she moved swiftly to the front entrance. She could've gone in the side entrance, but if Frank were there, her appearance would disrupt his prayer, and that's the last thing Kat wanted.

Just inside the front entrance there were six parishioners waiting to confess. Kat passed in front, greeting them with a smile. She turned left into the doorway at the far right side of the church, which became the right aisle of the nave, where the congregation sat during Mass. Rapidly surveying the pews, she saw no sign of Frank...and her heart sank. Remembering Our Lady's Chapel, she continued slowly, quietly down the aisle toward the front of the church where, in the center, was the main altar and sanctuary, and immediately to the right of the sanctuary was Our Lady's Chapel, a side chapel within the church. It was the only section currently not in her view, and the most logical and appropriate place for Frank to be.

As Katherine passed through the archway next to the sanctuary, she saw Frank kneeling before the side altar, which was a smaller altar installed specifically for Our Lady's Chapel. He was alone, except for the presence of God. Although kneeling lecterns flanked his sides, Frank knelt with perfectly erect posture, his hands clasped in front of his waist, using only the carpet.

The room was roughly 30 x 40 feet, in white stucco with an arched ceiling reinforced by wooden vaults. A single hexagonal chandelier hung from above. On the same wall where the side altar was situated, there were two small, rectangular stained glass windows, one on each side of the altar: the window on the left depicting Joseph, and the other, the Divine Infant of Prague. Directly over the side altar was a larger, round window of stained glass in a colorful symmetrical rose design. The far wall to the right was decorated exclusively by a window with an impressively colorful stained glass representation of the Virgin Mary nursing Baby Jesus. The window depicts Madonna looking down at the Son of God, who is looking directly into the eyes of any beholder. Below the window, there was an artistically embellished candleholder, about five feet tall, and an octagonal fountain used in baptism.

The side altar was made of marble, and was topped with two ornate gold objects of Roman Catholic significance. One was a tabernacle, a gold case in which the consecrated elements—holy bread and wine—of Communion are kept. The second was a monstrance, an intricately designed gold container in which the Host or Blessed

Sacrament is placed and shown to the congregation in a Roman Catholic Mass. There were also two candles on the side altar. Directly in front of Kat, a rear exit door led to a lane that separated Mary, Star of the Sea Church from Stella Maris Academy, the parochial elementary school directly behind the church.

Katherine silently inched her way around the corner into the chapel where a line of wooden chairs hugged the wall. In front of each chair was another, the back of which was equipped with a flip-down kneeling pad. Kat, making the sign of the cross, knelt on the one nearest her.

For at least five minutes she prayed in the darkness created by her closed eyes. Thanking God for all her blessings, a daily solemn observance, she then sincerely asked God's forgiveness for the manner in which she'd talked to her father, to whom she promised an apology and the assurance that it would never happen again.

She then talked to God about her relationship with Frank, periodically opening her eyes to make sure he was still there. Very carefully, trying to choose the correct words, she declared the depth of her love for Frank, expressing how much she wanted to be his wife. Finally, at the end of her prayer, she explained to God the primary reason for her being there, especially since she'd told Frank she'd wait for his call. Kat wanted God to know—no matter how much she loved Frank—she would never do anything to come between Him and Frank, that her marriage to Frank, if it indeed materialized, would bring them all closer together. That was her goal, to share and to be part of Frank's love for God for the rest of her life.

Upon finishing, she was relieved to open her eyes and find Frank there before her, still evidently engrossed in prayer. Now that she had explained her objective to God, she hoped God would assist her in conveying her commitment to Frank. She also hoped Frank was not about to pull an Uncle Gordon on her. The thought of being another Rebecca was unbearable.

In one last humble appeal, she silently spoke to Him, the only one who could help her now. "Dear God, please don't take Frank away from me. I love him more than I love myself. Please."

While kneeling there for another five minutes, watching Frank's motionless figure, she felt a magnetism beyond her control, pulling her closer and closer to panic, an emotional state completely foreign to her behavioral pattern. Having always prided herself as the calm, in-control type, she recognized, through her silence and lack of action, her destiny might be irreversibly altered. She decided, with or without God's help, she had to know her fate, and know it *NOW*.

Leaning forward from her kneeling position, attempting to place her face as close to Frank's as physically possible and still remain silent, she slowly opened her lips and quietly said, "Meow."

Frank's head moved slightly to his left, toward the rear door that was ajar. Then he looked to his right, toward Mary and Baby Jesus.

Now determined to know the outcome regardless of the heartbreak, Kat restated her love for Frank in kitty-cat language, "Meow."

That did it. Frank twisted around from his kneeling position, surprised as though seeing the face of God, and saw the beautiful living subject matter of his private thoughts. His face reflected a combination of astonishment and spiritual joy. Kat knew not to smile; it was inappropriate. Frank motioned for Kat to join him, to kneel beside him. She did. He took her right hand in both of his, kissing it quickly, then resumed his praying posture, holding her hand tightly in his left hand. She bowed her head and continued her prayers.

Two minutes later, unable to ignore the compulsion to verbalize her feelings, she leaned toward him and whispered, "Frank, I love you with all my heart and soul, but I would *never* come between God and you." He opened his mouth to speak and, once again, she covered it with her index finger. "If there's any possibility that could happen, I'll walk out of this church right now…and out of your life."

Their eyes laser-linked for 10 seconds. After making the sign of the cross, standing, then bending down close to Katherine's face,

Frank whispered, "Put your arms around my neck." After making the sign of the cross, she did so immediately, letting the side of her face touch his. He slid his left arm around her lower back, then, pulling her upward from the kneeling position, he moved his right arm under her knees, lifting her sprightly and whispering with a suppressed smile, "You're not walking anywhere…certainly not out of my life…not while I'm here. *Never.*"

Standing before the altar now, Katherine in his arms, Frank looked directly at the monstrance on top of the altar and whispered, "Thank You, Dear Father." He backed out the rear doorway, only a few feet away, letting the door close gently behind them, looked deeply into Kat's huge heavenly eyes, and spoke normally but seriously, "There's one extremely important question I must ask you, and I want you to think *very* clearly…before you answer."

Rather than waiting for the left side of her top lip to quiver, she quickly said, "What? Ask me, Baby."

"Will you marry me?"

Squeezing his neck ecstatically and screaming, "Yeeeees!"

They were standing at the top of a hand-railed, wheelchair ramp in the lane behind Mary, Star of the Sea. Frank swiftly sized up his surroundings before he started down the ramp with Katherine still in his arms. "Don't tell anybody," he said in a confidential tone, "but there're a couple of foxes in this alley."

Katherine pointed in the direction of her car. "Listen, Professor Schmeelburger—and never forget it: There are no alleys in La Jolla." Long pause. "But there *are* two foxes." Short pause. "And one of them sounds like a cat. Meow…and sometimes like a—quack, quack," imitating Donald Duck again.

At the base of the ramp, Frank gently released Katherine's legs so she could stand. They embraced and kissed affectionately, then walked hand in hand to her car where she deactivated the alarm, gave Frank her car keys, and slid in the passenger side of her car.

After Frank entered the driver's side and shut the door, he backed the car out of the diagonal parking space on Kline and proceeded a few yards to the intersection with Girard where he turned right, to the north, which would take them to Katherine's home.

At the next intersection, Girard and Silverado, they paused at the four-way stop sign for a seemingly eternal 30-second wait. Fortunately, no cars were behind them. Two sets of cars from both their right and left stopped and continued, while Kat's car remained motionless. Finally her Honda Prelude's left-turn signal came on and, instead of continuing straight toward Prospect and Katherine's place, they turned left onto Silverado. After stopping and then crossing Fay Avenue, they drove past Bishops Lane and turned left at Eads where, about eight cars from the corner, they found a diagonal parking space without a time limit. They kissed passionately in her car, then walked to Frank's garage apartment.

CHAPTER 13

Making love with Frank in his cozy apartment went far beyond Katherine's expectations. His sexual potency didn't surprise her. She knew he was healthy and physically strong. His coital technique, however, completely stunned her, as well as utterly satisfied her wildest desires. Her astonishment, naturally, was based on his personal history in the priesthood. She remembered her father's remarks...cautiously.

An hour and a half into their remarkably torrid session, some 45 minutes after her first nonmasturbatory orgasm in years (she'd had none with a man since the last of her many putrid hook-ups with Andy—only with her dependable dildo), Katherine rhythmically moved astride Frank's naked body, gripping both of his uplifted hands in hers, gazing voluptuously into his eyes, and feeling his marvelously erect penis sliding through her vaginal walls as she snapped her lower body back and forth over his. Fully aware that Frank had not yet climaxed, and enjoying every second of it, she elected not to raise questions about his commendable and evidently natural talent, and instead assiduously refocused her attention on the delightful sensations that vibrated throughout her body. She doubted that her father would understand her decision.

In another 10 minutes, correctly identifying the rapid approach of her second orgasm, Katherine fleetingly considered the likelihood of Frank joining her. Then he spoke.

"Baby, may I do it from the back?"

Smiling instantly, she replied, "I'd love it," and quickly placing her hands on his chest, lifted her excited vulva from his uncondomed penis. Before they got into bed, Frank had suggested that he should walk to Burns Drugs and buy some condoms, but Katherine convincingly persuaded him to skip it, that they were going to get married soon, and it didn't make any difference.

He stood by the side of the bed and helped her reposition on her hands and knees, with the latter near the bed's edge, her legs spread apart. Arching her back and lowering her turned face to a pillow, she reached through her legs with one arm and guided Frank's fully erect cock to the mouth of her stimulated vagina. From his standing posture, with the fingers of both hands grasping her naked hips, Frank gently and smoothly slipped the entire shaft of his cock deep into her vaginal cavity.

"Oh, Baby, you feel so good inside of me," she declared. "Move to me."

Frank happily followed her directions, gradually retracting his rigid penis several inches, then thrusting it forward more deeply. He systematically repeated this sequence, progressively escalating the speed of his movements as he alternately fingered the nipple of her right breast, then the left. When her unintelligible utterances clearly signaled the inevitability of her second orgasm, Frank slid his right hand over her stomach to her vulva and tenderly, but vigorously, massaged her sensitive clitoris.

Within 30 seconds, she clearly expressed her desire. "Fuck me, Frank…hard. I'm coming, Baby."

He adeptly complied with her wishes, demonstrating a flair that Katherine would only have associated with a seasoned adult film actor. She was sensually and emotionally overwhelmed. Feeling his withdrawal, she maintained her basically fetal physical attitude and flopped conveniently on her side, looking up into Frank's admiring eyes.

"Oh, Baby, that was...out of this world." She was still breathing heavily. "You are great. And I'm the luckiest woman alive..." Catching her breath before continuing, "but you didn't come, did you?" She looked directly at his completely extended penis.

"That's okay," he responded understandingly and without embarrassment, doing little to veil his prominent phallus.

Keeping her eyes on his penis, unwittingly comparing it with her ex-husband's, which she remembered to be small and unattractive, she noted that Frank's was visually appealing and exciting to touch—also impressive in size. "No, it isn't either. Go sponge off, and come right back. I'm gonna make you feel good." For the first time, she could admire his bare buns as he walked toward the bathroom.

Katherine sat up as Frank returned to the bed. She observed that although his erection had diminished somewhat, his eyes still reflected an animal hunger, and she intended to nourish it with a method she involuntarily learned from Andy, her ex-husband.

"Stretch out on your back, Baby, and relax. Leave the rest to me." She opened his legs and positioned herself between them, on her stomach, her face directly above his genitals. Cupping his scrotum with her left hand and firmly encircling the shaft of his cock with her right, she covered its head with her lips and began sucking strongly. Aware of his background, she anticipated his objection. There was none.

After 10 minutes, sensing his shaft becoming harder and the skin of his glans penis tightening, Katherine lifted her face and asked politely, "You like it, Baby?"

Propped up on his elbows, leaning his shoulders and head against a folded pillow that was between him and the headboard, Frank replied, "I don't like it, I love it." He was so preoccupied, he forgot to smile.

Katherine realized she loved it too. With Andy, she'd hated it, every second of it, because he made her feel it was her duty. The sensation was entirely different with Frank, even the palatable savor of his cock. Periodically, she lifted his penile shaft with the fingers of her right hand, dropped her head lower and, with her left hand, put his skin-covered testicles into her warm mouth where she gently fondled them with her tongue. In ecstasy, Frank looked toward the ceiling.

Then Katherine tightened the fingers of her hand around his cock and started moving them up and down the shaft while she vigorously sucked his cockhead.

Within 10 minutes, Frank knew there was no turning back…that he was about to orgasm. "I'm gonna come, Baby."

Rather than lifting her face, Katherine actually intensified both her sucking and the use of her tongue on the end of his cock. As Frank blissfully ejaculated, Katherine deliberately swallowed his semen. She'd planned it that way, and it was something she'd never done with Andy.

Looking up at him afterwards, "I want part of you inside of me, Frank. I've never done that." She passionately kissed his cock again, licking off all his semen. "Next time I want you to come deep inside of me."

"We should postpone that until after our ceremony, Katherine. My feelings are strong about that. I'd rather use a condom until we're married. I have enough to deal with as it is. Please understand."

She crawled forward on the bed, close to him, with her head next to his on the pillow. "Okay, Baby. I guess you're right. Hey, I'm so happy. It's like a dream. I wish I could stay longer, but I have to go home and prepare for tonight…and face my father."

"You plan to tell him our plans…right away?"

"You don't think I should?"

"Well…I'm sure he's gonna create a big scene, and…I don't feel like being part of it…at least for awhile. I wish…" He faced her directly and studied her eyes for several seconds.

"What, Baby? You wish what?"

"In the restaurant yesterday—Robilio's…you said you'd like to go with me to Hawaii—"

Sitting up quickly—the enthusiasm showing on her face, and her gorgeous breasts demanding Frank's attention, "Yeah, I'd love it, but you said it really wasn't necessary for you to make the trip, that you could do that research in the library."

As he talked, Frank fingered one of her nipples, then the other. "I've thought about it more carefully, and there's no question, being there and seeing the various spots that Jack has mentioned to me would be much better than reading about them from a book or on a computer monitor. Just like here, I've been to North Island, and I've seen the area where the Naval Training Center used to be. I can write about those places much more accurately and vividly than if I had just read about them."

"Let's do it, Baby. There's no problem." She took his hand from her nipple and rubbed it over her vulva. "You see, I'm part-time at Winthrop, and they can get a sub to fill in for me easily. And the same thing's true at the Gulls Nest. They've got a list of about 10 different entertainers who're dying to show their stuff at the Gulls Nest. And besides, after we're married I'm not gonna keep those jobs. I don't need to. I just want to be with you. I wanna be your wife, without any distractions." She pushed his hand strongly against her labia. "I told you that. It's just for fun that I do it. I'm very well off financially, Frank, and I don't want you paying for anything else. As a priest, you've probably been living like a pauper all your life. That's coming to an end, buddy. I'm gonna show you some fun. I've got so much money, I don't know what to do with it, but I've never had anybody to spend it with…to share it with." She started to kiss him, and drew back, smiling. "I need to brush my teeth and rinse out my mouth."

Shaking his head slowly and clearly agonizing, "Katherine, I appreciate your interest in my project...and your generosity, but..." his gaze was concentrated on her left eye, "the more I think about it, the more I realize how urgent it is for me to get started in Hawaii. I could leave Monday or Tuesday, and you can join me later at your convenience, after you deal with your father."

Completely nude, Katherine sprang from the bed, pulling the top sheet off of it and wrapping it around her body. "What? I can't believe this, Frank. You just proposed to me...and I accepted...we made love...and now you're off to Hawaii—just like that!" She snapped her fingers. "Without me? Are you serious?" Plainly, she was upset.

"Katherine," almost sounding like her father, "you don't seem to understand. Your father does not like me...and I'm having trouble dealing with that. I can see it in his eyes. I'm not accustomed to people looking at me in that fashion. And it's especially difficult, knowing that your uncle is a priest. I presume your father's Catholic, isn't he?"

Plainly deflated, "Yes, he is. This is terrible...right out of a soap opera." She sat on the edge of the bed. "I told you, Frank, my father does not run my life. If that's what it's all about, I can tell you right now, I'm going with you. We can leave Tuesday at the latest. Naturally, I have to perform tonight, but I'll explain everything to the manager. And regarding my French class, I can wrap it up with one phone call. As soon as my travel agent opens on Monday, I'll get our airline tickets. You've never been to Hawaii, have you?" Her smile was back. She permitted the sheet that covered her to drop on the floor, and she knelt close to him on the bed. Again holding his hand, she slid it over her thigh to her vaginal entrance and, taking one of his fingers into hers, she massaged her clitoris with it.

"No."

"I'll take care of all the details. We'll stay at the Halekulani. You'll love it."

"Do the units have common walls?"

"I…I'm not sure…what you mean." She was slightly distracted because Frank was now actively finger-fucking her.

"Can you hear the people in the next room listening to TV? I have to concentrate. That's why I picked this little apartment—it has no common walls."

"Yeah, I see what you mean now. Listen, the Halekulani has some individual bungalows. I'll get one for us." Fondling his cock with one hand, she vigorously increased the pressure of his finger on her clitoris with the other. "Baby, this is gonna be like a honeymoon. I'm gonna take care of you. And we're gonna make love every day." Moving one of her hands away from his pubic area and running her fingers over something on his skin, near his left hip, she looked at it. "What's this?"

"That's a mole. Had it since birth. Supposed to be lucky," he grinned and raised his eyebrows. "I've got two more on my left lat."

"Yeah, I saw those. They're brown, but this one's kinda invisible." Grinning back at him, "Baby, I don't think you really know how lucky you are…" She opened her legs wider, arched her back, and forcefully pushed her clitoris against his rigid finger. "And me too."

"I'm concerned about the expenses, Katherine. I have no idea how long it will take, and that makes me rather uncomfortable. As you can see from this place, I can rough it out, but I can't expect you to do that. My income is extremely limited."

"We're on no schedule, Frank. If it looks like we're gonna be there several months, I'll rent a house. Don't worry about it." Her other hand went back to his cock, which was getting hard again. "I told you…I have the money."

"I've learned the hard way that you can't write a personal check in another state. Nobody will accept it. So, you'd better think about that. And traveler's checks get to be a nuisance."

"Yeah, I hadn't really thought about it." Rhythmically moving her vulva over Frank's outstretched finger, she began to masturbate his hardening penis with amazing dexterity. "What do you suggest?"

"The most convenient thing is a standby letter of credit. It's like one big traveler's check that you can draw against in varying dollar amounts. You can get one in an amount that totals several thousand dollars. Then if you need, say, $1,500, you go into a bank in Hawaii that has what they refer to as a correspondent relationship with your bank here in La Jolla, and write a draft for the $1,500, and that's deducted from the total of the letter of credit. For example, if you decided to rent a house and you had to come up with the first and last months' rent, plus the cleaning deposit—like I had to do here—no problem. You just go into the bank and get it, in the form of cashier's check or cash. It's a real hassle when you start trying to have money wired from your bank. And they no doubt have ATMs all over Hawaii, but there're limitations connected to those. The standby letter of credit is the most trouble-free way to go. It's used almost exclusively in international business, so most people have never heard of it."

"I'm one of those people," she nodded and smiled. "You know a lot about this." She could feel his cock was fully erect now, and that, along with his skillful finger, heightened her arousal.

"I learned it the hard way…and, of course, vicariously through my parishioners, who've told me some horror stories. The nice thing too about the letter of credit is that whatever you don't use, you bring back in the unused portion of the instrument and re-deposit it to your savings account. It's sort of like having your bank with you, fully protected, in case of an emergency. As you know from your experience falling off the cliff, emergencies do happen. You were very lucky. I'd recommend that you get the letter of credit in a sizable amount to be on the safe side. Whatever you don't use, you simply deposit back into your account when we return—or when *you* return, if you decide to come back earlier."

"I'm not coming back earlier, Baby." A little upset again, but not letting it affect her body and hand movements. "Why do you say something like that?"

"Well…in case I have to stay longer than I bargain for. I certainly can't expect you to stay there indefinitely. I might start the ball rolling in the Catholic Diocese over there, as far as my leaving the priesthood. Depends."

"That's a good idea." Considering the subject matter, she removed her hand from his throbbing cock, stopped her body movement, but hoped he would leave his finger in her vagina. He did.

"I'm sure it has to end up in Chicago, but at least I can start things in Hawaii."

Gripping his stiff cock again and continuing her motion against his finger, "I'm staying with you. I'm crazy about you, Frank…and after making love to you, I'm even crazier." She started to kiss him again and remembered.

"Maybe…" This time he concentrated his gaze on her right eye, "I'd better go with you to the bank, so they won't give you the wrong instrument."

"Instrument?" she smiled, increasing the speed of her body movement and the intensity of her hold on his penis. "Nobody's gonna play this instrument but me."

Chuckling, "Negotiable instrument. That's what a letter of credit is, although this particular one is nonnegotiable—and it's strictly up to you—but something you should consider—again in case of an emergency—is to put me on as a signer. If some medical crisis came up and you were physically unable to sign—maybe temporarily unconscious—it would be good if I could get a few dollars quickly, so I could take care of the situation. It would be impossible for me to do it from my personal funds. I don't have that kind of money."

"Yeah, I'm gonna take you to the Pali Lookout, and the wind might blow me off. Man, you talk about a cliff…the one I fell from here in La Jolla looks like a street curb compared to the Pali. People from all over the world say it's the most spectacular view they've ever seen. You're right, Baby. I'll make sure you can sign. You come with me. We'll go to the bank together and you can tell them what we want—"

"What about Rocky?"

Katherine was getting very excited, and from the rigidity of his cock, she knew that he must feel the same way. "There's a place in the village. I've used it before. Rocky likes it. Well, I wouldn't exactly say he *likes* it. They're good to him. I know one of the girls there. No problem."

"You'd better go, Katherine." Frank smiled and appeared relaxed for the first time since they started making love. "You have to deal with your dad. I don't envy you. And if you tell him all this, I know I'll be making the trip alone."

"Hell, I'm not," momentarily she forgot about his dislike for profanity. "I'm sorry, Frank, I…I'm not gonna tell him anything…not today, anyway. Before I leave, I guess I should let him know where I'm going, but I'll be quite vague. I'm not giving him any details. I really don't care about seeing him in Hawaii. He's got that transplant on Tuesday. I'm sure he'll be gone tomorrow…could be already gone. We had a bad scene when I left him at my house to look for you at church. I kinda hope he's gone, tell you the truth. I don't feel like dealing with him either. If he's gone, can you stay with me tonight?"

Fingering the nipple of her left breast with his free hand, "I've got so many things to do, Katherine."

"Ooh, Baby, I'm so excited." She bent over and whispered into his ear. "Please fuck me one more time before I go. I'll be more at ease tonight at the Gulls Nest."

Frank chuckled. "You little rascal…if we're leaving Tuesday, I'd better get busy with my stuff. Fortunately, I'm paid up here through October—"

"This is only the 14th of September, Frank. You should check out of here right away…get that month's rent back. I'll come over and help you clean up tomorrow, so you can get the deposit back. You can stay at my place. I told you, I'm not stingy, just thrifty."

"I've got so much on my mind, I just don't want to have a disagreement with the manager. She's been very nice to me, and I want to keep it that way. And there's the possibility I might come back from Hawaii and stay here two or three more months."

"Frank…you mean you're not gonna live with me?"

"Not 'til after we're married, Katherine. You should understand that. Your father…remember?"

Perturbed again, but still not releasing his excited penis, "My father doesn't run my life, and he doesn't live with me."

"But he pops in whenever he feels like it." Putting his hand up to prevent her interruption, "And I understand that, perfectly. He's your father. I'll be marrying *you*, but whether you realize it or not, I'll also be marrying your father. He's your family. I accept it…but I'm not sure *he*'s going to accept me."

Determinedly, "Well, I'm gonna straighten this mess out. I'll tell you that right now."

"Please take my advice, Katherine, and don't try to straighten it out before our trip…*if* you want to go with me."

"Okay, Baby," sliding her hand gracefully up and down over his penile shaft. "What time can I call you tomorrow?"

"Maybe 11 or 11:30. I'm going to an early Mass. I need some time for prayer. If you want to, you can come back in the afternoon, and we can be together here."

Suddenly wearing a huge smile, "What do you mean, if I want to? I'm gonna be here, and I'm gonna dream about it tonight. Let me go brush my teeth and sponge off quickly." She gave him that irresistible Katsmile. "I'll be back in flash." She whispered in his ear as she squeezed his rock-hard cock. "Then will you fuck me again?"

Frank, lying on his back with his head propped on a pillow, smiled. "You're holding my answer."

"Baaad boy! I wonder if there're any more priests like you out there? Don't go away, Father." Completely nude, she wiggled her ass exaggeratedly and disappeared into the bathroom, closing the door behind her. Then, opening it immediately and projecting a voluptuous facial expression, "When I come back, I'll confess to you."

Frank's face reflected no emotion whatsoever, but his sexually stimulated cock twitched excitedly.

"Oooh, Baby, I got the message," with a huge grin, "and I love it." Then pointing at his demonstrative penis, "Tell him to stay right there—in that same position." She shut the door.

Staring blankly at the bathroom door, Frank mentally reshuffled his limited options. His master plan's objective was still clearly in focus, with ideal lighting and the correct background texture and shade. The key element in creating his masterpiece would be the film type and its speed. Frank decided on the slowest black-and-white.

CHAPTER 14

Before their departure on Tuesday, Frank had to take care of several important matters, one of which was relatively minor, yet something not to be overlooked: buying condoms. He did that following a Sunday Mass.

That afternoon in his apartment, he was glad he did so. They spent four hours in bed making love. Katherine seemingly couldn't get enough of Frank. She was especially intrigued by his countless repertoire of sexual positions and the flawless manner in which he implemented them. The uncanny ability to postpone his orgasm so he could prolong her carnal satisfaction was a distinctive delight, something from which she derived indescribable pleasure, making the most of her multi-orgasmic capabilities.

Earlier, when Katherine informed Frank that her father had left before she reached her home on Saturday, the relief in his face was quite apparent. She also told him that everything had been arranged concerning her two jobs, and there had been no trouble whatsoever. In the late afternoon, Katherine invited Frank for rainbow trout at Sammy's on the corner of Pearl and Draper. She then persuaded him to visit her place so she could show him the upstairs rooms, one of which she emphasized would be his private den for study and prayer. They ended up in her master bedroom, and within moments, were stripped and fucking on her king-sized bed. After two hours of mutual pleasure, with Frank keeping his orgasm in check because he neglected to bring the condoms, Katherine again happily performed fellatio. He returned later to his apartment where he spent the night alone in his whirlwind of thoughts.

Entering Bank of America Monday morning just after its opening, Katherine surprised Frank by suggesting they get a letter of credit in the amount of $100,000. He had been thinking in the neighborhood of $50,000 to $60,000, but she convinced him, based on what he'd told her, that the larger amount was on deposit in her savings account and "would cover just about any unforeseeable problem—so why not have it…to be completely prepared?" She joked that they might decide to go around the world…to escape from her father. He scolded her, but secretly was fascinated by the idea, even though it would be a deviation from his master plan.

The bank manager politely explained to Katherine, his valued depositor, the rarity of her request, that due to the popularity and global usage of credit cards, the letter of credit had diminished in usage, but, considering the dollar amount she was requesting to have on demand, he understood why she wanted this particular instrument. He emphasized that it was strictly an international banking instrument and normally would only be handled at the bank's downtown San Diego Main Office. However, because of her excellent relationship with the bank—meaning of course how much money she kept on deposit with them—and the lack of time before her intended departure, he would be delighted to have a messenger deliver her letter of credit to their branch later that afternoon. Then, he carefully pointed out, she and her friend could come in and sign, following the requisite withdrawal of money from her savings account that had to be transferred into the bank's name, and the transaction could be completed. After the manager made a brief telephone call to his Main Office, they decided on 2:30 p.m.

Next, they went to Katherine's travel agent on Fay Avenue. They got a Tuesday morning flight out of San Diego directly to Honolulu.

Katherine used one of her credit cards to pay. The agent explained that, because the date of their return flight was uncertain, they'd probably have to notify the airlines a few days in advance when they picked a specific return departure time, especially as the holiday season approached. "Anytime sooner than that," she explained, "or after the first of next year, no problem."

"Rocky," Kat decided, "should be boarded next, rather than waiting 'til the last minute. I don't want that hanging over my head. Let's do it." The goodbye scene at the kennel left Frank choked up…and Katherine in tears. Although Rocky shed no tears, he whined plaintively.

At 2:10 p.m. after salmon sandwiches at El Pescador on Pearl Street, Katherine and Frank returned to the Bank of America where her letter of credit awaited her. She withdrew the $100,000 from her savings account in order to complete the necessary financial mechanics of the transaction, and they both signed so that either could write drafts against that available total balance.

Kat and Frank then thought it best to split up during the remainder of the afternoon so they could each pack their luggage in preparation for an early departure the following morning. Katherine suggested that Frank bring a pizza and his luggage to her place in the early evening, spend the night there with her, then the following morning, Dan, from Jewel Transit, would take them to Lindbergh Field. When she told him the arrangements for the taxi service had been made, Frank appeared upset.

"You've already done that?"

"Yes, Baby, I did it last night after you left. They're very popular, and their schedule gets busy. I didn't want anybody else to take us. Did you have something else in mind?"

"Well, I was gonna drive us to the airport in my car and just leave it there."

"That could get pretty expensive, especially when we have no idea how long we'll be staying. Remember," she smiled, "we may go around the world...or to some exotic location. You can leave it at my place, Baby...no problem."

Frank's face registered concern. "Your house will be unattended during our absence, right...except for the security service?"

She paused. "Security service? Oh, you're talking about that sign near the back steps. That's phony. I've had it for years. It's just to keep the amateurs away. If a pro wants to break into your house, he does it. You know that." Then recalling what he'd told her, "Or *she* does it," with a silly grin. "But my housekeeper—I've never mentioned her—comes twice a week. I'm leaving her a note to keep an eye on everything, and to call the police if she sees anything suspicious. I'll let her know that the car belongs to my friend...and lover," kissing the air in front of her face.

Frank disregarded her humor. "On what days does she come?"

"Tuesdays and Saturdays. She'll be there shortly after we leave for the airport. She's excellent. I've had her for a couple of years. Don't worry about my stuff. It's all insured. And nobody'll bother your car. Remember, my neighbors are great spies. They don't miss anything. It's just from habit that I activate my car alarm when I leave it there."

"That's fine. I was just wondering." He seemed satisfied, but still a bit preoccupied.

The lovemaking Monday night had a special significance for Katherine. It would be the first time they'd spend the night together in her house...which she now considered theirs. Frank did remember to bring the condoms. And most significant of all, it was the very best screwing Katherine had ever had...period. Frank's sexual potency was nothing less than a 10. His cock seemed even harder and springier, especially when she sat on top and forced her clitoris against its shaft. Afterwards, however, Kat noticed that Frank appeared unusually pensive.

"Are you worried about something, Baby?"

His silent look at her was long and steady. She detected an unprecedented, arresting gleam that aroused her and, at the same time, slightly terrified her. Having just finished an eminently fervent coupling with the man, it was the latter impression that captivated her attention span.

"Hannibal is back." Playfully blocking his view with her open hand, "Please, I don't want a nightmare. This is a special occasion."

Finally, Frank smiled warmly and turned on his charm. "Hey, I'm a little drowsy. This is a completely new experience for me. You should understand that I'm somewhat overwhelmed. I'm making love to my dream girl. How many men can say that?"

"I'm glad to hear that. You're so sweet. Okay, Baby, let's go to sleep. We've got a long day tomorrow. Help me remember to call my dad before we leave. It's later there, and he'll already be at work, probably looking in on the transplant operation. I'll leave a message on his answering machine."

"Excellent idea," Frank chuckled, "but *please* don't tell him where we're staying. I can clearly picture him knocking on our bungalow door."

"Oh, I'm definitely not." She moved in closer, gently putting her arm across his naked chest. She kissed his shoulder. "Baby, I knew I was physically attracted to you, but I didn't have any idea just how sexy you are. You really surprised me. Talk about overwhelmed…I'm the one who's overwhelmed," drawing closer and licking his lips with her extended tongue, "and I just *looove* to fuck you."

"Well, you didn't surprise me. I knew you'd be a great lover, physically…and you are."

"Really?" Kat slowly slid her hand over his stomach, down toward his pubic area. "I can't keep my hands off you." She began exploring. "Baby, you're excited."

Kissing her ear, "You mean you can tell?"

She laughed softly. "I sure can, even if it was pitch-dark."

"Are you excited?"

Whispering, "Oh, yes, yes, yes. Can we do it one more time? I'll sleep better…and so will you."

Mimicking Katherine on a previous occasion, "Just relax, and leave the rest up to me." He opened her legs and positioned his upper body between them.

Katherine thought she knew what he was going to do, but, again, considering his background, felt that surely she was mistaken. It was the only way that Andy had been able to sexually satisfy her, and he'd been quite skillful at it, in contrast to his ineptitude at copulation.

Frank vigorously and expertly slid his open palms under her buns, firmly stabilizing Kat's hips and pelvic region. Then quickly, with a slight pause to admire her cleanly shaven cunt, he lowered his face and covered her vulva with his lips. From the moment he'd first felt this smooth, hairless area of her body, he'd wanted to get his mouth on it. Within three minutes, Kat knew that Frank was far superior to Andy at cunnilingus. The manner in which he softly used his tongue on her fully aroused clitoris delighted her. He started slowly and gently. Periodically, he pursed his lips and skillfully sucked her glans clitoris, the very tip. She was ecstatic. He then subtly increased the pressure of his tongue as he artfully moved its surface back and forth over her exhilarated clit. Ten minutes later, he began plunging his lengthy tongue deep into her vagina, curling it upward and, and with its tip, compellingly titillating her G-spot. Shortly thereafter, once again, she orgasmed dramatically.

He went immediately to the bathroom and brushed his teeth. When he returned, Kat was still breathing heavily. She embraced him tightly. "Frank, that was beautiful…like a wonderful, unforgettable dream. You made me feel great…like a real woman."

"Katherine, you are a real woman…if there ever was one. You are the greatest…the sexiest body I can imagine…the way you shave your pubic hair—that's great. Your labia and vagina—I love kissing it. And I love the way you fuck me too. And, what's even more important…I love you." Watching her eyes, "I surprised you, huh?"

He surprised her again, this time by using the *f* word and referring to her labia and vagina…and again by asking that last question.

"Frank, you *really* surprised me. I guess *stun* is the best word. You have to know what I'm talking about, Baby."

"I know." He looked away from her and paused, as if to make a decision. "I understand…and I have to tell you. You want to know the truth, and that's a mutual courtesy we both deserve from the outset."

She sat up, alarmed, but tried to joke it off. "Oh, Frank, you're not gonna play creative games with me again, are you?"

"No games. I promise. But…you should know the facts about my youth. And…if you decide to change your mind, and you don't want to marry me or go to Hawaii with me, I'll accept that. It's understandable. But this is personal information I have to share with you. You've told me everything…but I haven't told you everything."

Her mouth was open. Apprehension covered every inch of her face. She was afraid to listen. She thought her fairy tale was about to explode before her eyes.

"Katherine, I grew up," he continued, his eyes now focused on the ceiling, "in a brothel. My mother was a whore."

Kat didn't know what to say. She had no idea how to respond…or what to do. She remained silent. Her lip quivered.

"By the time I was 16…in the 10th grade at Tech High…I had screwed—I'll use the vernacular—that's the kind of language I grew up with…by 16, I'd screwed every whore in the brothel, which was in West Memphis, Arkansas, across the bridge over the Mississippi from Memphis. There were about 20 prostitutes working there, off and on. That's the way my mother wanted it. She never had a husband. I have no idea about my father's identity…and I seriously doubt she did. She wanted me to know everything about women. Well, the whores taught me well. They showed me everything there was to know about sex. I use *was* because times have changed. And I cannot honestly say that I didn't enjoy it, because I did. I loved it. They used to joke with me, and tell me I was a natural-born fucker…that none of their customers were in the same class with me.

I was proud of it." He chuckled softly. "And, of course, I had to keep it to myself at school. I don't think my mother really cared...but I did. No one ever knew...none of my buddies...only the whores...and they were all good to me...like a family...only I fucked them...frequently. I was ashamed of it though...and I was envious of the other kids who lived normal lives...at least I thought they were normal, until I became a priest and realized there's no such thing as a normal life. Some of the confessions I've heard...are absolutely unbelievable...as if they were straining their imaginations in order to make them up." He kept his eyes on the ceiling...and waited.

He didn't have to wait long. Katherine, on her knees, moved within inches of his head, and looked down directly into his eyes. Her exquisite naked breasts, with those delectable prominent nipples, partially framed Frank's visual perspective of her lovely face. She took his hands in hers, lifted them upward, placing his palms firmly over her nipples, and pressed them snugly against her bosom.

"Thank you for telling me that, Frank. I love you even more now. I want to spend the rest of my life with you. You've absolutely nothing to be ashamed of. Look what you've done with your life. I want you to know that I'm extremely proud of you." A slight smile came over her face. "And I love to make love with you. I'm absolutely crazy about your cock. Kissing it and sucking it is wonderful. It's beautiful." She lowered her face slowly and kissed him passionately. "Maybe those whores were the best thing that ever happened to you. I'm glad they taught you well."

CHAPTER 15

The flight to Honolulu went smoothly. A van from the Halekulani transported them to the lobby entrance of the hotel, and they actually completed their check-in while sitting on a colorful sofa with an attractive Asian lady in their spacious, luxurious bungalow, a pleasant deviation from the usual procedure at most hotels.

While unpacking, Katherine noticed how neat and well-organized Frank's clothing and personal belongings had been arranged in his luggage. She was impressed, but not surprised. He only opened one side of his suitcase. The sight of his swim trunks, which he'd completely surrounded with underwear, reminded her to make a point.

"Baby, I know the reason for coming here is your research, but," coming close to him and brushing her hand against his genitals, "can't we take a few days off and have sort of a mini-honeymoon? Huh?" The expression on her face didn't leave him many options, especially since she was footing the bill.

He dropped some rolled-up socks on the bed, and partially encircled her waist with his fingers, then gave her his phoxiest expression. "You mean I'm gonna tour Oahu on this bed?"

Now displaying the most lascivious look she could muster, "Your tour on this bed, young man, will be far more exciting than anything you'll experience on this island...or any other island in the world. I guarantee that." She French kissed him with a ferocity that indicated she was trying to outdo his whore/teachers.

After catching his breath, "That's not what the brochures say, but since you're covering the expenses, I'll leave that decision up to you."

"In that case, old boy, your research has been postponed to the *very* distant future." With her left hand, she found his cock and squeezed it affectionately. "I think we should spend a week or so doing nothing but eating, sleeping, and..." softly, in his ear, "fucking."

"What about drinking, pissing, and shiting?" he quickly added.

Swiftly, she removed her fingers from his cock and used that hand to stifle a laugh. "You are downright nasty, boy," looking at him in disbelief combined with amusement.

"Sorry, another inadvertent reversion to my youth, but...I am a realist." He fingered both of her nipples.

"I believe you." She gave him that bedroom look, then glanced down at his moving fingers. "Don't stop what you're doing. After we unpack, I'll close the drapes, and we can get...comfortably naked, climb aboard this magic carpet of a bed, and flyyyyyy to paradise." She laughed contagiously. "Is that a deal? Meow." Then like Donald Duck, "Quack, quack." Grinning grotesquely, "What's a fox sound like, Professor Schmeelburger?"

"In your case, a vixen," still using his fingers magically.

"What? That's a mean bitch. I'm not a vixen, Baby. I'm a sweet little foxy woxy." She knew he would scold her about the bitch word. He didn't. "I'm beginning to think maybe I've got some rabbit in me," faking embarrassment.

"Your predilection for flying to paradise on the magic carpet would certainly fit your rabbit heritage, but the first definition of a vixen, according to the dictionary, is a female fox. The second is a bad-tempered, vindictive woman."

Astounded, "Vixen? You gotta be kidding."

"Look it up...you cute little vixen."

"I didn't know that. I'm gonna get re-educated around you. Vixen, huh? Well...on the other hand, I can be kinda bitchy...sometimes...that fits too." She couldn't believe he hadn't jumped on her choice of words.

Frank looked toward the window, the one facing the beach. "There's still plenty of daylight left. Sure you don't want take me for my first swim at Waikiki Beach? It's kinda special for me. I grew up dreaming about it when I was a kid...even *before* Pearl Harbor. I used to look at National Geographic in the elementary school library." Kissing her nose. "I grew up dreaming about a girl like you too."

Instantly taken aback, "With my skin color? You'd better think again, Buster. Remember, you're a priest. God is watching."

Frank lifted her chin so he could see those marvelous eyes. "Hey, I was an innocent, unknowing victim of my social environment."

She kissed his nose. "Spoken like a true...honky." She laughed and tickled his armpits at the same time. "Be careful how you respond to that." She feigned gravity. Then she wrapped her arms tightly around him and looked into his face. "I'm only joking. I don't care what you call me. You can even call me...the *n* word...if you want to," suppressing a giggle, "because I'm crazy about you."

"Be quiet. Don't talk that way. That word is *not* part of my vocabulary...and never will be."

Egging him on, "Do it, Baby, please. I want to hear what it sounds like...just for fun." Rubbing her lips against his, "Come on, I'm asking you to."

There was nothing but admiration in his eyes. "I love you...*n* word."

She laughed. "Aw, heck, you're spoilin' my fun."

"Never used the word in my life, and I'm not about to start with you. Can you imagine what your father would do? He'd reduce my butt-beating to *one* second flat...maybe zero."

"Oh, I can just picture the look on his face." French kissing him, "I love you, honky. I'm your little nigger."

Focusing on her tits, he grinned. "You're my *big*...you said it, not me."

They both laughed, then kissed lovingly.

"And you know something, Phoxy?"

"What, Kat?"

"Hey, that's the first time you've called me that. I love it. Katherine's so formal. And besides, that's what Dad calls me. We're very *in*formal now." She whispered, "In fact...don't tell anybody, but we're fuckin' buddies." She grimaced clownishly in preparation for his mini-sermon...but didn't get it.

"I know," he confirmed.

Pleasantly surprised, she continued. "And I love it. We're *the* greatest nigger/honky couple in the world."

"I know that too, and I knew it," pressing his fingers into the small of her back, "when we were walking on Girard, on our way to Robilio's."

Exhibiting genuine pleasure, "Really?"

"God is my witness."

"That's beautiful. We have a beautiful story, Frank. Let's go for a swim."

They finished unpacking first, then moments later, Katherine appeared in a daring yet tastefully designed blue bikini. It left little to the imagination, but also stated with no doubts that this was a woman with a perfect figure.

Observing Frank in his one and only swimsuit, "I'm not gonna embarrass you, am I?"

"Of course not. You have on more than when I met you."

Katherine cracked up.

"And this is Waikiki Beach," he pointed out. "Turn around." She did, and he looked at her derrière, again absolutely sure it was the all-time greatest ass in the world. "What you have on is appropriate. Actually, you'd be overdressed at Ipanema."

"Whoa, you astonish the devil out of me."

"If *he*'s coming," Frank joked, "I'm getting out of here. Any red-blooded man knows where the thong originated…even a priest."

Shaking her head as she smiled approvingly, "You are really something, Frank Taylor. I'll bet my uncle doesn't know. Oh, wait a minute, he probably does. I'll bet my father doesn't."

"I'll let you ask him. I'm staying out of that one."

"Skip it," waving her arm. "Let's go for a swim."

"I've got the door key here in my pocket." Frank patted the side of his swim trunks. "Did you put the letter of credit in the safe?" Their accommodations included a combo-safe, built into the wall.

"I zipped it up in an empty garment bag in the closet. If somebody stole it, he'd have to identify himself when he signs for the money."

"Hey, careful with your genders. The prisons are full of female thieves and robbers. There're some pretty slick chicks, as well as dudes, out there. That's your decision. It's your money, but a hundred 'thou' would be a nice heist."

Franks choice of words amused and, again, surprised Katherine. "Oh, come on, Baby, we're not gonna be gone that long. We don't even need to take towels, do we?" she asked.

"No, we'll just swim for awhile and come back."

It was only a few yards to Gray's Beach, which bordered the hotel grounds. Typically, the sky was filled with magnificent cumuli and miles of blue, which the ocean's surface faithfully reflected.

As they approached the tidemark, Kat motioned to their left. "There's Diamond Head."

"Oh, look at that," Frank remarked. "I've seen so many pictures of it…and there it is." Then he affectionately clasped Kat's hand. "I'm so glad you came, Katherine. Thank you."

"Thank *you*, Baby, for inviting me."

Wading in up to his knees, Frank commented, "The water's perfect. Feel that temperature. Must be 75 degrees or more."

"That's usually about it. Let's swim out to the flag," nodding in that direction.

Raising his face, immediately locating it, "That's a pretty good swim. I'm not gonna race you, Baby, you're in better shape than I. Let's just take it easy and unwind. Is anything out there, or do we just turn around and swim back?"

"Depending on the tide, you can usually stand, or sometimes sit, on a slab of concrete. It's a little over 200 yards to the flag. I asked a local beach attendant once—looked like a pure Hawaiian—and I think he said 220 yards. Straight out and back, the bottom is sandy and coral free, but if you get off to the side, there is coral, and it's easy to cut your feet, so let's stay together."

They did stay together, both using a relaxed breaststroke. Occasionally, Frank turned around to admire the view of Oahu. Kat was very much thinking of her initial meeting with Frank. The tide was cooperative; they were able to sit comfortably on the concrete and take a break.

Facing the island, Frank carefully took in 180 degrees. "I've never seen anything this beautiful…except you."

Below the water surface, she coiled her arm around his waist and pulled her body closer to his. "This whole thing is incredible to me. You realize it was only five days ago that we met. I can't believe it, Baby. I thank God with all my heart that I met you, Frank." She saw that mysterious look in his eye again. "Is something wrong? I've only known you for five days, but I can tell that something is bothering you. It's obvious. Can't you share it with me? I've told you not to worry about anything…especially money. So it's obviously something else."

"Katherine, I just have a lot on my mind. I have two projects now. I've gotta make a formal application to the diocese, and it's…it's tough. That's the only way I can express it. It's the toughest thing I'll ever do."

Seriously, along with perceivable compassion, Kat asked, "You're not getting cold feet, are you?"

"No, no, no, it's not that," Frank asserted at once. "My decision is final. I've already wrestled with that. That's between God and me. I've put all that in His hands. It's just the paper work and dealing with human beings that bugs me a little. I'll get over it. Please bear with me." He looked out to sea toward the horizon, then down into the water. "Any sharks around here?"

"No, Baby. There's a big reef way out there. They've never had a shark incident here…at Waikiki, that is."

"Kinda spooky out here," he said. "No other swimmers around. A guy could drown, and nobody would even know about it."

"Careful with your genders," she teased. "No, they watch the area pretty well." She focused her eyes back on the beach. "See that really brown guy with the red hat on? He's got binoculars. I think he's looking at us now."

"Oh, yeah. I see him. Maybe you're right. Well, that's fine as long as he doesn't twist around and zoom in on our bed."

Moving her head closer to his, she licked his ear. "If he zooms in there about an hour from now, he's gonna get an eyeful."

Frank smoothly turned his head and kissed her. "Is that a promise?"

"You better believe it, boy. I'm gonna get you. But the drapes'll be closed, so don't worry about the guy in the red hat. Just worry about me…'cause I'm gonna eat you up."

"Oooh, that sounds like fun." Frank wiggled his eyebrows. "I'm gonna use the backstroke returning…in case a large female fish with penis envy tries to put me out of commission."

She muted a laugh. "You sexy clown. Those West Memphis whores were right on." It was hard for Katherine to accept the dramatic reversal Frank had made regarding his tolerance of her word choices…and his own usage. "You're the funniest *priest* I've ever known—that's for sure."

"Now wait a minute, Your Honor, that's prompts a key question." Frank was playing games again. "Just how many priests have you *known*, young lady? And to what extent?"

Licking his ear again, "I haven't known *any* priests as intimately as I know you…Father." That got a chuckle out of Frank. "The ones I've confessed to haven't been funny at all, believe me."

"Aha, confession. Now we're getting to the nitty-gritty. We're not supposed to be funny when we listen to confessions. I certainly wasn't. A bit of humor at the beginning of a homily, of course, helps some of the congregation to stay awake throughout the remainder, but…during confessions I customarily left any wit up to the parishioner."

She rubbed her nose against his cheek. "Yeah, I'll bet some of those confessions you heard were mind-blowing. You ever have a person tell you…they've murdered someone?" For a split-second she saw that look in his eye again.

"No," Frank answered solemnly. "And if I had…I couldn't tell you. You know that. Let's go for a swim."

He playfully squirmed away from her, and gracefully launched himself toward the beach. Katherine followed his frog-kicking legs.

After transferring the letter of credit to their built-in safe, having double-checked the combo number in her purse, Katherine and Frank took their first shower together in a roomy, glassed-in stall. A mini-spa, easily capable of accommodating two people, was only a few feet away. Katherine was enthralled by the shower experience, particularly the skillful manner in which Frank dexterously lathered her vulva and buttocks, frequently entering her vagina and anus with a soapy finger or two. By combining that with sporadic soul kisses and powerful sucks on her nipples, he brought her close to orgasm, but knowingly eased off at the proper moment.

Attempting to appreciatively reciprocate, Katherine concentrated her lathering on his scrotum and fully engorged penis. After rinsing the soap and sea salt from his genitals and the rest of his body, she pulled a hand towel over the top of the shower stall, knelt on it, and began fellatio. Feeling his fingers comb through her wet hair, thereby sensing his gratitude, she intensified her tongue movement and increased her suction. Frank politely avoided orgasm by lifting her head and pulling her to a standing position. They kissed ardently and long, then started drying each other's bodies.

Katherine used an electric dryer on her hair, Frank a towel. Then within moments, their nude bodies tightly joined on the bed, both resumed their mutual sexual gratification. Having already told Frank she was unable to get enough of him, she clearly demonstrated it by following his guidance on an almost endless series of coital postures, all of which seemed second nature to Frank. Emotionally, that bothered her momentarily, but his application and movements were so physically thrilling that she philosophically chalked it up to his brothel upbringing. Kat judged herself an extremely fortunate woman, most definitely when he piloted her into the most dramatic and intense orgasm of her life, one she could unmistakably sense that he physically shared with her, even though he wore a condom. She had been right.

The highly regarded La Mer, offering the best of French cuisine, is on the grounds of the Halekulani. Katherine treated Frank to a dinner that was nothing short of a gustatory delight. Because he was required to wear a jacket in La Mer, the same blazer he'd worn to the Gulls Nest, they returned to their bungalow after eating and changed into something more comfortable for walking in the balmy evening air, to the extent of leaving their shoes. Kat took Frank in the sand along Waikiki Beach, past the Sheraton, the Royal Hawaiian, and the Outrigger Hotels to the Moana Surfrider, where they cut through the elegant, old-world lobby—still barefooted—and exited by way of the hotel's front entrance onto Kalakaua Avenue.

At the first appropriate shop along the street, Kat bought each of them a pair of flip-flops to finish their stroll on the sidewalk. Throughout the eight-block walk—approximately a third of a mile—alternating from one side of Kalakaua to the other—Kat pointed out several points of interest, and explained how everything would look so much better under tomorrow's blue Hawaiian sky. The air temp was 75°. Before they turned left off Kalakaua and proceeded on Lewers to the Halekulani, Katherine spotted an Islands Bank branch on the other side of the street.

"Oh look, there's an Islands Bank office. That's convenient. When we need some money, that's where we can go with that credit letter thing, right?"

"Yeah, that's one of the correspondent banks listed," replied Frank.

Back in their bungalow, Kat could see that Frank was a bit fatigued and, although she wanted to make love to him again, she diplomatically suggested they both sponge off and try to go to sleep. With reference to herself, she emphasized the word *try*, and Frank knew exactly what she meant.

Approximately 10 minutes after they got into bed, Kat began fondling Frank's penis and kissing his shoulder. He knew what was coming, and decided they would both sleep better if he sexually satisfied her. She asked him to lie on his back and let her straddle him. He complied, and she showed her appreciation in a way that brought a smile to his face, and obviously gave her an orgasm. They did sleep better.

CHAPTER 16

The next morning Frank was pleasantly awakened by a dream of a beautiful woman performing fellatio on him. It was no dream, of course; it was Katherine.

Removing her mouth and lifting her face, she politely apologized. "I'm sorry, Baby, you woke up. I guess the truth is that I'm sex starved and didn't know it—plus you make me feel so good...beyond anything I've ever dreamed. I really didn't know what making love was all about...until you."

Running his hand through her hair, "Don't apologize. I understand...and I'm happy about it. Let me wash my face and brush my teeth." He went promptly into the bathroom.

When he returned, Kat got up. "I have to go too."

While he waited, stretched out nude on the bed, Frank's mind whirled almost out of control. He tried to frantically reorganize his agenda, one that was drastically changed at Katherine's home in La Jolla. Learning that she had already made reservations with Jewel Transit, and that her maid was scheduled to clean her house Tuesday morning shortly after their scheduled departure, forced him into a new game plan. He could've easily accomplished in La Jolla what he now had to do here in Hawaii, over 2,000 miles away. Past experience had taught him not to panic however, to visualize his objective and to calmly let the pieces logically fall into place. He learned years ago that the human brain, especially his, was extremely adaptable. There was always a successful method out there somewhere. It was merely a matter of sensibly applying his mental faculties to locate and to put into motion the one that would spell victory. So far, he had never failed. He'd come close to failure on several occasions, but through meditation, concentration, and complete confidence in himself—the latter attribute being without doubt his most important and strongest—he'd always managed to come through.

His immediate quandary, however, had nothing to do with the success of his master plan. On the contrary, there was no doubt in Frank's mind that it would work. The problem was—and this is what was presently eating away at his alter ego like a school of sharks—did he now really want the master plan to work? At this precise point in his life, considering his newly awakened feelings for Katherine, which he had to confront and to honestly admit to be genuine, did he want to see it through? Or would he prefer to trash his plan and, for the first time in many years, permit his alter ego to guide him…guide him into a soul-mate existence with the most beautiful woman he'd ever known…and the only woman he'd ever loved…except one?

Returning to bed, Katherine nimbly aligned her body with his supine position, sliding her right arm under his neck and looping her naked left leg over his waist. She covered his lips with hers, thrusting her tongue deeply into his open mouth, while lovingly stroking his tumescent cock with her left hand over the curve of her ass.

Frank questioned his ability to fulfill her carnal needs in a copulatory fashion. As she withdrew her tongue and devoured his eyes with hers, he gracefully wriggled toward a cunniligual posture. Katherine instantly and correctly interpreted his message, placed her head on a pillow, and invitingly spread her gorgeous legs. Frank thoroughly captivated her attention for the next half-hour, then once again cathartically brought her over the orgasmic threshold with his empirical expertise. There was something about her hairless pubic area, dark skin, and deep red flesh in the folds of her vulva that held a special attraction for Frank. That combination, along with a distinctive aroma and flavor during cunnilingus, was a different and delightful experience.

"Baby, Baby, I love it! You're wonderful," she exclaimed. "I've never felt so alive. I've never been this happy. Now I think *I'm* the one who's dreaming."

Gently, subtly, he continued using his tongue in an expert fashion. Then pausing, and looking up at her, "You're the one who's wonderful, Katherine. I love you. I've never really loved anyone before." And he knew that was the truth…almost.

Frank had been impressed with the atmosphere at the Moana Surfrider, so Katherine took him back for breakfast. Still mentally and physically pretty much on Pacific Standard Time, they had awakened early as far as the local time was concerned, and even though they had made love for over an hour, it was not yet 9 a.m. when they entered the Moana restaurant.

Katherine watched with fascination as Frank put away egg-covered pancakes, plus a large bowl of bite-sized Shredded Wheat and orange juice.

"You've got a great appetite, boy," she joked.

"I told you breakfast is my favorite meal."

They walked down the steps, then under the huge banyan tree to the edge of the sand. It was indeed a breathtaking sight: the myriad hues of green and blue in the water, those gigantic fluffy clouds floating majestically, and one of Hawaii's icons, Diamond Head, off to the left.

Katherine moved close to him. "You feel better now?"

"Much, thank you. I'm one of those strange animals for whom breakfast is a necessity. If I don't have it," he gesticulated dramatically by flipping his hand from one side to the other, "an hour later I just keel over in a dead faint."

She laughed. "Really? I'd have to see that to believe it."

"It's true, but I feel great now. Test me."

"I was hoping you'd ask." In her light khaki shorts, burgundy halter-top and high-heeled mules, she pressed her bosom against his chest. "Let's go back to bed, Baby."

Grinning broadly, "I was hoping *you*'d suggest that."

"Where's your little itsy-bitsy camera?" she asked. "I haven't seen it."

"I forgot it. Left it in a drawer in my La Jolla mansion."

"Oh, Baby, I can't believe you did that. Hawaii's a photographer's paradise, and you need one to take pictures for your project. I'll get you another one, but one that's a bit larger and easier for me to use."

They took the same route down Kalakaua, this time more slowly on the ocean side of the street, window-shopping and people watching. Just prior to turning off toward the beach at Lewers, immediately after Katherine pointed out the accessible location of the Islands Bank branch again, Frank glimpsed the face of a woman on a tour bus that had just pulled away after stopping at a traffic signal. The woman stared keenly at Frank, as long as her view from the bus's moving window permitted. Frank abruptly turned his face. Katherine saw none of it. As they rounded the corner at Lewers, Frank noticeably increased the speed of his gait.

"Hey, I like a man with enthusiasm." Holding his hand tightly, she followed suit.

"I kinda thought you might." Grinning again, "I'm a man with an important objective."

Beaming back at him, "And I *love* the objective."

"Yeah, I sorta get that impression." Frank looked back over his shoulder. "You think it could be serious…and possibly incurable?"

Walking even faster, she grabbed his neck and whispered near his ear, "If you mean nymphomania, I hope so, and I hope it's incurable, 'cause I *looove* having it. It's fun. I don't want to be cured. I refuse to see a doctor. Sure as hell, don't want see Dr. Churchill." Now she was laughing.

"Maybe I've been stricken with satyriasis." He kept a straight face.

"What?" Making a funny face, "Here we go again, professor. What's *that*?"

"The male equivalent."

"Of nymphomania?"

"Yeah."

"Oh, boy. I hope you have a *baaaad* case...and it's incurable too. That would be a fantastic combination." She lowered her voice. "We'd be the perfect fucking couple."

They both laughed.

As they entered the grounds of the Halekulani, Frank took one more look over his shoulder. "Let's stop at the front desk for a second. I want to make sure we're not interrupted. When I have an objective, I don't like distractions."

Squeezing his hand, "I like the way your mind works, Schmeelburger. We can put the tag on the door knob," she assured him.

"We can do that too, but I like to communicate—make it official, with no room for error. After all, we're talking about top-priority logistics."

In the lobby, the same lady who checked them in was behind the counter. "Oh, hi there. Is everything okay in your bungalow?"

"Superb. Couldn't be better," Frank answered. "I noticed a brochure on one of our tables said you have maid service *twice* a day," stressing the twice.

"That's correct," she smiled, "morning and afternoon."

"Why don't you tell the housekeeper," Frank continued, "to skip our unit until about...2 p.m. *tomorrow*?" He emphasized the last word so there could be no mistake that he meant 2 p.m. today.

Katherine looked away in embarrassment, trying unsuccessfully to fight off a smile.

"No problem, sir." The desk clerk smiled radiantly, the subtle twinkle in her eyes letting Frank know that she understood exactly what he had in mind. "I'll take care of it for you, Mr. Churchill. Should you need anything else, please let us know."

"Sure will." Frank ignored her mistake with his name, preferring to leave it that way, then thinking of something else, turned back. "Oh, one other thing: We'd appreciate it if you'd put a stop on all incoming telephone calls. We're not expecting any, but…just in case, take a message, and we'll call them back after 2 p.m. tomorrow."

She gave him her same knowing smile, thinking, "Wow, this couple is serious," then responded to Frank, "I'll leave a note for everyone on the desk staff."

"Unless, of course, there's an emergency," Frank added, noticing *CATHY HIGA* on her nametag and figuring she was of Japanese ancestry. "If the Japanese attack Pearl Harbor again, we'd like to know about that."

Katherine's eyebrows went up, and Cathy Higa gave Frank a twisted smile with her reply. "If that happens, Mr. Churchill, I'll personally knock on your door."

Katherine and Frank walked toward their bungalow. Once out of the lobby, Katherine put her arm around Frank's waist. "I've got you to myself for 27 hours. Prepare yourself. I'm gonna get you now, boy."

"You really think so?" He stuck his face in her hair and inhaled its aroma.

Playfully ominous, "You just wait and see, honky. You ain't seen nothin' yet. I heard a comedian say, 'Once you go black, you never go back.'" She muted a giggle. "Of course he was black."

Using his key to open the door, Frank was relieved to see that the drapes were still drawn. As soon as he closed the door and locked it, he asked Kat, "What's that?" He motioned toward the dresser. When Katherine looked in that direction, Frank struck her rather forcefully at the back of her neck, using the side of his palm, karate style, instantly rendering her unconscious. Quickly seizing her armpits, he kept her from falling to the floor.

"Sorry, Katherine. I have no options."

He dragged her to the colorful sofa, the one on which they sat when they registered. Gingerly, he positioned her body on it, sincerely attempting to avoid further injury to her neck, and removed her high-heeled mules. First, he brought a wooden straight chair from the bedroom. Then, from his suitcase, he swiftly jerked open the drawstring of a dark brown, cloth bag from which he pulled a roll of two-inch-wide, gray duct tape, a black sleep mask—the kind used by passengers on airliners—and a new package of nylon rope, 100'x¼". Along with a razor blade from his shaving kit, Frank was able to use the tape and fashion a clean-cut, secure gag over Katherine's mouth, leaving ample space for breathing through her nose.

After tying her bare feet tightly together at the ankles, Frank lifted her into the chair, with her head flopped forward, and tied her wrists together behind her back. Then, working frantically to finish before she regained consciousness, he systematically wrapped separate pieces of the white braided, nylon filament strategically around her body to bind her to the chair and thus minimize the possibility that she could disentangle herself.

He reinforced the tape on her mouth by wrapping additional pieces completely around her neck, then, dragging her—chair and all—into the bedroom closet, he tilted the chair against the back wall so that its front legs, as well as Katherine's feet, were off the floor. Placing the index finger of his right hand under her nostrils, Frank confirmed she was still breathing. On the closet shelf, he noticed two folded, tan velour blankets, probably for guests who prefer to sleep with the air conditioner turned on high. Jamming them tightly under the elevated two front legs of Kat's chair, he thought that might prevent her from later rocking forward and trying to snake her way out of the closet on the floor to the bedroom telephone, with which he purposely did not tamper.

Arranging a bath towel behind Kat's neck, he tried to provide a cushion for meager comfort. Considering her athleticism, in a final stratagem to preclude her getaway, Frank securely roped the top of her chair, near her neck, to the long metal hanging rod in the closet.

Katherine groaned. Frank stood a few feet away from her and tried to think of anything he'd overlooked. Lifting her head slightly and looking into his eyes, he heard her desperate, muffled attempt to communicate.

"Easy, Katherine." Frank knelt on one knee before her, and kept the volume of his voice down. "Listen to me."

Again, she repeated her attempt, this time with a combination of hatred and hurt in her eyes.

"Goddammit, shut up and listen to what I have to say." Frank's tone of voice and countenance revealed a persona with whom Katherine was totally unfamiliar. She was clearly startled and her eyes reflected it. "I'm running out of time fast. I've got a lot of things to do, and I don't have time to fuck around with you anymore." He gradually moved his face in closer to hers. "You're gonna hate my guts for the rest of your life, and there's nothing I can do about that. You're gonna find out all kinds of shit about me now…things I'm not proud of by any means, but I did them, and it's done and over with, and there's nothing I can do to change it. But someday…when you're 80 years old…and still beautiful…long after I'm dead and gone…there's one thing I want you to remember about me—if you don't remember *anything* else. I don't want there to be any question in your mind…I love you, Katherine Churchill. You'll never understand that, but I love you with all my heart and soul—and believe me, I do have a soul, contrary to what the authorities are gonna tell you. I've never loved another human being…" Frank was getting choked up with emotion now, "but I sincerely love you. If I could kidnap you, and take you to an island and spend the rest of my life with you, I'd do it in a fucking heartbeat, Baby…but there's no way it can be done. It's impossible. Our relationship is history…and I'm sincerely sorry about that."

He put one of his hands on her bare foot. She didn't flinch. "I'm a hunted man…have been for years. I can't make excuses for what I've done, and I'm not trying. Somebody spotted me on the street a few minutes ago. That's why I'm doing this so abruptly. It's just a matter of time now. They'll have an APB out on me, and I'll be trapped like a goddamned rat on this island." For 10 seconds, without blinking, he looked into her eyes, first the left, then the right. Then he removed his hand from her foot. "I have to go now. Sorry about the 100 grand, but I need it a lot more than you. Your dad's gonna be highly pissed, but he was anyway. Just tell him he was right, that I'm a no-good bastard. That'll make him feel better…not *good*, but better. Nothing makes him feel good except his fucking medical practice. That's…why your mother left him. She was bored shitless."

Frank pointed to the rope that tied her chair to the closet's metal rod, and lied to her very convincingly. "I've got this rope rigged to your chair so that if you get a little rambunctious and move around too much, you're gonna have one helluva unpleasant surprise. Take my advice and don't do that…relax. Don't trigger my setup. You'll be very sorry if you do. Try to sleep if you can. It'll be tomorrow after 2 p.m. before the housekeeper comes. I could've done all this shit much less painfully for you in La Jolla, but your maid was scheduled, and so was Jewel Transit. That was beyond my control, and *not* the way I planned it. I know you'll never believe this, but this morning, when we were having breakfast, I had decided to dump my plan altogether—I mean every fucking bit of it. I was gonna persuade you to take me on an around-the-world cruise so we could be inseparable every goddamned second—because," he came very close to breaking down, "I'm absolutely fucking crazy about you…but I guess it just wasn't meant to be." Looking into her beautiful eyes and knowing he'd never see them again, he wanted to put the whole world on pause…then he continued, "Oh yeah…when nature calls, I'm sorry, Baby. Please forgive me. You'll have to make the best of it."

Kat growled her disapproval at his last remark, but her eyes were flooded with tears from everything else he'd said.

"I've got some unfinished business to take care of before I leave." He pulled the black sleep mask from his pocket. "You won't be seeing me anymore. I'm gonna cover your eyes with this. Sorry, but I'm not gonna hurt you. That's something I could never do. Never, never." Before he put it on her, he kissed her forehead. She didn't resist. More tears flowed over her cheekbones onto the tape. "I love you, Kat. I sincerely mean that. They're gonna tell you I'm nuts, that I'm a psycho. That's a batch of shit. *They're* the psychos. I'm a smart son of a bitch—smarter than any of those assholes, but…something happened a long time ago…in a far off place…in a dark alley…and I guess I never got over it. I never will." With one last look into her eyes, he stretched the elasticized band over the back of her head to keep the sleep mask in place. Then he bent forward and checked to make sure she couldn't see under it.

At the top of his agenda was the letter of credit. He went directly to the safe, used the combination that he'd memorized, and removed the letter of credit. Placing it on the bed next to his opened suitcase, he then reached into one of the expandable liners that bordered the interior of his luggage and removed a rolled-up pair of black socks. He quickly unwrapped and separated the socks, sticking his hand into one of them and fishing out a gold band, which he promptly slipped onto the third finger of his left hand. From the same compartment of his suitcase, he lifted two pairs of neatly folded trousers that covered a dark brown, zippered, imitation-leather briefcase, which he put on the bed. He'd purposely avoided making this trip with anything metallic. That's why he left his camera in La Jolla.

Frank then yanked open a partition that had been Velcroed closed in the other half of his large suitcase, and removed black shoes, black trousers, and all the other articles of clothing, including a Roman collar and complementary black vest, necessary to dress like a priest. Beneath all that, was a tan pith hat, inside of which was a plastic sandwich bag containing a fake mustache, a small plastic jar of liquid adhesive, and an applicator brush. From another plastic bag inside the hat, he removed a U.S. passport. Observing Katherine's purse on the dresser, he opened it, jerked her wallet out, and counted four 20s, two 10s, three 5s, and four 1s, which came to $119, which he put on the bed.

Frank then sat on the bed and opened the yellow pages of the city telephone directory. First, he checked the section for banks and found that Islands Bank's main branch was on Merchant Street. He then looked in the front part of the book and spotted a map showing the entire island of Oahu, and another with the streets of Honolulu. He verified that Merchant Street was in downtown Honolulu. Then, on the Oahu map, moving his fingertip across the island from Waikiki, where he was now situated, to the opposite side of the island, he saw what looked to be another community or town called Kaneohe. Quickly he flipped to the church section, specifically Catholic, and searched for a Catholic Church in Kaneohe. There was a St. Ann's listed on Haiku Road. He closed the book and organized his thoughts for a few seconds.

Within 20 minutes, Frank was faultlessly attired as a mustached Catholic priest, wearing a pith hat for protection from the strong Hawaiian sun, and carrying a briefcase. He went to the closet door and checked his appearance in the full-length mirror, then looked at Katherine.

"I'm leaving, Baby. Try to remember one or two good things about me. I'm not 100% bad. I'm sorry I had to hit you. I wouldn't do anything in the world to harm you. I love you. Good luck. I'm not gonna let the sons of bitches lock me in a cell for the rest of my life, so I'm outta here. I'll never forget you, and...I'll never stop loving you."

Sincerely hating to turn away from her, he did. He checked through a window in the living room first. He had previously noticed a Dumpster behind the bungalow and, not wanting to be overly generous to Forensics, would love to have thrown his suitcase, clothes, and toilet articles into it, but figured someone from the hotel staff would no doubt see him do it. For that same reason, he didn't try to exit with the luggage. He would just leave it. He also knew this would be the first time he'd left fingerprints, and that would present problems for him in the future. "Fuck 'em. I'll outsmart the stupid cunts anyway." Then he slightly cracked open the entrance door, viewed the area around the lobby, taking extra care that Cathy Higa was nowhere in sight, and departed, making sure the door was locked and the "Do Not Disturb" sign was securely hanging from the outside doorknob.

On Lewers, a half-block before reaching Kalakaua, he spotted a cab and hailed it, requesting in a passable British accent to be taken to Islands Bank's main branch on Merchant where, he told the driver, he was late for an appointment.

CHAPTER 17

"I know how you feel, Miss Carlyle, but you have to realize what we're up against." The man speaking had a large, wide Asian face. They were sitting in an unmarked white car, just outside the entrance to the Royal Hawaiian Hotel, in a no-parking zone. "I've issued an all-points bulletin, but here again, we have no recent photos of the guy—"

"But I know it's him," the woman expressed with absolute certainty. "It's Brian Clement. I can identify him. He's Australian. As soon as he opens his mouth and talks, there's no question about it. I looked directly into his face, and he looked back at me. He knows I saw him. He knows who I am. The bastard murdered my sister." She was in the mid-forties, blonde, overweight, bespectacled, with pockmarks on her face...and plainly upset.

"Everything points in that direction. Our database indicates there's DNA evidence now to prove he did it, although there's never been any fingerprints on the guy, but keep in mind, there are thousands of people here at Waikiki. We can't take you door to door, attempting to identify this character. That's impossible. You say he was with a local girl?"

"No, no, I didn't get that good a look at her. I'm not positive about that. She could be from Bombay, India as far as that goes. I was focusing on him. She definitely has darker skin, but I really didn't see her face. She has a nice figure, and was wearing shorts, and her hair—dark—is short."

"Probably his next intended victim." He scratched his partially bald head as he watched an elderly couple come out of the Royal Hawaiian. "This guy's a cunning psychopath, responsible for eight homicides that we know about—all women...plus he robs them—that's the main reason he murders them, so they can't identify him. What about your sister, did he get any money from her?"

"About $120,000, plus a very expensive sailboat—which you folks recovered after he'd already sold it to somebody—and some pricey jewelry," she replied dejectedly.

"Your sister's body was never found, right?"

"That's correct."

"Oh boy, that's terrible. We don't run into much of this over here. The island's not that big, and it's not that easy to get off. Surveillance at our airport is pretty good, especially since 9/11. The problem with this guy is that we really don't know what he looks like now. He's reportedly a master of disguise...not only that, he speaks different languages and can use a variety of accents. For your information—not that it makes any difference—the guy's *not* Australian. He's got the longest list of aliases I've ever seen and, being a computer whiz, he's able to make very passable copies of driver's licenses and passports that he uses all those aliases on. Would you mind if I send a sketch artist to your room?"

"That's fine, but...I'll do what I can. I'm not sure I can help though."

"Maybe the two of you can come up with something useful for the airport personnel. Her name's Patti Chin. She's very nice, and very talented. Just listen to her questions and try to describe what she wants. Sometimes it works and...sometimes it doesn't. What are your plans now here in Hawaii?"

"I've already toured the other islands. I'd planned to stay here at the hotel for another week, but I'm going home as soon as possible. You think he might come after me?"

He took a deep breath before answering, and tried to pick his words carefully, not wanting to alarm the woman, but at the same time, feeling he should level with her. "I really don't think so. First of all, he probably has no idea where you are. However, we're dealing with a very dangerous individual. And, since he now knows that you saw him, he realizes you're gonna report him. So you're gonna change your flight schedule and depart as soon as you can?"

"Yes, I am. I won't be able to sleep or anything," shaking her head. "I'm a nervous wreck now. I'm sure you understand."

"Of course…but I'm very sorry your trip got messed up. On the other hand, we're very appreciative that you called us. Too bad you had to get off the tour bus to do it. I'd like to put a 24-hour watch on you until you leave, if you don't mind, Miss Carlyle."

"That's very nice of you, Mr…what's your name again?"

"Horikawa. Larry Horikawa. I've been with the bureau 24 years. I've got your home number and address. If we catch the guy, I'll let you know. If we don't come up with anything in a few weeks, I'll call you anyway, just to make sure you're okay."

"You're so thoughtful."

"Will you be in your room for the next couple of hours?"

"Yes, I plan to."

"Then I'll have Patti call first and set up an appointment. We won't waste any time. That's important if we want to nab this guy before he leaves Oahu. Within one hour, we'll have somebody keeping an eye on you, but you won't be aware of it." He extended his right hand.

She shook it and got out of the car. "Thanks again, Mr. Horikawa, for responding so quickly." She walked toward the entrance of the Royal Hawaiian.

Frank paid the cabby, waved him off, and entered the attractive lobby of Islands Bank's home branch, removing his pith hat and propping it under his left arm, the same one he used to carry his virtually empty briefcase. He immediately looked toward the wall opposite the commercial side of the spacious office, the one across from the tellers, and quickly identified the manager's desk. Because of the large amount of money involved, he knew it would be a waste of time to talk with anyone else.

The nameplate on the desktop plaque read, "NANCY OSA, VICE PRESIDENT & MANAGER." A beautiful Asian woman in her mid-thirties, she smiled brightly at Frank's approach.

"Good morning, Father. Is there something I can help you with?" Her right arm was fully extended, and she warmly shook Frank's hand. "Please have a seat."

"Hi, Nancy. I'm sorry to barge in on you like this." Frank sat in the chair next to her desk and faced her directly. "I'm Monsignor Frank Taylor...pastor of Mary, Star of the Sea Church in La Jolla, California."

"Oh, that's a *very* nice place. I've been there twice. If I ever had to leave Hawaii, that's the only place I'd want to go. Is everything all right this morning?"

"As a matter of fact, it couldn't be better," Frank beamed. "Pardon my excess enthusiasm, but...I'm here in town representing one of my generous parishioners who's decided to make a much needed contribution to a project you've probably read about in the newspaper."

"There're so many different things going on, Monsignor. I'm not sure which one you're referring to."

"We're having ground-breaking ceremonies Saturday at St. Ann's in Kaneohe. It's not only going to be a home, but also a school, for abused girls. They'll have excellent personal tutoring in computer skills and a variety of other subjects. For example, they'll be shown how to dress properly. Also, social conduct will be covered at length. It'll be a marvelous opportunity for some of your less-privileged local girls to break into the job market…rather impressively."

"That's fantastic. I hadn't heard about it."

"My parishioner, Katherine Churchill, wanted to get the ball rolling with a $100,000 gift. She sent me with a standby letter of credit on which I'm a signer." Frank pulled it out of his coat pocket and unfolded it. "She asked me to take a close look at everything, because of my past experience in these building programs, and…if things are in order—and according to what I see, they certainly are—get the money into the hands of the three different subcontractors so they can start right away and finish on schedule." He gave the letter of credit to the manager.

"Don't see many of these, but…" she quickly noticed the dollar amount, "considering the total dollar amount, I understand why she and her banker chose this instrument." She examined it very carefully, from top to bottom. "The *general* contractor," looking straight into Frank's eyes, "customarily controls disbursements."

Unfazed, as if he had anticipated that point, "That's true, and that's the reason I came directly to you. This is a deviation from normal procedure, not only because of the manner in which the disbursements are made, but also the fact that I'll be making them in cash." Frank glanced over his shoulder in a secretive fashion as if to confirm that no one was listening, and then noticeably lowered the volume of his voice. "All three subcontractors—and they're all Catholics—are giving us a *very* handsome discount…*if* they get the so-called front money in cash." He lowered his voice even more. "Has something to do with their taxes. I'm not very knowledgeable on that subject."

She waved her hand. "That's really none of my business." Giving him a warm informative smile, "I'll pretend I didn't hear that. My father's a CPA so actually I know exactly what you're talking about though." After a slight pause in which she inquisitively studied his greenish-brown eyes, "So you want all of this in cash…all $100,000? That's…uh…rather dangerous, isn't it?"

Plainly minimizing the peril, "Not really. I'm going directly to St. Ann's as soon as I walk out of your bank, and that'll be the end of it, *but*…the beginning of something extremely worthwhile…something I'm quite proud to be part of, frankly…and now *you*'re part of it." He never removed his eyes from hers, and that wasn't difficult because hers were hypnotically alluring.

"May I see your ID, Monsignor? I realize, according to regulations, all we're supposed to do is compare your signature on the draft that I'll have you sign with the signature on the letter of credit, but…this is a lot of money. I'm sure your generous parishioner would want me to do that. Then I can indicate on the instrument that I did so. And since you're requesting the full balance that's available, we retain the letter of credit, and return it to your bank. You understand all that, I'm sure."

Frank opened his wallet, "Of course," and removed his fake, computer-generated California driver's license.

She gave it a careful look, viewing both sides. "It's brand new…and you're a Scorpio."

With a slight chuckle, "I'm not into astrology. And yes, I had the laser operation to get rid of my glasses, so I could have the 'glasses required' notation taken off my license, and I had to get a new one."

Nancy pointed at her own eyes and smiled. "I had that too. I love it. You like it?"

"It's great…especially when you're swimming," Frankly actually envisaged cunnilingus with the sexy woman he was talking to, "and other activities." He smiled involuntarily and mentally toyed with the likelihood of Nancy's promiscuity. He also wondered what her confessions would be like.

"That's true," returning a smile that clearly indicated she was two moves ahead of him. "Just about…anything you do is more fun without glasses." That confirmed it. She was obviously enjoying the game, but surely had no suspicions about the monsignor's actual thoughts. "Scorpios are interesting people," she went on, leveling her unblinking gaze on Frank's receptive eyes. "Charles Manson is one."

Frank responded instantly. "He may be one, and he may be very interesting, but I don't know if I want to put him in the people category."

She grinned.

"Are you Catholic?" Frank had to know, particularly since she was so cooperative...and sensual...not that her answer would've made any difference.

"No, I'm not."

"That's okay." Frank flashed a little of his charm. "You're excused."

She chuckled and removed a packet of bank drafts from the bottom right drawer of her desk. Peeling the top one off and placing it on her desk near Frank, she cordially directed him, "Just complete this in the amount of $100,000, and sign it so that your signature matches the one on the letter of credit, and I'll do the rest. Make it payable to cash so you don't have to endorse it again on the back."

Frank twisted his body so he could fill in the draft while seated. Her watching him didn't seem to make him nervous. On the contrary, when he finished and added his rather flamboyant signature, he looked into her gorgeous Asian eyes, making no effort to conceal his physical attraction for her. "How's that, Nancy? Pretty good forgery job?"

She chuckled again, placed the completed draft next to the letter of credit, and scrutinized the signatures. "If I go to La Jolla again, I'm gonna make a special visit to one of your Masses...even though I'm not Catholic."

"We'll let you in, Nancy," projecting his best non-priestly grin at her. "Just don't forget to drop something in the collection basket."

Now exceeding Frank's grin, "You're amusing." She was obviously entertained...and attracted, even though Frank was supposed to be a priest. "Have you ever considered relocating in Honolulu?"

"Any possibility of converting *you*?"

She was definitely into Frank's game now. "Well, I don't know about that." Her eye contact was incredibly sensuous, reminding Frank of his most memorable and kinkiest fuck, a 25-year-old Thai girl, Khiam Tansrivong, he'd murdered in Bankok. "I might convert *you*." She laughed aloud, and it was just as contagious as Katherine's.

"It's a strange world out there." He couldn't resist, even at the risk of $100,000. "You never know. What are you, a Shintoist?"

"No, my grandparents are. I'm...not sure what I am. Haven't made up my mind yet." Chuckling again, "Maybe nothing."

Her last word made Frank want to see her with nothing on. He was having trouble pulling himself away from the conversation...until he allowed that Nancy could purposely be trying to keep him at her desk, pending the FBI's arrival. Again, momentarily dwelling on her last word, "Nancy, if there's one thing in the world you are *not*, it's nothing." His eyes were glued on hers. "You are indeed *something*. You're an intelligent, beautiful young lady...with a bright future." Apologetically, "I have to go. The subcontractors are waiting, unless they went for a beer. If I were staying over on Sunday, I'd invite you to Mass at St. Ann's, but I'm flying back right after the ceremony on Saturday. I have Masses scheduled for Sunday in La Jolla. We'll meet again someday. I'm sure of it—maybe when my parishioner makes another donation."

"I hope so." Her smile diminished, and it was back to business. "How do want the money...in what denominations? All 100s?"

Frank had memorized his answer to that. "I'd appreciate nine straps of a hundred 100s. That's $90,000. Then $5,000 in 20s," he watched as she scribbled the figures down on a pad, and gauged his verbal instructions on the speed of her writing, "$3,000 in 10s, $1,950 in 5s, and $50 in 1s."

"I don't understand why they couldn't have you keep it in $100 bills, especially with only three subcontractors."

"You'd have to ask them. I'm just doing it the way they requested. They'll probably re-subcontract some of their work out to other subcontractors. Your dad can explain it, no doubt."

"I suppose." She looked across the office. "See the vault door over there?"

Frank stood and looked in that direction. "Yes."

"I'll place your order with the vault teller and double-check her. It shouldn't take too long, unless we're low on $100 bills, but I doubt that. When it's ready, it's better if you go over there, rather than loading your briefcase here where too many people can see you. Just relax and I'll let you know." She left with the letter of credit and the draft.

Frank remained standing so he could try to see what was going on. In particular, he wanted to make sure that Nancy didn't go to a telephone or intercom transmitter. He liked the way she moved her ass walking to the other side of the office, and was sorry there wasn't a sufficient time frame in which to get much better acquainted with her. He knew she'd be a great fuck, and he'd never been wrong about that specific estimate. "Confirmation," he thought, "would have been so delightful." Asian women had always turned him on. The only reason he'd reluctantly killed Khiam Tansrivong was because she had planned to rat on him, and that would have meant his certain death by execution. Had there been any realistic options, he'd never have taken her life. At least twice a year, he had vivid dreams in which he thoroughly fucked her. Khiam no doubt had a Master of Arts degree in prolonged and deviant sex, and made fun of Americans for their fast food and fast sex.

During the bank manager's absence, although Frank kept his visual awareness directed toward the vault door, he further formulated his plan to escape from Oahu. After picturing various scenarios in his mind, ones involving changes in clothing, he determined his best choice was to stick with the priest outfit. Racquel Yancey's sister had seen him dressed casually, walking with Katherine on Kalakaua. If the FBI took her to the airport, she would be able to identify him...*if* she saw him. The last *if* is the one Frank had to gamble on. At Honolulu International, there was an abundance of carriers going to different parts of the world, with numerous queues of people waiting for tickets or to pass through security. To watch all of these individuals, even with the updated, sophisticated optical surveillance equipment in use since 9/11, would be impossible. Also, the chances were fairly good that Minnie Carlyle wouldn't recognize him in the priest outfit with a mustache, even without the pith hat, which would certainly be a red flag to security personnel if he kept it on his head.

Another obvious warning signal would be checking in without luggage. That would be a dead giveaway, particularly since the "Shoe Bomber" had done it on a Paris-to-Miami flight in December of the previous year. The solution for that would be to make a quick stop at the nearest department store, after leaving the bank, and buy a suitcase, along with the appropriate clothes to, at least partially, fill it. Frank mentally added that to his agenda.

Nancy waived from the vault door, and motioned for him to come. She introduced him to the vault teller, and directed him to a private cubicle where the strapped bundles totaling $100,000 were neatly placed on the table. She invited Frank to count it all. He courteously declined, but took note of how many strapped bundles of what denominations were there, as he neatly placed them one by one into his briefcase.

Once again, Nancy cautioned Frank about the danger in which he unnecessarily placed himself. "That's a lot of money, Monsignor. As you said, it's a strange world out there. Not everybody is Catholic. You're in a predominantly Asian environment."

"Listen, it's just a bunch of paper," he again downplayed the danger potential. "Absolutely nothing of significance in our relationship with Him." Frank pointed his finger upward.

"You know what?" Nancy asked suddenly. "I want to drive you to St. Ann's. I'll feel much better, if you don't mind. Plus, I'd like to see the building site." Plus, she wanted to get better acquainted with Monsignor Taylor. Although he was a monsignor, there was something devilishly attractive about the man. She had also heard that Scorpios were interesting in bed.

"I think you're the sweetest lady I've ever met…and the most beautiful." Frank's mind was reeling in an attempt to come up with a polite, acceptable refusal. Hoping the vault teller was out of earshot, he continued, "If I'd known you 50 years ago, before I started seminary, my life would've been entirely different. Of course, 50 years ago your father was about five years old." Frank chuckled. Finally, the right answer clicked into place. "I've got a rental car parked down the street. The rental fee's hefty enough. I don't want a parking ticket on top of it. Thank you very much though, Nancy. It was a good thought." He signaled a low-five from his waist, and backed out of the cubicle. "Drive over Saturday for the ceremony. It's at 10 a.m. sharp."

"I just might do that, Monsignor. You be very careful. Can't you phone me from the church *after* you disburse the money? I'll feel better."

Frank knew what would make her feel even better, but…"I'll send you a postcard from La Jolla. Bye, Nancy." He started to embrace her, but didn't want to press his luck with regard to keeping his mustache perfectly straight. Plus, he was on the verge of an erection. "Thanks again for all your help…and the money."

She watched him put on his pith hat as he exited the front doors, knowing there was something decidedly special about the man. There was no doubt whatsoever where she'd be at 10 a.m. Saturday. She was extremely disappointed that she missed driving him to St. Ann's, and the gleam in her eye suggested the possibility she had priest seduction on her mind. Suddenly, a mixture of both shame and amusement came over her as she mentally noted the word *pedophilia* popped into her mind when she first looked up and saw Monsignor Taylor approaching her desk.

CHAPTER 18

Frank didn't have far to go. Turning left after his exit from the bank, he stopped an attractive, fashionably dressed woman in her mid-40s, more than likely of Chinese lineage, walking toward him.

"Pardon me, but could you tell me if there's a nice department store in the area?"

"Yes, of course, Father." Looking in the direction from which she came, "Just go one block in that direction, then turn right, and about two and a half blocks on the left is Liberty House. They have excellent merchandise. I know you'll like it."

"Thank you. Liberty House. Very appropriate."

"Where're you from, Father?" Her question represented congenial small talk more than inquisitiveness.

"Here we go again," Frank thought. "Nova Scotia," he shot back.

"Oooh, chilly place, huh?" Her smile was engaging, and she feigned shivering.

"Actually…" On closer inspection, he now became aware of her sex appeal, especially her nipples showing through a sheer blouse, and playfully responded, "more like tamales."

Her face froze for a second while she construed the semantic connection between her chilly and his tamales. Then she burst into laughter after realizing he'd comically inferred that her chilly had been the Mexican chili that one eats. "You're very funny."

"It's more fun that way."

"I'm Catholic too," still grinning with charm.

"Really? Well...I just retired. I'm not available for confession." Frank moved past her, backing away, en route to Liberty House.

Another hearty laugh. "You have to visit my church. Our pastor's not very funny."

"Tell him you're broke. That'll get a laugh."

She giggled this time.

"What parish are you from?" Frank inquired.

"St. Ann's."

"In Kaneohe, right?"

"Oh," surprised, with a cute smile, "you've heard of it?"

"Of course. I'm not senile...yet."

A glow came over her face. "Listen, you look...healthy...very strong."

Frank identified that familiar gleam in her eyes, the one he'd seen on numerous occasions from an endless variety of sexually hungry females. "You married?" He expected that question to startle her...or physically arouse her. Possibly both.

The subtle curl of her lips revealed her inner feelings, and Frank instantly recognized that she was an eager candidate for bedding. "I'm a widow."

Unable to turn down a provocative game, "Which Mass do you attend?"

"The 10 a.m., Sundays." The gleam turned into an invitation. "I'll be there this Sunday."

"Maybe I'll come incognito, wearing a Hawaiian shirt." He lifted the pith hat from his head, revealing his hair. "Would you recognize me?" Then he replaced it.

"Easily. You'll be the most...attractive man in church."

Her eyes filled in the pause before attractive with the word, *sexually*. "Hey, talk about incentive...maybe I'll confess you, after all." Frank had read about certain women whose top priority was to seduce a priest. Strangely, according to what he'd read, most of the women were devout Catholics.

"You'd probably be disappointed." The gleam intensified. "I'm...a very nice lady."

Frank remembered that some of the best fucks he'd ever had were with self-proclaimed, "very nice" ladies. "Hey, nothing disappointing about that. And, incidentally, I already knew you're a nice lady...and...extremely beautiful."

At that precise moment, the woman confessed to herself that she was carnally attracted to Frank. "Thank you. What's your name, Father?"

It was testing time, and Frank couldn't resist...with his straightest face. "Boris Freidhofer...and I'm not, and never have been, a pedophile."

After a highly analytical pause with a completely blank face, she began laughing...quietly but uncontrollably. Using the same approach as with Katherine, and an interminable roster before her, Frank maintained his straight countenance and permitted the beautiful lady of Chinese descent to regain her composure. Several passers-by took notice of her gleeful public display and facially expressed their delight.

"I'm so sorry, Father. This is embarrassing," she admitted.

"You don't like my name?" The next step always was to squeeze a little shame out of the woman by challenging her, then to watch her squirm in an attempt to verbally weasel out of it. Frank, however, suddenly realized the $100,000 in his briefcase could turn into a bitter memory if he didn't get his ass in gear.

"No, no, no, that's not it," she insisted. "It's just that..." gesturing cheerfully with her hands, "the name doesn't...somehow, go with your face...or personality. I guess I shouldn't say that, but I'm a very candid person."

Frank wondered if she was candid enough to admit she wanted to screw him. "Perhaps subconsciously that's why I became a priest." Seeking swift closure, Frank politely lied, as usual, and let her off the hook. "It's only a joke. My name's Tom Walker. It's been a pleasure talking with you, Mrs...what's yours?"

"Mimi...Mimi Ching."

"I love it." He lied again. "Nice name. What's your maiden name?"

"Chung."

"Chung to Ching. Only a one-letter difference," he pointed out. "Alphabetically backwards, but...no matter," shrugging his shoulders.

"Yes, I kept my same initials."

"No relation to Connie?" Frank inquired.

"No...none at all," she replied pleasantly. "I like her very much."

Frank took two steps back toward Fort Street Mall. "Thanks again for your assistance, Mimi. I'll try to make it Sunday, but if not, perhaps some other time. Sorry to run off, but I have some urgent shopping to do. Goodbye."

"Goodbye, Father Walker. I'll look forward to seeing you Sunday."

Frank turned away in disappointment, knowing that, minutes apart, he had permitted two legitimate sure-bet lays to slip away. "And goddammit, they're both Asian—my favorite fuck." Then he thought about Katherine, and the possibility of changing his racial preference. He remembered Katherine's quote from the black comedian and smiled approvingly. "Maybe the bastard was right."

He followed Mimi's directions and found Liberty House with no difficulty. Just as she'd said, it was a very nice store. He was impressed. First on his list of immediate objectives was to transfer sufficient soft currency from his briefcase to the clothes he wore—without being seen—so he wouldn't have to open the briefcase again until he arrived at his garage apartment in La Jolla. In

Men's Clothing, he picked out three pairs of cargo pants, the kind sporting large pockets with Velcro fasteners on each side of the legs.

He knew his size, but purposely went to a fitting room so he could switch the money in privacy. Inside the closed cubicle, he quickly but unobtrusively looked for hidden surveillance cameras. He saw none. After hanging the pants on a clothing hook, he placed the briefcase on a built-in bench and opened it. The sight of all that valuable green paper still fascinated him. He put his wallet next to the briefcase.

According to plan, he took ten $100 bills from a pack, placed them in his wallet, and then put the remaining 90 bills in the left inside pocket of the coat he was wearing. He basically did the same with the 20s, putting $200 in his wallet and the rest of the pack in the right inside coat pocket, and repeating the procedure with the 10s, putting the remainder in his front right trouser pocket. He had intended to do the $5 bills too, but saw that his wallet was full and felt he already had enough to pay for clothing, a suitcase, cab fares and the airline ticket to San Diego. If not, he could use the $100 bills in his coat pocket.

Due to heightened security since 9/11, in case his bag should be checked at the airport, he selected some socks, underwear, two shirts, and a belt without a metal buckle. When he told the sales clerk he planned to purchase an appropriate piece of luggage for island hopping, she suggested he leave what he'd selected, then bring his choice of luggage back to her counter and pay for it all at once.

Frank picked an inflexible type suitcase, one with hard sides, because he planned to put his briefcase inside of it. He also bought a small lock with a key. If he went through security at the boarding gate with his briefcase, he felt sure they'd routinely examine the contents, and that would be the end of his freedom...for the rest of his life. He'd just have to take a chance on his checked luggage not being lost, stolen, or flown to another destination.

Back at Men's Clothing, he went to the same clerk, an elderly Caucasian. He asked her, "Since I'm going directly to the airport, would it be all right—if I keep my sales receipts handy to show at the exit—to remove the sales tags and manufacturers tags here and pack my clothing, so I won't have to do it at the airport?"

"Of course, Father. I'll be glad to help you." She got scissors from a drawer under the counter, and as she rang up each item on the register, she cut the tags free and gave the clothes to Frank, who in turn folded them neatly and placed them in the suitcase. After folding the last pair of undershorts, Frank could see there was still too much empty space in the suitcase. He picked out a plain blue, cotton robe and had the clerk ring it up. As soon as she cut the tags off, Frank wrapped it around his briefcase, put them both into the suitcase, closed it, and locked it. Along with all the tags she had cut, she gave him the total bill. He paid it, and she was nice enough to walk him to the exit.

From this point on, his plans panned out with precision. His first stop inside Honolulu International terminal was the waiting area near Japan Airlines, where he inconspicuously left his pith hat on an empty seat. His need for it was over. He then swiftly walked to the ticket counter at United Airlines, the carrier that reportedly had the most flights from Hawaii to the Mainland. Luckily, he only had to wait 90 minutes for the next departing flight to San Diego. Using his new ID, a passport he'd made in La Jolla with some rather sophisticated computer software, he successfully represented himself to be Antonio Miguel Gonzalez, born in Chihuahua, Mexico. Figuring there were at least 1,000,000 men with that name in Mexico, his intention was to soon become one of them. He began his conversation with the United Airlines sales agent in fluent Spanish, but learned shortly, with no surprise, since she appeared to be of Japanese ancestry, that she didn't speak Spanish. Frank then switched to broken English with a very pronounced Spanish accent, and was able to be understood. Naturally, he paid in cash, and also checked his suitcase for that flight, with the cash-filled briefcase inside. Paying in cash could have been another red flag, but he had no option. His priestly attire, he trusted, would cover that potential suspicion.

Following a quick visit to the restroom, where he gave himself the once-over in the mirror after urinating and washing his hands, he watched the security line for the passengers boarding his particular flight vary in length. He purposely chose to get in line when there were more waiting passengers, hoping to thereby minimize any difficulties he might have, counting on the potential temporary inattentiveness of stressed-out security personnel. There were no difficulties. He briefly thought of Katherine again, and felt guilty about her discomfort, especially if she had to "pee pee." He sadly recalled their wonderful afternoon at La Jolla Shores Beach.

The flight to San Diego seemed an eternity. He took a cab to the edge of Katherine's property on Prospect. It was dark now, and Frank moved quickly to his car, threw his suitcase in the backseat, and drove to his garage apartment. Once inside, his number one priority was to open his suitcase, then his briefcase, and to confirm that all the green stuff was still there. It was.

Next, he turned on his computer and, after deleting his own images from the Zip disc that Katherine had photographed with his digital camera, he reformatted the hard drive. Knowing he couldn't take the computer with him on the next flight, he realized any savvy agent or detective could recover his stored data, even if he'd deleted all files, including those in the Recycle Bin. Against his better judgment, but because he truly loved her, Frank decided to take the Zip disc on which Katherine's digital photos were still recorded. Her images would be permanently branded on his brain, yet there was nothing like seeing them in living color on a monitor screen…nothing except being next to her and holding her in his arms, but he lamentably accepted the fact that it would never happen. He knew he'd never forget her, that she was indeed someone very special. That she would now hate him for the rest of her life was heavy on Frank's habitually hardened conscience.

Next, he changed into casual clothes, temporarily losing his priest's identity. He would take the sacerdotal garments with him, along with the gold band, just in case he needed them later. The plan now was to neatly stuff all the packets of cash into every available pocket of his cargo pants, in addition to those of the nylon jacket he would wear into Mexico. He also threaded his belt through the loop on the back of the small case that contained his digital camera. After re-packing, he now had two full suitcases, one of them with his empty briefcase inside.

On a piece of scratch paper, he scribbled: "Japan Airlines. LAX. Saturday," and stuck it in his shirt pocket. He then locked his apartment and drove off with his two bags. Within 15 minutes, Frank was in the huge parking lot at the Trolley Station in Old Town. He removed the piece of paper from his shirt pocket and placed it under his seat, where he knew an agent or cop would find it. Leaving his car unlocked and hoping someone would steal it, he walked with his luggage to a payphone about 35 yards away and ordered a cab for the Tijuana Airport, on the other side of the Mexican border, where he would take a plane to Acapulco, Mexico. With a little luck, Antonio Miguel Gonzalez might find a rich, sexually desirable woman there, who will share her wealth with him...whether she wants to or not.

CHAPTER 19

Katherine had several hours of solitude to think about her relationship with Frank Taylor, something her father had urged her to do on two or three occasions. She retraced her dialogue with Frank over and over, attempting somehow to salvage her self-respect and, if nothing else, pinpoint her stupidity so she would never make this mistake again. At the end of each torturous review she would come to the same conclusion: There had been absolutely nothing in his behavior or his words that would even remotely suggest this could happen. There were only pluses...not one minus. She could only see his sensitive face...and feel his arms wrapped passionately around her...and that marvelous part of his body deep inside of her. She knew that, although she would undoubtedly despise him for the remainder of her life, she would also love him forever for what he could have been. She would never stop loving the person she sincerely believed he was. And then she cried like a baby. She pleaded for God to explain why this could happen to her. They were basically the same pleas she had made when she found out about Andy, the same as when she learned her mother had left her father, the same pleas she had made the previous year on 9/11 when thousands of innocent people lost their lives.

Katherine knew there would be no answer, no explanation from her spiritual father. She knew the answer had to come from within her being. The answer was in the form of faith. So Katherine began to pray, not by asking God for help, but by thanking him for all her blessings. She convinced herself, and verbally expressed it to God, that all this happened for a good reason, a reason that someday He would make clear to her.

Then suddenly, with the same determination Katherine called upon to learn the piano, the French language, and certain sports—perhaps aided by the need to urinate—she made up her mind that, no matter what happened, even if she died doing it, she was going to escape from this closet and bungalow. She had no idea what time it was, but she made a decision not to wait until 2 p.m. the next day for the housekeeper to find her bound and gagged.

Unable to budge her chair backward or forward, she started rocking aggressively from side to side, putting the pressure of her weight on the rope that tied her chair to the hanging rod in the closet. In one final lunge away from the rod, her chair toppled, due to her body weight on the rope, breaking the rod from its placement, causing it to fall to the carpeted floor where one end of the smooth metallic cylinder slipped through the knotted rope. Katherine, firmly tied to the chair, fell in the opposite direction, landing heavily on her left shoulder and banging her head on the carpet-covered concrete. Although she felt the sharp pain, it didn't faze her mentally. If anything, it riled her into more intense action, fueling her resolution.

Feeling the carpet next to her facial skin, she instantly scraped the sleep mask briskly against the carpet's pile, freeing it completely from her head. Now she could see, despite the relative absence of light. Fiercely, grunting like an animal, she forced her body to roll sideways, taking the chair with her, thereby focusing the brunt of her pain primarily on her knees, shoulders and head. Katherine steeled herself swiftly and repeated the roll. Near the closet's open entrance now, she had to make adjustments because of the door's width. Straining to raise her head, she could distinguish in the extraneous light the vague outline of the table where the phone was, and that alone gave her psychological impetus to inch her body forward in snake-like fashion. If football is a game of inches, then Katherine's plight was an exercise in centimeters, but slowly and surely she appeared to be winning.

The inability to roll her body, with the chair tied onto it, through the open closet door lengthened her ordeal considerably. Her reptilian, headfirst thrusts through the closet exit took another 15 minutes. Once she cleared the threshold, the rigorous rolling motions were resumed and, within moments, Katherine was at the base of the telephone table, exhausted and in pain, but knowing the end of her confinement was in sight.

At this point, she simply rammed her body against the nearest table leg with as much force as she could muster. Her first effort proved successful, and the phone's receiver, along with its base, fell to the floor two feet from her head. The ringing at the other end was clearly audible as Katherine frantically wriggled closer.

The third ring was interrupted by a woman's voice. "Good evening, this is Alice at the front desk. How may I help you?"

Fortunately, the transmitter was angled toward Katherine's face, and although the duct tape covered her mouth securely, it wasn't soundproof; therefore she gamely attempted to convey her predicament to the desk clerk in muffled, unintelligible exclamations.

"I'm sorry, is this Ms. Churchill? I can't understand you. Maybe there's something wrong with your phone. We have a note not to disturb you, as per Mr. Churchill's request."

As loud as the tape permitted, Katherine exploded with, "Uh-huh, uh-huh, uh-huh."

"Oh, my," replied the clerk, her voice reflecting alarm, "it sounds like you're agreeing with me—that I should not disturb you."

Just as loud, but more emphatically, Katherine responded, "Uh-uh, uh-uh, uh-uh."

"Oh, you want me to disturb you, right?"

Even louder, "Uh-huh, uh-huh, uh-huh."

"All right, I'll send a bellman. Maybe he can find out what the problem is."

"Uh-huh, uh-huh."

In less than 60 seconds, there was a firm knock on the bungalow door.

Again Katherine tried her best to scream, "Come in, come in," but no one at the entrance door could have heard her, much less understood her.

The knock was repeated, and Katherine replied even louder. The sound of what must have been a master key was heard in the door lock, the door opened, and the ceiling light went on. A cute teenage male of Asian descent, in a bellman's uniform, entered the living room. Katherine continued her stifled appeal for help. The bellman heard it, and moved cautiously toward the open bedroom door. As soon as he turned on the bedroom's overhead light he spotted Katherine on the floor.

His handsome boyish face was right out of a TV commercial. Immediately recognizing the seriousness of Katherine's situation, he jumped backward a step or two and glanced around the room, expecting to find the villain ready to pounce on him.

"Oh, wow. Let me get security."

"No, no, no," Katherine struggled to express, shaking her head exaggeratedly. "Help me, untie me," she ineffectively communicated.

The closer he moved toward Katherine, the more aware he became of her shapely legs and ample breasts. Instinctively, he started removing the duct tape from her mouth, if for no other reason than to touch her physically attractive body.

When her lips had been uncovered, "Oh, thank you so much. Hold the phone next to my mouth." He did. "Alice, are you there?"

"Yes, Ms. Churchill, are you okay?"

"I'm fine, Alice. I just had a little accident. The bellman is helping me. I'll send him back to you in a few minutes, all right? Thanks for helping me. Bye." Without waiting for Alice's reply, she looked at the bellman and whispered, "Hang it up, please." He did. "Okay, untie me, sweetie, and listen to me very carefully while you're doing it." He started. "What's your name?"

"Hank."

"Hank what?"

"Tatsuhara. It's Henry Tatsuhara, but..." he was clearly distracted by the sight of her prominent nipples showing through the material of her blouse, "everybody calls me Hank."

"Hank, hurry up and untie me. I'm about to pee in my pants—and you don't want to be around when that happens—but listen, this is between you and me. I'll give you a $100 tip, but you've got to promise me you won't tell *anybody* about this. My boyfriend and I had a big fuss, and he really tripped out on me. This is his idea of a joke, but I don't think it's funny at all. He's hoping I'll report the whole thing, and that it will get into the news media. He'd love that. But that's what the $100 tip is for, to keep your mouth shut, okay? Will you do it?"

"Oh, sure." Hank had freed her hands, and was looking forward to doing her ankles so he could get a closer look at those extraordinary legs, and see if she was wearing a thong. "It's nobody else's business. Don't worry about it. He didn't beat you up though, did he?"

"Hell no. He didn't touch me. I probably got a little bruised from rolling on the floor, tied to that chair. Look at my face. It's fine, isn't it?"

Breaking into a great smile as he studied it, "It's beautiful. You're a beautiful woman." Hank couldn't help looking once more at her lovely breasts. All the ropes were now untied.

"Aw thanks, Hank. You're a doll." She stood slowly, getting the kinks out of her back. "I gotta pee, Hank. Wait for me. I'll be right back."

She moved gingerly toward the bathroom, testing her legs. She noticed Frank's open suitcase on the bed. Seconds after the door shut, the sound of her urinating was more like that of a horse rather than a beautiful woman. Hank grimaced. He heard the toilet flush, followed by the running water as Katherine washed her hands. Seconds later, she left the bathroom and headed toward her open purse on the bed.

She removed her wallet, opened it, then looked carefully for something she evidently was unable to find. "Shit! I cannot believe this. That son of a bitch."

"What happened?" Hank asked.

"That bastard took most of my cash. Fortunately, he didn't take my credit cards." Throwing her wallet on the bed next to her purse and turning to Hank, "Listen, Hank, I'm not a flake. I know I'm looking and acting like one right now but, believe me, I'm a decent person who has a few bucks, so you're gonna get your tip that I promised you. When I check out—which is gonna be very soon—by the way, what time is it?"

Checking his watch, "It's 10:39."

"Jesus, no wonder I had to pee. Is there a hotel near the airport?"

"Yes, there're two directly in front…Honolulu Airport Hotel and the Best Western-Plaza Hotel."

"Oh, hell, that's great. Okay, this is what we're gonna do, Hank." She picked up her wallet again and removed her American Express card. "Take this to Alice and have her check me out. I don't give a shit if she charges me for all of next week—that's not important. The main thing is, I've gotta get the hell out of here quick. There's some damage I did inside the closet. Tell Alice that can also be charged to this credit card number when they determine how much it is. Just be reasonable, don't charge me for remodeling the whole goddamned bungalow, okay? She can verify easily enough that I have a $25,000 limit on my card, so there's no big deal. Tell her I want $500 cash back after my room bill is paid. I'll give you the 100 bucks from that—don't tell her that though. I'm gonna get ready fast—I'll gather all this rope and tape, and throw it in the trash. There's more in the closet."

Hank promptly jammed her credit card into his pocket, and immediately started picking up the pieces of rope and tape.

"Oh, thank you, sweetie. Please don't tell her about any of this. It's our little secret, okay?"

"No problem," Hank agreed, checking out her ass.

"Ask her to order a cab for me to the airport. I'll be ready in 20 minutes. I doubt I can get a flight out tonight, but you never know. If not, I'll stay in one of the hotels you mentioned."

Hank had already picked up a trash can and had it 80% filled with rope and tape. "I'll throw this in the Dumpster out back, and leave the can at your door on my way to the office. Then I'll go over everything with Alice. We'll get your cab. Is there anything else, Ms. Churchill?"

"No, Hank, except that you're an absolute doll. You a student?"

"Yes…at the university."

"What are you studying?"

"I'm in pre-law…poly-sci major."

"Terrific. Where're you going to law school?"

"I want to go to Duke…if I can swing it."

"Really?" The school name gave her a queasy feeling.

"My uncle practices law in Memphis. He's trying to help me."

Katherine tried to control her reaction, but it was difficult. "I'm sure you'll succeed, Hank. You'll make a fine attorney. Thank you so much for your assistance. Tell Alice I'll be right out. And one last thing, Hank…after I leave, please take *his* suitcase," pointing to it on the bed, "and anything else you can find in the room that belongs to the son of a bitch—check the dresser drawers, etc.—and throw it all in the Dumpster too."

"Will do," he lied. He'd put it in Lost and Found in case the guy comes back later. That could mean another fat tip. "Thank you, Ms. Churchill. Just call the front desk when you're ready, and I'll help you with your luggage."

"Okay, Hank."

She watched him go through the living room and out the entrance door. Then she turned and swiftly walked to the wall safe, which was slightly ajar. She opened it completely and saw, as she expected, that it was empty. "Fucking goddamned thief! And I was in love with the turd."

Turning again and looking at herself in the bedroom mirror, she queried aloud sardonically. "Duke and Memphis in almost the same breath? Shit! I think the White Lady's after my ass." Temporarily forgetting her emotions, Katherine then monitored herself physiologically. "Jesus, I'm constipated." She walked closer to the mirror and looked into her own eyes. "Yeah, sure, you know who's to blame for all this crap, don't you?" Pointing an index finger at her image in the mirror, "You, you dumb fuckin' broad. When are you gonna wise up, Shithead? How in the hell are you possibly gonna explain all this crap to Rocky?"

CHAPTER 20

There were two strange cars in front of her home when Dan of Jewel Transit brought Katherine from the airport. Relieved that she hadn't stopped to pick up Rocky on the way, she was nevertheless concerned, especially when she noticed that one of the cars had what looked like a government license, and the other appeared to be a rental car. The fact that Frank's car wasn't there told her he'd preceded her. The only surprise was that he would come anywhere near her home after what he'd done.

Dan put her two bags by the entrance, and Katherine paid him. Purposely waiting until he left, she approached her front door, with all her psychic antennae clearly announcing her father's presence.

"That could explain the rental car. I didn't mention on his answering machine that I was flying out of San Diego, so maybe he thought I'd used my car. The government car would probably belong to an FBI agent or a detective from the San Diego Police," she surmised. Choosing not to walk in and rudely interrupt them, even though it was her house, and especially if they were burglars, she decided to ring the doorbell, giving them a chance, if they were unlawful intruders, "to get their asses out of her home." The absence of Rocky's whine seemed unreal. After waiting for what Katherine thought was too long a period, she was about to insert her key when the door opened. It was her father. Othello's face reflected a combination of distress and deliverance. Of course, the sight of her father was comforting to Katherine, rather than looking into the face of a criminal intruder.

"My God, Katherine, you're okay." He hugged her more affectionately than she could ever remember. Over her father's shoulder, she saw a diminutive, gray-haired man several feet away. Her father pulled back from her and looked deeply into her eyes. "You *are* okay, aren't you?"

Katherine began crying. She embraced her father again, clinging to him like an eight-year-old who'd been lost at Disneyland.

"I'm so happy to see you, Baby." Othello was crying too. "I was worried sick. Did he hurt you?"

Unable to speak yet, Katherine uttered her best, "Uh-uh."

"Do you know where he is?" Dr. Churchill ventured.

"No…It's all over, Dad. You were right about everything." She resumed crying.

"Easy now. Try to calm down. I want to introduce to someone." Her father turned toward the man behind him. "Katherine, this is Inspector Hodges of the FBI. He said to call him Al."

Katherine extended her right hand. "How do you do, sir? Sorry about the emotional display."

He shook her hand. "Quite all right, Katherine. I understand."

Dr. Churchill picked up Katherine's bags. "Let's go into the living room. Al has a lot of information on Frank Taylor, but he needs more, and thinks you might be able to help him."

Katherine, a bit confused about why Frank was the subject, shut the door after her father entered. He put the bags on the floor nearby, and they all went into the living room area where the gray-haired man sat at the end of the sofa. On the table next to him there were several sheets of paper in a stack.

"Why don't you sit next to Al, Katherine. He'll want to show you some of that stuff on the table."

She sat on the cushion next to the man, and her father sat in the stuffed chair that faced them. The man was very soft-spoken. He started the conversation.

Looking at Katherine, "You just arrived from Hawaii?"

She was visibly taken by surprise, and glanced at her father first, then back at the man. "How did you know I was in Hawaii?" Trying to make light of it, she tacked a comic inflection on the end of her question.

Hodges answered, "The man you were with—you know him as Frank Taylor—he has about 35 aliases—was seen yesterday walking on Kalakaua Avenue with a woman who fits your description. The lady who saw both of you from a tour bus, and immediately reported it to the FBI, is the sister of his most recent murder victim. Do you know where he is?"

From the beginning of Hodges's statement to the end, Katherine's expression went from surprise to horror. To her father, "No." She then turned to the man in utter astonishment. "You're telling me that Frank Taylor…murdered someone?"

He gave her a sheet of paper from the stack. "This is a copy of a composite sketch by a forensic artist in Honolulu, created with help from the lady who reportedly saw him."

Katherine's hands were slightly trembling as she held the paper and carefully studied the artist's representation. The resemblance to Frank was remarkable. "The woman who saw us, did she say what time it was?"

"Before noon…Hawaiian time."

"Did she notice if Frank saw her?" Katherine remembered that, after they turned off Kalakaua onto Lewers, Frank started walking faster, and she even teased him about it, thinking he was in a hurry to fuck her.

"She said he definitely saw her. There's some…" Inspector Hodges continued, "rather conclusive evidence connecting him with eight homicides…all wealthy, attractive women. Your father tells me this sketch looks a lot like the man you know as Frank Taylor."

She dropped the paper on the agent's lap and covered her face with her hands. "Jesus, this is a nightmare." She resumed crying.

"Take it easy, Baby. I know how you must feel." Her father's empathy was stronger and more sincere than Katherine could possibly know at this point.

"You're very lucky to be alive, Katherine," Hodges added. "This man's mentally sick and quite dangerous. He's also extremely intelligent…cunning, I suppose, is the right word, like a fox. We've been after him for years, but we don't have any photographs of him—none that were taken in the last 25 years. Although we have no fingerprints of his, we do have DNA samples, but that doesn't apprehend him…it only helps identify him and strengthens the specific evidence we have against him."

Lifting her tearful face, "Who is this bastard? He sure as hell isn't a Catholic priest. He told me he grew up in Memphis, Tennessee…that his mother was a prostitute—"

"Excuse me, Katherine," Hodges apologized. "Would you mind if I turn on my recorder?" He pulled a small Olympus recorder out of his coat pocket. "Some of what you know could be instrumental in capturing this man, and without the assistance of people like you, we'll never catch him."

"Go ahead. Flip it on. I might get very profane though."

He did, and held it between them.

"Told me he grew up in Memphis," she repeated, "and was raised in a brothel where his mother was a whore."

"That's fabrication," Hodges inserted. "We have factual information on his childhood. He came to Memphis with his parents when he was 10 years old…from Torreon, Mexico."

"What?" Katherine was astounded.

"He was born there in Mexico. His father was actually from Helsinki, Finland, and somehow migrated to Torreon where he became employed at the Cook Cotton Company, which was headquartered in Memphis. His mother was Mexican, and *his* real name is Erik—with a K—Kukka…with three Ks and a U."

"Oh, my God." Katherine listened open-mouthed. "Sounds like one of the names he would make up."

"He made up a lot of names, believe me, but this one's real. His father was transferred to Memphis when Erik was 10. His mother, by the way, according to our data, was a very nice lady…and quite religious…Catholic, naturally. Erik was an only child.

"He grew up speaking Spanish and Finnish. Then when they moved to Memphis he learned English. Went to Bellevue Junior High School and—"

"Memphis Tech High School," Katherine filled in without missing a beat.

"He told you about Memphis Technical High School, right?" Hodges smiled, glad to see that Katherine was recovering.

"Oh, yes. Played basketball. His nickname was Phoxy, with a PH." She rattled it off humorously. "In the 10th grade they got kicked out of the league for some harebrained violation the coach committed. His teammate, Jack McRae, urinated in the Superintendent of City School's face, and they were reinstated and went on to—"

"Hold it. Wait a minute." Hodges, laughing, waved her off. "He played basketball, and his nickname was Phoxy. And they *were* kicked out of the league, but what you said Jack McRae did, and the reinstatement…" he shook his head. "that's all fiction."

"Fiction?" Katherine was stunned. "You mean Tech High School didn't win the Tennessee State Basketball Championship?"

"Not Memphis Tech," he clarified. "They were kicked out…and didn't play until the next season. Erik did play then. And Jack McRae…well, according to our files, he and Erik weren't acquainted until the late 60's in Quito, Ecuador."

"Quito, Ecuador?" Katherine repeated. "Unbelievable! This is getting out of hand." She looked at her father, who was a very quiet

Othello. Then back at Hodges, with a rapid verbal delivery, "What about Jack McRae in Boot Camp here in San Diego, and in Korea on the battleship New Jersey?...as a photographer? And as a student at Duke University? Maybe you just don't know about that."

"That wasn't Jack McRae." He cleared his throat. "That was Erik Kukka," Hodges assured her. "He was in the navy here...a photographer on the New Jersey. He also went to Duke University."

"Oh, no, this is too much." Katherine shook her head slowly. "I can't believe this. The man's a real nutso." Then it occurred to her, "What about Jack McRae getting into a fight with...oh, hell, I can't remember these names. Anyway, it was at a Christmas party in Illinois. Jack was visiting his Duke girlfriend, and he and the girl's hometown boyfriend got into a fight, and Jack killed him and was sent to prison...where he is now. Don't tell me that was Frank." She stopped cold and looked at Hodges for a reaction.

He shook his head. "Don't know anything about that. Maybe this is a homicide that hasn't been reported."

Katherine stood quickly and crisply enunciated each word. "You mean Jack McRae isn't in prison?"

Hodges cleared his throat again. "Jack McRae was murdered in Quito...sometime before 1970, and it's from that point on that our biographical info on Erik rapidly deteriorates."

Dr. Churchill never took his eyes off Katherine. He'd made a promise to himself that he'd never say "I told you so" to her. He knew the conversation at this stage was primarily between his daughter and Hodges, but later, when information of which Katherine was now unaware was presented, his presence would be appreciated.

"Well, was...hell, I can't call him Erik. I know him as Frank. Was *Frank*...Honorman of his company in Navy Boot Camp?"

"Yes."

"Did he receive a Letter of Commendation from the Chief of Naval...something or other?"

"Operations, yes."

Placing her hands on her hips, and in rapid fire, "What about the Japanese girlfriend in Hawaii? Was..."

"That was Erik...or Frank."

"Why that...son of a bitch. No wonder he...and he told me he'd never been to Hawaii. And he went to Duke. That bastard! I questioned how he could remember all that crap. The old salt, yeah...shit...and Jean. So, he's the no-good asshole who left her—oh, I'm sorry—I forgot about the tape. I don't normally talk this way...but I'm very upset. No wonder...it was *him*. He told me he graduated from Loyola and Fordham. Now, wait a minute. If he didn't kill the girl's boyfriend, what happened then? Did he get booted out of Duke for promiscuity...probably screwed the school president's daughter, huh?"

"No, matter of fact, Erik was president of the campus theater group, the Duke Players, and actually graduated in three years...instead of the usual four. Was on the Dean's List his senior, or third, year. Then he went to the Pasadena Playhouse in California on the last year of his GI Bill. While there, he won a scholarship as the outstanding actor in his first-year class and graduated with honors."

"Pasadena Playhouse!" She twisted and strode three paces toward the windows, then stopped abruptly and about-faced. "He's a pretty damned good actor—I'll tell you that. If they ever made a movie, he could play the hell out of his own character...except for his age."

"I'd say he's practiced and perfected his craft over the years." Hodges suggested a smile. "Dustin Hoffman was in the class ahead of Erik at the Playhouse, and Gene Hackman left the year before Erik got there. A well-known actor of Japanese ancestry—I can't recall his name at the moment—was Erik's classmate. In an interview, this actor told us Erik was just a regular guy, that he played a lot of table tennis with him and, when Erik's car was stolen, he loaned him his. They were also in two or three plays together. Evidently Erik wasn't good enough, or lucky enough, to find work in that field after he graduated from the Playhouse, so he took a job with Bank of America and stayed with them for about seven years. Ended up in international banking and was sent to Quito. That's where the problems started and, shortly thereafter, his bio fades."

"What kind of problems?" She sat again.

"That's where he met Jack McRae. We don't know exactly how. McRae was a civil engineer who worked for a road construction company. He and Erik formed a verbal partnership and bought a couple of taverns that featured topless dancers. This was against the bank's policy…as well as the construction company's. The taverns were financially successful though, and that led to a string of brothels and, based on the info we've gathered, the guys made a huge bundle of money, which in turn led to the cultivation of poppies and the production of heroin—plus marijuana. Sometime near the end of 1969, Jack McRae was found in a dark alley with his throat cut. No one seems to have seen Erik, or Frank, since, except the women he's murdered, along with Minnie Carlyle, who is the sister of Raquel Yancey, reportedly his latest victim…and you." Glancing at Katherine's father, Hodges stated, "I'm doing all the talking." Then back at her, "Let me ask you about a couple of things. Did you take any photos of Frank on your trip?"

Katherine leaned back in the sofa. "No, I don't even have a camera. One day at the Cove, here in La Jolla, we took pictures of each other with his little digital camera."

"I'm sure he's got that…plus the pictures. What about his car? Your dad said he had one."

"Yeah, it was parked next to mine out front when we left here for Hawaii. It's not there now."

"Did you come back from Hawaii together?"

"No way. We split over there."

"Well, I'd appreciate it if you'd tell me basically what happened…in Honolulu."

Katherine traded looks with her father, then tried to organize her thoughts. She'd decided earlier not to give the details on being tied up in the closet, or even mention the $100,000 he stole from her. That was her personal business. Only Hank Tatsuhara knew about the closet, and he disposed of Frank's clothes and other stuff that was in his suitcase. Unless she filed a report, Katherine presumed the bank would never know that the money was taken against her will.

"We had a big fight yesterday…verbal, nothing physical. He never laid a hand on me. In fact, he couldn't have been nicer to me. I'm sure my father's told you I was very much in love with him." She almost broke down again when she heard herself say that. "It just ended…with me telling him to get out…to get out of my life. It came to the point where I realized it couldn't possibly work. My father tried to warn me. I didn't listen." She looked at her father. "Sorry, Dad. I know you were trying to help me. I knew it then, but I was also absolutely sure you were dead wrong. Of course, I was the one who was dead wrong. But, at least, I'm not dead. And it sure as hell sounds like I could be."

"It's okay, Baby." Dr. Churchill smiled weakly. "I love you, and I'm so happy you're safe and alive."

"I love you too. I'll always listen to you in the future." Then back to Hodges, "I have no idea when Frank left Honolulu. Apparently, pretty soon after I kicked him out. He packed his bag and left in a huff."

"Where he stayed here in La Jolla…I suppose you know where that is?"

"Of course. It's only a few blocks away…on Bishops Lane, behind the Empress Hotel…a garage apartment."

"You know the address?"

"Aw, gosh, I…never really paid attention…to the numbers. I can take you over there though. I don't have a key, however. We weren't that cozy."

"Okay, later. That's fine. What about his phone number? You know it?"

"Yeah, it's in my book over there," nodding toward the phone table, "and in my phone's memory."

"I'll get it later."

She got up again and faced Hodges. "Is this gonna be all over the news? Am I gonna have to go through all that crap? I think I've experienced enough bullshit."

"Actually, there's no crime connected with you. I don't see any reason why it should be in the news. However, as the investigation progresses, and particularly when we catch him—and we will—we don't have any control over the media or the paparazzi."

"Well, when you find the rotten bastard, why don't you just bring him to me and I'll save the taxpayers a helluva lot of money." Emphatically and wide-eyed, "I'll kill his ass right on the spot...and you can drag it away and throw it in a goddamned Dumpster as far as I'm concerned."

He smiled and turned off the recorder. "That would be a pleasure for me too, Katherine, but unfortunately it isn't permitted. If the rules were up to me, however, I'd bring him over in a heartbeat...maybe even let you use my pistol."

Katherine shook her head again. "This is all very difficult to accept. All this talk he gave me about his friend, Jack McRae, being in prison for 40-some-odd years—that's a bunch of garbage he made up. The man's loony, and I believed him. That really pisses me off. I believed every frigging word he said. You wouldn't believe all the details he went into. Or I should say, you *would* believe it because he told it so...credibly. Hell, I could write a book about Jack McRae now—and he was dead—it wasn't even him—it was Frank, or Erik whatever-the-hell-his-name-is. He rattled off all these hundreds of details. And why would he tell me his mother was a whore, for God's sake?"

"It's a twisted sort of talent," Hodges explained, "that comes only from a sick mind...but a slick mind. He was probably trying to suck you into his sympathy tank...so you'd feel sorry for him...at least subconsciously. You'd think there'd be some rough edges somewhere along the way that would give him away, but apparently he's as sharp as a tack...and quite smooth. According to our psychiatrists, who're experts in dealing with this mental condition, one of the reasons these people are so convincing...is that they completely believe *themselves*...and all the lies they tell. To them, in their diseased way of thinking, it's all the truth...they're not telling lies."

"That must be correct," Katherine agreed. "That would explain it. Oh, he's got a precision mind—no question about it...has an excellent vocabulary."

"He's well-educated. Too bad...he took the wrong route. Probably could've amounted to something." Hodges picked up one of the other pieces of paper and referred to it. "He's passed himself off as a professor, coach, writer, airlines pilot, international businessman, movie producer, newspaper editor, literary agent, computer expert," looking up at Katherine, "which he is, according to some of the bogus IDs he's made and used—and now, a Catholic priest. Only God knows what he's going to be next."

Katherine sprang to her feet and visually bore down on Hodges in a courteous way. "So he made fake IDs...like driver's licenses and things of that nature?"

"Absolutely. That's one of his many talents. Passports included."

Katherine, now smirking, "So that SOB isn't 71 years old, is he? I knew that was a big batch. He didn't fool me." She looked back at Hodges, to get an approval of what she'd said.

Hodges gazed into the living room space and performed some mental arithmetic. "Well...he was born in Torreon, Mexico...on November the 5th of...1930. That would make him 72 this November."

"Shit!" Katherine turned and walked toward the large windows and, in perfect Donald Duck language, said what sounded like, "Son of a bitch."

Hodges looked with puzzlement at her father. "What's that all about?"

Hearing him, Katherine turned back and told him, "Sorry, that's a private joke."

Hodges cleared his throat again and asked, "Where did you stay in Honolulu? Which hotel?"

Visibly upset, Katherine raised her voice and addressed him for the first time with his given name. "Aw, come on, Al, what the hell have you got to know that for? That's history. I want to forget about that experience. Can't we just leave Hawaii out of this?"

"The FBI doesn't leave anything out, Katherine." He gave her a serious look. "You know that. The unit you stayed in probably has a wealth of DNA and, especially, fingerprints. It'll all add up to a positive ID. We need to get an evidence team in there as soon as possible. Give me the name of the place, and I'll call Horikawa at our Honolulu office right away. Then, if you'll take me to his apartment here, I'll get some people over there. And since he's been in here, according to your father, we'll have to look your place over."

"Wait a minute," Katherine aimed the fingers of her right hand at the ceiling, "there's something I don't understand, Al. When this woman's sister saw Frank on the street in Honolulu, she reported it there. Then they phoned you at your office here—"

"No, I work out of D.C. They called me there, and I flew out here. I just got here a few minutes before you arrived."

"What?" Plainly confounded, Katherine slowly walked toward Hodges. "Why did you come to my home. You didn't have any information that connected me with him." Then, training her eyes on her father, "And, Dad, why are you here? This is confusing the hell out of me. There must be something you—"

"Tell her, Al." Dr. Churchill rose and took one of Katherine's hands in his. "She has to know sooner or later, and it might as well be now."

"Know what?" She grabbed her father's shoulder with her free hand. "For God's sake, you're not gonna unload something else on me?"

"Your father's right, Katherine." Hodges stayed on the sofa. "Please sit down and I'll—"

"No, no, no, I want to stand. I don't want to sit. What are you gonna tell me now, that he murdered Rocky?"

"Where is Rocky?" Dr. Churchill asked.

"He's in the kennel, where I always take him when I go out of town. Okay, Dad, what is it I should know sooner or later?" Turning to Hodges, "No, you're gonna tell me, right?"

Hodges brushed his fingers over his right temple. "Frank Taylor—the man you know as Frank Taylor…murdered your mother."

All signs of life seemingly disappeared from Katherine's face. There was no expression there, only a blank. Her body language confirmed what amounted to a temporary emotional death. It was that seconds-long gap that separates the removal of a hand grenade's safety pin from the moment when the time fuse functions and the explosion occurs. In this case, three or four seconds later, the heart-wrenching eruption took place. She buried her face in her father's embrace and bawled unstoppably.

Both men had anticipated as much, and fully understood the outpouring. Her father made no attempt to curtail her outburst, and Hodges waited patiently. Finally, 90 seconds later, Katherine coughed—it sounded more like a choke—and went to the end of the sofa away from Hodges. Reaching into the nearby table cabinet, she removed an open box of Kleenex, sat on the sofa, and wiped her face with facial tissues.

Finally gaining adequate control over her feelings, she asked Hodges, "How do you know Frank killed my mother?"

Her father spoke first. “Katherine, you remember I told you about the guy—the imposter—who was arrested at his wedding rehearsal?” He sat in the chair again. “I’d read an article in the newspaper about it weeks ago. He’d been all over the U.S., fooling people with assumed identities, posing as a college instructor, a pro athlete with a Super Bowl ring, etc. Remember?”

“Yes, Dad.”

“After I read that, I started thinking about your mom…the way she disappeared, even though she left me a note. My business partners didn’t want any tabloid sensationalism disrupting our practice, and you talked me out of it too, as far as reporting it to the police, but my conscience got the best of me. I called the FBI at home and discussed it with the headman—Miller’s his name. He came by the house. We had a long talk. He sent a forensic specialist over, and I gave him several things that belonged to your mom, things I had put in a bag and stuck away…that I hadn’t mentioned to you. Her hairbrush, for example, and the razor she shaved her legs with, toothbrush, comb—a few other things I can’t recall—female stuff. Also, there was clothing…robe, blouses, jackets, shoes—all kinds of stuff—and dental records from Dr. Barksdale. Anyway, he took them with him. Al, you can explain what happened after that better than I.”

Hodges looked compassionately at Katherine. “Are you okay?”

“Tell you the truth, no…and I never will be for the rest of my life.” The solemnity registered on Katherine’s face was of the first magnitude. “I want to know about my mother though. I want to know what happened. She was my mother, and I think I have a right to know.”

“You certainly do, Katherine. There’s no question about that.” Hodges rose, quickly glancing at the paintings on the opposite wall, and walked two paces beyond Katherine, then turned back to face her. “But, because you’re her daughter, you have to realize that talking to you about her death is rather difficult for me. I’m with the

FBI, but I'm also a human being who had a mother and father, and who has a wife, three daughters, and one son. I'm not a robot. I'm Alvin Hodges, the guy who happens to be in charge of the case against Erik Kukka." He fleetingly admired the impressive seascape through the large windows.

"Just throw the facts at me, Al," requested Katherine, "I think I can handle them now...please."

"The Bureau has a vast computer database that contains both fingerprint and DNA records. We also have intelligence files with biographical data on selected criminals, ones like Erik Kukka, with their particular MOs and skills. It appears that your mother, like Erik, never had her fingerprints recorded. At least, they were not in our system. And, of course, that's not unusual for a person in her age category who has never worked for the government or been in trouble.

"At any rate," he slowly paced back and forth in front of Katherine as he spoke and thought, "when your mother's body was found—"

"When was that?" Katherine immediately asked.

"Nearly five years ago...not too long after she left your father."

"Where?"

"Sanibel Island."

"Sanibel Island? Where the hell is that...the other side of the world?"

"Gulf of Mexico, just off the coast of Florida...near the Cape Coral/Fort Myers Beach area. There's a bridge going over there, so it's pretty accessible."

"What was she doing down there? I'll bet she'd never heard of the place."

"Only Frank Taylor could answer that."

"How was she killed?" Katherine still wasn't ready to accept that Frank had done it.

"Strangled. She was found in some bushes on the side of the road...wearing only an unlabeled negligée. He'd taken her life elsewhere and dumped her body there. The label had been cut off."

Visibly shaken, Katherine fought back her tears and raised her voice, as if challenging Inspector Hodges, "How do you know Frank did it?"

"There wasn't any doubt about that. Forensics found his skin cells under her fingernails...where she'd scratched him, trying to fight him off. The DNA was a perfect link up with his previous samples on file. We knew it was him. We just didn't know who your mother was. Your father hadn't filed any missing-person report, so..." shrugging his shoulders. "But we saved samples of everything, and filed them away...some of her hair, for example...some blood, some skin cells, and so forth...and her fingerprints, for which there were no matches in our database. When your dad finally called our office in Indianapolis and they collected some of her personal things, it was just a matter of time until we fed everything into our database and watched the match-ups connect."

Dr. Churchill sat next to Katherine on the sofa and took her hand in his. "Al phoned me in the early evening yesterday—right after I got home from work—and went over everything with me. When he told me the guy's age, I got a chill—the red flag really jumped out. Then he started telling me how intelligent and crafty the guy is, and while we were talking, he received the all-points bulletin from Hawaii with the sketch. I told him about the message you left me on your answering machine and about the guy you'd just met—which was the main reason I had called the FBI in the first place. He quickly reasoned that the guy had known about you and your financial status from your mother, and had put you on his future agenda. He faxed me the sketch that was made in Hawaii. I looked at it...and almost died on the spot." He hugged her ferociously, sobbing like a kid.

Katherine kissed him on the cheek, looked at Hodges, and spit her words out, "We stayed at the Halekulani in Waikiki." Then pointing toward the bookcase, "I know he picked up one of the Thomas Hardy novels in the bookcase, and he also picked up that frame with the photo of my parents and me. He touched a lot of other stuff in here too. So you're gonna get your fingerprints. When you're ready, I'll take you to his apartment." Now she was angry. "Let's catch the bastard. I don't want him killing someone else. He needs to be put away…forever."

"I'll put round-the-clock surveillance on you, Katherine, until we have a better feel for what's going on," said Hodges. "We're not sure the guy's out of the area. Probably is…probably halfway around the world by now…but I don't want to take any chances." Then Hodges fixed his eyes steadily on Katherine's. "The really puzzling part for me is…why the guy didn't kill you? I suppose it's because he didn't manage to get the large sum of money from you that he got from the others. But even so, based on his usual method, he would have taken your life to make sure you couldn't identify him." For the first time then, Hodges carefully studied the attractive women before him, analytically evaluating her gorgeous face, her hands, hair, shapely legs…breasts. He didn't overlook anything. "On the other hand, Katherine, maybe the guy was actually in love with you, and decided he wanted you to live…regardless of what happened to him. When we catch him—if we don't kill him doing it—maybe he'll answer that question for us. It's something I'd like to know. And I'm sure you would too."

Dr. Churchill asked Katherine, "I'd like to stay here for a few days, Katherine, if it's all right?"

"You know it is, Dad." She embraced her father warmly. "Poor mom. She didn't know what she was doing, Dad. Please forgive her." Katherine was lying and she knew it. There was no question in her mind that her mother had known exactly what she was doing…and had been having the time of her life…getting the best fucking she'd ever had…until Frank killed her. Katherine was an authority on that subject.

CHAPTER 21

Four Months Later—Acapulco, Mexico

The view from their private cottage at *Las Brisas* was spectacular. Most of the city and the bay were clearly visible through the large bedroom window. The couple, however, apparently had no interest in scenery at the moment. On the spacious bed, both completely nude, their close bodies a stark contrast in skin pigmentation, they conversed in a relaxed fashion about something obviously mutually attractive.

The blonde female laughed loudly. "I swear ta God, Greg, that's exactly the way it happened. I woke up that mornin', and there he wuz, rat there next to me in bed…dead as hell." Her accent was thick, and suggested a connection with the southern part of the United States. "I'd never been in bed with a dead man before, so I tell ya rat now, I wuz scared shitless." Another big laugh. She jumped out of bed quickly, sweeping her long blonde hair back over her shoulders with both hands. Her skin was extremely fair. "I'm gonna turn up the air, honey. Gittin' kinda warm in here. I'm sweatin' ma ass off. You don' wont me ta sweat all over ya while you're fuckin' me."

The wall thermostat was only a few feet away. The dark-skinned man, appearing to be Mexican and sporting a dense mustache in a deep shade of brown, raised up enough to watch the provocative movements of her ass and breasts as she fulfilled her objective.

After resetting the thermostat, she playfully twisted her naked body toward his gaze, hands on her hips. "Ya like me like this?"

Looking at the diamond affixed to her bellybutton, he smiled, "*Me encanta, mi amor. Tu belleza es maravillosa.*"

She pranced back to the bed, rolled onto it, and cuddled next to him, her face within inches of his. "Aw, come on now, don' talk that Mexican shit ta me. I don' know wut the hell ya mean." She flashed a breathtaking smile, focusing her liquid blue eyes on his.

"You absolutely enchant me," he clarified. "Your beauty is…astonishing." Curling his leg over her hip, he rubbed his hand against one of her nipples and French kissed her passionately. Then, "I am completely captivated by you." His Spanish accent was heavy. His dark hair was rather long.

The girl stared for a moment into his greenish brown eyes, which were accentuated by his dark skin. "Me too, honey. You rilly turn me on. I jes' love the way ya fuck me."

"Tell me what happened then," he asked.

"Well, hell, I'd only been married to 'im fer seven months. I had ta go thooh all that legal bullshit. One good theng though, he didn' have iny family…and I didn' have iny idea hi much money the sombitch had. He wuz loaded…and I got every fuckin' bit of it. A lot a goddamned taxes though, but…hell, when it's that much money, who gives a shit. My daddy helped me a lot. He advised me on wut ta do…up ta a point. Rat after that, ma fuckin' daddy died. That wudn' all that much of a surprise though 'cause he'd been sick fer quite a while. But I wuz shocked when ma husband died…although he *wuz* a helluva lot older than me." She looked 25.

"*Commo yo*—like me," the brown-skinned man affirmed, wearing a gigantic grin.

"Oh, honey, there's no comparison with you." She fondled his partially erect penis. "You still got it, babe. When I first married tha sombitch he was okay…well, not bad…but in the last couple a months, shit, Viagra didn' even work. He jes' couldn' git it up…so," another stunning smile, "I s'pose everytheng happened fer the best…'cause I do like fuckin'." Squeezing his cock affectionately, "But tell me the truth now, ya rilly think I kin play that part?"

"*Sin duda, mi amor*…without doubt. There is absolutely no question in my mind," he asserted. "I wrote the screenplay, and…I will be directing the movie…*if* I can raise the 250,000 dollars."

Excitedly, she added, "I saw *Selena* three times, honey. It wuz a great movie. I sure never thought I'd meet the director…'specially in bed makin' love to 'im." She ended the last sentence with an infectious laugh.

"*La vida*—life," he shrugged, "is full of many surprises." He then gently fingered her clit.

"Oooh, honey, I jes' love them kinda surprises. Gimme some more." She kissed him. "Jennifer Lopez wuz rilly good in that part. Directin' her…wuz it easy? No problems?"

"None whatsoever. She is a very talented young lady."

"And she hadn' done much, had she?"

"At that point, no. It was a breakthrough performance for her…and she deserved it."

"Butcha helped her, didn' ya?"

"*Por supuesto que sí*. Of course, it's my responsibility, among many other things. A movie director is like a god…of the particular movie he directs. That movie becomes his creation." He smiled, using his finger again. "And I am a very caring god."

"You sure are," nibbling his nose. "I jes' love the way ya ate me, then fucked me. I never felt that good in my whole damn life. When I started comin', ya musta thought I's goin' crazy, but I jes' couldn' help it, hon." With a sly smile, "An' *you* didn' even come. Does that mean we kin do it agin in a little while? Hell, I kin have a orgasm jes' about iny time I wont."

"Yes, of course, my dear. I only want to satisfy you." He lowered his face, and began sucking her left breast.

"Feels so good," she cooed. "I was in one high school play. That's about it, as far as ma actin' experience. Ya think I could be as good as Jennifer Lopez, if ya help me and I try rill hard?"

"*Mejor, en mi opinion*—I'm sorry—better, I think, simply because the role is more dramatic. You'll play the part of an American mistress of a drug lord here in Mexico. She's a real bitch. Although, in reality, you are a very nice young lady, I can teach you to act like a complete bitch. Believe me, I can do it. There is a scene near the end of the story," his description is quite dramatic, "where she cuts her lover's throat, ear to ear…and she watches him trying desperately to hold in the blood that is gushing from his severed jugulars. It's a marvelous scene, and the man's part is outstanding too. I have someone in mind who can play it masterfully. But your part…oh ho! It is Academy Award material."

"No shit? The Oscar?"

"Yes indeed. I wrote it that way. The role actually runs the full gamut of a woman's emotions. When the audience leaves the theater, they will be completely drained…and they will *never* forget you…never. *If* I can get the money, this will be the greatest…the *greatest*…Mexican motion picture ever made. It will change the history of movie making in Mexico…a country I truly love."

"But, Greg, I never been in a movie before."

"Well…did you see the film, *Finding Forrester*, with Sean Connery?"

"Yeah, 'bout the kid who wonts to be a writer?"

"Precisely. The young fellow who played the kid had never made a movie…and had no acting experience, but the director, Gus Van Sant, gave him excellent guidance. You saw the results…outstanding. That's not to diminish what the kid did, no. What I'm trying to say is, that under another director, the young actor's performance may not have reached that level of excellence. That same director, incidentally, was responsible for *Good Will Hunting* and, although Matt Damon and Ben Affleck co-wrote the screenplay, they'd had very little acting experience. Look where there are now. The same will be true of you, my dear. I guarantee it. You have my word...and I always keep my word. Ask Jennifer Lopez."

"When ya gotta have the money, baby?" She was stroking his penile shaft now, and watching it increase in size.

"*Mañana.* Tomorrow at the latest. Otherwise...the deal will probably collapse. They're getting very anxious...and I don't blame them."

"You gonna make the movie 'round here...in Acapulco?"

"No, primarily in *Distrito Federal*—Mexico City—and Cuernavaca...with maybe one or two scenes in the Oaxaca area."

She raised up on one elbow. "And the whole theng's gonna be in Mexican?"

"Spanish, my dear. There is no such language as Mexican." With a forced grin, "That is your lesson for the day...but there will be many more. I'll teach you everything you need to know...to win the Academy Award."

"But I don' speak iny Mexican—I mean Spanish. Idn' that gonna be a...problem?"

"No, no. As I mentioned, you are his American mistress. Most of your dialogue will be in English, spoken as you speak it. Where did you grow up?"

"Tupelo, Missippi."

"Mississippi?" He accentuated the additional set of s's.

With a giggle, "Well...we don' say it that way in Tupelo. Least not in my family...or inybody I know."

"I can easily write your accent into the script," he assured her. "Then the limited amount of Spanish that will be spoken by your character can be dubbed. There are several Mexican actresses who specialize in that."

Gliding her fingers over his scrotum, "I thought bein' a director, they would jes' pay ya such and such money fer the job. Hi come they're makin' ya put your own money in it?"

"That's an excellent question and, coming from you, I am not surprised...you are a very intelligent girl. That's one of the reasons I want you for the part...aside from your commanding beauty and...your intoxicating sensuality, which I am certain can be captured on film by the cinematographer. You see this is my project. I wrote it, and I'm instigating the entire artistic vehicle. The producers, on the other hand, who happen to be good friends of mine, will be investing millions of dollars—in pesos of course. It's a major production. They feel—and I understand it perfectly—that because it's *my* project, that I should be willing to invest some of my own money. They feel it's my way of financially showing I have faith in the project. And that's the way it should be. But the truth is, I don't have that kind of money...nowhere near it. So...unless you can help me, the deal is history. I will chalk it off as a missed opportunity...not only for me, but more importantly, for you, my dear."

"Honey, You ain' chalkin' inything off,...not as long as I'm here." She wrapped her fingers around the base of his cock and felt it swelling. "Will ya go ta the bank with me tomorrow in the mornin'...not too early though?"

"I'll accompany you, my dear...but I don't think it's wise for me to get involved personally. Tell them it's for an investment here in Acapulco, and that it has to be in large peso bills. I have a briefcase you can use. In what city is your U.S. bank located?"

"Tulsa. It's oil money. That wuz ma husband's life...oil...and money." She could feel his shaft hardening quickly. "Frankly, there's other thengs that interest me. Oh, what's this I feel?" Without releasing his penis, she rubbed his side, over his left hip, with her other hand.

"That's a...how do you say it?...mole. I've had it since birth. They say it's good luck."

"Well, I hope ya have all the luck in the world, sweetie. An' I wonna be rat there with ya when yer havin' it...fuckin' ya upside down an' backwards." She squeezed his cock with a smile on her face.

"This ain' no fuckin' mole." She laughed wildly. "Is it okay if I kiss it first, Greg?"

"*Sí, mi amor*. Of course...I would love that."

"Then later, after ya go down on *me,* hi 'bout fuckin' me rill good, honey. I jes' cain' git enough a ya. And listen, if ya don' rilly feel like comin'," she put her face as close as possible to his without touching it, "jes' wait'll tonight and we kin do it agin, and I promise ya I'll rilly make ya feel good."

As she repositioned herself, preparing for fellatio, the man studied the artistic Aztec design on the ceiling and considered what his next alias and destination should be. Antonio Miguel Gonzalez had brought him to Acapulco, Frank Taylor had got him through La Jolla and to the island of Oahu, and now this lovely girl thinks he's Gregory Nava, well-known motion picture director.

With Mexican pesos worth $250,000 in U.S. currency, maybe he would simply move to another distant part of Mexico. Perhaps Veracruz, on the Gulf of Mexico, would be a wise choice. On second thought, in order to increase the possibility of finding a rich, gullible American woman, maybe Cancún would be a better choice. He could easily become Gustavo Martinez, a novelist from Paraguay, doing research for his 10th book, a sexy murder story that takes place along Mexico's eastern coast. Martinez would be originally from Barcelona, Spain, with light skin, thereby obviating the periodic need to apply sunless tanning lotion over his entire body, including his private parts. That had been a supreme nuisance. But taking into consideration the pleasurable favors he had received from this physically attractive and well-endowed girl, and particularly the special financial gift tomorrow, it had all been worth his while.

At this point, he was unable to determine whether or not he could spare her life. That would depend on several factors over which he had little control. It was not, however, customarily part of his modus operandi. Katherine Churchill had been an exception. She was the only human being he had ever loved...except Jean. He wondered if Jean was still alive.

Then suddenly, when he felt that marvelous sensation of the girl's moist lips, mouth, and tongue enveloping his throbbing cock, he decided to postpone the decision concerning this talented girl from Tupelo, Mississippi until...*mañana.*

CHAPTER 22

It was the bench on Coast Walk that Katherine had made a special point of showing to Frank before they had started walking from her home to Robilio's. The same bench she referred to as "our bench," where she and Rocky had spent hundreds of hours together, as they were at this moment, looking out toward the Pacific Ocean, over the exact spot from which she fell that day she'd remember as long as she lived.

The air was cooler now—it was February—but the sky, the ocean, and the rugged coastline combined to form a partial panorama that was hard to match.

With Rocky's head on her lap, Katherine enjoyed the serenity and beauty of the scene, feeling the unquestionable presence of God. She frequently sat here with Rocky like this, and silently thanked God for letting her live through that unfortunate episode with Frank Taylor. She invariably asked God to forgive her mother, to bless her soul, and to grant her a peaceful existence in eternity.

Affectionately stroking Rocky's head, Katherine couldn't help but wonder where Frank was...what he was doing...and whom he was with. She knew she was supposed to hate him for what he'd done and, based on the facts as they had been related to her, she did, in a certain fashion, but was unable to erase from her mind the wonderful things he'd said to her. It would be impossible for her to categorically conclude that everything he told her was a lie. And she readily accepted that she would be lying to herself if she denied ever having loved him. The truth was…that she had loved him like no other man before…and probably any she'd meet in the future. It was still inconceivable that he purposely deceived her. All the memories she had of their talks at the beach, at Robilio's, the Marine Room, walking on this path, sitting on another bench that's closer to the snork pad…how could all of that have been lies and deception? His final words…what he told her to remember when she was "80 years old…and still beautiful"…how could he possibly have lied about something like that? He could easily have left her that final day without saying a word…but he didn't…and those words would echo through her mind for the rest of her life. He could have easily taken her life…but he didn't.

The tears formed on her eyelids, as they had many times in the past. She was learning to control them, little by little. She solicited Rocky's assistance. "You have to help me, Rocky. I'm tired of crying. I'll be an old lady before I know it…an ugly old lady whose face is wrinkled from too much sadness. You don't want me to look like that, do you, Rocky?"

He raised his head and looked understandably into her face, then licked her hand. While sitting on the bench, whenever a human form approached from either direction on the path, Katherine consciously invented a scenario in which that human form materialized into Frank. She would not scream. That was a vow she had made. Realizing there was no longer FBI surveillance—she had voluntarily discontinued that after the Christmas holidays—she would remain calm and quiet, and simply listen to what he had to say. She'd listen to each of his apologies, especially the one concerning the death of her mother. Then, wearing a sweet smile, she would inform him there was something special she wanted him to have as a memento of their relationship. Then, with the self-confidence of an actor who had repeatedly rehearsed a scene, she would remove from her shoulder bag the Beretta 950, which an FBI agent had taught her how to use, and put eight rapid rounds into the upper body and face of the man she had loved so passionately.

"There is no way I could do that, Rocky..." stroking his little head, "not a way in the world. He would just have to kill me. It isn't in my nature to take someone's life...and certainly not his."

From her left, the direction of The Cave Store, a jogging figure advanced toward her on the Coast Walk path. It was a large man in blue-and-gray warm-ups and, as he neared, Katherine could see that he was African-American, and quite handsome. Usually she made it a rule not to establish eye contact with strangers along the path, but there was something almost regal about his carriage as he smoothly trotted closer. Rocky lifted his head and watched suspiciously.

The jogger smiled and waved politely with his right hand. Katherine, now seeing that he was definitely up there at the top of the charts as far as looks were concerned, flashed back her incomparable "Katsmile." The man went a few yards past her, then stopped in his tracks, turned his body around, and addressed her.

"Excuse me, is this a dead-end path or will I be able to get through to that big beach," he motioned toward La Jolla Shores, "over there?" He walked back closer to the bench.

"You can get through okay," Katherine responded. "Just follow your nose. That white wooden bridge," she pointed to it, "is basically the end of this dirt path...but you can cross it—no problem—then, as you can see, there's a short paved street, Coast Walk, that intersects Torrey Pines, one of the main drags for getting in and out of La Jolla. Turn left there, and you'll have one block of carbon monoxide until you hit the next street, which is Princess. Turn left again and follow Princess down the hill, and it becomes Spindrift Drive when it curves off to the right. About a block from there you'll see the Marine Room, a restaurant, on the left side of the street." She pointed toward the La Jolla Beach and Tennis Club. "You see that group of structures with the red tile roofs?"

"Sure, right there."

"Okay, the section closest to us, at this end, is the Marine Room. You can see the windows from here. It's a very scenic place to dine."

"Yes, I can see them."

"Just this side of the Marine Room—you can see at the corner of that first building where it ends on the beach—there's a walkway that runs along the edge of the restaurant, and it starts on Spindrift Drive, where you'll be jogging. So when you get to the Marine Room, don't jog past it, take a quick left down that walkway. If it isn't high tide—and I don't think it is—no, I can see from here that it isn't—you can go down to the beach on that walkway and run your brains out."

His laugh was genuine and spontaneous. "You're funny…and you give great directions. You live around here?"

Katherine had no intention of revealing that kind of information to an absolute stranger. Rolling her eyes a bit, "Are you kidding?"

"Will your dog attack me if I sit for a minute?" He nodded toward the empty space on the bench.

"I don't think so…unless you're a villain." Kat gave him the once-over. "He's pretty good at sniffing out villains." She grasped Rocky's collar tightly, just in case. "We're about to leave anyway." Rocky stood on the bench and faced the man.

"Oh, come on, don't let me run you off. I'm not a villain, but I guess that's what a villain would tell you." Smiling, he extended the back of his hand to Rocky's nose, and got it licked. "Just want to take a quick break before I continue…and I like dogs too. I'm in town for a job interview, and thought I'd take in some of this great scenery…and get some exercise along with it." Rubbing the top of Rocky's head, "What is he, a Jack Russell? He looks a little different." The stranger sat on the bench.

"Half that, and half rat terrier."

"That explains it. His legs look longer. Has a very intelligent face. Talks with his eyes." For the first time, he looked deeply into Katherine's eyes. "What's his name?"

Deciding to keep up the masquerade, "Herbie," without the New Jersey accent.

Stroking Rocky's head vigorously, "Hey, Herbie." Rocky growled. The man swiftly withdrew his hand. "Oh, I don't think Herbie likes me. I'll keep my distance. Maybe he thinks I'm a big rat." Looking back into Katherine's eyes, and shaking his head, "This is incredible." He studied her face carefully. "You know who you look like, don't you? I bet you get tired of people telling you."

Katherine curled her fingers under Rocky's mouth. "I think we'd better go, Herbie." Rocky growled. "This is beginning to sound *very* familiar."

Raising his fingers upward, "Oh, no, please…I guess it does sound like a line. But I swear to God, I'm sincere."

When Katherine saw his brilliant smile and the sparkle in his eyes, she knew she was looking at the most handsome man she'd ever seen.

"You mean to tell me," he was persuasively challenging her now, "nobody has ever told you that you look like…" He paused, giving her a chance to fill in the blank.

Playing the game, but with her rules, "Halle Berry?"

"No, Halle Berry's a fine looking woman, and great actress—won the Oscar last year—but you look exactly like…Vivica Fox…and she's gorgeous…and so are you."

"Vivica Fox?" Katherine tried to appear surprised. "She is gorgeous. You must be interviewing for a sales job."

"No way. That's one thing I'm not, is a salesman. You sure you don't have a fox head tattooed on your left shoulder, and you're just putting me on?"

Now Katherine was honestly surprised, and a bit upset that a perfect stranger knew about her tattoo. "What are you talking about?"

"Vivica Fox has a fox tattoo, right here," pointing to his left shoulder. "I've seen it many times in photos, and when she's interviewed on TV. It's kind of her pet trademark…that goes with her name."

"I didn't know that," Katherine honestly admitted.

"Yeah, the funny part is, I saw her on *Hollywood Squares* about a year ago. They asked her a question…something to do with what a vixen is…and the right answer was a female fox. She missed it. She didn't get it right, and I think she was *really* embarrassed. I bet she never forgets that. Anyway, I can't believe that nobody's ever told you about the similarity in your looks."

Katherine was definitely warming up to his personality, and enjoying it. She also sympathized with Vivica Fox because Katherine hadn't known that a vixen was a female fox either until Frank told her. "What job *are* you interviewing for?"

"The coaching staff for the Chargers. That's my field, football. I've been working in Buffalo, New York for several years. I'm tired of walking and driving in the snow, and freezing my tail off." Looking out toward the ocean, "This is February, and it looks and feels wonderful to me." Then, focusing on Katherine's eyes again, "This is my kind of February weather. It's gotta be a great place to live, if for no other reason than the weather." Then looking back at the view, "And you've got this scenery to go with it."

"It is a great place. You'll love it. You think there's a chance you'll get the job?" Katherine now felt comfortable with this stranger.

"Yeah, I was recommended…from the inside. It's all about salary now. I'll have to make a decision. You like living here?"

"Very much. Wouldn't want to live anyplace else. You get spoiled." She noticed him looking at her ring finger as a couple of matronly women walked by.

"I can believe that. Grow up around here and you probably wouldn't want to leave." Now he was concentrating strictly on her face: her nose, lips, ears, hair, then her eyes again, first the right, then the left. "On the other hand, if you grew up here, you might not appreciate it."

"That's a good point," she agreed. "Human nature, I suppose."

Then aware that he was virtually hypnotized by her huge bewitching eyes, and that he was dangling at the end of a thin thread that seemed about to break, he couldn't think of anything else to do or say but..."Well, it's been nice talking to you. I...guess I'd better..." He got up reluctantly, "move on."

Katherine could tell that he was struggling, and frankly enjoyed his lack of glibness. She found it refreshing to see a man working hard mentally to express his thoughts. "Good luck with your interview," throwing him a verbal lifesaver.

"I've already had it, actually. They're supposed to call me tomorrow with the salary figure. Then it's my decision."

"Oh, you've got it then...unless they want you to work for free." She grinned. "Hope you've done your homework. Life in the San Diego area is kinda expensive, definitely if you're thinking about living in La Jolla."

"Yeah, I checked a few things. My buddy's told me a lot too. I think I'll be in pretty good shape financially." Giving her that look again, "I really want to live here...now."

The last word said it all for Katherine. She got the message, but it made her slightly uncomfortable. Her experience with Frank essentially removed any possibility of her ever completely trusting anyone again, certainly not with the same surrender of self that she unhesitatingly offered to Frank. The reservations about starting a new relationship with this man were perhaps irreversibly entrenched. Katherine, however, was unable to take her eyes off his.

"Listen..." He sat again. "My name's Nate Harrington...I, uh..." He shook his head and laughed out loud. "God, I feel like an idiot...I've never done anything like this in my life."

A guy in a baseball cap with a golden Labrador retriever went by. Katherine held Rocky's collar tightly.

"Is there a problem here," she ventured, "that I'm not aware of?"

"Yeah," he laughed and appeared more relaxed, "the problem is...I want to meet you. I want to get acquainted with you. I want to know you, and everything that comes out of my mouth sounds...stupid. Even what's going on in my brain is stupid. If I get up and continue on my way to the beach, I'll never see you again. I know that. And I'll remember this moment for the rest of my life...and how stupid I was not to be able to express myself. So that's the problem. And it's my problem...not yours." He was on a roll now. "Isn't there...some way? I don't even know your name. Can I...take you to lunch? I'll take your parents too, if you want me to. I just want to be able to get better acquainted with you. I want you to know who I am. You must be thinking I'm a wacko...and I'm not. I'm a decent, intelligent hardworking guy."

"Why," giving him one of those microscopic, analytical looks that she no doubt inherited from her father, "do you want to get better acquainted with me, Nate?" Rocky was quiet and motionless. "There's something," she orally underlined, "called infatuation, and I don't want any part of that. I've been there, done that."

"So have I." He practically jumped on her last remark as though he was happy she made it. "I'm 38 years old. I've never been married, but I have been infatuated, and I know exactly what you're talking about. The first few minutes of our conversation, yeah, I think that's what it was...I was overwhelmed by your physical beauty. I admit it...the fact that you look so much like Vivica Fox. I actually thought you might be her...here on vacation. But that's not what it really is. You're very special. I can tell. And I want to know you. I've never felt these vibrations with any woman...and I have never said those words to any woman. I swear to God...and I'm Catholic."

This guy was saying all the right things, and Katherine was getting that old feeling back. But still..."We're talking now, Nate. I come here frequently with...Herbie." Rocky gave her a strange look and growled softly. "You'll see me again. If you accept the job offer, you'll have to go back to Buffalo for a spell, I'm sure. Then, when you return, you'll see me here again. I promise." She glanced at her watch, a new one that her father gave her for Christmas. "I've got an appointment, so I have to go now, but…"

"So that's it, huh?" His disappointment showed like a traffic signal. "There's no way I can see you later, after your appointment, or tonight? Like I said, your parents are invited. I'm serious. I'm not just saying that. We can all have dinner together, and they can take you home—if that's what you're concerned about. I know I'm a complete stranger and, if you were my daughter, there's no way I'd let you do it alone."

Admiring him in a different light now, "You really mean that, don't you?"

"Of course, I do. I totally understand the situation from your standpoint." Meeting her intense look head-on, "And…if you have no interest in me, I certainly understand that too. I'm a realist."

"Maybe you *should* be in sales," smiling. "Where are you staying?"

"The Empress, on Fay. That's where they put me up."

"You like it?"

"Very nice. The rooms are spacious and quiet…very friendly staff. And the restaurant there, Manhattan, is excellent."

"Do you know where Hotel Mallorca is?"

"That's the building with the older, kind of interesting, architecture…and the fancy old-fashioned lobby, with the little fenced-in elevator?"

She smiled. "That's it. There's a cocktail lounge upstairs called the Gulls Nest. I work there part-time, and I'll be there tonight, if you want to drop by."

His chin dropped a little, and she could see the wheels of his brain churning. "I don't drink," he acknowledged.

"As a matter of fact, neither do I, but it's a job and…it's a nice respectable place. They serve iced tea, orange juice, and Cokes…or just bottled water. It's not a joint."

"Oh, I didn't mean that. I'm sure it's a very nice place...especially if it's in that hotel. You wait on tables there?"

"Sort of...but I do other things." She clearly saw that his appraisal of her was now in abeyance...and she liked that. He didn't come across as one of those guys who're looking for an easy lay. He was gathering information so he could make a rational judgment, the same process he had been using with reference to his job application.

"What's a good time for me to come...and should I wear a coat and tie? I would imagine so."

"Oh, 8:30, 9. A coat and tie would be fine, but if you didn't bring that, don't worry. It's not that formal. Some of the older people dress up." She extended her right hand. "My name's Katherine."

Her eye contact carried more significance now, and Nate could sense it. He also wondered if he was getting involved with a cocktail waitress who had a shady past. The firmness of her handshake told him she was a woman of character. Now it was up to him to find out what kind of character.

"I get a break around 10 o'clock," she added. "We can talk for a few minutes then. When do you go back to Buffalo?"

"Probably right after I get the phone call, or as soon as I can get a plane out."

"Well, if for some reason you can't make it tonight, maybe I'll see you here on the bench some other time. I hope everything works out for you."

He got up again. "Thanks, Katherine. I plan to see you tonight. I'll definitely be there." Then, in a different tone of voice, "Okay, Herbie. Take care of Katherine." Rocky stood on the bench seat and growled. Nate pulled back. "Hey, I can't believe this...first dog I ever met that didn't like me."

"He'll get used to you." Katherine smiled. "He's kinda funny about strangers. He had a disappointing experience."

"See you tonight then." Nate backed away from her on the path, grinning broadly. "You made my day, Katherine." He jogged off in the direction of the white wooden footbridge, toward his beach destination.

Watching the departure of her new acquaintance, Katherine thought, "I like the way he moves. Nice butt too. Absolutely beautiful man. And if things worked out, Dad would be overjoyed."

Rocky sat on the bench facing her.

"Forgive me, Rocky. I won't use that *other* name anymore." She stroked his head tenderly and looked into his eyes. "What do think about Nate? Tell me the truth now…yes or no?"

After a slight intelligent pause, Rocky nodded.

Katherine grinned approvingly at Rocky. "Why didn't I think of asking you that before? Would've saved me a helluva lot of trouble. But maybe you were fooled too."

Rocky stood on the bench seat and turned away from Kat. He began sniffing and licking a spot on its surface.

"No, no, Rocky, there're germs on the bench. You're my baby…I don't want you to get sick."

Although he was a half-breed, like most full-blooded Jack Russell terriers, Rocky was stubborn. He gave no sign of abstinence. Katherine gently pulled his body away from the spot that drew his attention, and slid her own closer for inspection. Looking down and running her fingers over the area, she could clearly see and feel a series of alphabetical symbols that had been neatly scored into the wooden surface. She immediately broke into tears and began sobbing uncontrollably, without taking her eyes off what she saw. Instantly pulling Rocky's body closer to hers and affectionately soothing his feelings with her palm on the side of his face, she asked, "What're we gonna do, Rocky?" She looked out over the ocean. "It's not fair."

Her mind flashed backed to a scene in September. She was straddling Frank's thighs at La Jolla Shores Beach, gazing into his greenish-brown eyes, and he was telling her, "'All's fair in love and war.' I'm sure you've heard that before."

Rubbing her fingers across the inconspicuous carved-out letters, she looked down at them again, able to see them only intermittently through the fitful stream of tears. She brokenheartedly pronounced the words aloud:

PHOXY LOVES KAT
& ROCKY
À TOUTE JAMAIS

Chaotically thinking of all the possible time frames in which Frank could have done this, Katherine's sobbing, nevertheless, worsened. The inscribed words were at the opposite end of the bench from where she and Rocky customarily sat, but she was amazed at not having noticed them until now. One could plainly see that the handcrafted letters were not recently made. That would indicate Frank had done it weeks or months ago, presumably around the time she had last seen him, conceivably the same morning on which he so thoughtfully recovered her emerald bra. Or else, the Sunday morning before they left for Hawaii, the one on which he claimed to have attended an early Mass, would've been another opportunity.

Across the dirt path, over the ice plant—to the exact spot from which Katherine fell last September—then across the expanse of La Jolla Bay, Katherine's tearful visual focus concentrated on the stretch of sand that constituted La Jolla Shores Beach, the same location to which she'd just given Nate Harrington directions. Her memory was suddenly invaded by a range of vivid, one-second vignettes that spanned the yardage between the Marine Room and the plot of sand by the sea wall where she and Frank had their romantic hours-long, expository tête-à-tête.

Coaxing Rocky closer, she caressed his little head with her trembling hand. Then, looking again at the words on the wooden surface, she read them silently in the sanctum of her inner being: "Phoxy Loves Kat & Rocky *à toute jamais*."

Fully resigned now to her inescapable state of heartache, Katherine dazedly cruised her focal point along the distant horizon of sea, sky, and hills, pronouncing aloud, in perfect French, the last words of Frank's sentimental affirmation: "*à toute jamais*."

Another set of tears collected on her lower lids. The left side of her top lip began to quiver, and she audibly translated the French into English: "forever and ever."

She now had Rocky's undivided attention. Keeping her moist eyes on the horizon, her mind raced through the splendid highlights of the relationship with Frank, from the instant she had seen him while falling from the cliff over the White Lady to the last words she heard from him: "I'm not gonna let the sons of bitches lock me in a cell for the rest of my life, so I'm outta here. I'll never forget you, and…I'll never stop loving you." She knew now, regardless of his past, that every minute she'd spent with him was priceless, and she'd never forget the Frank Taylor she'd known and loved. She didn't know Erik Kukka or Brian Clement, or any of his other fictitious characters—and she didn't want to know them. The Frank Taylor she knew was real—in every way—and that's the one she'd remember until she died.

Directing her attention now to a large white cumulus cloud over La Jolla Shores Beach, she softly whispered, "I love you too." The tears cascaded over her lovely cheekbones and down the sides of her marvelous face. Even in grief, as Frank had told her, Katherine Churchill was a stunningly beautiful woman.

Rocky promptly rose to a standing position, undoubtedly thinking she'd spoken those magical words to him. He opened his mouth as if to respond, then, after a thoughtful pause, seemingly understood that Katherine's words had been intended for someone unseen, and sat.

She looked down into Rocky's expressive eyes, stroked the top of his head with obvious affection, and smiled, "I love you too, Rocky…*à toute jamais*."

0-595-25377-6

Printed in the United States
15722LVS00003B/61-66

9 780595 253777